WHITE LIE

WHITE LIE

John Templeton Smith

POCKET
BOOKS

LONDON · SYDNEY · NEW YORK · TOKYO · SINGAPORE · TORONTO

First published in Great Britain by Pockets Books, 1999
An imprint of Simon & Schuster UK Ltd
A Viacom Company

1 3 5 7 9 10 8 6 4 2

Simon & Schuster UK Ltd
Africa House
64–78 Kingsway
London WC2B 6AH

Simon & Schuster Australia
Sydney

A CIP catalogue record for this book is available
from the British Library

ISBN 0–671–01603–2

Permission to use lyrics from the song *Release* granted by
Smith & Eurgubian Music, Hollywood, California.

Typeset by Palimpsest Book Production Limited,
Polmont, Stirlingshire
Printed and bound in Great Britain by
Caledonian International
Book Manufacturing, Glasgow

For Deirdre, Sacha, Georgina, Sootie & Tess,
– with love

'A better knight cannot die, though he might in a better cause.'

— John Winter, a.k.a. Sibelius One

'We conduct our activities and ourselves according to the highest standards of integrity, morality and honour and according to the spirit and letter of our law and Constitution . . . you have my word.'

— Tanner Williams, Central Intelligence Agency

'The drink? The drink lessens the pain, that's all.'

— Major Charles Riker, USAF (Rtd)

ACKNOWLEDGEMENTS

My grateful thanks to the following, without whom this project would never have got off the ground:

Daniel and Oscar and Ursula and Margarita, for the extended South American tour – especially the less well-travelled roads of Colombia, legal and otherwise.

Dr Terry Phelps, Oklahoma City University, for his scholarly advice on the many aspects of this work.

Deirdre Graziella Smith RN, for the medical advice.

Michael Sissons, my agent for the past seventeen years, for his continued faith in my abilities.

Martin Fletcher, my editor at Simon & Schuster, whose creative insight helped lay the foundations for this story.

Lastly, to those friends in my former profession – the aviating game (sadly too numerous to mention) – for the anecdotes and the technical gen . . . and above all the memories.

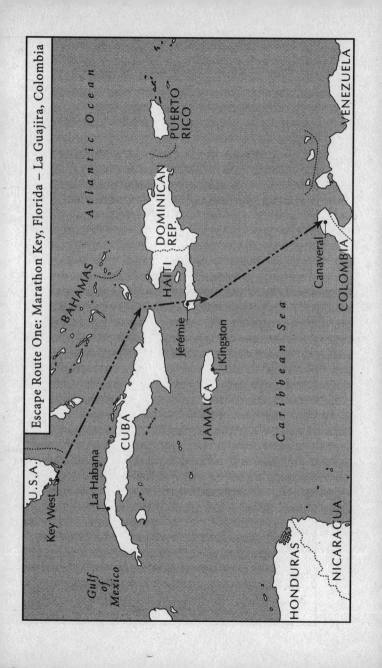

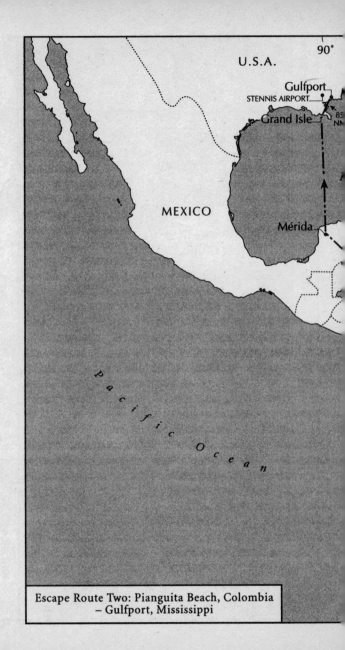

Escape Route Two: Pianguita Beach, Colombia
– Gulfport, Mississippi

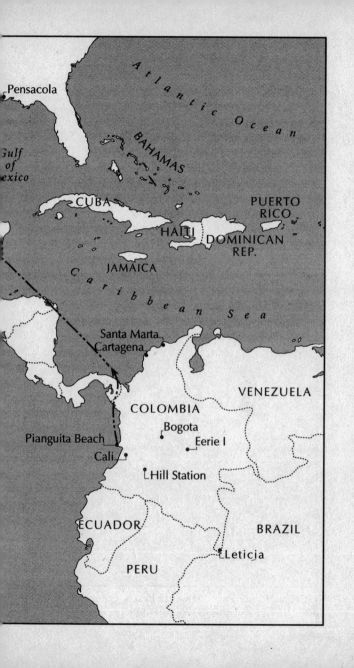

Briefing

Three apparently unconnected events had their beginnings during that twenty-four-hour period in late September.

The first, in Oklahoma City, was the lead news story on the local television stations and concerned the violent rape and murder of a TV presenter. The thirty-five-year-old woman, Julia Somers Carroll, had been reporting on drug pushers targeting metro-area schools. Early indications pointed to a city drug gang as suspects in the homicide.

It was two days later that an OB unit from Channel 9 – a CBS affiliate – ran a piece on the murdered woman's husband: a professor at Oklahoma City University, a softly spoken man in his early fifties with long untidy blond hair, who had lectured on European History at the university for six years and who had been married to Julia for just eighteen months. He had the shell-shocked air of a man who hadn't yet taken it all in. Except perhaps for his parting words to those responsible – 'They will all be brought to justice, of that they should have no doubts' – which sounded implausibly like a threat.

Following the murder of Julia Somers Carroll there was a series of 'druggie' killings in the three-month run-up to Christmas, four in total. One every three

1

weeks. The city police – with a pathologist's report showing that the killings followed the same MO, death being the result of a sharp instrument entering the base of the skull, where the spinal cord joined the brain (the perfect spot: quick, quiet and clean) – were no nearer discovering the killer when a young detective, finding that the personal effects of Julia Somers Carroll (a wristwatch and a wedding ring) had not been returned to her husband, tried to contact the professor at his university, only to be told that he had resigned his position and returned to his native Ireland. They gave him a forwarding address. The detective soon found out that no one called Professor Deavas Liam Carroll lived, or had lived, at the address in Dublin, Eire.

Going the extra mile he ran a check with King's College, Cambridge, England, where according to Carroll's c.v. he had been a lecturer prior to taking up the American post, and where perhaps he might have returned. In fact he had never really left. The clipped, very British message that came back – via fax – was from the Provost's office and stated, 'Professor Carroll D.L. MA (Hons), died as a result of injuries received in a motor car accident at Finchley, north London.' Attached was a copy of the death certificate. The date was interesting. *Six years earlier!*

The Oklahoma City PD suddenly had a chief suspect to tie in with the recent slayings.

A man that didn't exist.

The second, in Key West, Florida, concerned a dishwasher at a local diner. He was known on the street as Ugly Charlie. That night was the first night that two kids – Latino illegals fresh from a dirt-poor country, drawn to the land of the soft touch, America – beat him up for his day's wages.

The old man didn't fight back, so the punks put him on their regular list. The beatings were superficial; they wanted the victim to be able to work and earn money after all. They never considered that a scar-faced old dishwasher, uglier than hell, could have a friend more chilling than their worst nightmares. But why should they? They had found another easy touch.

Their first mistake would happen some months later when they would incapacitate the old man, temporarily ending a weekly pay day.

They would – regretfully for them – make a second.

The third was in Washington, DC. A memo circulated to heads of departments of the DEA (Drug Enforcement Administration) nationwide stated, 'It is a long way from the Californian mansions of elite North American dealers to the Bolivian Indian peasant villages in Chapare where the manufacture of cocaine begins. Snow blows north – from the high Andean plateaus of Bolivia and Peru, where most of the coca crop is grown, to Colombia, where historically it has been refined into cocaine, to Panama and the Bahamas whence it is trans-shipped via southern Florida to final markets across North America.

'With the recent and dramatic reduction in drug trafficking related arrests in southern Florida, we could be forgiven for thinking that we have won a major battle in the drug war. Sadly this appears not to be the case. Department analysts have today produced figures that show the annual $100 billion black economy in the US is alive and well. If anything, on the increase.

'In conclusion we must therefore assume that the Colombian cartels have changed their export/import arrangements.

'The implications are grave.'

PART ONE
Old Pros

1

The northeast trade wind had slackened by the time it reached the end of the island chain, where now, little more than a whisper, its final act was to stir the white concrete dust on the Key West International airport ramp and blend the scents of aviation fuel, sea salt and mud flats, with the whine of spooling-down jet engines: a four-foot-above-sea-level greeting to the disembarking passengers from the morning Miami service.

The first passenger to leave the American Eagle flight – a man by the name of John Winter – tilted his face briefly towards the cloudless sky. A nod of recognition. He knew the smell, the sound – was for a moment back in a cramped cockpit, running final instrument and control checks, nodding his head forward to his wingman at the start of a take-off roll.

An ex-pilot returned to the fold.

Except it was more than that. There was a term for odd twists of fate: synchronicity. Most ordinary men might have accepted a chain of incidents as being hinged together by simple coincidence. Chance encounters. God moving in mysterious ways. Would have turned their backs. Let it lie.

But then Winter was no ordinary man.

He checked his watch – a little after ten – and went into the terminal to collect a set of car keys from the Avis desk. Ten minutes later he eased the red Chevrolet Lumina out of the airport, turning right on South Roosevelt.

Sarge's Airport Diner was modelled on a 1950s eatery: black-and-white-tiled floor, long red plastic-finished counter with matching red vinyl-covered swivel chairs. A chrome jukebox in the corner was pumping out old fifties music. On the whitewashed walls were framed pictures of some of the stars of that era: James Dean, Marilyn Monroe, Elvis, Bill Haley, Buddy Holly. An original red Coke machine, rusting slightly, stood alongside the wall near the door. The smell of bacon and eggs drifted through the serving hatch from the kitchen and mingled with the cigarette smoke, which was whirlpooled throughout the diner by four-blade ceiling fans. A few customers were sitting in the booths by the streetside windows.

Winter found a free stool at the end of the counter and ordered coffee. He took a pack of Particulares from his pocket and lit one. He hadn't smoked in seven years. But then he hadn't been in Key West for seven years. The two seemed synonymous.

A heavy-set man with tattooed arms, a shaved head, and the battered face of an ex-boxer appeared from the kitchen and took two plates of bacon, eggs and hash browns to a couple sitting in one of the window booths. As he came back, Winter called him over.

'Wonder if you could help me. I'm looking for a guy called Charles Riker. I was told he worked here.'

'Wrong place, buddy,' the man growled and started to move away.

'Badly scarred face, might have been working under some other name.'

The man stopped and turned around. 'Ugly Charlie you mean. Had to let him go some time before Christmas.'

'Can I ask why?'

'You can ask, but who I hire and fire is my business.'

'How about a home address.'

'Same deal. So who are you?'

'Friend of his.'

The man laughed. 'Ugly Charlie, friends! Life's full of surprises. I figured you for a cop or something, but then the accent. Australian?'

'Nearly . . . English.' Winter took out his wallet and put a fifty-dollar bill on the counter. 'Seems he could use a few friends, wouldn't you say?'

'Keep your money, pal. Like I said, I know nothing, okay? Get you a refill on the coffee?'

'No thanks.'

The man shrugged, muttered, 'Have a nice one,' and moved off in the direction of the kitchen.

Winter finished his coffee and left the diner. Of course the guy knew where Riker lived. Just didn't like talking to suits. Jeans and a sweatshirt might have produced better results.

He had parked the car in the shade of palm trees near

the diner. He was unlocking the driver's door when a middle-aged woman, dark hair, thin face, wearing a greasy blue-coloured smock, came out of a side door of the diner. She leaned against the wall and lit a cigarette, all the time watching him.

'You looking for Charlie?'

Winter said, 'Maybe.'

'I run the kitchen; overheard you asking Sarge about him. Wasting your time with him, one of those *semper fi* meatheads . . . you know, ex-Marine.'

'So I gathered from the tattoos.'

'You a cop?'

'A friend.'

The woman thought about that. Studying the tall, serious man with military-short blond hair and sad blue eyes, as if trying to reconcile herself to the fact that Charlie had friends who wore city suits and drove new cars. 'You still up to paying a few bucks for information? He don't pay too well either. Minimum wage, and if you want a burger you pay regular price. Great life, ain't it?'

'What's your name?'

'Nancy.'

'Yeah, great life, Nancy. What did Charlie do here?'

'Handyman, dishwasher, that kind of thing. Then he got beat up some time before Christmas. Some kids robbed him or something. Bust him up pretty bad. He didn't show for a few days, and when he did Sarge had found somebody else.'

Winter's face was bleak as he took the fifty-dollar bill from his wallet and offered it to her.

She came across the narrow street hesitantly. 'He's not in trouble or nothing?'

'Not any more. I've come to take care of him.'

The gentleness in the man's voice convinced her. 'Lives on Seidenberg Avenue. Head east up that street, Flagler.' She pointed. 'Make a left on 10th. When you get to Seidenberg you go right. About the fifth house down on the right. There's a rusted yellow Volkswagen parked outside the house. He's got rooms there. I try and help him once in a while, you know, take him food and stuff. Ain't easy. He's a nice guy, though.'

'One in a million, Nancy.'

'Tell him I said hi.'

'I'll do that.'

The clear grey eyes smiled. 'You know, I had the feeling he was somebody once. Sarge figured he was a bum.'

Winter got into the car and lowered the window. 'August 1970, President Richard Nixon conferred upon him the Congressional Medal of Honour at the White House. Talk to a reporter on your local newspaper. Tell him to check out Major Charles Riker, United States Air Force. He'll be able to verify it.'

Winter left an open-mouthed Nancy and drove away in the direction of Seidenberg Avenue.

It was an old and decaying street in which Winter parked. The weather-worn wooden houses had stood since earlier in the century, built by ships' carpenters, using wooden pegs instead of nails, the style predominantly Bahamian. Spanish lime, sapodilla and Geiger trees lined what would have once been a pretty street. Now the trees did little more than give shade to the stray cats that foraged along the cracked sidewalks.

Winter went up the pathway, kicking back the overgrown saw grass. The house had been split into two – up and down. There was a flight of rickety stairs on the side of the building, alongside which someone had written in red paint, long since faded, the name Riker with an arrow pointing upward. He went up the rotting steps slowly, checking each one in turn, pausing at the top, where he surveyed the shabby street, checking for traffic. Then he knocked on the door.

'It's open,' a voice shouted.

He stepped inside out of the bright sunlight, closing the door behind him. The room was hot and airless and in total darkness. It took a moment for his eyes to adjust; then he saw someone sitting next to a window, the curtain drawn so that only the faintest daylight filtered through. 'Major Charles Riker?' Flawless English.

The figure stirred slightly. A nervous voice said, 'Who are you?'

'Christ, Charlie, how many Englishmen do you know?'

The man got up slowly from the chair and drew the curtain back. Harsh light flooded into the small dusty room. Winter noticed the handgun on the arm of the chair, a Colt Woodsman with a custom polished, hardwood grip. Long silenced barrel, .22 calibre. Effective when used with hollow-point bullets at short range. As for the man himself, he would hardly have recognised him; he had aged alarmingly. A small bent figure with a few tufts of grey hair on the right side of his scalp. The scar tissue which covered the left side of his head had pulled his left eye into a narrow slit. He shuffled forward.

'Wint! Where the hell did you come from?' Both men laughed and embraced. 'It's been a long time,' Charlie said.

'Know what the date is?'

Charlie looked around for a newspaper. 'January close enough?'

'Friday January fifth. Seven years to the day on Sunday.'

Charlie shook his head. 'Hell of a memory you got. Seems like yesterday . . . Have a seat, have a seat. So what you been doing . . . ? No, stand by on that.' He went over to the far side of the room to a broken-down Coldspot refrigerator and pulled out two bottles of Red Stripe. 'Last two, but enough to celebrate on.' He knocked the tops off on the edge of the breakfast counter and handed one to Winter. Then he opened the window and the door, allowing a cooling breeze to circulate through the room. 'That's got it.' He sat down and raised his beer. 'To the old days.' They drank.

'So what brings you here?' Charlie asked. 'Going into the treasure-hunting business?'

'Treasure hunting?'

'Sure. The old Spanish treasure ships. Guys out there every day. They run down to the Marquesas, usually by way of Mule Key and Boca Grande. After Boca there's a wide channel, beyond that the Marquesas. Lot of Spanish gold and silver down that way. Made a lot of guys rich over the years, and a lot more poor . . . and I guess taken a few as well.'

'No, nothing to do with that.'

'So why'd you come?'

'To see you.'

Charlie lit a cigarette with great care, as if needing

time to think. He was a man without friends. A loner.
His only visitors were people like debt collectors, repo
men, and the usual assortment of salesmen selling
everything from customised condoms to Caribbean
timeshares. No one came to see him, not even people
he had once known whom in an alcoholic moment
he might have considered friends; well maybe Nancy
stopped by once in a while, but she was the only
one. And now Winter had appeared after all these
years. The tall, elegant Winter. A gentle man until
you crossed him, or were unlucky enough to be on
the wrong side. He hadn't changed that much either.
The blond hair had greyed slightly at the temples. A
few more lines, sun spokes around the blue eyes. A
little more gaunt perhaps. The clothes looked expensive. Charcoal-grey suit, white button-down shirt, soft
red-patterned tie. Sure, the Chevy that he had seen
parked outside the house was not the choice of a rich
man, but Wint never had been one for flashy cars.

He flicked ash at the ashtray and looked up. 'How'd
you know I was still here?'

'Made a few enquiries via the old net – you know
how that goes.'

Charlie looked out of the window towards the street.
He started to say something then stopped.

Winter continued, 'I just called by the diner. Nancy
confirmed your address. She sent her regards by the
way.'

'Yeah, thanks, she's a nice lady.'

'She mentioned that you got roughed up by some
punks before Christmas. Anything I can do to help?'

'No, let it ride. They only got a few bucks.'

'How about your face?'

Charlie fingered his right cheek. It was scabby, but healing. 'Kind of matches the other side I guess.' He laughed. 'Anyway, how long you staying?'

'Depends.'

'On what?'

Winter swirled the last of the beer around the bottom of the bottle. This was the difficult part. How much did he tell? More than that, was this the same Charlie he had known all those years ago? He put the bottle down on the floor and looked steadily into the other man's eyes. 'Feel up to a short drive?'

'Sure, where we going?'

'I'll buy you an early lunch.'

'Give me five minutes to tidy up.' He went through to the bathroom and tugged off the stained sweatshirt. He ran some hot water into the sink, drawn as he was every day to the sickening reflection in the mirror. His nickname Ugly had been given him by the local kids, the left side of his face and scalp being scar tissue which gave his face a lop-sided appearance, especially when he smiled. Charlie didn't mind. If they had seen his body they would have run home screaming to their mothers. It, as he often remarked to himself in the shower, looked like hell. Sixty-eight per cent of it had received third-degree burns. But that had been a long time ago, back in the days when he had had a family and friends. After a few drinks he often thought he had really died in that crash near Bien Hoa and was now living in a parallel dimension, atoning for past mistakes or some such crap. Each time he sobered up, he considered psychiatric help, or, easier yet, putting a gun to his head.

Incipient suicide.

Likely to remain so, he thought. He didn't possess that kind of courage.

He scraped a razor carefully around the right side of his face and brushed his teeth. Then he went through to the bedroom and sorted through a basket of laundry. He put on a pair of faded jeans and a white sweatshirt. He couldn't find any clean socks, so he slipped his bare feet into a pair of worn canvas sneakers. Lastly he pulled on a dark-blue baseball cap. A quick glance in a dusty mirror, an old Air Force vanity about checking your dress before leaving your quarters, and he was ready to find out what had brought the Englishman back after all these years.

2

At precisely the same moment Ugly Charlie was joining Winter for lunch in Key West, an elderly man was arriving at a snow-covered terraced house in one-way Jackson Place, Washington, DC. His name was Oscar Porteous.

He went immediately to his office off the main hallway. The furnishings were antique and quite breathtaking, from the two French Rococo chairs in one corner of the large room, to the *bureau du roi* with the intricate marquetry and elaborate ormolu mounts. On the wall above the bureau hung a cartel clock by Juste Meissonnier. Even the fireplace was antique, an exquisite limestone creation, imported in the postwar years from Alencon where it had graced the drawing room of a French château for nearly four centuries. Before the fireplace a beautiful blue and gold Savonnerie carpet, and at either side of the hearth two high-backed *caquetoires* – conversation chairs – designed centuries earlier for ladies to sit and gossip in.

His secretary, Alice, an ageing woman with cropped iron-grey hair and an unsmiling face, appeared in the doorway. Porteous said, 'Coffee, lots of coffee.' She nodded and started to close the door. 'Do you know if Mr Williams is in?' The woman replied in the affirmative. 'Good, tell him I'd like to see him. Give me ten minutes.' The heavy oak door closed.

Porteous slumped into one of the high-backed *caquetoires*. Staring straight ahead. Lost in thought. The knives were out – he knew that. He also knew they were all pointing at him. He was certain it was the new Director who wanted to close down his operation, the man who had said at today's meeting a new broom sweeps clean. He had even suggested restyling the South American CIA stations along the lines of Israel's Mossad, which had good human-resource intelligence penetrations. That was the problem with self-made men, Porteous thought, no class.

Porteous was old-school. The smooth H YP – Harvard, Yale, Princeton – type. Refined, well tailored in manners as well as dress. He was also a jealous man, jealous of those younger and brighter than himself. He had destroyed many careers in his thirty years with the Company; not that he saw it that way – to him it was simply playing the establishment game. He was very good at it.

His job description was not so easy to define. He was the CEO of Lafayette Antiques, Inc., a company that supplied the finest antique furniture to politicians, embassies, and even on occasions to the White House. A company that would send its discerning buyers all over the globe to inspect and purchase a vast range of antiques. The reality, however, lay somewhere quite different.

White Lie

There are three levels on which the CIA interacts with the world of war, business and finance. One derives from the need for facilities for transferring funds to finance covert operations, military, political, and economic. The second, closely related, derives from the need for the clandestine investment of the agency's earnings from its front companies. The third, that of corporate cover, derives from the need to generate the illusion that agents engaged in covert action are actually ordinary employees of legitimate businesses.

Lafayette Antiques, then, was a commercial cover for SACO (South American Covert (Black) Operations), one of those 'technically legal but little else' units within the CIA. Black Ops was split up into global theatres, like the military, and mainly concerned infiltration under false cover into hot spots around the world to provide both critical and counterterrorist support. They were operations that never officially took place, although if a line was needed for the press it came under the heading 'token nonlethal assistance'. Only a handful of senior officials were aware of the precise number and identification of members within the unit, as well as location of offices, safe houses and multiple overseas fronts.

The antique company had been Porteous's life for more years than he cared to remember. It was all he had. All he wanted. It had become his empire, small and efficient, and when required, lethal. If they closed him down, what would be left? Back to the Virginia countryside? His mausoleum of a house, institutionalised by the smell of disenfectant and the whisper of oxygen; his ailing wife, Ursula, who chattered incessantly about trivial matters, who hated him under her feet, who had a fetish for cleanliness, who forbade smoking in every room but the library – a room she never visited – and who had slept in her own room for more than two decades now. Their relationship then was a career one. A partnership of social graces. No love.

Physically he was an unprepossessing man, small and portly, even though he had become anaemic and lost weight in recent months. Coughing up blood had been one of the early signs. He had consulted a private doctor, who had mumbled phrases like: upper GI bleed . . . coffee-ground emesis. Porteous had asked for medication. The doctor had said they would need to carry out an EGD (Esophago Gastro Duodenoscopy) first to establish cause: bleeding ulcers, vein or tumour. Porteous had declined. He was too busy. Even so, he had taken some of the doctor's advice and reduced his daily eighty-cigarette consumption to half that. To ease the smoker's cough, he had taken to drinking vast quantities of honey-and-lemon cough mixture. It was a medical condition he kept to himself, enduring bouts of pain in stoical silence. Not that pain was the real problem, more the fear of not being at the helm – he had never missed a day's work in his life because of sickness, and he was not going to start now.

Other than that he was completely bald with a heavily jowled face. Small flint-grey eyes set in a sallow face. Round silver-framed glasses which gave him the appearance of a small-town banker.

Alice appeared with the coffee tray, two white bone-china cups and saucers with matching coffee pot and a bowl of sugar lumps. 'Leave it,' Porteous ordered. 'I'll see to it myself.' She put the tray on the small Reisener cabinet and silently left the room. Porteous poured the coffee. Black, three sugars. Something he would pay for later in pain, but for now he needed to be alert. He returned to his chair and considered Tanner Williams for a moment. A former Navy commander, who had at the end of his service been the assistant naval attaché in Stockholm. His naval file had read: Gifted with high intelligence, courageous, ruthless, a brilliant sailor. He was also a heavily decorated man. Navy Cross, Silver Cross and two Purple Hearts. He had been with SACO for five years and had been Porteous's deputy for the last two of those years. The promotion had been political. Porteous considered him a threat.

The man who entered the room some minutes later, carrying a blue-stripe folder under his arm, was tall and lean and elegantly dressed in grey slacks and double-breasted navy-blue blazer. The white shirt with lightly starched collar was immaculate, as was the green silk tie. The Bally loafers he wore around the office were for comfort; on the street he wore highly polished Oxford brogues. His features were strong and his skin the colour of polished ebony. His ancestry went back to the Hausa people of northern Nigeria, a gentle race more likely to be the scholar than the warrior. Tanner Williams was both. A brilliant scholar who had distinguished himself on the field of battle.

He was also on that day a man in a hurry. It was his twenty-fifth wedding anniversary. A celebration had been arranged. Family members had flown in from as far as San Diego.

'We have problems, Tanner,' Porteous remarked.

'White Knight?'

Porteous nodded. 'Congress is today pushing through

an amendment to ban covert CIA assistance in Colombia. This following the recent bombing of clandestine airstrips which resulted in a number of civilian casualties.'

'Since when did civilian casualties—' Williams started.

Porteous cut him off. 'Not least of which were two government ministers and their entire families. The South American press is reporting it as an attempt to overthrow the government.'

Williams said, 'I was of the opinion that the operation was a limited success. After all, we did take out about fifty per cent of the cartel's operations.'

'"Causing a brief disruption of the real-estate market in Atlantic-coast resorts where the owners of luxury villas precipitously left," to quote the Director, and to paraphrase the remainder, which has left the major traffickers enjoying an open-ended vacation in Panama, pleased that a government operation has helped relieve the glut which was depressing prices.'

'And the source?'

Porteous gave a wheezing laugh. 'Source! You tell me. Probably nothing more informed than the *Washington Post*,' Porteous snapped, 'The new Director and his entourage playing politics with all the finesse of a bunch of mental retards – passing the buck for his predecessor's indiscretions. Don't you agree, Tanner?'

A muscle fluttered in Williams's cheek. Even though he often disagreed with Porteous's thinking, he was not in a position to question. Nevertheless, it made him feel uneasy when he spoke that way about some of the nation's most powerful people. He was keenly aware that the espionage business did not begin and end with the Central Intelligence Agency; indeed, there were other government bodies and even newspapermen out there equally capable of planting listening devices.

Porteous continued. 'More than that, a report from the DEA has indicated that the cartels have changed their import arrangements. Southern Florida is off the list. We have been asked to gather up-to-the-minute intelligence on this.'

'Not easy, we need time for things to quiet down.'

'Something we don't have, Tanner. We are being held responsible for the last fiasco. Which means we need to put somebody in on the ground yesterday.' Williams was silent, thinking. 'That for me?' Porteous indicated the folder Williams was carrying.

Williams looked at the 'blue-stripe' folder in his hands as though temporarily unsure how it had got there. It was so called because of its wide blue stripe, denoting a sensitive human source, 'blue stripe' or 'bigot' list, access being something available to a narrow select group of people with a need-to-know status. 'Maybe nothing,' Williams started, 'but we received a report from the DEA on a series of drug-associated killings in Oklahoma City. A woman TV reporter was slain by a drug gang. Following her murder, four drug pushers were executed in the city. It seems likely that her husband, a university professor, was responsible.'

Porteous said, 'Police work, Tanner.'

'My thoughts initially. Except police investigations discovered that the professor – a man named Carroll – had died as the result of an auto accident in England six years ago. By the time this came to light, the man passing himself off as Carroll had disappeared. It came across our side for assessment, where it was found that the man masquerading as Carroll was someone called John Winter.'

'Who did the assessment?' Porteous asked.

'Jack Kendall. European specialist. Good man.'

Porteous waved him on. Williams opened the folder and began reading. Pertinent points only.

'John Paul Winter. a.k.a. Jan Zikmund Winter, a.k.a. Sibelius. British mercenary. Planner in a number of Third World coups. Earliest information records him in the early 1970s moving back and forth through Checkpoint Charlie, Berlin, liaison with known KGB agents. Southern Philippines in 1974, working with the Marcos government to overthrow Marxist elements. Nigeria in 1976, photographed at the Kaduna Air Force base with Russian advisers. He then appeared in Tel Aviv with the Israeli Army in November 1978, a prelude to restructuring Zaïre's armed forces with PLO weapons stockpiles, and to train a brigade to defend Shaba province. La Paz, Bolivia, engineered the military coup that overthrew the first woman president, Lydia Gueiler Tejada. At the time of the Falklands War he was photographed at Cherbourg airport, France, with an Egyptair 707 freighter being loaded with Exocet missiles, which were routed via Cairo to Buenos Aires. In the late eighties he was in the Marshall Islands, apparently talking with two radical senators who were preaching revolution over the failure of President Amata Kabua to get the US to fund a major clean-up to make Bikini Atoll habitable again following the 1946 A-bomb testing. From there he went to the French islands of New Caledonia, possibly seeking support for his latest venture. Nothing more was heard of him after that time. Reports stated that he had been shot by the French.'

Porteous took the white handkerchief from his breast pocket and held it to his mouth, fighting to suppress a cough. 'And we're assuming he put out that final French report himself and assumed the new identity. Correct?'

'Yes.'

'Early background?'

'Made sergeant in the British Army, did a spell with the 22nd Regiment of the Special Air Service – the SAS – then he got into trouble in Northern Ireland at the beginning of the troubles. He shot one of his own officers.'

'I take it this is leading somewhere, Tanner?'

Williams closed the folder. 'I think so, sir. You see, the unofficial version of the Irish business indicates that the officer had shot two young Irish children who he maintained were Provisionals. It seems Winter knew differently and tried to stop him. He failed but later found the officer and killed him. He was arrested and taken back to England for trial. He escaped and went into the war business for himself. Something of a scholar, apparently, fluent in half a dozen languages. Which brings us to the present situation. His wife of eighteen months was raped and butchered by a drug gang in Oklahoma City. He, very quietly and systematically, finds and kills the four responsible.'

'Meaning?'

'Meaning he's been flushed out of retirement. Back across the line of justice and morality.'

'Meaning he could be of use to us in Colombia!'

'If we could somehow feed him the right information, yes.'

'Do we know where he is?'

'No. But I'm working on it.'

Porteous coughed into the handkerchief. Longer this time. 'How much time?' Porteous asked. It was a sophomoric question with no good answer.

'Weeks,' Williams said.

'How many weeks?'

'Difficult to assess.'

Porteous stood up and went over to the limestone fireplace and inspected the ornate carvings. He wondered for the thousandth time who the stonemason had been all those centuries ago. The artistic intricacy, from the first blocking out of the work with a bouchard, to the drill to produce the final small points of shadow. Breathtaking. 'I'll give you seventy-two hours to come up with something, Tanner. Three days, no more. I suggest you phone your wife and tell her you will be staying here until that time.'

Porteous waited until the door had been closed before going to his small private bathroom. He locked the door, switched on the extractor fan, lit a much-needed cigarette, Camel unfiltered, and recalled the new Director's last remark at the closed-door session with the Committee. 'You have to look to the future and, learning from the past, make sure that you don't make the same mistake again.' Without doubt another pointed reference.

In a small office on the second floor – furnished with little more than a grey metal desk and credenza, functional office chair, high-definition TV monitor, secure computer terminal and three telephones — Tanner Williams paced methodically backwards and forwards. His jacket was buttoned, and his tie was perfectly in place. He never relaxed.

Three days! What was the man thinking about? It was an impossibility. He picked up the phone and called his wife. He got the answerphone, which probably meant she was out at the airport collecting family members for the evening's planned celebration. He left a message explaining they had a situation, and that he would not be home for at least seventy-two hours. He said how very sorry he was, as this was their silver wedding anniversary, but that he would make it up to her. Promise. He loved her very much.

Then he took an address book from the top right-hand drawer and made a call to the United Kingdom. Edeyrn Caradog Owens, known as Ed by most Americans, Eddie or Edward by Brits, was a former SIS (Secret Intelligence Service) agent whom he had known from his time in Stockholm. They had played intellectual trivia games together, games which the old Welshman invariably won. Perhaps some of that trivia might lead to the whereabouts of John Winter.

Both calls were made on a Secure Telephone Unit (STU), which prevented the information content being exploited by hostile elements.

27

3

It was midday as the soft thunder of twin Rolls-Royce Tay engines carried a Gulfstream GIV away from Colon's France Field in Panama, on course for its destination: Cali, Colombia. It was as the aircraft commander was executing a smooth right-hand climbing turn in accordance with the SID (Standard Instrument Departure) and switching to departure frequency that a porter at Colon's Hotel Washington, situated at the end of Avenida del Frente, found the splatter of human blood, flesh and splintered bone in the east courtyard. He notified the assistant manager on duty. The Colon police were called. A squad of uniformed *policias* and two detectives arrived.

The late Pablo Ruiz, Mexican citizen according to his passport, had checked into the Hotel Washington the previous day, taking a suite on the fourth floor. He paid cash for the one-night stay. The same night he had patronised the no-limit salons of the Los Panama gaming casino. He had played roulette all night, eventually losing over 700,000 dollars. Enraged, he created an ugly scene, shouting that the wheel was fixed. Casino attendants were forced to eject him bodily – soon after 3 a.m., they said.

The night clerk declared that Ruiz had returned to the hotel in an agitated state and taken the stairs, presumably going to his suite. The exact time at which he changed into his red silk pyjamas and jumped from his bedroom window on the fourth floor was an open question, although it was thought to be close to the noon checkout time.

No credit cards or traveller's cheques or airline tickets were found in Pablo Ruiz's suite. Among his effects, there was less than two hundred dollars in cash, not even enough to pay his airline fare back to Mexico.

'*Suicidio,*' the senior detective shrugged, but wrote that the Mexican had fallen out of the window accidently: the standard practice wherever gambling casinos operate legally, for the simple reason that stories of suicides by gamblers who have lost everything deter other gamblers who would otherwise come in droves in the hope of winning something. No one considered the fact that Colon – the most dangerous city on Earth in terms of crime – stood little chance of attracting droves of gamblers, even if they offered the chips at half price.

By the time the Colon police – drinking free coffee from fine china in the lounge of the elegant turn-of-the-century grand hotel – had arrived at their conclusions, the GIV had descended over Colombia's westernmost mountain range, the Cordillera Occidental, and made a visual approach and landing at Cali's Palmaseca Airport. The sole passenger, Emilio Figueras, President of CALIMA CORP., was met by his eldest son, Luis, a practising attorney. They left the noisy crowded airport in a black Cadillac limousine, with dark, tinted, bulletproof windows, which took them at high speed and in air-conditioned comfort along the dusty roads of the Cauca Valley towards the family hacienda high in the green mountains.

Luis took off his glasses and rubbed his eyes. He looked and felt nervous. He turned to the white-haired patriarchal figure at his side. 'It went well in Colon, *Padre*?'

The bull-necked old man stared fixedly ahead. No one had seen him smile in the last three months. What they had witnessed instead were periods of long gloomy silences punctuated by moments of violent rage. It was there now as he reached inside his lightweight alpaca suit jacket and removed a Walther P-38 automatic with a white, pearl, inlaid handle, from his waistband. The big, raw, brutal hand made it look like a toy. He handed it to his son. 'Battle-spoil,' he snarled, his dark eyes flaring savage light. 'It belonged to a man – a *caco* – who failed me.'

Luis replaced his glasses. 'I take it he has reformed?' His tone chancing amusement.

'He is being reformed in hell, my son. I gave him three months after all, was not that fair? Three months to find and bring to me the man who killed your younger brother. And when he fails he runs away, steals from me, takes a new identity . . . thinks that I will forget.'

'What now, *Padre*?' The amusement was gone. Replaced by fear. His father was such a man. No forgiveness.

The old man reached across and laid a hand upon Luis's cheek. A short sharp pat. Violent enough to bring tears to the lawyer's eyes. 'Now? Now, Luis, I give the task to you. After all, it was you who suggested that Francisco go to Norteamerica to check the distribution network. But for that he would never have been in Oklahoma City.' The voice was full of bitterness.

The slimly built Luis, who had studied at the University of Southern California and Harvard, who had weak eyes, and was mocked by some for having the gentleness of a woman, made no reply. He was thinking of his younger brother, Francisco, the wild man who had no doubt killed the TV woman just for the fun of it. Just like his father would have done. He looked down at the Walther in his unsteady hands, Ramon's gun. His brother-in-law Ramon, the streetwise hard man, a natural-born killer who could frighten you to death just by looking at you. Ramon, who had married into the family, but who had cracked under the pressure of being given an impossible task. Who had run away, but not before stealing from his own family. A *caco* – a thief – was one thing. A thief who stole from the head of the Cartel de Cali another. Ramon, a.k.a. Pablo Ruiz.

I'm going to be sick, he thought. Dear God! How can I succeed where Ramon failed?

4

They drove down towards First Street talking about the old days, Winter occasionally making remarks about the town and asking questions on its history while checking his rear-view mirror every thirty seconds. It was a habit that had easily returned. They parked and walked the final two blocks to Sloppy Joe's. The bar was crowded and noisy. Cigarette smoke hung in a moist, warm haze that the labouring air conditioner could only slightly mitigate. A sign by the door said that Sloppy Joe's had been the once favourite haunt of Ernest Hemingway, but then the same sign probably hung in every bar in the Key. According to legend Hemingway had been a heavy drinker.

They found a crab-trap table in the corner. Winter ordered beers and the conch chowder then took a pack of cigarettes from his pocket and offered one to Charlie. He lit it and started to choke immediately. 'Sweet Jesus, Wint, what are you trying to do, kill me?'

'Particulares. Argentinian. Black tobacco. You get used to them after a while.'

Charlie stubbed the cigarette out. 'You may have asbestos lungs, pal – I'm operating on the non-fireblocked system. So, you were going to tell me why you're here.'

'Short check list or the amplified one?'

'Try me with the mnemonics. Short attention span.'

Winter smiled and leaned closer. 'I need to get out of the country.'

'Cops or Feds?'

'Probably both.'

'Money?'

'Not a problem.'

'When?'

'Immediate.'

'Shit! Perhaps you'd better give me the other version.'

'After we quit the merc business going on seven years ago, I decided I was on too many dictators' grey and black lists around the world, so I got a new identity. I became a college professor.'

'You what?' Charlie asked. 'Then again you always did have your head in a book. What did you teach? No, let me guess, either geography or history. You always did know more about those mosquito-haunted places at the end of the world than the people who lived in them.'

'One of the things that kept me alive, the maxim: "You have to know where you have been to know where you are going".'

'History, then.'

'Specifically Medieval European History. Even so,

the students were more interested in the drinking habits of the Cistercian monks in Saxon times than the kings and the politics. Seems they've adopted the pledges, *Woesheil* and *Drincheil*.'

'Same old stories you used to tell us, what was it? Your health?'

'Health to thee, and the response, I drink thy health.'

Charlie laughed. 'Had their priorities right those guys; so how did you manage the switch into the teaching game?'

'Borrowed somebody else's c.v. New identity and papers, and then spent a year brushing up on my subject, and applied for a position at a university in Oklahoma. I got the job and continued with my studies as I started lecturing. I was a bit shaky at first, but after a year or two even I was convinced that I was a reasonable facsimile of an academic. It was during my second year that I met Julia; she was a TV journalist. We hung around together, then moved in together, and then eighteen or so months back we got married. Everything was going fine until last September. She was doing a series of programmes on drug pushers infiltrating the metro schools. It was the evening that they ran the third programme in the series that she was picked up by a city drug gang. They raped her in a back alley . . . and then killed her.'

'Jesus,' Charlie exclaimed. 'I'm sorry to hear that. You okay?'

Okay? He would never be okay. He could live for a thousand years and would still wake up in a cold heart-wrenching sweat in the middle of the night. Hearing her voice. Her cries for help. Seeing her mutilated body. Not just mutilated, but sexually mutilated, her breasts removed piece by piece, her vagina opened up to her stomach, obscene words cut into her buttocks, her back, her thighs. Knowing she had died very slowly and very, very painfully. 'Yeah, I'm fine now.'

'What happened then?'

'I went after them.'

'Who?'

'The drug gang. I took them out one by one.'

'How many?'

'Enough.'

'What the hell does that mean?'

'It means those I considered responsible.'

Charlie had picked up the change of tone in the voice, the coldness in the eyes. Knew when to change the subject. He stared through the window onto First Street, watching the tourists for a moment. A pretty girl with spiky blonde hair and a ring in her nose, hand in hand with a slim Latino type; both wearing shorts and T-shirts, both it seemed without a care in the world. Two obviously gay men, talking and laughing, the older one caressing his partner's backside. 'Used to be a nice place this, years ago. Even better back in Hemingway's day, I'd bet. Now the weirdos have moved in and it's gone tits up.'

'I think that goes for most of the country, Charlie, and most back in Europe. Too many people, high unemployment, gives rise to a growing underclass, the classic ingredients for civil unrest, for war.'

'You figure?'

'We're hanging on by our fingernails, old friend . . . just a matter of time.'

They stopped talking while a waiter served the beer and the conch chowder. Charlie sprinkled salt on his, and they ate for a while.

'Were you followed here?' Charlie asked between mouthfuls.

'No. Went cross country to California, then doubled back.'

'Yeah, I should have figured you'd done that. I guess what you need is some false papers and head down to South America.'

'To do what?' Winter asked. 'Rot away in some forgotten backwater like La Paz; take my morning coffee in that old café on the corner of Ayacucho and Camacho and watch the sunsets across the Altiplano flatlands?'

'It was called Café Le Paz,' Charlie said reminiscently, 'the best iced coffee and cheese pastries in town. Do you remember that?'

'And where Klaus Barbie hung out until they expelled him in the early eighties. Yes, I remember. Got pretty cold in the evenings, didn't it?'

'I quite liked Bolivia – nice low-tech existence, like living in the nineteenth century. This damn place has gotten too crowded. You get tourists even in the summer now.'

'You could always move to Havana,' Winter suggested lightly. 'The way things are going, Fidel will soon be the only one left down there.'

'La Paz sounds better, I was happy there.' Charlie mopped up the last of the chowder with a piece of bread, while Winter ordered two more beers from a passing waiter.

'So how about it?' Winter asked, taking a sip of the

fresh beer. 'You find a plane and take me over to Colombia. From there I'll get a ride to Brazil, Africa, and find a way back up to Europe.'

Ugly Charlie nervously patted his pockets, found a crushed pack of Marlboros and lit one. When he looked across at Winter, his eyes were sad and full of tears. 'Colombia! Look at me, Wint – take a good look. I'm an old man, old and crippled. Jesus, even my hands . . .' He held them out; they were shaking, as was his voice now. 'I . . . I can't straighten them any more. Besides that I've got one good eye and another that can see about as far as that door. Fly an airplane! Shit, we'd end up in a ball of fire at the end of the first runway I negotiated. Besides, you were a pilot once.'

'Not with your background, Charlie.'

'You know what a bird of passage is, Wint? It's a homeless creature that spends most of its life on the wing. Flight-planning new destinations year in, year out. New hunting grounds. That some of its number get killed by larger predators does nothing to deter it from its chosen lifestyle; only one thing does that: fitness. When that fails, the bird makes its final landfall.'

'And rolls over and dies, you mean?'

'Or is permanently grounded. Fatigue life doesn't just apply to airplanes, buddy.'

'I'm not talking Mach numbers and high-g combat missions. Just a few hours low level.'

'Like I said, you were a pilot once.'

Winter looked around and his voice dropped. 'I was the planner, remember. I arranged the little wars, the coups for the Third World dictators. Flying was a necessary evil. You taught me a few tricks, but I'm thinking it will need more than that to get out of here undetected.'

'I guess it will at that. The customs authorities and any other ex-Hitler Youth geniuses will be watching every port and airport to make sure you don't leave the country. Then again they'd be looking for a college professor – you used another name, didn't you?'

'I did. But anyone checking up would soon find out that the background I had belonged to a guy who died years ago. From there it's just a matter of time until someone comes up with my true identity.'

'Don't get me wrong on what I'm about to say, Wint, but I could maybe fix you up with a ride down to Colombia. Unofficial.'

'How unofficial?'

'There's an old flying buddy of mine in the Everglades; haven't spoken to him in years, but if he's still alive and kicking, I'm sure he'll help you out.'

'You didn't say. How unofficial?'

'He does a bit of running between here and Colombia. Zero feet, under coastal radar.'

'Running? You mean drugs?'

'Yeah, but—'

'No buts, Major Riker. That kind of people killed my wife. You expect me to ride in the same plane with them?'

Charlie's half-open mouth snapped shut. It was as though he had opened a door into some other place, and he had seen something his mind had locked away. Winter's hands balling briefly into quivering fists of stone, the eyes focusing on something he could not see. The pallor on his friend's face not shock, but rage. Then the face had changed again. Comprehension replacing the blind, killing rage. What he saw finally belonged to other times, other places. It was still the most dangerous sight he had ever witnessed. Then the door closed. The eyes shut briefly, and when they opened again, the face was unnaturally serene.

And he knew beyond any shadow of a doubt what he had seen in the other man. He had seen the face of Death. Controlled. Planned. Disciplined.

They finished their beers in silence and went outside into the muggy afternoon and the smells of mangrove, salt ponds and mud flats. To the west, clouds were building. A storm was moving in.

5

It had taken Tanner Williams a little over six hours to track down Edeyrn Owens by phone, not at his home in England as he had supposed, but at the Alexander Hotel in Miami.

'Lovely to hear from you,' Owens said. Lilting Welsh accent.

'You're a hard man to find, Edeyrn.'

'The joys of retirement, one might say, the opportunity to travel on one's own timetable, to one's own destinations.'

'Would have thought you could have found a better place than Miami to spend your vacations. You need to be careful down there – lots of street gangs and drive-by shootings and not enough law enforcement to handle it.'

'Thanks for the tip, Tanner, but I rarely stray much further than the hotel bar. Besides I'm leaving tomorrow, going down to the Keys. My wife and I went once when she was alive, so I suppose one could put this down to a foolish old man's pilgrimage. Anyway, how's life with you? Still in the antique business I take it?'

'My wife thinks I should take an early retirement.'

'Ah, sounds like Oscar and his thirty-hour days.'

'Too much work and not enough play according to my wife, but I guess you're right at that: Oscar does get pretty impossible with his work ethic. Didn't realise you knew him that well.'

For a moment the voice took on a serious edge. 'Oh yes, we go back a long way Oscar and I . . . I think your wife is right by the way.'

'About what?'

'Taking an early retirement. It's our wives who suffer in this business, Tanner. It's only when we lose them that we realise how much we have neglected them, and by then it's too late. Anyway, what can I do for you? As charming as it is to hear from old colleagues, I'm sure you haven't gone to the trouble of tracking me down to advise me on the wisdom of my holiday arrangements, and my sister-in-law, bless her cold unforgiving heart, would have serious misgivings about any advice I offered on matters matrimonial. Or am I wrong?'

'I'm looking for someone.'

'Ah! And you think I may be able to help?'

'Or know someone who can.'

'There would of course be a fee for my services.'

'I'll take care of that.'

Owens laughed. 'No, no, boyo. The game. "They aimed at producing cleverness and efficiency rather than wisdom and goodness, and they charged fees for their services, since people take seriously what they have to pay for."'

Williams thought for a moment, then replied. 'Which

in effect stated, "Knowledge is impossible, but I can show you how to make the most of yourself." Ancient Greece . . . the Sophists!'

Owens laughed again. 'You know, Tanner, for an American you never cease to amaze me.'

'One of your backhanded compliments, right?'

'What the hallowed halls of academe lost, dear boy! I always told you you were too much of a scholar for this business. So who is he?'

'Englishman. Name: John Paul Winter. We are anxious to know of his whereabouts.'

'Background?'

'Mercenary. Ex-British Army. Served for a time with the SAS.'

'Not really my province. Photographs?'

'I'll send you what I have by courier tonight. You'll have it early tomorrow morning. What time were you planning on leaving?'

'Early afternoon, say one o'clock.'

'I'll call you at ten then. And thanks for this.'

'Quite all right. A word to the wise, however: I wouldn't mention my name in any reports you might draft. It could upset your gallant leader.'

'You in particular, or the Brits in general?'

'Bit of both, I fear. Well, must run. I'm having dinner with a banker from Milwaukee.'

'Sounds like a barrel of laughs.'

'I should have added, lady banker, early forties, long legs, very attractive.'

It was Williams's turn to laugh. 'Now why doesn't that surprise me? That Welsh charm at work, I guess.'

'Nothing like that, alas. I'm an old man; I pose no threat. Until tomorrow then.'

White Lie

Williams replaced the phone and made a notation in his desk diary. It said simply, 'Saturday a.m. — Flowers.' Owens's words about neglected wives had struck a chord.

6

It was in the early hours of Saturday morning when the squall line moved in on Key West. Thunderclaps rumbled in the distance, wind gusts banged the shutters of the house on Seidenberg Avenue, and the rain slashed across the sky in sheets.

To Ugly Charlie, fast asleep after a heavy drinking session with Winter, it was the sound of distant guns and the damp pungent air of a Vietnamese night. He was crawling back into the burning fuselage of *Blue Satin*, the operational name for an ancient C-47 that had made her last flight. Five times he went back to pull out the injured Special Forces guys he had picked up earlier from Loc Ninh, an up-country jungle airstrip; the last time the second set of tanks blew. There was a vague recollection of lying under wet dripping trees . . . except there were no familiar smells of rotting vegetation that marked this place, instead the distinct aroma of frying meat . . . trying to orientate himself with his surroundings . . . a pyjama'd figure with a coolie hat shining a flashlight in his face . . . trying to

close his eyes and finding for some unknown reason
he couldn't . . . raising an arm as a shield against the
light and seeing his own flesh . . . burned black . . .
melting from the bone . . . then the pain kicked in,
and he started screaming.

He woke with a start, soaked in sweat. He sat up
and switched on the bedside light and checked his
watch. Five after three. He sighed and got out of
bed, stretching for a moment. Grimacing against the
arthritic pain that throbbed in his finger joints. 'Fucking drink,' he mumbled to himself. He had learned
at an AA meeting, which he'd attended in one of
his more lucid moments, that lots of drinkers had
horrific night visitations not connected with DTs. This
normally after the drinkers were jolted awake by a
drop in blood sugar, or by withdrawal syndrome. The
tormentors could take any gruesome form: spiders,
snakes, rats. His were memorable visits to that one
place in his past and the fire that had sought to
engulf him. He saw the flames now, dancing around
the foot of the bed, heard the hiss of barbecued flesh.
The smell filled his nostrils. He screwed his eyes
closed, remembering what an ex-drinking buddy had
told him. 'You gotta learn to ignore the vodka gob-
lins, Charlie. It's not for you: it's for the other guy
that lives upstairs.' Easy to fucking say, but then he
didn't share the recurring dream. And how did you
put fear into words, when there were no words to
describe it?

Through shuttered eyelids he pulled on a grubby
terry-towel bathrobe and shuffled through the flames
to the kitchen.

Winter was sitting on a stool at the breakfast bar,

drinking coffee and reading a book. He looked up.
'Couldn't sleep either, eh?'

'Nightmares,' Charlie mumbled.

'You're still getting them, then.'

'Yeah, I'm still getting them.'

Winter poured a second mug of coffee and passed it
to him. Charlie helped himself to two heaped spoon-
fuls of sugar and stirred the drink. He lit a cigarette
with unsteady hands and sipped the coffee. 'What you
reading?'

Winter turned the slim book over. '*Manual of the
Urban Guerrilla.*'

'And which military dictator's ass you planning
to kick?'

'I'm not.'

'Just bedtime reading then?'

Winter was silent.

Charlie eyed the Englishman for a moment. Thinking. The look in the bar earlier that day. *Oh shit!*
'You're not . . . you're not considering wreaking some
kinda revenge on those guys down south?'

'Take the enemy by surprise, Charlie.'

'What about "Know the terrain of the encounter
better than the enemy"? For Christ's sake, Wint, your
wife's dead. Hell, I'm sorry, real sorry, but you said
you'd taken out those responsible. Why not quit while
you're ahead?'

'I did a deal with one of the druggies in OKC.'

'You what? What sort of deal?'

'Information for his life. He gave me the name of
Colombia's chief cocaine baron, address, company
front, and a lot more. His life story, more or less.'

'And you let him go!'

'I lied.'

'And you figure to go in solo and take out this guy, right?'

'Element of surprise, Charlie.'

Ugly Charlie put his coffee mug down on the breakfast counter and paced up and down the room. 'You know how well these guys are guarded? Shit, you'd never get within half a mile of their fucking fortress.'

'Not on foot I grant you.'

I'm not talking Mach numbers and high-g combat missions. Just a few hours low level. 'You're not talking air strike!'

'Why not?'

'How about they probably run their own paramilitary outfit, like Gomez did down in Bolivia? Shit, what did that guy have! Fifteen hundred soldiers, elite guard trained in Libya . . . an air force of three Harrier jump-jets, twelve fighter bombers, some reportedly fitted with Exocet missiles . . . and he reckoned he was just a cattle rancher!'

'Element of surprise, Charlie.'

'Don't keep saying that. Sure, you might get one bite at the cherry, but what are the odds of the head honcho being at home?'

Winter went over to the window and opened it. Rain dripped from the roof, and out at sea lightning crackled. He loved the rain and the smell of the sea. It reminded him of his youth in a faraway English seaside town. His attic bedroom that had looked out over the harbour. The muted sounds of the foghorn on dark, mist-shrouded nights. The violin screech of gulls. 'I'm doing it for my wife, Charlie, and for all the other husbands who lost wives that way, and for parents who lost kids to drugs. You know, I'll be fifty-three this year. Fifty-three! I spent Christmas by myself in a motel somewhere in Arizona, and for the first time I realised how fast this life goes. I also realised what I'd missed all those years: a wife, and a home. A newspaper boy delivering the morning paper and saying good morning! Can you ever remember anyone out in those Third Worlds wishing us good morning? No, of course you can't because it never happened. We were the hired guns, people were afraid of us, gave us a wide berth.' He drank a little more of his coffee, then put the cup down and closed the window. 'Going back to your question, Rule 4 of the IAs: Your information service must be better than the enemy's.'

Charlie made an explosive sound, a mixture of anger and incredulity. 'I'm not talking Initial Advantages. What about mobility and speed? You may get in and unload a few stores, but those recycled cocadollars sure as hell are going to be up your ass in Mach time.'

'So, what would you suggest?'

'Apart from borrowing a Stealth fighter from my old air force, with next to no radar signature, I'd say forget it.' Charlie finished his coffee and stubbed out his cigarette, and tried to massage the stabbing arthritic pain from his finger joints.

'That's the problem, isn't it? Everybody is doing just that, forgetting it, putting their head in the sand hoping it will go away.'

'Best left to the government.'

'You don't really believe that, do you? You don't think that any fat-cat politician is going to get off the fence and risk his multimillion-dollar investments getting involved with the dirty business of drugs, especially when the electorate is split on whether or not to legalise it. No, they'll wait until public opinion becomes strong enough either way to guarantee them their re-election before they lift a finger to do anything.'

'And what would you do? Send in the Marines? The Army? The Navy? The Air Force?'

'A better knight cannot die, though he might in a better cause.'

'What does that mean?'

'What it says. We pour all our money and military might into worrying over people like Saddam Hussein — who in reality is nothing more than a pimple on the face of humanity, but who threatens the oil investments of the Western cartels — when the planet is going the equivalent of HIV positive on drugs. Another hundred years and there won't be anything to govern. Half the world will have OD'd, the rest will be too high to care one way or the other.'

'You should have been a politician.'

'Too honest.'

Charlie laughed. 'Anyway, I'm going to turn in. Couch comfortable enough?'

'Fine. Just fine. See you in the morning.'

'Yeah. 'Night.'

Winter went back to his reading for another thirty minutes, then washed up the coffee cups, before lying down on the couch. He adjusted the cushion beneath his head. Charlie had changed a lot in the past half-dozen years, from the days he had flown operations for him in Third Worlds. And all the money he had made – what had happened to that? Winter's had been carefully salted away into various offshore corporate tax company accounts around the world in places like Geneva, Monaco, Luxembourg and Panama – legal and tax-free. Charlie didn't have enough to buy the groceries; an empty fridge with a half-drunk bottle of cheap vodka in the door rack seemed to confirm that. He had seen the pile of bills on the breakfast counter, had sifted through them. The phone had been cut off for nine months. The rent was three months past due. A local bank was threatening repossession of his twenty-year-old Volkswagen Beetle unless the balance of six hundred dollars was paid immediately. Mostly, they were final notices warning of legal action. Lastly there was a letter from an enterprising local law firm suggesting that for eight hundred and fifty dollars they would take care of all his problems by filing bankruptcy for him.

Eventually, he reached up and switched off the wall light and lay back, staring through the darkness, remembering Julia. Seeing her smile, the short ash-blonde hair, the green eyes beneath the perfectly shaped dark eyebrows, her voice when it was filled with laughter, the perfumed softness of her body when she lay in his arms at night and asked him to tell her about his day, and when his voice became filled with tiredness, how she would slowly stretch across his body and turn off the bedside light. And touch her lips lightly to his. Sometimes refusing to stop.

How she had been before the last time.

And the last time.

It was not the first body he had been asked to identify, yet he had thought that part of his life was something left far behind. Other people were there to support him, but there was no consolation at a time like that. A priest had been summoned to give the last rites, words that hadn't really registered or even been heard. He walked out of the city morgue, aware of the eyes upon him. A police officer quietly explaining that everything was being done to apprehend those responsible. Just a matter of time, he had said, the same words he must have used on many occasions before to many innocent people who had seen their world come to a premature end.

But that wasn't the only sadness. She had been married to a man named Deavas Carroll, a history professor. She had never known the truth. And as the events of love and trust had overtaken him, he had been too afraid to tell her for fear that he would lose her. Now it was too late.

In the darkness the tears came as he suffered the utter, dejected loneliness that had been with him every waking minute since. The same darkness in which he made his silent promises to her.

The rain beat in flurries against the window. After a while, he slept.

PART TWO
Vital Actions

7

It was snowing the following morning in Washington, DC. Williams had just returned from a late breakfast at the Hay-Adams hotel on H Street. Alice had brought him a cup of coffee, and he was now placing a call to Owens in Miami.

'Who am I talking to?'

'Edeyrn, it's Tanner – Tanner Williams.'

'Good morning, Tanner. Just got in from my early-morning swim.'

'Lucky for some – it's snowing here. You received the package okay?'

'Yes. Eight this morning. I took it down to the pool and went through it over breakfast.'

'You're making me envious.'

'You should bring your wife down for a weekend break, do you the world of good.'

'I have two kids in college, Edeyrn. Have you any idea what that costs?'

'Two days, Tanner, you'd go back a new man, and your wife would start baking cakes again.'

Williams smiled to himself. Sophie didn't bake cakes, never had. Preferred eating out. His mother had been altogether different, but that kind of woman didn't exist any more. Especially inside the belt-way. 'Perhaps, if I can get away. Anything on this guy Winter?'

'Spoke to a colleague of mine, Harry Tait, at Century House twenty minutes ago. He knew of him.'

Williams gave an audible sigh of relief. 'Any idea where we might find him?'

'Records show he's dead, Tanner.'

'Supposition.'

'Possibly.'

'Well?'

'If he's still alive, you don't want to know. If you were serious when you said you were thinking of an early retirement, then do it. Leave this for some-one else.'

'You make him sound quite lethal.'

'London had reason to think so. That's enough for me.'

'Any idea where he might hide out?'

Owens laughed. A rich, fruity sound. 'Winter hide out! Oh no, boyo, apparently he never does that. If you're looking for him, he's probably already got you in his sights.'

Williams looked out of the second-storey window at the thickly falling snow and felt a chill run over his body. 'I don't think so, Edeyrn. You see, he doesn't know we're on to him – yet.'

'In that event you're fortunate. Nothing known on whereabouts, but as he has, or had, an amazing knack for escaping the hangman's noose one must consider that he is constantly on the move.'

'How about associates?'

'Loyal lieutenants you mean. As a matter of fact he did have one. One of your people.'

'Name?'

'Riker. Major Charles Riker. Badly burned in Viet Nam. Invalided out of the Air Force. They said he'd never fly again; a few years later he proved the pundits wrong and passed his aircrew medical, what you would refer to as a flight physical, I think, although it was restricted, which meant he couldn't fly professionally. It was some time after that he teamed up with Winter in the mercenary business. Last heard of in Florida.'

'Where exactly?'

'Near a place called Ochopee in the Everglades. What used to be called Camp Alpha. Your people built it as a Top Secret base for training Cuban refugees. They were to form "hunter-killer" teams, infiltrate Cuba, and assassinate Castro and his principal aides. The operation, code-named "Havana Cigar", was eventually abandoned and the site sold off to a private consortium. Riker was involved with the new owners it seems. Mind you, that was all six or more years ago.'

'You're still leaving this afternoon, I guess.'

'Actually no, I've decided to rent a car and leave tomorrow morning. It's such a pleasant drive down through the Keys. Something I forgot to mention by the way, it seems your Major Riker picked up the Medal of Honour in Viet Nam; you might want to bear that in mind. You know what the press are like these days, hallowed ground and all that.'

'Yes, valid point. Anything else?'

There was a short pause. 'Just checking a few notes I made. Other than Winter preferring Gurkha *kukris* in the field – doubtless the result of some venerated old sergeant major conditioning his chaps into believing that cold steel strikes fear at the heart – it seems he only operates in Third World environments. It's just that I can't see him getting involved with your people. You're quite sure he's your man?'

'Quite sure.'

'Your report tallied with London's that he was reportedly killed in New Caledonia six or so years ago; but you know differently, is that correct?'

'Probability only.'

'No point my asking how all this came to pass?'

'Classified, I'm afraid.'

'Quite, quite. Well, if there's anything else, don't hesitate to contact me. The hotel manager here is a personal friend – Welshman, would you believe? He takes messages for me. I phone in daily whilst I'm touring around.'

'I'll do that, Edeyrn. Have a nice day . . . oh, and thanks for all this.'

'Think nothing of it, Tanner. For the only genius I've ever known, the very least I could do.'

8

To the forty-year-old Luis Figueras, being a bachelor
and not being currently involved in any serious love
affairs had advantages. He had no need to make apologies or excuses for spending the weekend in his city
office. Even so, he still found the time to stop at
the Iglesia de la Ermita, the beautiful Gothic-style
church overlooking the parks on the River Cali by the
Avenida Colombia, to light a candle for his mother,
who had passed away two years earlier. His mother,
who had suffered for years with atherosclerosis. Who
had taken nitroglycerine pills, among others, for her
condition. Pills that during the weekends, when his
mother's private nurse was off duty, only his father
was allowed to administer. Except on the occasion of
the last episode of angina there had been no little white
pills in the dark-brown bottle in the medicine cabinet.
By the time the doctor had arrived at the family home
it had been too late: the angina had developed, and his
mother had suffered a fatal heart attack. His father had
said nothing of the incident. Had shed no tears. Had

moved on with his life as though his wife of nearly fifty years had never existed.

Luis had learned of the absence of the prescribed drugs quite by accident. An overheard conversation by the nurse who had been employed to look after his mother. And Luis had made a simple vow: his mother's death would not go unpunished.

There was on this particular day, however, a secondary reason for his visit to the church. To give thanks to the Holy Infant and the Lady of Mercy, and to request another small miracle. To find the man whose name he had been passed by a contact in Washington, DC, the night before. And even though in the context of law the evidence that John Paul Winter was responsible for the death of his brother was as yet circumstantial, gut feelings told him otherwise. He took the rosary from his pocket and looked at it for a moment. His mother's rosary. Something she had had since childhood. He fingered the worn wooden beads and offered up the silent prayers as he knelt before the beautiful marble altar, never for one moment considering that God would deny his request. After all, wasn't he simply a pious son, who kept his mother's memory sacred? A hard-working man, who earned a great deal of money, but was more than generous in his gifts to the Mother Church?

The facts were somewhat different.

Narco-terrorism had resumed in Colombia in July 1992 when Pablo Escobar Gavira – one of the leaders of the Medellin Cartel – escaped from the La Catedral jail following the government's bumbling attempts to move him to a more secure prison. Over the next year and a half, the elite 1,500-man Search Block sought

Escobar, tracking down and killing most of his close aides and collaborators. Finally, in December 1993, after 499 days of searching, the special unit located Escobar and shot him dead. The government heralded its victory as the beginning of the end of the drug war. The proclamation was premature. Drug trafficking didn't diminish as the government hoped it would – on the contrary, it increased. And while Colombia's elite force concentrated its resources, hunting one man and persecuting one cartel, other cartels were quick to take advantage of the opportune circumstances.

The Cali Cartel, which developed during the 1980s, swiftly moved into the shattered Medellin Cartel's markets, and became Colombia's largest drug trafficker. The Cali organisation, led by Emilio Figueras and his sons, ruled the industry in a quieter, more businesslike manner – no less ruthless than its Medellin rival, but certainly more discreet and sophisticated, avoiding open violence and terrorism if it was not 'necessary'.

Luis chose to ignore what he termed government propaganda and media hysterics; he was the chief attorney of CALIMA CORP., a respectable trading company.

A palliative in a dangerous world.

It was twenty minutes later when he parked his dark-blue Mercedes S600 in the Plaza de Caycedo at the heart of the old city and went into the Banco Industrial Colombiano building.

Ana Lucia Rubiano gave credence to the fact that Cali was noted for the beauty of its women, *las caleñas*, or so thought Luis Figueras as he went into her office on the fourth floor. She was, as seemed the case with most bank employees, happy to work under neon strip lighting with the venetian blinds tightly closed – shutting out God's sunlight, or perhaps the distractions it offered – tapping busily away on a keyboard before a full-size computer VDU.

She stopped typing the moment he entered the air-conditioned room and came around her desk to greet him. She liked this man, not so much physically, in that he was very average – medium height, slim build, thick dark hair flecked with grey; the cool grey eyes were nice though. The business suits he always seemed to wear were very smart, but perhaps a little austere. No, it was none of those things. It was the little-boy-lost look that he sometimes had when he spoke to her, something that stirred deep untapped maternal feelings.

'*Buenos días*, Señor Figueras, it is a pleasure to see you again.'

'*Cómo está*, Ana.' He touched his cheeks lightly to both her cheeks, suddenly aware of the expensive perfume, the scent of shampoo in her shoulder-length raven hair, the slim body beneath the high-necked white blouse and elegant black skirt. 'You mentioned it was urgent,' she said, returning to her Eames chair behind the desk.

He sat and took a piece of paper from his inside pocket. 'I am trying to contact a gentleman who did some business with CALIMA a few years ago. Our chief accountant recently discovered that we failed to make a payment to his bank account. The sum is rather large . . . I was wondering if you could help.'

'Of course, but how? If you already know his account
. . . Perhaps it is with our bank.'

Luis removed his glasses and rubbed his eyes. 'And
that is the problem. We . . . that is our accountant has
checked the files, but for some reason the bank and the
address of the bank seem to have been deleted from
our computer listings.'

'Ah! Indeed a problem.'

'The money we have sent him has on one occasion
at least been sent from our account with your bank.
Perhaps your records might show this.' God forgive
me for lying to such a beautiful woman, he thought.

'Perhaps.'

Luis replaced his glasses and slid the folded piece
of paper across the desk.

Ana picked it up and unfolded it. 'Señor John Paul
Winter. This is all you have?' Surprise in her voice.

'And the date and amount of the last known transaction through this bank.'

'*Si*, but that was more than three years ago.'

'He is English.'

'*Inglés, si.*'

'I do recall he had offshore accounts in Panama
and possibly Switzerland. I thought if you cannot
find anything in your files, you could perhaps run
a check through some of your correspondent banks
overseas.'

'It is very difficult, I think.'

The attorney got to his feet. 'But not altogether
impossible, perhaps?'

She came back around the desk and walked with
him to the door. 'I will try, Señor, a favour to you.' She
smiled warmly.

'*Gracias*, Ana. And thank you for coming in on your day off. It is very much appreciated. Any information . . . you know where to reach me.'

She laughed. 'Everyone knows: at your office seven days a week. You should relax more.'

'That is what my mother used to tell me.'

'And you did not take your mama's advice.'

Luis looked sheepish. 'Perhaps . . . perhaps when you find my customer's bank . . . I could take you out to dinner?'

She laughed again, the even white teeth showing off the coral lips. 'Is that a promise?'

In a move that was completely out of character for the shy and conservative attorney, he placed his hands on her shoulders and kissed her on the lips. 'A promise, Ana,' he whispered. '*Chao*.'

She stood for a full five minutes after he had left. Believing and not believing. Had Luis Figueras, one of the richest and most powerful men in Cali, really kissed her? Promised her dinner?

For Ana Lucia Rubiano, twenty-eight, single, who had been raised in the slums of Cali, and had long ago set her sights on a rich and powerful husband, it was a dream come true. Almost.

For Luis Figueras, driving along Cali 12, it was simply a matter of criminal interpretation. His logic dictated that a man who had lived a number of years under a false identity had something to hide. A man who (allegedly) would avenge the death of his wife in a series of highly efficient killings, a professional. And the clever professional killers, active or retired, had one thing in common. They conducted their business through offshore companies, or at least held private offshore accounts. It was a long shot. But you had to start somewhere.

He stopped at the intersection of Cali 12 and Avenida Colombia and lowered his window to heat, car horns and salsa music, all excessively high. The place where people had changed the order of the letters to make 'Locombia', the mad country. His country. He waved over a gamin who was selling newspapers – probably stolen, he thought with a wry smile. He took a copy of *El País* and *El Occidente*, gave the street urchin a two-dollar tip for his enterprise, slipped the walnut wood-trimmed gearshift into drive and accelerated away in the direction of the Hotel Intercontinental, where he had a lunch meeting with an American attorney. An old friend from his days at Harvard. A man from a well-connected Boston family, who had as expected risen rapidly through the ranks of wealth and favour and was now chief legal counsel to the President of the United States. A man who had high political aspirations of his own, something Luis could help him with. Naturally the favour would be returned.

His thoughts drifted back for a moment to the beautiful Ana. They were very pleasing thoughts.

9

The Dry Tortugas lie sixty-eight nautical miles west of Key West in the Gulf of Mexico. Discovered by Ponce de Leon in 1513 and called Dry Tortugas because they lack fresh water, the small island group was for centuries inhabited by pirates. Garden Key is where the construction of Fort Jefferson was begun in 1846. After nearly thirty years it was still incomplete and was abandoned in 1874 following a damaging hurricane and a second yellow fever outbreak.

It was to this Key late that Saturday morning that a small blue and white Cessna 185 floatplane made its final approach. The floats skimmed the water before making a perfect touchdown. The pilot taxied in towards the wooden jetty. A matter of yards out he cut power to the three-hundred-horsepower Continental engine and climbed down onto the left float, tossing a line to a young boy.

Winter and Ugly Charlie climbed out and made their way down the pathway to a small deserted beach area. 'Told you you'd enjoy it,' Winter said, putting a wicker hamper and Styrofoam cooler in the shade of a scrub tree.

'I never get up until lunchtime on a Saturday,' Charlie complained. 'And that damned engine did nothing for my hangover.'

Winter opened the cooler and took a bottle of Red Stripe from the packed ice. 'Try that on for size. Want something to eat? Chicken or salad?'

Charlie took the beer. 'Where the hell did that come from?'

'Went out early this morning – that was after I'd phoned the Seaplane Service and booked a couple of seats. You were still sleeping. Been here before?'

'Hell no, this is for tourists.'

Winter lit a cigarette. 'Thought we'd do a bit of diving. Waters are quite shallow according to the pilot. He mentioned there were a few Spanish wrecks hereabouts.'

'And sharks and rays.'

'How dangerous are they?'

'Dangerous enough.'

'Two divers would be better than one, though.'

'What do we do for diving gear?'

'In the plane.'

Ugly Charlie finished his beer. 'Don't suppose there's any way I can talk my way out of this?'

'You're the expert, Charlie. I'm relying on you to show me the ropes.'

Half an hour later they were on a small boat being ferried out to the reef. They pulled on orange diving suits, strapped computers to the lines of the air-pressure gauges. Velcro wrappers firmly around the waist. Diving gloves. Masks rinsed and adjusted to their faces. Then they stepped off the stern into the sea.

The water was incredibly clear. Brilliant blue. The two men swam round to the anchor rope and started down, following the line. The sensation of floating in space a joy that Winter had long forgotten. A silent world which bordered on the unreal. The sunlight faded as they descended. The reef where the anchor was caught was a forest of coral and sea grass; fish of every conceivable description: yellow-tail snappers, angel and parrot fish, sergeant majors.

Winter checked his dive computer. It not only indicated his depth, but told him how long he was safe at that level. Charlie tugged his arm and pointed. A barracuda, at least five feet long, turned towards them threateningly. Winter eased back. Charlie grinned and signalled it was okay: he knew the 'cuda was seldom a threat to anyone.

They swam on for thirty minutes more, occasionally pointing out fish and exotic coral formations to each other. At one point two rays in close formation sailed gracefully by above them. The magic touched both of them, making them regret their slow climb back towards the sun. A by-the-book ascent, one foot per second, hands sliding up the anchor line. They left the line at twenty feet to swim under the boat and surface at the stern.

'What did you think?' Winter asked, dressing in his white shorts and tennis shirt. They were back at the patch of sand and scrub trees where they had left the hamper and cooler. Winter had broken out the beer and paper plates with chicken and salad.

White Lie

Charlie was noncommittal. He tugged a long-sleeved flowery shirt over his scarred body. 'I think I'm going to ache like hell in the morning. These old bones of mine ain't up to all that exercise.' He could have said, *Loved every minute. I'd forgotten how much fun it is to dive. One of those things that somehow found its way from the front burner to the back woodshed of exotic memories, like flying, I guess.* But what was the point? The past was past – it did no good to dwell on it. He pulled on the baggy lightweight cotton trousers and then sat down to put on his sneakers.

'I'm surprised you never bought a boat; must be quite a bit of charter business with all the tourists you mentioned.'

'Something I should have done once, I guess.'

'So what's to stop you now?'

Ugly Charlie made no reply. He was a proud man. Penniless but proud. That his wife had cleaned out his bank account all those years ago and moved in with a Mexican playboy was nobody's business but his.

Winter smiled to himself and settled down to eat his lunch. He knew Charlie better than Charlie knew himself. 'I've reconsidered your offer, by the way.'

'What offer?' Charlie asked, defensively.

'About the guy you know getting me a ride to Colombia.'

'What changed your mind?'

'Intelligence, Charlie. What better way to get through the door than being apparently involved with the people who do business down there?'

'You know what they think of gringos in Colombia?'

'I know.'

'Riding the wave of enthusiasm, huh?'

'I can swim.'

'So can the fucking piranhas.'

After the picnic lunch, washed down by six Red Stripes, Charlie lay back on the sand and slept. Winter cleared up the empty bottles and the paper plates and scraps and put them into a trash bag, which he carried back along the pathway to a large garbage container.

Then he went down to the water's edge and looked out over the Gulf. The sky was filling up with puffy cumulus. Wind swirled around the point and created tiny waves, while further out whitecaps rolled across the reef. The sun beat down. The clean salt air filled his lungs.

It was perhaps a little sad that such places existed, he thought. Especially as he and Julia had never had a real honeymoon.

She would have loved this.

10

Tanner Williams received two telephone calls that afternoon. The first was from Florence Bell, a naturalised Nigerian-American, who worked for the FBI in DC and had long had a soft spot for Williams.

'You're sure it's him?'

'Deavas Carroll, yes, the credit card number checks.'

'And he took a flight from where?'

'American Airlines from LAX to Miami late on Thursday evening. Friday morning he connected with an American Eagle flight to Key West.'

'Round trip?'

'No. One way. Coach.'

'Is that it?'

'No, he rented an Avis car at Key West. Chevrolet Lumina. Red. You got a pen?'

'Yes.' He copied the tag number. 'How long was the car rented for?'

'One week.'

'Being returned to the same place?'

'According to the Avis contract, yes. But it doesn't necessarily follow . . .'

'Yeah, I know, Florence. Look, thanks for this.'

'You owe me, Tanner,' she breathed seductively. 'Dinner sometime soon, perhaps?'

'I'm a married man, Florence.'

'And I'm a married woman; so what's that got to do with it?'

'Yeah, sure, least I can do. Give me a couple of days, I'll call you.'

'I'll be waiting. 'Bye, Tanner.'

Williams replaced the phone and immediately tapped information into his computer. Edeyrn Owens had been wrong about Winter. The guy might have been good as a low-tech Third World operator, adviser to generals who wouldn't make corporal in the US Army, but in this place he was just another dumb civilian. Credit cards left a trail a mile wide in this world.

The second call, thirty minutes later, was from a man named Palmer who was returning Williams's earlier telephone request. The call was made from a mobile phone. The place: Ochopee, Florida. The information was scant but informative. 'Charles Riker lives in Key West. Address as follows . . .'

When Williams terminated that call he was a happy man.

It was late afternoon and still snowing when Oscar Porteous returned to the house in Jackson Place. Williams waited for five minutes and then went to see him. He was seated in his usual conversation chair. Handkerchief to his mouth. Coughing. The room was in near darkness, curtains drawn tight. The only light came from the log fire crackling cheerfully in the vast limestone fireplace. Shadows danced off the walls and the numerous gilt-framed paintings. Faintly, from a music centre concealed in an antique cabinet, came the sound of classical music. Williams recognised the overture to Wagner's *The Flying Dutchman*. A ghostly ship rushing headlong through the raging storm – Williams wondered if Wagner's creation of a dramatic atmosphere, and Porteous's choice, was purely coincidental.

'I hope it's urgent, Tanner.' A hint of impatience.

'I think it is.'

Porteous waved to the chair opposite him. 'You'd better sit down, then.'

Williams took a deep breath. 'I think I've located Winter.'

'On file?'

'I'm still working on that. I thought you might want an immediate update.'

Porteous held the white handkerchief to his mouth and coughed again. 'I'm listening.'

'It seems there is every chance he is in Key West.'

'Any reason that we know of for him going down there?'

'Nothing certain. Could be a jumping-off point for an unofficial boat ride to Cuba.'

'What else?'

'One Charles Riker, who was on the Winter team some years ago. Seems he might live in Key West. Could be helping him to get out of the country.'

'What action have we taken?'

'Nothing yet. I do have someone in Miami, though, who could possibly act as a go-between.'

Firelight glistened off Porteous's bald head as he turned to look directly into Williams's eyes. 'I wish I shared your optimism, but long experience has taught me to see calamity in every opportunity. I therefore suggest that you take a few days' vacation. They say the Keys can be rather pleasant at this time of year.' A threatening tone had entered his voice when he added, 'I was at a private meeting this afternoon and I was asked how things were progressing with the Colombia business. I said we would have some answers very soon. When I next see you I expect that to be the case.' He lifted a small remote controller from his lap and pointed it into the darkness.

Wagner filled the room, but not before Williams had heard the deep, retching cough.

11

Most of the tourists were out on the dock near Old Mallory Square watching the sunset, leaving the bars on Front Street and the imaginative cafés on Duval Street quite empty.

Winter and Ugly Charlie were at Sloppy Joe's, drinking Red Stripe with vodka chasers, at the corner table they had occupied the previous day. They had been back from the Dry Tortugas for nearly two hours and had been with the pilot of the float-plane to the yacht club to look at his thirty-four-foot Chris-Craft. The pristine white boat was for sale.

'Nice boat, wasn't it?' Winter said.

'I guess,' Charlie replied.

'So how about it?'

Charlie lit a fresh cigarette from the butt of the old one. 'Jesus, Wint, don't you ever take no for an answer? I'm no good to you. Over the hill. Burned-out case. You pick the epithet. I can't do it any more . . .' He could have added, 'Sometimes I dream I'm maintaining formation on a jitterbugging wingtip at night in the

middle of a thunderstorm . . . and when the formation
light disappears, wondering if it's bounced up in
turbulence . . . or if the leader's turned and we're
about to collide . . . and I'm scared and I feel my
bladder going and I can't stop it . . . and I wake up
and find I've wet the bed and I'm still scared . . .
a fucking dream and I'm shaking all over.' But he
didn't. Pride. Instead he said, 'Look, I'll make a call
to Johnny Shoosh from the Pier House Hotel, get you
a ride out. Maybe he can suggest someone for you to
team up with. Any number of good guys would take
a boat like that in payment.'

'I don't want drug runners, Charlie, I want professionals. Men with the discipline of fighting guerrilla
wars. Military-trained pilots who know the enemy
better than the enemy knows himself. Somebody I
know – and trust.'

'Don't knock those druggies. You've got to be pretty
damn slick to get through coastal radar into the States.'

'And a lot get caught. I need a one-hundred-per-
cent foolproof operation. Besides, what else are you
doing?'

'I'll get a job.'

'Doing what? Washing dishes? Sweeping the streets?
Come on, Major Riker, you're too good for that.'

'Was, buddy, was.'

Winter changed tack. 'Yes, maybe you're right. Your
ex-wife Susi said something along the same lines.'

Charlie's head jerked up. 'Susi! What . . . what are
you talking about?'

'I ran into her in Los Angeles – lives near the
university in south central. That's how I found out
where you were. So what was it? She took all the

money you made when you worked with me, and when the pay cheques stopped, shacked up with that Mexican divorce lawyer guy.'

'Go to hell, Wint.'

'And ever since then you've been drowning in a sea of self-pity. The war hero who got badly burned in Viet Nam, who lost his good looks saving a bunch of shot-up Special Forces guys, who hides in dark rooms and takes menial jobs. What is it, Charlie? Did some born-again Christian tell you to wear sackcloth and ashes and do penance for the rest of your life, that the big airport in the sky is really all that is important now?'

'Go to hell.'

'You already said that. Come on, Major Riker, you can be more imaginative than that. I remember ten years ago seeing you standing before a bunch of Third World fighter jocks, briefing them on ground-strike missions in obsolete ships that were more dangerous than the enemy. Those guys would have followed you to hell if you'd asked them.' Ugly Charlie stubbed out his cigarette and stood up. 'Where are you going?'

Charlie's voice was quiet. Defeated. 'You don't get it, do you, Wint? It's not what you want or what I want. My body has quit on me; it's had enough. The systems have started shutting down. In the Air Force you had a way out – eject. Here there's no such luxury – you just stay with the ship and auger in. You asked where I was going. The Pier House. I promised you I'd call Johnny Shoosh and fix you up with a ride out of here. After that you're on your own.'

'I'll go and pick up the car. Wait for me at the hotel.'

Ugly Charlie raised a hand and was gone.

It was half an hour later when Winter turned onto Duval Street. He had taken his time collecting the car, walking past the parking lot a couple of times, looking for the unusual, waiting for night to settle. When he was sure it was clear, he drove away quickly, heading the opposite way for a few blocks before swinging back in the direction of the Pier House.

His headlights picked out the scuffle on the sidewalk. Kids drinking too much, getting into a fight. Christ! The night had hardly begun. He had driven past the incident before he realised it was Charlie. The baseball cap. The flowery shirt. He slammed on the brakes and leapt out of the car.

There were two of them. They had taken Charlie into a side street, had him down on the ground, going through his pockets. Winter stooped and picked up the baseball cap, dusting it off on his thigh. His head was lowered, his eyes up, fixed on the youths. His voice was just loud enough to be heard. 'I think you're making a serious mistake, boys. I'm the one you want.'

The two youths stopped, turned towards him, and moved apart.

The first one slashed a knife blade through the air. He took a step towards Winter, a grin forming on his face. '*Buenas noches, Señor.* You have money also?'

Winter backed off half a step, coming up to an erect stance, eyes locked on the thin-faced youth. The first lunge with the knife was clumsy. Winter parried the arm aside and stepped expertly inside the arc. A stiff, straight right to the solar plexus deflated the mugger's lungs, winding him. Even so, the youth swept the knife hand out wildly. Winter grabbed the hand, twisting and extending the arm, then stepped over the falling body. A sickening, tearing, cracking sound confirmed the dislocation of the youth's shoulder. Winter continued the move, rendering the arm useless. The youth lay on the ground writhing and moaning in pain.

Winter picked up the knife and moved towards the second youth, who stood transfixed by what he'd just seen. 'Go to the car, Charlie. I'll be right with you.'

Ugly Charlie scrambled to his feet, retrieved his baseball cap, and stumbled off down the alley.

'So what did you take from my friend?' Winter asked, circling the second mugger.

The wild eyes looked around, trying to size up a way out, yet somehow knowing it was not possible. He dropped the knife held loosely at his side and backed up against the wall. 'Nothing . . .'

A big hand grabbed his throat. The knife blade stroked his cheek. 'Why should I believe you?'

'It is truth . . . I swear, I swear on my mother's grave . . . this time nothing . . .' The strangled voice stopped. The wild eyes registered the mistake.

'This time? You have stolen from this man before?'

'*Si* . . . yes, Señor . . . perhaps once.'

Winter rapped his head sharply against the wall. 'How many times?'

'*Seis* . . . *diez* . . . I cannot remember . . . please, we will give the money back.'

'You deal?' Winter asked.

'Deal?' The eyes puzzled over that for a second. 'Ah deal . . . *si* . . . you want crack?'

'What else have you got?'

'Cocaine . . . it is best, Señor . . . very best.'

'You sell to schoolkids?'

'*Si* . . . Americano kids have lots of money.'

'Lots of money,' Winter agreed. 'You like America?'

'*Si, mucho buenos.*'

'And you'd like to stay permanently in this wonderful country, is that right?'

'*Si* . . . yes . . . we would like to stay very much. You can get me and my friend green cards perhaps? We pay you well.'

'Better than that,' Winter replied.

Ugly Charlie glanced across at Winter as they turned towards Roosevelt Boulevard. 'Thanks, Wint, I owe you one.'

'Why didn't you wait?'

'Thought I'd save a bit of time by coming to meet you.' He put his hands onto his knees. 'Can't stop my damned legs shaking.'

'Were they shaking before those punks grabbed you?'

'No.'

'It's just adrenaline, then. It'll stop soon.'

'I got through to Johnny Shoosh by the way.'

Winter, checking his mirror for following headlights, said, 'Any luck?'

'He's got a flight out on Monday night. He'll pick you up from Marathon Key.'

'Destination?'

'Colombia . . . strip called Canaveral. That's a code name used by the guys in the drug-hauling business. The flight will be at low level to avoid Cuban radar.'

'What about radar this side?'

'Northeast of here they run up a balloon, called

an aerostat, to fourteen thousand feet or so. They look down with radar. It's not going to be up on Monday night.'

'He told you that?'

'Yes.'

'How does he know?'

'They pull it down in bad weather. Apparently they lost one once due to leaving it up in a storm. That cost the government fifteen million bucks. Now they reel it in. Course, you'll have to stay low-low to avoid military primary radar.'

'He's expecting some weather on Monday night then?'

'According to the satellite stuff he's picking up and local television reports, yes.'

'And the low-low, how low would that be exactly?'

'Oh, I don't know. Twenty . . . thirty feet . . . until you're past Cuba.'

Winter made no reply. Low flying was one thing. Low flying at night in bad weather with a man you didn't know was something else entirely. He took a pack of Particulares from his shirt pocket and lit one. 'Want one of these?' Charlie shook his head; his hands were still clinging to his knees. Winter lowered his window and felt the soft night breeze on his cheek. Soothing. 'What time out of Marathon?'

'Johnny figures the front'll be passing through about twenty hundred hours. That's when he'll be coming in. I've got to confirm with him on Monday afternoon.'

'And how well do you know this guy Shoosh?'

'Well enough. Served with me in Nam.'

'What sort of pilot is he?'

'Old.'

Winter frowned. 'What's that supposed to mean?'

'Means he's still around. Don't worry, he's the best.'

'Can he do anything about finding me a good operational pilot?'

Ugly Charlie fumbled in his shirt pocket and found a crushed Marlboro pack. It was empty. He dropped it on the floor and went back to holding his knees. 'Maybe. It'll take money, though.'

'That's not a problem.'

'I'm coming with you,' Charlie said suddenly.

'You what?'

'I'm coming with you.'

'Look, Charlie, you don't owe me a thing; those punks back there I mean. I would have done it for anyone.'

'I made my mind up before that. Something you said to me back at the bar. I guess I just needed someone to believe in me again – you know what I mean.'

Men made poor decisions under the influence of emotion. In the SAS's world, emotion had been a perverse word. But uncontrolled emotion had put Winter here in this place, so he couldn't really blame Charlie for his decision. Besides, hadn't he come here expressly to recruit the man? Even so, he didn't show his feelings. 'Don't give me that sentimental crap, Charlie. If you're coming along I expect results. No thanks, no tears, no prisoners. Okay?'

'Okay.'

Winter flicked his half-smoked cigarette out of the window. 'Does that car of yours run?'

'The Volks? Yeah. Just needs some gas, no tag or insurance, though. Why'd you ask?'

'A small strategic problem we might have.'

'Like what?'

'Guerrilla warfare, Charlie – you know what that's about. Ducking and weaving, and running for a better day.'

Winter went on to outline the problem, and his plan to overcome it.

12

Tanner Williams's *vacation* started on the Monday morning. He had been taken to Andrews Air Force base in a dark government Oldsmobile, where he had boarded a grey and white T-39 Air Force jet. After take-off a young lieutenant crew member had served him with a cup of black coffee and then returned to the front of the aircraft. Williams had declined the small, clinically wrapped tray of sandwiches, happy to sip on the strong, sweet coffee. He toyed with the gold Dunhill cigarette lighter in his jacket pocket for a moment. Pity he had stopped smoking more than a year earlier, he reflected. Made the lighter obsolete. He carried it anyway, something of a good-luck charm. Something his wife had given him in happier days.

Things were going quite well, he decided. Of course the use of plastic had been Carroll's or Winter's – or whatever his real name was – undoing. Which meant he had been lucky. His report to Porteous, however, had been modified to remove any suggestion that luck had played even the smallest part. Which of course meant that Oscar would have to grudgingly agree that he had performed the seemingly impossible.

He finished his coffee and went aft to the small toilet in the rear of the cabin. He ran hot water into the aluminium basin, soaked a flannel, then, wringing out the excess moisture, held it to his face for a moment. He then inspected the reflection in the mirror. Good, strong features, hair greying slightly at the temples, which of course was to be expected at fifty-two. Even so, he had held back the years pretty well. And Grandmother Baba had said all those years ago that there was no escaping the *gandu* fields, that the master's farm would always be there. She had been an old woman at fifty-two, worn out by too much work. She had died before she could celebrate her fifty-third birthday. He wished she were still alive to see how successful he had become. Not so with Sophie – she expected success, felt it was her birthright, and his as well. Now she was insisting that he take an early retirement. She wanted to travel while she was still young enough to enjoy the world. One part of him agreed, especially if it meant saving their marriage, the other, career-orientated, eying the chance to take over Oscar's job. Something he had worked long and hard for. Perhaps there was a compromise, something that would satisfy his wife. What it was he didn't yet know, but if such a thing existed, he would find it.

He went back to his seat and strapped himself in and opened his briefcase. He checked off the phone calls he had made that morning, then swore softly when he saw the notation he had made about flowers for Sophie. He had forgotten. Never mind, he would be home soon. He would deliver them in person.

Thirty-five thousand feet below, lost beneath a deck of rumpled cloud, Charleston, South Carolina, slipped by. The jet being vectored by military radar altered heading slightly as it was given a direct track for EYE – Key West International. The time was 1100 EST.

13

Ugly Charlie was sitting on his bed at the Econo Lodge motel on North Roosevelt looking at his watch. He needed a drink. Winter had been gone all morning, and he was getting edgy. The change of address had been Winter's idea. They had moved out on Sunday, taking the Volkswagen and leaving Winter's rental car outside the house, and driven to the Econo Lodge, where they booked two adjoining rooms. Charlie hadn't been convinced that they were being watched, at first. Then Winter dropped the bombshell. Told him about the paper trail he had left. That had got Charlie's attention. He asked why? Winter had smiled in that enigmatic way he had, and said, 'The seventh sin, Charlie.'

It was like other times. The tethered mule and the 'body' in the sleeping bag, alongside the dried-up river bed in Afghanistan, the Soviet Mi-24 helicopter manoeuvring into position for its gunner to engage with machine-gun fire, and Winter perched high on a mountain ledge, firing the Redeye missile that went down through the rotor blades at supersonic speed.

The destruction of one or more of the five rotor blades meant the pilot had no chance of autorotation. The helo plummeted to the ground and was engulfed in flames, killing the pilot and the gunner instantly. One of Winter's traps. Set and sprung. The seventh sin was where you *failed* to plan things and to act out of improvisation. Winter's actions translated in Charlie's mind to: Only a matter of time before the feds know my identity. Therefore, I give all assistance leading them where I want them to go. Thus, I have the advantage.

Charlie heard a car pull up. He shuffled over to the window and eased the curtain back a fraction. It wasn't Winter. Just a black Lincoln backing into a parking space. An old man with short, thinning, grey hair and wearing a blue sports shirt and white pants got out and walked towards reception. Tourist. Charlie checked his watch again, and unable to take any more, and against Winter's express instructions not to leave his room under any circumstances, pulled on his old baseball cap and slipped out of the door. There was a gas station less than a block away. He would pick up a six pack and be back in ten minutes.

It took him fifteen, and still Winter hadn't returned. He popped the top of one of the Red Stripe beers and put the rest into the refrigerator. He sat on the edge of the bed and drank. Then again there was Johnny Shoosh. He had told him one passenger outbound. As for Wint, he hadn't been altogether truthful. He hadn't decided about going with him until that very moment in the car, when his legs had been shaking uncontrollably, and the thought had occurred to him that with Winter he would at least be safe. It didn't really matter where they went. Anywhere but here.

Here he was going to sit and live out his last years thinking about the good times, knowing they were all past and what remained was nothing more than an empty room to fill the empty days. No one to talk to. No women to hold. No excitement.

He picked up the phone and dialled Shoosh's number in the Everglades. He needed to confirm the ETD. He also needed to confirm that the light plane would have room for a second passenger. As internal fuel tanks, to extend the range, would have been fitted, payload would be a critical factor.

He finished his beer, got a second from the refrigerator, lay back on the bed and took the slim booklet from between the folds of the newspaper on the nightstand. Winter had suggested, because he was back on the strength, he should at least be up to speed on guerrilla warfare techniques. Some fucking joke – between them they had written the book a dozen times over. Even so, he started reading:

To compensate for his general weakness and shortage of arms compared to the enemy, the guerrilla uses surprise. The enemy has no way to fight surprise and becomes confused or is destroyed.

The technique of surprise is based on four essential requisites:

a) We know the situation of the enemy we are going to attack, usually by means of precise information and meticulous observation, while the enemy does not know he is going to be attacked and knows nothing about the attacker.

b) We know the force of the enemy that is going to be attacked and the enemy knows nothing about our force.

c) Attacking by surprise, we save and conserve our forces, while the enemy is unable to do the same and is left at the mercy of events.

d) We determine the hour and the place of the attack, fix its duration, and establish its objective. The enemy remains ignorant of all this.

Ugly Charlie lowered the booklet and opened the South America pilot's route chart that Winter had given him. It was sparse in content, and carried no topographical information, giving only track distances in nautical miles between major cities. Ways of escape following the strike. Provided they could find the right type of military aircraft. Provided it carried the right type of ordnance. Provided they could find someone to give them a thorough and detailed checkout on the military hardware.

But it wasn't those things that concerned him. Winter was Winter. A man who had a happy knack of achieving the impossible. Doubtless he already had sufficient intelligence in his back pocket to negate initial problems. As for the element of surprise, he was right about that. There might be a few seconds' warning for the enemy, but nothing more. The problem would be in egressing the area safely. There seemed no obvious solution.

He picked up the booklet and started reading again.

14

Tanner Williams arrived at Key West at 1201 Eastern Standard Time. The arrival of the jet had been delayed by some minutes due to the need for radar sequencing in traffic for their approach. The weather was hot and muggy. He was collected on the ramp by a black Lincoln town car, which proceeded through the main gate security check and turned towards the old town. The driver was Edeyrn Owens.

'Good flight, Tanner?'

Williams dabbed at the sweat on his face with a handkerchief, then looked across at the driver. An amazing man. Sure the grey hair was a little thinner on top, the cheeks hollower than he remembered. But the permanent smile, that hadn't changed – as if he had found some inner peace. There was nothing in his appearance or demeanour to suggest that he had once been a spy in the employ of the British Secret Service. In fact dressed in the pale-blue short-sleeved shirt and lightweight white cotton trousers, he looked like a retired American worker on vacation. 'Not bad, Edeyrn. Nice to see you again after all this time.'

Owens chuckled, 'Except you wish it were under more auspicious circumstances, isn't that the case?'

'I remember you telling me about Vladivostok and sitting in a car half your life waiting for one of your Russian Mafia pals to appear out of the shadows. Always backing your car into a parking space so it was poised to make a quick escape. Always making mental notes of every unlighted window. Always suspicious of every locked door. Didn't seem like much of an existence.'

Owens said, 'Oh, it wasn't that bad. Good times, bad times. One charming marriage, an unlimited supply of vodka in the bars on Lenin Street. Of course, the people were hard. When the Tsar dispatched his pioneers to open up his vast territories in the mid-nineteenth century the weak ones ended up in Siberia, the tough ones reached the sea – Vladivostok.' There was a moment's reflection in his voice. 'Of course, I would have preferred Berlin and ice skating at the Europa Centre and Saturday nights at the opera. But no, I understand what you mean, and I'm afraid, boyo, they've got you by the short ones. I told you in Sweden, before you got involved with the Company, that you had to be careful about stepping on people's toes, especially our sort of people; they have long memories.'

'Whose toes did I step on?'

'You know what I mean. Yale graduate. Navy hero. You're too brilliant – you frighten people.'

'You forgot black.'

'That makes you twice as frightening.'

Williams smiled. 'Perhaps I should wear a loincloth and carry a spear.'

'Perhaps you should have followed the academic path. You're too clever to be in this business.'

'Run away you mean?'

'Is that what you call it?'

'Maybe. Anyway, I don't altogether agree with you about stepping on people's toes. I consider my record pretty good.'

'Except you're here, boyo. Back in the field. Civil war among the gods, and violent quarrels and fights, and a great deal more of the same kind, I shouldn't wonder. Oscar never could delegate very well, could he? Always liked a finger in the pie. And to send his number two on such a minor errand of finding the artist of religious pictures, especially on the robe which is carried up to the Acropolis at the great Panathenaic festival . . . if one believes such stories of course. Or perhaps there's more to this than meets the eye!'

Williams permitted himself a half-smile. There were no easy answers with Edeyrn Owens. A reason he looked on the old man as a father figure, his case officer, even. They both possessed natural brilliance. Had similar academic backgrounds. And in their day had lacked the necessary family background to take them to the top. A genetic Peter Principle. 'Perhaps. So where is he?'

'Winter, you mean?'

'Winter.'

'With Riker as you surmised. They're leaving tonight in a light aircraft from a place called Marathon Key. The aircraft is picking them up at twenty hundred hours.'

'I'm impressed, how did you—'

'Find out? You know, Tanner, age is a curious thing. On the one hand the body slows down and becomes more or less an imperfect copy of its former self; at which point we are sent away from the workplace into some sunlit green pasture to await whatever it is our faith has conditioned us to believe in. Our minds on the other hand have assimilated all this wonderful information. Decades of wisdom. A library of little black books full of answers. And suddenly and quite inexplicably it is all useless, obsolete. So let us accept that I've been doing this for rather a long time and, modesty permitting, one might add I'm rather good at what I do.'

Williams took the slim Dunhill lighter from his pocket and turned it over in his fingers. 'So what's the plan after they're picked up?'

'A little clandestine jaunt down to Colombia. Place called Canaveral. Quite popular with the drug-running fraternity, although your DEA people are quite familiar with all that goes on there.'

'South America. That figures. Easy place to get lost in.'

'One thing that puzzles me, however.'

'What's that?'

'This is not the Winter that I've heard about. He's not doing a very good job of covering his tracks.'

'Getting old, careless. It happens.'

'Possibly, possibly.' Owens turned right on Whitehead Street. 'I've booked you a room next to mine at the Pier House, by the way. Have you eaten?'

'Not since breakfast.'

'Good, we'll have lunch then.' Owens braked gently

to a stop, reversed the car into a parking space outside the Pier House and switched the engine off.

Williams said, 'You see, you're still doing it!'

'Doing what?'

'Backing into parking spaces, ready for the quick getaway.'

Owens laughed. 'A spy's balance sheet summed up in a single sentence. And people think we lead romantic lives. If only they knew.'

Williams reached up and pulled down the sun visor and checked his eyes in the vanity mirror. They felt gritty. His suspicions were confirmed – the left eye was bloodshot. He tried to remember if he had packed eyedrops in his toilet case. 'Where's the plane coming in from?'

'Everglades. I flew down as soon as you contacted me early Sunday morning, rented a car and have spent most of the last twenty hours in it, sitting, watching and listening. Primary focus Riker. He's the weak link. Alcoholic. But if I might, in the interests of an early lunch, précis it, there is a man called Johnny Shoosh who resides in the Everglades. He's the pilot bringing the aircraft in tonight. ETA twenty hundred hours local.'

'You spoke to this guy Shoosh?' Williams was concerned.

'Naturally. When you want information in a specific field you go to the top. Of course, he was rather indignant at first, asked me what the hell I was talking about, and who the hell did I think I was. I imagine I rather caught his attention when I mentioned FBI in a passable American accent, especially when I assured him that I was not interested in his operation, more in catching up with a friend of Major Rikers. Mr Winter.'

'And he agreed to help! Come on Edeyrn, nothing's that simple.'

'Well, I did agree that we would turn a blind eye to his dealings for the foreseeable future. And that we would take his name off the list.'

'What list?'

'Customs and immigration shit list, as the Fibies so eloquently put it.'

'He's on that?'

Owens chuckled. 'Not that I'm aware, but I made it sound rather convincing.'

Williams adjusted his tie in the vanity mirror, then flipped the visor up. His hand fell on the door handle. 'How long were you with British Intelligence, Edeyrn?'

'Thirty-five years.'

'A long time.'

'Think of it as thirty-five Christmas presents, boyo. Thirty-five pairs of socks or ties no one would be seen dead in. Not so long.'

'And the CIA? I've read a lot of stuff; a lot of antagonism toward SIS.'

'I'm sure you have. I remember something we developed called RAFTER, back in the fifties. By the time we let your people in on it the Russians had it, and most of your Polish section was blown. But if you're asking about allegiance, which I assume you are, don't worry – I'm helping you because you asked, nothing more.'

'You're certain?'

'You've got a suspicious mind.'

'Through working in the *gandu* fields.'

Owens laughed and winked an innocent, conspiratorial wink. 'The master is lucky to have a *Hausa* man.'

'True . . . it is only the *Ibo* tribe who eat people.'

'You never told me how you found Winter.'

'And as you're now on the payroll . . .'

'I should share the poisoned chalice – unofficially.'

'Off the record then,' Williams said. And outlined the Oklahoma situation and the follow-up investigations.

'And you really think you can recruit him?'

'Why not?'

Owens chuckled. 'Not his style, Tanner.'

'Neither is street violence, killing civilians. Druggies or not. Perhaps he might be receptive to some sort of amnesty if we can get the police off his back.'

Owens thought differently. He too was a widower. Remembered the pain of losing his wife, Eleanor, who had remained at their home in deepest Surrey, tending her small flower garden, while he had been shunted off to the Far East to work with the Russian Mafia, the behind-the-scene rulers in the eastern seaport of Vladivostok. And there he had remained over all those years, slipping in and out of the Russian city from the Chinese side, picking up titbits of information at the seafront hotel, the Amurski Zaliv. Handing over packets of black-market dollars for raw intelligence on Soviet Fleet movements. It was later, standing in a bleak English cemetery, that he had placed the event. Time-slipped away the English hours. He had been doing a deal with Andrei – the little Russian with gold-plated teeth who could smell a KGB man a mile off – in the Amurski. Sinking a few vodkas. And she, unable to cope with her own company any more, had taken a bottle of sleeping tablets. There had been a note. Nothing dramatic – she was not that kind of person. It had ended, 'I'm so terribly sorry.' *She, apologising to him.*

The pain never went away. It visited him on the long nights. And the truth. He had failed her. Had left her alone, childless over too many years. He would have done anything to start again. Anything! That was what Winter had done. Exacted a price. Answered his pain in a positive manner.

Three a.m. introspection. No place here. The deceptive smile was back. 'You're thinking of talking to him?'

'I was, but subject to his movements, I think a change of plan is called for. We'll discuss it over lunch.'

15

'Coffee?' Winter called from the kitchenette that made up part of the motel room.

Ugly Charlie was standing by the window, curtain drawn back a fraction. High cloud cover had moved in from the west. Precursor to the front. The window was open a few inches. He could smell the salt ponds, the mangrove, the mud flats. He suddenly realised he was going to miss it. Perhaps after this trip he'd come back and buy that boat and go into the charter business. He half turned and called back, 'Thanks.'

'Regular or unleaded?'

'Regular. When we leaving, by the way?'

'Plenty of time. We'll eat first — tomato soup okay?'

'Sure.' He walked over to Winter. 'So what kept you so long? I was getting worried.'

'Oh, the usual. Banks. I had a number of large bank cashier's cheques to cash. They wanted to go through the verification process; even the suit didn't convince them I was legit. After that I did some clothes shopping, bought us both some new kit, and . . .' He opened a briefcase on the small table in the corner of the room and pulled out a sheaf of papers. He handed them to Charlie. 'I paid all your bills. You're up to date plus one month in advance on your utilities. They've even turned your phone back on at the house. You'll also find a lien release from your bank on the Volkswagen. You now own it.'

Ugly Charlie slumped into a chair by the table and looked at the paid bills in his hand. He couldn't remember the last time he had been clear of debt. 'Thanks, Wint. I really appreciate this.'

Winter gave a small smile and opened a can of tomato soup. 'No thanks, Charlie. I'm not a charitable institution. You'll earn every penny. There's an envelope in the briefcase with your name on it; you'll find seventy-five hundred dollars in it, various denominations. Call it travelling expenses. We'll talk about payment for your services once we get the show on the road.'

Charlie picked up the mug of coffee with shaking hands. He wanted to say something, but knew that Winter didn't go in for the sentimental stuff. 'What about your rental car over at my house?'

'Taken care of. Being collected in the morning. That way if someone's hoping I'll come back to pick it up, they'll be disappointed.'

'I was thinking about this airstrike idea of yours,' Charlie said.

'And?'

'What do we do for airplanes, number one? Number two, when did either of us last fly operationally?'

'You know the area called Los Llanos in Colombia?'

'Heard of it. Flat land in the east, isn't it?'

'Yes. Low-lying savannah, stretching from the eastern mountain range – the Cordillera Oriental – into western Venezuela. Rainy season April to November. Anyway, there's a disused airfield down there, used by the Medellin Cartel's own private air force back in the seventies and eighties. There's also a number of old military fighters and spares. Haven't been flown for some years apparently. My idea is to make two aircraft and two pilots operational by the end of March, before the rains hit.'

'What type of fighters?'

'Don't know for sure, other than jet.'

'Information from the kiddie in Oklahoma City?'

'Yes. He also said that it's an eerie place, lacking any notable topographical features, and that as the dry season gets under way after December, the sun bakes the soil and the winds blow dust all around. No people in that area. No communications. And plenty of dust. Perfect cover, Charlie.'

'What about fuel? Any jet fuel left in storage tanks would have degraded over a number of years.'

'That could be a major problem. We'll need to check all supply points in eastern Colombia and western Venezuela before we go in. Once we've located the base and checked the status on what's there, we'll make arrangements for a few tanker loads.'

'Roads?'

'I'm guessing trails. But as the savannah is very flat – and dry – shouldn't be a problem.'

'What about manpower? According to what you've just said, we need minimum two airplane mechanics . . . and say, a few good foot soldiers.'

'Remember Red Stevens?'

'The Aussie?'

'Yes. Lives in Caracas these days. I've already spoken to him. Anything we need, he can supply. Anything else?'

'We'll need a light aircraft for communications transport.'

'I'll mention it to Red. You might want to mention it to Johnny Shoosh tonight on the flight down. He's sure to know of something. Hell, all the druggie aeroplanes are stolen in the first place. Must be a few spares lying around down there that somebody would part with for money.' Winter poured the soup into two bowls.

Charlie sprinkled a little salt into his and stirred it in with his spoon. 'And if not, we could always steal one back.' He laughed at the thought. 'How hot does it get down there in the dry season?'

'Similar to here. Few degrees warmer, I'd guess.'

'I was thinking about flying. We'll need to operate around the dawn hours for training purposes.'

'What about the mission itself?'

'Depending on distance to the target, I'd figure we launch in the dark and plan to "splash" the target just before sunrise. False dawn light should be enough to eyeball it in. Even the guards should be asleep at that hour.'

Winter said nothing more. After a while he cleared the dishes and washed and dried them, finally stacking them away in the cupboard above the sink. Charlie sat smoking a cigarette, watching him. Winter, he decided, was a very methodical man.

They were packing. Winter had made a careful inventory of essential requirements. He checked off the small pile on the bed. Penicillin tablets, morphine-loaded syringes, salt tablets, antimalarial tablets, anti-histamines, glucose candy, aspirin and dysentery and diarrhoea pills, water-sterilising pills. Potassium per-manganate (add to water and mix until pink to sterilise, deeper pink to make antiseptic, full red to treat fungal diseases – such as athlete's foot), butterfly sutures, plasters, condoms (good water bags, hold one litre). Solid fuel tablets, mini-signal flares, pencil flashlights (with batteries reversed to prevent running down if accidently switched on). He finally came to the last two items. Handguns. One a Soviet Makarov; the other a Heckler & Koch P9S, nine-millimetre Parabellum cartridges, double-action with a thumb-operated cocking/decocking lever on the left grip. He took this through to Charlie in the next room. 'You'd better have this. It's loaded. Safety's on.'

Ugly Charlie hesitated, then took it. 'Where did you get it?'

'Pawn shop.'

'I thought there was a waiting period . . . fifteen days or something.'

'That's what the guy told me until I offered him twice the sticker price. Seems business is a little slow.'

'Rather have my Colt,' Charlie said, weighing the gun in his shaking hand.

'Too lightweight. You'll have the H & K.'

'I'll have the H & K,' Charlie mumbled.

'We leave in ten minutes,' Winter added, going out of the room.

'Why so early?'

'Why do you think?' Winter called back.

Think? It didn't matter what he thought. All right
for Winter. He went where there was fighting. Bought
round-trip tickets. Crossed the line of departure with
nerves of steel. Set his clever little traps like a poacher.
And then patiently waited for the kill, picking up a
suntan along the way. What do you think? He didn't
want to die, not that way at least. He'd had his wars.
One more perhaps. Close to Winter. Close enough for
the luck to rub off.

16

The plane was late.

To Winter it was a bad sign. It gave him time to think back to a time years earlier when he and Ugly Charlie had set off on a not too dissimilar night for Bolivia. He had never considered failure then. Just lately he had been thinking about it every day. The years at the university had softened his body, his reflexes, his language. How many years before you passed the point of no return? A valid question, to which he had no answer. His thoughts drifted off to Julia. Seeking sanctuary. If only for a few moments.

They were sheltering under some scrub trees twenty yards from the upwind end of the runway at the small Marathon airport, located in the Florida Keys. Both men were dressed in identical clothes, all black, including black windcheaters with lightweight plastic hoods zipped into the collar. The hoods were up now, pulled tight by drawstrings. Camouflage smears on their cheeks and foreheads. They were practically invisible. Out of the darkness came the flying hiss of the wind along the wave tops. The rain, which had been relentless for the past hour or more, had eased a little.

'He's not coming, Wint.'

Winter remained totally still. Listening. Trying to pick out the sound of aircraft engines. 'He'll come, Charlie. Besides, when did you ever hear of a flight being on time? And we're not exactly talking Pan Am Clipper service to Rio, are we?'

Ugly Charlie didn't answer. On a cold wet night he was soaked in sweat. The shakes, which never really left him, had got worse in the last half-hour. He needed a drink.

They had been on station ever since dark. Lying motionless in the rain and the wind, checking periodically through the single-lens night scope for movement across on the airport. There had been no aircraft arrivals in that time. Pilots did not fly into uncontrolled airports in such weather. Winter had left the Volkswagen two miles up Highway 1, concealed behind a stand of stunted trees and rocky outcrop, keys taped under the front left wing. Should anything go wrong they headed out down the beach – the opposite way. Winter knew that if anything went wrong it would be a direct result of their being tailed, and if they had been, the followers would have been smart enough to have located the Volkswagen. Finally, Nancy – Charlie's friend from the diner – would travel out the next morning by taxi, and if the car was still there, drive it back to Key West.

'See anything over by the terminal?' Charlie asked nervously.

'Nothing.'

'Told you you were imagining things. Nobody's following us.'

But Winter wasn't listening. His peripheral vision had caught a glimmer of light in the sky. Aircraft was his first thought. Then he saw another, and another, and another. 'Stars, Charlie. The front's clearing.' He motioned with his head.

'Which means the Feds will be hoisting the aerostat back up. What do you figure – cancel?'

Thunder rumbled distantly out of the east, down towards the islands. Winter rolled over and checked the luminous dial on his watch. Shoosh was thirty minutes late. If he was coming at all. 'We'll give him another ten minutes.'

'Then what?'

'Find a motel and a steak and a phone. You can call him, check what the problem is.'

Ugly Charlie squirrelled down deeper into his wind-cheater, the movement causing a trickle of water to get inside his hood and run down his neck. He swore, then fumbled through his pockets for a cigarette before deciding Winter would not permit it. Cigarettes and lighters were too conspicuous after dark.

Winter heard the sound first. A faint sound flickering in and out of the gusts. Engines. Not car or truck though. Aeroplane. The resonant sound grew gradually nearer, then took on a more urgent note as the pilot increased the props to high r.p.m. The landing lights came on last. Two white beams scything through the blackness. Both men watched as the lights grew nearer and the engine noise died to a low burble as the high-wing twin drifted across the boundary, flared and made a perfect touchdown.

'Better late than never,' Charlie muttered, as they both moved out quickly in the direction of the ramp. He lowered his hood and pulled on his blue baseball cap.

They were fifty yards away when Charlie, following Johnny Shoosh's instructions, signalled the letter R (for Riker) in morse with his flashlight. No response. He tried again: dit-dah-dit. A momentary pause and the aircraft responded: dit-dit-dit – the letter S (for Shoosh) – from its right landing light, as it came to a stop at the edge of the backlit ramp area. The engines died. They both watched as the door opened.

'It's a woman!' Charlie said with surprise, grabbing at Winter's sleeve.

'I can see that.'

'What about Shoosh?'

'One way to find out, Charlie – let's ask her.'

They quickly walked the short distance down the edge of the ramp to where the twin-engine Aero Commander stood. The clouds had cleared completely now, being replaced by a sky full of stars.

Charlie spoke first, 'Hi, where's Johnny?'

'You are Charlie Riker?' Slight figure. About five-five. Olive complexion. Unsmiling mouth. Her eyes dark and direct. The accent – Spanish. Not soft and feminine though – more hard veteran.

'Yeah, and this is Winter,' Charlie replied, indicating the Englishman.

She nodded, her long dark hair falling like a shadow across her face. 'Johnny is ill. Influenza, I think. He asked me to pick you up.'

Charlie gave Winter an uncertain look, before turning back to the woman. 'You been down that way before?'

'*Si*, I was born there.'

'I meant the flight. From what Johnny told me . . .' the voice trailed off, leaving sufficient innuendo as to indicate the difficulty of such a mission.

She shrugged, her face remaining expressionless. 'It is not too difficult, I think. Johnny told me to turn right after Cuba.'

Charlie laughed nervously at the throwaway remark. 'Sure we do. What do we call you, by the way?'

'Maria Espinosa.'

'Okay, Maria, Johnny mentioned that the aerostat — the radar balloon down by Key West — was reeled in in bad weather; problem is, the front's gone through, which to my way of thinking means they're putting it back up right now.'

'It is not a problem. Johnny pays a government employee at the aerostat location to keep him informed. The balloon is down for servicing. It will not go up until tomorrow morning. You have some luggage?'

'Over there,' Charlie said. He pointed to the dark area near the runway where they had left their bags.

'Good. You fly right seat for the first half of the journey, then Mr Winter can take over if you feel tired — an extra pair of eyes to watch out for shipping, you understand?' Her voice carried a measure of authority.

Charlie nodded and walked back towards the scrub brush with Winter.

'I don't like it,' Charlie said unhappily. 'Something doesn't feel right.'

'The guy's ill. What's the problem? You don't like flying with women, is that it?'

'Johnny would have said something if there was the slightest chance he wasn't going to make it.'

Winter did another sweep of the terminal area with his night scope before gathering up his baggage. 'Make your mind up, Charlie – it's now or never!'

'Simple as that,' Charlie mumbled to himself. 'The old black-and-white world.'

Five minutes later they were airborne. Winter was wedged in a tiny back seat with the baggage. In front of him was a square fifty-gallon fuel tank with enough room to squeeze by to get to the pilots' seats. Maria Espinosa was an able pilot. She initially flew the aircraft around the Marathon pattern with all the aircraft lights on, calling up over the hand-mike from time to time on the Unicom frequency. There was no air-traffic controller on duty at this time of night – this was just a common frequency which aircraft used to warn other aircraft of their intentions. To any watcher below it was a light plane doing night-flying training. It was on the third approach that she retracted the gear, and switched off the landing lights and position lights and banked sharply to the east. In the dim glow of instrument panel lights Winter saw her right hand advance the throttles as the plane dived towards the sea. From a side window he saw the vague outline of a couple of masts of boats rocket past, then nothing but inky blackness.

He put his head back against the bulkhead and closed his eyes, and thought of similar night-mission briefings – flying low over water is dangerous, especially at night . . . it is too easy to become disorientated . . . you forget where the horizon is . . . and if you keep looking out of the window instead of checking your instruments you can drive the aeroplane right into the water.

White Lie

He hoped the woman up front was as good as Johnny Shoosh believed her to be.

The plane caught up with the storm half an hour after setting course. For Ugly Charlie it was like sitting inside a hollow metal drum being deafened by the rising and falling thunder of rain. That and the pitching and rolling and yawing motions as the woman next to him fought to maintain the dangerously low height over the waves. Something he had had a lifetime of doing. Something which had once been 'operations normal'. Now he was scared shitless. Dry-mouthed, bowel-churning-shitless.

He needed a drink badly. Except the bottle was in his kit at the back of the cabin. Twenty times over the next few hours he thought about crawling back through the space at the side of the fuel tank and digging out the bottle of vodka. As once or twice he considered speaking to the woman, but each time he checked himself. His old training told him you didn't disturb a pilot flying at a suicidal level, especially at night. Nor did you move from your seat and cause a trim change. Okay going back when the change would be in a nose-up direction. Returning might prove fatal. At one point in those few hours the plane slipped briefly out of the weather into calmer air, and he thought he saw lights off to the right of the aircraft. Cuba perhaps. Names like Sagua la Grande, Moron, Nuevitas and Sagua de Tanamo, came to mind. Voices and places from the past, except it didn't seem to belong to him and that far-off youth. It was as though he had always been old and crippled and afraid, and the young man he sometimes imagined he had been was a total stranger, someone out of an old movie he had once seen. He squinted out again, looking for the lights. But they had been swallowed up by the night.

It was later. Fatigue had finally overtaken him and his eyes had closed when the engines increased in power and the aircraft started climbing. That was when a grateful Charlie made his way to the back of the cabin. 'Go talk to Maria, I need a beer and some shuteye.'

Winter said, 'Where are we?'

'Haiti. Just climbing to miss a bunch of high ground ahead, Massif de la Hotte, if that means anything to you!'

'What about their radar?'

'Maria reckons they're all asleep at this time of night. If not they'll probably mistake us for local traffic.'

Winter poured some coffee from a green Stanley thermos and took it forward.

Maria accepted the cup wordlessly. Her eyes two prisms of concentration fixed on the instruments. Winter slipped into the right seat, found a cup holder for his coffee and fastened his seat harness. The plane levelled off at ten thousand feet. That was when she switched on the radios and turned up the instrument panel lights. 'Oxygen deprivation,' she said, as if to herself. Winter nodded. At night you could tell when oxygen content in the air was getting low in an unpressurised plane by the fact that the instrument panel lights appeared dimmer. Ten thousand feet seemed acceptable enough. He looked across at her. A small slight figure. She was perhaps not as young as he had thought when they first met. Sun spokes emanated from the corner of her dark eyes, or what the medicos termed crow's feet or periorbital lines; 'sun spokes' was kinder, more feminine. Good complexion, high cheekbones. Pretty pert nose. A few lines around the neck. As for putting an age to the face, that was difficult. Some races carried the years better than others.

'Charlie told me you were from England,' she said without looking away from the instruments.

Charlie would. Charlie talks too much.

'Odessa – on the Black Sea.' Winter replied matter-of-factly.

'You were born there?'

'No. I was born in Prague.'

'Ah.'

Winter settled back in his seat and pulled a book from within his windcheater. The 'ah' was enough to convince him she had no idea where Prague or Odessa was, or if she did she didn't give a damn. He opened the book, tilting it towards the glow of instrument panel lights, and began reading.

She persisted. 'But you have lived in England?'

'No.'

'Funny, I have delivered planes over there. Your accent is very distinctive.'

'Berlitz tapes,' Winter smiled. 'They're very good.' Then changing tack he added, 'I didn't know they had lady ferry pilots these days.'

She glanced across at him. It was a brief look, dark eyes challenging. 'Charlie also said you had been away from flying for a lot of years, so what brought you back?'

'Money,' Winter lied, turning the book over at the opened page and laying it face down on his lap. 'Or should I say lack of it.'

'Ah, yes.'

'Any more weather?'

'No. We left the south edge of the front perhaps forty miles back. Now it will be clear all the way.' She waved a hand at the windscreen, indicating a night sky stained with stars.

'And this place Canaveral, how much further would that be?'

She reached forward and switched on one of the radios. Winter watched as her fingers turned various knobs and certain sequences of yellow-lit numbers and acronyms scrolled across a small screen. 'There,' she said. 'Four hundred and twelve miles. In time approximately two hours.'

Winter pointed at the navigation system. 'Loran?'

'No, GPS. Global Positioning System. Gives us range to any airport in the world or any other waypoint we program in. Also our groundspeed and time to station as well as track to fly. It also computes fuel burn and gives spot winds. Better than the old ways, I think.' She took a map from the side of her seat and passed it to Winter.

He partially unfolded it. It was a pilot's topographical chart. A Lambert Conformal Conic Projection. Scale 1:1,000,000. The top section covered that part of the Caribbean south of Jamaica and Haiti, neat squared grid lines on pale-blue paper, sloping isogonals showing magnetic variation, a few small disputed islands (claimed by both Colombia and the United States) and coral reefs and shipwrecks away to the west. He turned it over and found the chart's lowest thirty degrees of latitude featured the Peninsula de la Guajira – their destination. More alarmingly, surrounding the peninsula and marked with the legend SKR8, was a heavy blue border: Special Use Airspace – Alert, Danger, Military Operations Area, Prohibited, Restricted, Warning Area.

He didn't need to ask if they had permission to enter.

He glanced across at her. She was settled back in her seat. Motionless. Eyes quietly scanning the instruments, her left hand feeding in gentle corrections to the control yoke from time to time, the other hand balancing the cup of coffee on her thigh. He wanted to ask her what she was doing in this business. He had always imagined the drug-running fraternity as grizzled old men chewing tobacco and spitting out the reddish-brown fluid from time to time, guns and knives tucked in the sides of their flying boots, a few days' growth of beard on their leathery faces. Anything but young women in tight-fitting jeans and sweatshirts. How did you ask such a question of a stranger? He pushed the thought from his mind and in the warm red glow of the instrument lights picked up the book and began to read again. After perhaps ten minutes his eyes flickered and closed. And he slept.

It was nearly two hours later that they started their descent. Maria had dimmed the panel lights down to their lowest intensity and was staring out through the windscreen.

Winter stirred and opened his eyes. 'We there?'

'*Si* . . . twenty-five miles out,' Maria said, picking up the hand mike. 'Canaveral from Tricky Five Five. Colour Indigo.'

Silence.

She tried again.

A sleepy drawl crackled over the cockpit speaker, 'Tricky Five Five . . . pass your message.'

'Tricky Five Five, colour Indigo . . . ETA in seven minutes.'

'Okay, Señorita . . . flare path coming up.'

Maria throttled back and started running through approach and prelanding checks. 'Harness tight?'

Winter checked. 'Tight. What was the "colour indigo", by the way?'

'We are landing due west; tell me if you see a flare path.' She could have told him that 'Indigo' was the colour code of the day, identifying them as friendly; even that the callsign Tricky Five Five was Johnny Shoosh's signature from his Viet Nam days when he had been an F-105 'Thud' jock. But as far as she was concerned that was her business.

Winter leaned forward, the inertia-reel shoulder harness allowing his upper torso to move. The altimeter was now passing fifteen hundred feet. He tried to remember how big or how small a flare path would look from this height, but it was all too long ago. The plane jinked suddenly hard left.

'Tricky Five Five . . . visual,' Maria said into the microphone.

Winter looked to the left and saw nothing. Nothing but black night. And they were going down fast. He tugged his harness tighter. A ball of something close to fear wound up inside his gut. He strained his eyes looking for something that she could see and he could not. How good was this woman? He focused on what appeared to be a few flickering orange pinpricks of light. Nothing else. Surely to God that couldn't

be a flarepath – too short, too damned short. He
pressed himself further back into his seat, all the time
bracing his body as they sank rapidly towards the tiny
flarepath. He wanted to ask her about landing lights,
but then realised the stupidity of such a statement.
Illegal flights do not advertise their arrival. In his
peripheral vision he saw her right hand snatch back
the throttles – the engine note changed to a muted
burble as the plane skimmed over the tops of what
seemed to be dark tree shapes. Then the flare path
was coming up fast – flaming torches, ribbons of
black smoke rushing up towards them. They hit hard
– carrier landing – at a high angle of attack. Then
the nosewheel was on, Maria standing on the brakes
slowing the aeroplane down.

Two yellow electric marshaller's wands beckoned
out of the darkness, and she let the plane roll towards
them, adding a touch of power. The wands crossed
and remained still, indicating stop; then one wand
went across the throat, signifying 'cut your engines'.
Maria brought the mixture levers back to idle-cutoff
and the engines surged and died, a gentle shudder
resonating through the airframe. Shutdown checks
complete, she knocked off the battery switch and the
faint glow of instrument panel lights died, leaving
only the whine of gyros running down against the
silence.

'Nice landing,' Winter said. Maria unfastened her
seat harness in silence. 'You never told me what
"Indigo" meant!'

'Not your concern, Mr Winter – enjoy your stay in
Colombia.'

*   *   *

Drummer was a stocky black Spanish-speaking Panamanian. He was nicknamed Drummer because of the
pair of old drumsticks he carried in his hip pocket,
and whenever he wasn't working he would 'sit in' on
a scratchy old recording of Dave Brubeck's 'Take the
A-Train', beating out time on anything that came to
hand. He was also the man who ran Canaveral. He
introduced himself briefly before he and two other
men pulled a camouflage net over the aeroplane, then
shouted something at them in Spanish. Both men ran
down the airstrip, dousing the flare path.

'Catch up with you inside,' Winter said to Charlie
before walking over to intercept Drummer.

Charlie went to the long wooden trailer home, which
was also under camouflage netting. Just inside the
doorway were a couple of rickety chairs. A ceiling fan whirred softly, rustling weighted-down yellowed papers on a cluttered desk. The tiled floor
was obscured by dried mud, cigarette butts, flight
bags, pieces of ancient magazines, and the remains of
Christmas decorations. The air was dank and oppres-
sively warm. Even so, he was glad to be down, glad
to be away from the engines that had pounded away
at his ears for hour after hour.

A voice at his side said, 'Come, I will show you your
bunk.' It was one of the young boys he had seen out on
the strip.

Charlie followed him down a narrow corridor to the
end of the building and into a small room; vertical
in greatest area, the distance from tiles to cracked
plaster ceiling being considerably more than from
wall to wall. In comparison to the rest of the shanty-
town building, however, it was neat and tidy, the

open window circulating a slight breeze. A two-tier bunk with clean white linen stood against the wall opposite the window. Charlie dropped his bags on the floor and turned to thank the boy, but he had gone. He went over and tried the bottom bunk. The springs creaked, and the mattress was lumpy; the top bunk was no better. The sheets had that feeling of cloying dampness found only in the tropics. He moved across to the open window and listened to the sound of ground crickets. He now knew beyond a shadow of doubt that he had returned to the world of aerial Gypsies. A dangerous place to the uninitiated.

He had showered and changed into fresh jeans and sweatshirt and was lying on the lower bunk, baseball cap over his eyes, when Winter eventually arrived. 'How's everything?'

'So-so,' said Winter.

'What does that mean?'

'There'll be a DAS guy here in the morning to stamp our passports.'

'DAS? Customs?

'Departamento Administrativo de Seguridad – the security police. Also responsible for immigration.'

'How much?'

'Five grand.'

'Shit!'

'For that you get a port-of-entry stamp showing Cali, backdated forty-eight hours.'

'Anything for money, huh?'

'Drummer also mentioned to keep an eye on our bags at all times: nothing's safe according to him.'

'What's new? Like Africa – when you had to leave a

guy to guard your airplane, or you'd sure as hell find
a wing missing when you got back.'

Winter went over to the window and lit a cigarette.
'Drummer said there are no tourists on the peninsula,
only drug dealers. He said the place is wild; get
your pocket picked or your throat cut for a dollar
bill. That's why the army doesn't come here. Can't
say I blame them. Anyway, we're here. First obstacle
overcome.'

'And the next?'

'Intelligence gathering.'

'What about cover? Just in case we run into some
real police guys.'

'I've got letters of introduction in Spanish on my
old university's letter-headed paper. Lots of copies.
Lots of signatures. We're writing a wildlife feature for
National Geographic on the threatened extinction of
the *caiman del Orinoco* – crocodile to you, Charlie. In
fact the largest American crocodile, more than eight
metres in length. Virtually decimated now, thanks to
ranchers killing them for their skins. Which of course
gives us a reason to be carrying cameras.'

'When did you get those done?'

'The letters? Before I left the university.'

'For me as well?'

'Yes.'

'Pretty sure I'd drop everything and come along,
weren't you? What is it? Some people lead, some
people follow. Good old Charlie, born in the year of
the fucking Sheep.'

'Crap, Charlie, and you know it. You were the best
man for the job.'

'And if you hadn't found me?'

'Easier to throw something away than worry about producing it later.'

'What about transport?'

'Drummer's got a Dodge Ram Charger. I thought you or he might drive me as far as Santa Marta. Avianca runs flights to Medellin with a connection to Cali.'

'Reconnaissance?' Charlie asked.

'I'm hoping for the "no worthwhile reconnaissance is ever wasted" line my army used to preach. Aerial photography. I've got a Sony Handycam, compact video with ten-to-one zoom. Might even find a light plane I can pick up cheap. Pilot even.'

'Not a good idea. We can't very well bring a local guy in to fly the plane. That means we'd have to take him out to Los Llanos.'

'To look for crocodiles.'

'What about the military strip?'

'He could drop us there and return in seventy-two hours. Give us enough time to check out the base. If we think we can trust him we can take him on. If not I'll get one of Red's guys out of Caracas.'

'Why not get Red to send a plane and pilot to meet us back here? You return from Cali. I pick you up at Santa Marta. Everything in reverse.'

'Except Red's plane would be on a Venezuelan registration. I don't want anything to stand out if at all possible. I want everything to appear for real. We *are* doing a feature for *National Geographic*. We are *only* interested in those poor bloody crocodiles that are being hunted to extinction. I'll even pay a visit to the appropriate government offices in Cali to pay my respects.'

'Don't you think that's going a bit too far?'

'Innocents abroad, Charlie. We are not a threat. We do everything by the book. What you used to call left-handed truth.'

'Don't you think "One Up" is a bit risky in Cali?'

The military term for someone travelling solo on a surveillance mission did not escape Winter. 'If I could take someone with me to watch my back I would, but I need you here to liaise with Red in Caracas if the need arises, and to plan the flight into Los Llanos.'

'Going back to renting a plane and pilot: still think that's risky.'

'What do you suggest? You told me you were unfit to fly a plane yourself, so we'll have to take our chances the other way.'

'So if anything goes wrong it's my fault! Is that it?'

Winter took a towel and a wash bag from his valise. 'Showers?'

'Down the corridor, on the right.' Winter started through the door. 'You never answered me – is that it?' The only reply was Winter's footsteps receding down the corridor.

It was later. Winter had gone out saying he needed to talk with Drummer again. Ugly Charlie made his way down the corridor to the kitchen. He had put a six pack of beer into the fridge earlier. They would be chilled by now. He drank two in quick succession, knocked the top of a third and was making his way back to his room when he ran into Maria coming out of the communal bathroom. Her hair was damp. Her face scrubbed to a shine. A grey-white towel was draped round her neck, covering the front of a skimpy bra. She stopped.

'You have known Mr Winter for a long time?'

'Yeah. Why do you ask?'

'He asks a lot of questions. If I did not know better I might think he was working for the Federales.'

Ugly Charlie laughed, 'Feds? Hell no, just a pilot buddy in a fix. Needs work, money.'

'You are sure?' Probing.

'Well . . . yeah, sure I'm sure.' He cursed the uncertainty of his own voice.

'He has been questioning Drummer also since we arrived. Why would that be?'

'Trying to find us a cargo plane to fly somewhere. Work. You know the sort of thing!'

'Then there was the book he was reading on the way in.'

'Book?'

'*Manual of the Urban Guerrilla* it was called. Pilots I know never graduated beyond Jeppesen let-down plates and the centrefold of *Playboy*.'

Ugly Charlie felt her eyes probing his as she spoke the words. He felt uncomfortable. Questions from strangers did that to him. 'Dangerous place, so we've been told. He likes to know about problems and how to deal with them.'

'And I always thought Englishmen were quiet and reserved.'

'Exceptions in every race, Maria.'

'He said he was from London. Something like New York perhaps. Harder men.'

'You got it.'

She shrugged mute acceptance and walked away down the corridor. Hips swinging.

'Thanks for the ride, by the way.'

She raised a hand in acknowledgement. No words.

Ugly Charlie decided she was one tough bitch. Pretty but tough. He had run into a few of her type in years gone by. The type who would come to you in the night at one of these lonely outposts, lift their skirt and drop down onto you. They never spoke, just screwed you, then dropped their skirt and took off. They could be more like animals than any man. Even so, he went to bed thinking about what she had said: 'If I did not know better I might think he was working for the Federales!'

Some joke!

PART THREE
Intel

17

As they lay close in what had become a silvered darkness, Luis's eyes sought out her slim, almost wiry body, the small perfectly formed breasts, the dark hair at the base of her stomach. Lastly he came back to her eyes. She had been watching him.

'You will know me next time?'

'Yes, my Ana.'

A small smile in the voice. 'You are sure?'

He wrapped an arm around her waist. 'I'm sure.'

'How?'

He moved a hand and ran it across the swell of her breasts. 'Touch and smell.'

'What else?'

He ran his tongue down across her belly into the mound of dark hair. 'Taste.'

She laughed. 'And what do I taste like?'

'No words I know.'

'Good words?'

He moved her beneath him and kissed her parted mouth. 'Pretty words.'

'I did well for you, Luis?'

'Yes.'

She wrapped her legs around his back, drawing him into her, the sudden intake of air through her parted lips, a small gasp of pain, repeated over and over and over again. Each cry a little faster and a little louder than the one before. Until the last one. That lasted a full ten seconds.

It was later, as she slept, that he left the bed and went over to the window; the curtains were open, the three-quarter moon that had shone over the city earlier had set, the streets were deserted, the car horns and the music finally offering a temporary truce to another Colombian day. Soon it would be dawn. And he thought the disjointed thoughts of one who was only half awake. The clock had turned the world into a more organised place, except perhaps for his country, which had only loosely taken to the notion. Exceptions? Always those . . . if money was directly involved – working hours and all they entailed were more likely to be adhered to . . . which was why Colombian banks ran like Swiss watches . . . which was why Ana Lucia Rubiano was now lying asleep in a tangle of white satin sheets, a smile upon her lips . . . she had done as he requested, quickly and efficiently . . . and he had been lucky . . . computer data banks had located, via a convoluted trail, an account of the man called John Paul Winter at the Marshall Islands Bank on the island of Majoro Atoll . . . they could give no further details but would gladly receive deposits on behalf of their customer . . . she had called him, excitement in her voice . . . he had been pleased, had invited her to dinner that very evening . . . she had arrived at his luxury penthouse apartment wearing a sensuous red dress with a tight-fitting bodice and flared skirt . . . the dinner and the champagne had been catered from a nearby hotel restaurant, and when the waiters had gone he had taken her to the bedroom . . . the lovemaking had lasted most of the night . . . and still it was not over.

He went back to the bed, kneeling at its side, drawing back the sheet from her sleeping form, running his lips lightly across her shoulders, her neck, her breasts, her belly. Thinking, Such a pity, my sweet and beautiful Ana, such a pity.

Her fingers touched his hair. A sleepy voice said, 'What is a pity, Luis?'

He started, unaware that he had spoken his thoughts. 'Nothing . . . only that it is nearly five o'clock, Ana, and you have to go.'

'So soon!' The voice wide awake now. Urgent. She slipped from the bed and knelt beside him in the darkness.

She kissed him hungrily, and he started to pull away, but she clung to him, her nails digging painfully into his back, burying her head in the hollow of his shoulder. 'Please, my darling . . . please.'

He smacked her buttocks playfully. 'Not now.'

'You will see me again, Luis?'

He returned her kiss. 'I will see you again,' he promised.

'Tonight?'

'Not tonight, I might have to leave today to fly to the Marshall Islands.'

'Your customer?'

'Yes. I was thinking, perhaps if I go in person they

will give me an address. Some way to contact the man. The least I can do is offer him an apology in person.'

'I think it is not possible, Luis. You know how strict the banking laws have become: it is almost a paranoia with them now.'

'So how can I find this out?'

'The Marshall Islands come under US Pacific Trust Territory. Certainly they have violated security laws and attracted the scrutiny of the US comptroller of their currency, but they are aware that American IRS men have visited other US Pacific Trust territories and bribed clerks into letting them see accounts which are then used to prosecute. I think with these people, Luis, you will have a very serious problem. They are very secretive.'

'Perhaps you should come with me. You know the ways of international banking.'

'They would not tell me; they would not even tell the *presidente* of my bank.'

'The *presidente* is not as beautiful as you.'

Ana laughed. 'You think anyone will pay attention to a pretty smile?'

Luis reached down and kissed her small breasts. 'Maybe not a pretty smile, but there are other ways, perhaps.' He took her back to the bed and covered them both with the satin sheet, stroking her body, kissing her all over.

She lay very still. Her body rigid. When she eventually spoke her voice was a mixture of anger and disbelief. 'You want me to whore for you, Luis? Is that what you are asking?'

He stopped kissing her and laid his head back on

the pillows. 'No, Ana, that is not what I am asking. I would never ask any woman to do such a thing.'

If there was hurt in his voice, she did not recognise it. She leapt from the bed, stumbling in the darkness, collecting her clothes, which were strewn across the floor.

'Where are you going?'

'Home.'

'Wait, I will take you.' He got out of the bed and moved towards her.

'Please, Luis, no. I will take a taxi.' Her clothes clutched to her naked body, she ran from the room.

Luis swore violently, something he never did, made the sign of the cross and asked God's forgiveness for his blasphemy, uttered, he assured Him, in a moment of weakness. He gathered up his mother's rosary from the dressing table and twined it around his fingers. And went back to bed. And slept.

18

It was dawn. Winter was standing outside the trailer home in the smoky yellow dawn with a mug of coffee in his hand. He hadn't been able to sleep, the thought of getting to Cali foremost in his mind. He had fixed the coffee in the kitchen and stumbled outside into the cool morning. Everywhere was still. A tin-roofed portable building had been positioned halfway down the solitary dirt runway; a few pigs were rooting in the makeshift airstrip a few yards away, and a number of scrawny roosters were likewise scratching at the dirt, searching for food – from the air this place would look nothing more than a poor man's hacienda in the boondocks.

He found the B-25 under a camouflage net similar to the one they had put over the Shrike Commander some hours earlier. He stared in disbelief. Drummer had assured him the previous evening that the aeroplane was in good airworthy condition.

What he saw contradicted everything he had heard. The thin, box-sided, square-cut plane with the long transparent nose might have been good and airworthy once, but that would have been a long time ago. The Plexiglas nose had gone smoky and was crazed with thousands of tiny veins. The bare aluminium fuselage and wings were covered with gritty white lichens of corrosion. The parts of the plane that had been painted were dulled and flaking, and the hydraulic system appeared to have a major leak because the bomb doors and the flaps were drooping. The dented and patched engine cowlings were full of walking rivets, all trailing thin streams of black oily grease. Other than that there was an excess of oil on the ground beneath the engines.

What the hell, he thought, in an attempt to reassure himself, if it flew in here from somewhere, it's got to have something going for it. He finished his coffee and placed the mug on the ground, then ducked under the belly of the plane and climbed up through the open hatch forward of the bomb bay. The smell caught him first. That smell peculiar to all military aircraft: hydraulic fluid, avgas, oil, leather and metal, all combining to form an exquisite musky scent loved by flyers. Ahead, up a high step, the dawn light filtered in through the glass roof above the pilots' seats. Standing above the hatch Winter surveyed the interior of the fuselage. Pipes, cables, electrical junction boxes. What had once been an upper gun turret had been filled in, the aluminium modification unpainted. A number of utility passenger seats filled the confined area, as well as a new-looking internal fuel tank obviously fitted for the mission it had come here on. He idly wondered what sort of range the old ship had. To the front was a dark tunnel which ran under the pilots' seats to the bomb aimer's position in the transparent nose.

He moved forward and took a step up, swinging himself into the pilot's seat. The green leather was old and cracked. The harness webbing was no better than the seat – ancient, mildewed and rotting. The instrument panel a nightmare of corroded instruments and switches and blank gaping holes staring into a darkness of looms of electrical wiring. And now he knew what it was that worried him. She was the woman he had heard about all his life. The hooker who had lain with more men than was decent. She was the old hag full of disease. The old hag with the painted smile who promised everything if you were prepared to take the risk! His fingers reached out slowly, tentatively, until they touched the metal. She wasn't, he decided, so much an aeroplane any more, more an accident waiting to happen.

He looked across at the copilot's seat. There was an untidy pile of dog-eared logbooks and various operating manuals. A part of the life story of an aeroplane that had doubtless been flying before he was born. He gathered up the books with a sigh and went back to the shack.

Drummer was waiting in the doorway. Bleary-eyed, dressed only in a pair of dirty white trousers with a sheathed machete attached to a snakeskin belt. He was absently scratching his naked potbelly as Winter approached him.

He grinned, showing perfect white teeth, '*Buenos dias, Señor.* You have found the airplane, *si?*'

'*Si.*'

'She is a pretty one, eh?'

Winter pulled a face. He could think of plenty of adjectives for her, none of which was pretty. 'How many more planes here?' he asked.

'*Tres* . . . three. The Señorita's and two other Americans. The Señorita and one other leave in two days. The other I do not know.' A heave of the shoulders.

Winter drew Drummer away from the door, noticing for the first time the smell of the man. It triggered a distant memory of West Africa, and how some of the natives in that part of the world ate dog flesh, the result being a rancorous body odour emanating from their sweat. He distanced himself a little from the Panamanian, turning his head to breathe the slightly fresher air. 'How about the owner? When will he come?'

Drummer shrugged, 'Tonight after dark perhaps, maybe *mañana* . . . it depends.'

'I see,' Winter replied, understanding that in these places terms for time did exist but their interpretation was not necessarily what Westerners might expect. *Mañana* – literally tomorrow, better understood as 'in an indefinite future'. All Third Worlds suffered from it, where a 'moment' is both flexible and unpredictable; it may mean five minutes or five hours – or even five days. 'Good job you guys don't have to haul the sun over the horizon every morning – we'd still be operating by candlelight.'

'*No entiendo, Señor.*'

'Small English joke.'

Drummer smiled as though he understood, then said, 'You have the money for the plane, Señor?'

'I have the money.'

'The owner said I should first see it, before he comes.'

'You call the owner and tell him if he wants to sell his aeroplane to come out here and talk with me. He will see the money then.'

Drummer's eyes narrowed, his right hand moving slowly to the bone handle of the machete. 'The owner is an important man. He does not like his time to be wasted,' the Panamanian insisted, his voice hardening.

In reply Winter slipped his hand inside his blue nylon flight jacket and pulled out the Makarov nine-millimetre. Flicking off the safety, he half turned, aimed at one of the roosters scratching around in the dirt some fifty yards away, and fired. The explosion made Drummer clasp his hands to his ears. Winter swung the smoking barrel of the gun back towards the Panamanian and smiled. 'As I said, Drummer, when the owner comes he will see the money – understand?'

Drummer grinned nervously, '*Si . . . Si, Señor . . . entiendo.*'

Winter slipped the safety on and put the enlarged Soviet copy of the Walther Model PP back into its holster. 'Next thing, I need to run the engines on the plane – maybe taxi it up and down the runway, check the brakes, part of the prepurchase inspection . . . *tu entiendo?*

'*Si, entiendo.* We can move the building from the runway, but it is not safe in the morning.'

'This afternoon then?'

'*Si,* when people are taking their siesta. That will be good.'

'What about fuel?'

'She is full, Señor. . . and also the ferry tanks inside the plane, they are full.'

'Oil?'

'There are two spare cases . . . under the wing.'

'How much fuel did you put on board?'

Drummer shuffled back into the shack and searched through the stack of yellowed papers on his desk. 'Two thousand gallons, Señor. Here is the paper.'

Winter checked the figures and gave the sheet back to Drummer. 'You have a radio?'

'*Si*, an HF transmitter.'

'In case we need to check up on weather.'

'Any time, Señor, please help yourself. You like some breakfast now?'

'What have you got?'

'Bacon and eggs.'

'Good. How much do I owe you for the dead rooster by the way?'

'*Señor, no entiendo.*'

Winter tried again in broken Spanish.

Drummer laughed. 'Another English joke, *si*? There is no charge.'

The sound awoke Ugly Charlie. A sharp explosion; a gun? Or perhaps a car backfiring. He lay for a moment listening, but only silence came back. He turned over and tried to go back to sleep, but it was no good – his mouth was dry. Parched. He needed a drink. He climbed out of the bunk and pulled on a pair of pants and a shirt and his baseball cap, slipped his feet into his sneakers, and made his way down the corridor. He paused by a half-open door, and in the half-light of the room saw Maria sitting at an antiquated radio transmitter speaking rapidly in Spanish. He moved on to the kitchen, ignored the black Panamanian, nearly gagged on the nauseating smell of frying bacon, took a beer from the fridge and went outside. Winter was sitting on the steps to the shack, quietly reading a book.

'There you are,' he said, rubbing his eyes, 'Thought I heard a noise, gunshot or something.'

Winter glanced up. 'Just showing Drummer how effective a nine-mill Soviet Auto Pistol cartridge is.'

'Oh,' Ugly Charlie said, sitting down next to him. He knocked the top off the bottle on one of the steps, took a long swallow of the cold beer, belched, and said, 'Anyway, you're about early.'

'Couldn't sleep.'

'What you reading?'

'B-25 flight manual.'

Charlie's mouth dropped open. 'B what? What's the deal?' he said, warily.

'According to Drummer a B-25 came in here about three weeks back with a couple of young American boys at the controls. Seems they went off to Cartagena to do some drug dealing. They never returned. Drummer figures they were robbed and killed. He was pissed off because he'd loaned them a truck; he didn't get it back.'

'And the plane?'

'There's a drug dealer called Werner Stock who lives in Santa Marta; it seems he's laid claim to the aircraft. Told Drummer the kids owed him money, even has some papers to prove it. It's for sale.'

'And you're thinking of buying it?' Charlie snorted.

'A World War Two bomber? Come on, Wint, get real.
You remember the old commandment about military
airplanes – built by the lowest bidder!'

'Backup plan in case I don't find a plane in Cali.'

'What tail number's it got?'

'US.'

'I thought we needed a Colombian registration. Try
and merge in with the scenery.'

'I was just looking at options. A way to get us in
to Los Llanos and carry enough supplies for three
months.'

Charlie slapped his hand on his thigh. 'Jesus, Wint,
you're not listening to me, are you? You're talking
about a ship that was thrown together more than
half a century ago by a bunch of bicycle mechanics
pressed into service to supplement the war effort.
Its life expectancy in those days over enemy territory was about seventy-five hours. That this one
survived is probably down to the fact that it missed
the war; stayed at home to train crews or something.
The point is it was never meant to last for ever. As
for the kids who flew it in here, five'll get you ten
they stole it from some airplane graveyard, and with
more luck than judgement arrived here in one piece.
Notwithstanding all that, they probably overboosted
the engines and God knows what else . . . Sure, we
need transport to get in and out of Los Llanos, but
no fucking point killing ourselves doing it, is there?
Where is it, anyway?'

'Over there.' Winter pointed. 'Under the camouflage
netting. I thought you might want to check the oil, run
the engines and do taxi checks.'

'Waste of time,' Charlie said, sullenly.

'Maybe, but there is a consolation. It's fitted with internal ferry tanks. Total fuel load is two thousand gallons, and according to the book of words here we should burn about a hundred and forty gallons an hour. At one eighty knots that would give us a range of around two thousand five hundred nauticals.'

'What you thinking?'

'We need a way out of the country once we've finished what we've come here to do.'

Charlie finished his beer, belched again, tossed the empty bottle to one side, and searched through his pockets for the pack of Marlboros. He lit one and stood up, mumbled something under his breath about crazy Englishmen, and shuffled off in the direction of the plane. 'There was another commandment,' he called back.

'What was that?'

'Don't climb in the cockpit with someone braver than yourself.'

'I'll leave the final decision up to you, then, Major Riker,' Winter replied.

'That'll be the day,' Charlie muttered, and went in search of the old bomber.

It was two hours later that Ugly Charlie dropped down next to Winter on the step. There was one epaulet and several buttons missing from his sweat-stained khaki shirt. He took off his baseball cap and fanned his face.

'How was she?' Winter asked.

'Reminded me of an old hooker I used to know in downtown Manila. Great with a paper sack over her head.'

'Real time, Charlie.'

'Oh, I've seen worse, only thing is they were usually in a smoking heap at the end of a runway,' Charlie said in a concerned voice. 'Half the engine gauges only work intermittently, and there's more oil outside the engines than should be in them. There's a hydraulic leak on the left strut; they should never have left it sitting there with all that fuel on board – too much weight. On the plus side both engines run, although there's a big mag drop on the right engine; could be plugs oiling, but more likely to be a bad magneto.'

'Any chance of finding spares?'

'Spares!' Charlie laughed. 'Always the comedian, eh, Wint? Sure, why don't I just run down to the local K-Mart and pick up an overhauled engine or two? Then again there could be an airplane graveyard down at Santa Marta; who knows – we might even find a wrecked B-25 that backed very gently into a mountain. As I told you back in the Keys, this place is only good for white powder, white slavery and black money.' He picked up the airframe logs and squinted at the writing on the front cover; at the callsign – N4777. So much fiction. He wondered what other lies had been written up to make this collection of corroded metal parts temporarily airworthy. 'Even with a few new engine parts it'd be Warbird Airways' first and last flight. The worst safety record in aviation history. One hundred per cent fatal.'

Winter got up and stretched, looking around the flat barren wilderness. 'Hell of a place,' he commented. 'See why they don't get a lot of tourists out this way. The police guy came and stamped our passports, by the way.'

'I guess that means we're now here legally. Something to be thankful for.' Charlie dragged himself tiredly to his feet, hitched up his trousers and moved towards the door. 'Need a beer or three. How about you?'

'No, thanks. Need to find Drummer and arrange a ride into Santa Marta. Can you manage for a couple of days?'

'Sure. You serious about that heap of junk, then?'

'I'm thinking about it, that's all. I'll fly down to Cali and do what's got to be done. You stay here and see how airworthy you can make it. If I find something more modern, like a twin-engined Cessna, we'll go that route.'

'You still figuring getting a local pilot?'

'Maybe. If that guy Werner Stock drops in, by the way, keep him in the hold until I get back.'

'You got it,' Charlie said, disappearing into the shack.

19

Tanner Williams pointed to the sheets and said to Owens, 'You want to pull the strings?'

'The what?'

'Work the sheets.'

'Aye, aye, skipper,' Owens said, moving to the winch.

When they cleared the jetty, Williams brought the sloop up on course to weather. When he tacked for the first time, he yelled, 'Ready about!'

'Ready, skipper!' Owens shouted back.

'Hard a-lee!' Williams called, noting that there was hardly a luff before the old man trimmed the jib.

The tack was silky and fast. The sails roared, then filled, and they were jetting forward again, away from the harbour and the bobbing boats at anchor, a silver plume of spray in their faces.

'What do you think?' Williams shouted from the helm.

'That you're enjoying every minute.'

'It's been a while, Edeyrn. You get a bit rusty.'

Owens laughed. 'I'd noticed.'

The big sloop – with a displacement of ten thousand five hundred pounds, a very long waterline and a planing hull, and a furling one fifty – sped southwest in the sunlight, glinting like a knife, down towards the Marquesas, where the water dramatically changed to midnight blue.

'You think it was Winter – the Key West television report?'

Owens said, 'Certainly fits with the killings in Oklahoma City. Don't quite follow the reasoning, though.'

'Are we dealing with a psychopath?'

'Unlikely. A psychopath is a person unable to deal with life – he sees life in a very different way than the rest of us.'

'His wife's murder could have done that to him.'

'According to the Key West police they were known drug pushers. Winter might just be teaching the fraternity a lesson. But whichever way you look at it he's playing right into your hands. What was the latest news from Colombia, by the way?'

'He's on his way to Cali. Two-day trip, apparently.'

'Nothing else?'

'No. Except the Cali Cartel is the main player in the cocaine business these days; they've also diversified into opium poppies and heroin, keeping up with the consumer habits back in the States, I guess. I've got a hunch he's gone down there to do a bit of intelligence work.'

'For what reason?'

'You tell me, Edeyrn.'

'I think our Mr Winter is a very complex man.'

'You think there could be another reason for him going to that place?'

'Perhaps. Perhaps not.'

'I think you . . . or your people, at least, overrate him.'

Owens laughed. 'Is there an opposite to overrate, as sleeping is opposite to waking?'

'Sure.'

'What is it?'

'Underrate.'

'So if they are two opposites, they come from one another, and have their processes of generation between the two of them?'

'Of course.'

'Very well, then,' Owens said. 'I will state one pair of opposites and the processes between them; and you can state the other. My opposites are sleeping and waking, and I say that waking comes from sleeping and sleeping from waking, and that the processes between them are going to sleep and waking up. Would you agree?'

'Yes.'

'Now you tell me in the same way about overrate and underrate. You do agree they are opposites?'

'I do.'

'And that they come from one another?'

'Yes.'

'Then what comes from underrate?'

'Overrate.'

'And what comes from overrate?'

'Underrate.'

'And the processes between them?'

Williams paused. Staring out at the empty blue

ocean. Tasting salt in his teeth. 'Knowledge . . . skill perhaps!'

'So the wise man confounds you by making you believe the opposite. Is that not skill? Knowledge?'

'Party trivia, Edeyrn. An attorney friend of mine plays the same word games in court every week. An ex-soldier with the rank of sergeant may be equipped to handle those Third World environments you spoke of. This is different.'

Owens said, 'We'll see.'

'I'll grant you that much at least.'

'Lovely day.'

'Beautiful.'

'Nice of the admiral to lend you his boat.'

'Not exactly lend: he'll send his bill in when we return it.'

'The wheels of commerce, Tanner, never let go, do they? But, going back to those Third World environments we were discussing, where in the table of developing countries would you put Colombia?'

'Word games, Edeyrn. You talk and I'll listen, but they're still word games.'

The forty-foot sloop with the name *Belinda Jane* painted in gold letters on the stern flashed onward in the late afternoon, playing its own games with the silvery translucent flying fish off her starboard bow. A moment of enchantment before sunset.

Satellite tracking towards a CPA on the western tip of Cuba. And from that Closest Point of Approach, a course for Cartagena de Indias.

20

Emilio Figueras had a personal fortune of two billion dollars, amassed by dealing in narcotics. It had been more than forty years since he had ventured into the business. Quite by accident. It was in 1951 that Klaus Barbie – the 'Butcher of Lyons' acquired in 1945 from the Gestapo by US Army Intelligence and put on the payroll to mould clandestine Nazi cells in Eastern Europe into anticommunist spy rings – was given a new name and a false passport and sent to Latin America to help the US combat communism, especially in Bolivia.

Emilio Figueras was one of Barbie's early contacts and from that initial association they ventured into the dope trade together. Their business was never big. Never too high-profile. High-profile figures were generally targets for the next coup. Things might have progressed in that comfortable vein had it not been for the July 1982 coup which put in power a group of military officers, who were seen internationally as incapable and dangerous. The concern was great enough for the US, among others, to back Hernan Siles Zuazo, who carried not a little high-level political prestige, and would be coming to power untainted by association with the drug barons. And this was where Emilio Figueras was at his best. Being a cautious man he had an uncanny ability of living in the present but thinking a long way into the future; so much so that the July 1982 coup had for him been the writing on the wall for his ventures with Barbie in Bolivia. He withdrew completely and poured all his efforts into his Cali company, but not before he had sold out Klaus Barbie. Not for money. He had plenty of that. Favours sometimes yielded higher rates of interest. In his case he produced false documents, put together over many years as a kind of insurance policy, to show that Barbie had been defrauding COMIBOL (Corporacion Minera de Bolivia), the Bolivian state mining monopoly, of tens of millions of dollars, and even suggested to Siles Zuazo that Barbie should be extradited to France, where he was wanted for war crimes. That Bolivia had no extradition treaty with France was not a factor. Siles Zuazo was shrewd enough to know that this gesture would result in increased financial and military aid from the French, as well as other Western govern-ments, and ease the burden – if only temporarily – of the Bolivian foreign debt.

For Emilio, who with the help of Barbie had in the early days bought the coca paste in Bolivia and Peru, and transported and sold it to his old friend Pablo Escobar in Colombia; who had then refined it in a clan-destine laboratory hidden in the jungle and distributed the pure cocaine product to the USA, mainly through Florida (the early and primitive smuggling methods being to pack the cocaine into shoe heels, or to sew consignments into the linings of suitcases or coats and smuggle them overseas by *mulas* – paid couriers – on regular airline flights), it was the beginning of a new chapter.

The boom years in Colombia coincided with Bolivia being seen as cleaning up its act. That was when the Medellin Cartel became the principal mafia – temporarily. Its leaders – Pablo Escobar, Jorge Luis Ochoa, Gonzalo Rodriguez Gacha and Carlos Lehder – lived quietly in freedom and luxury. Escobar founded a newspaper and, in 1982, was elected to the Congress. By 1983, Escobar's personal wealth was estimated to be in excess of two billion US dollars, making him the richest criminal in the world. He financed the construction of a barrio for 200 poor families in Medellin, and for this and several other benevolent actions, came to be known as 'Robin Hood Paisa'.

In mid-1983, Tranquiandia, the largest cocaine laboratory in history, went into production on the banks of the Rio Yari in Los Llanos. It had fourteen independent, fully equipped laboratories, a water and electricity supply, roads, dormitories, and its own airstrip. It produced 3,500 kilogrammes of pure cocaine per month.

The climate in which such laboratories could operate changed in August 1983 when Belisario Betancur appointed Rodrigo Lara Bonilla, Minister of Justice. Bonilla launched a campaign against the drug trade, which led *El Espectador*, one of Bogota's leading daily newspapers, to publicise some of Escobar's former crimes. The war between the cartel and the government began.

What very few people knew was that Emilio Figueras had worked very closely with Bonilla in feeding him information on Escobar. Not an altogether improbable scenario as the Figuerases and Escobar had worked closely together in the early days, when Figueras had supplied Escobar with vast amounts of coca paste from Bolivia.

His connections with Bonilla were even closer. He was his first cousin.

Once Emilio Figueras had sown the seeds of discontent and the government persecution of the Medellin Cartel had begun, he slipped into the shadows of Cali, and with the help of his sons set up a number of legitimate businesses, trading mainly in oil and coal and coffee. He had then, in secret, formed a newer, stronger Cali Cartel, who waited in the wings to take over as the largest drug cartel in the world. Now, he was set to exceed the reported wealth of Escobar in his heyday. The vehicle for this being the new export/import arrangements of pure cocaine into the USA, the subject of the breakfast meeting that Wednesday morning at his mountain hacienda one hundred kilometres west of the city.

The hacienda was built in the popular Andalusian style within a three-hundred-acre walled estate. The house itself was a large, two-storey, whitewashed building with a balcony around the entire upper floor, the red-tiled roof sun-faded to a rusty pink. Guard towers with a three-hundred-and-sixty-degree field of vision were elegantly disguised as supporting pillars to the massive gates, and were spaced at three-hundred-metre intervals around the walled property. Beyond the walls a two-hundred-and-fifty-metre perimeter of cleared land, seeded apparently with crops. In reality, antipersonnel mines.

The breakfast table, set with sparkling white linen and gleaming silverware and crystal, was on the east balcony. Three men sat at the table. Emilio Figueras at its head. Luis, his son, on his right. And a heavily built American with grey hair, matching beard, and sad brown eyes, addressed always as Mr Walker, to his left.

Emilio Figueras, who spoke little at these meetings, turned to his son, and waved an impatient hand. 'So, Luis. Perhaps you would explain the new shipping arrangements to Mr Walker.'

Luis removed his glasses and rubbed his eyes for a moment. 'Quite simply, and as we are all aware, US Customs, the FBI and the DEA have made Florida, as an importation centre, a no-go area. Notwithstanding that, they have in recent years used military jets to shoot down suspected drug-running flights.

'Naturally, we have always been prepared to take some losses. An arbitrary figure of twenty-five per cent was set by our company five years ago. Last year the annual loss figure escalated to forty-one per cent. That was when we decided that our contingency export plan should be put in place.' Luis paused, replaced his glasses, and took a sip of orange juice. 'The new arrangements call initially for four bulk cargo transactions per year. Fifty thousand kilogrammes per cargo. Each cargo will travel by seagoing coal freighter from Cartagena to Liverpool, England. The freighter will leave one day earlier than shown on the manifest and will route up the mid-Atlantic. It will rendezvous at a prearranged location with a freighter out of Montreal.

This freighter, owned by the Canadian mining company VANCO, will take on the cargo by ship-to-ship transfer. Following the transfer the VANCO freighter will continue its journey to a small island called Amitsoq, very close to the coast of southwest Greenland. This island is the site of a disused blacklead quarry, and as of last year was leased to VANCO.

'The cargo will be shipped back to Canada with actual rock samples being shipped for geographical evaluation. Once in Canada the cargo will be reduced to smaller amounts for shipment into the US. Any questions so far, Mr Walker?'

Walker stroked his beard. His accent when he spoke was markedly southern. 'One or two, I guess. I'm assuming the mining company, VANCO, is a part of your group of companies?'

Luis nodded. 'Yes.'

'Might it not be a little risky moving such large amounts in a single shipment?'

'The only risk would be from our own government, Mr Walker, and that I can assure you is taken care of. As far as Greenland is concerned we have no problems. Likewise Canada: we have a legitimate mining company transporting vast rock samples. This has already been running for nine months and we are certain we have . . . ironed out – is that right? – any wrinkles. If there are to be any problems it will be with border crossings into the USA. Which is where your expertise will be invaluable.'

'My pleasure, gentlemen, I assure you. However, concerning the ship-to-ship transfer in open ocean, it occurs to me that such a manoeuvre might be picked up by satellites. Could raise unwanted questions.'

White Lie

Luis said, 'A valid point. The transfer will only take place under certain weather conditions, that is, total cloud cover. Contrary to popular belief, satellites cannot photograph through cloud.'

'What about the shipping schedule? You said the ship was leaving a day early.'

'All sailings will be dependent upon long-range weather forecasts. That is, those that guarantee the cloud-cover conditions I mentioned.'

'May I enquire as to what you're mining in Greenland?'

'Gold, Mr Walker.'

Walker looked up in surprise. 'For real? In that godforsaken place!'

Luis smiled. 'There is another Canadian mining company by the name of Platinova that has had some success on the east coast of Greenland. We are seeking to emulate that success – at least in the eyes of those watching.'

'What about the cost of the operation? Sounds pretty high to me.'

'Shipping costs are absorbed by the other companies. The cost of the mining setup on Amitsoq is acceptable – that is, it will run at three to five per cent of our projected gross annual profit. Far better than the forty-one-per-cent losses we incurred in the last fiscal year, I am sure you would agree.'

'I'm impressed, sir. Most impressed. This island you mentioned . . . Amitsoq. It's got deep water, I guess, for shipping.'

'We have barges to offload from the freighter one kilometre from the island. Also, we have cleared an airstrip on the north side of the island. Mining officials fly into one of the Greenland airports and then take a smaller plane or a helicopter to the island.'

'Why not go directly to our own airstrip?'

'Procedure, Mr Walker. We use the airbase at a place called Narsarsuaq which has police/customs facilities. Up until now I have been told that no flight crews have seen a customs man. Greenland Air operations officers handle all the paperwork and refuelling and arrange for the charter of one of their helicopters. We feel comfortable with these arrangements.'

'Where is the rock sample taken to in Canada?'

'Montreal by ship. By road to our factory near Winnipeg.'

'But surely we're running the same sort of risk as Florida. What happens if the Canadian Customs discover we're using their back door?'

'They won't, Mr Walker. We have a senior Department of Transport official on the payroll. He gives us the green light to offload at night, at a specific point on the St Lawrence. The consignments are moved to safe houses, shall we say, legitimate businesses once again. From these safe houses they will make their way to various border crossing points. Ones you will establish. Which leaves US Customs. What is their coverage on the American side?'

'Generally pretty strong. They were running Operation Exodus for some years, creating highway checkpoints plus coastal ports and airports. The operation is still in place, except they're dealing it under a different name, Operation Change Up . . . new President likes baseball, I guess. Therefore I think we'd be better to move the stuff over toward Calgary and take it down through the Rocky Mountains into Oregon. From there, a straight shot into California.'

'How foolproof would this be?'

'Something I'd need to check out, sir. Even so I feel we need to put a number of alternative arrangements in place at the same time – what I'd call fail-safe options.'

'Keeping one step ahead, Mr Walker.'

'You got it, sir.'

Luis turned to his father, who was sitting stonelike at the head of the table. An imperceptible nod of the white-haired head, nothing more. Luis removed his glasses and polished them for a moment with the corner of his napkin. 'Excellent, Mr Walker. I will leave those details up to you. Perhaps you could advise me of the precise procedure once you have put it in place.'

Walker smiled. 'Not a problem, sir, I assure you.'

Breakfast of eggs and fried maize pancakes and fresh coffee was served by two smiling young girls. The men ate in silence.

It was half an hour later that Emilio Figueras had left to take the American to his car and driver, and Luis was enjoying a last cup of coffee before driving to his office in the city. He stood up and walked across to the edge of the balcony, breathing deeply of the mountain air. Such a beautiful day, he thought. A small red and white aircraft appeared out of the east. It passed within a mile of the house, making a slow turn onto a southerly heading. Luis briefly envied the pilot of the single-engined aeroplane. What freedom there must be up there on such a morning.

He turned his attention to the courtyard and the sound of the car engine. Mr Walker's dark Mercedes swept through the gates and down the dusty mountain road.

It was minutes later, as he was collecting his briefcase in the hallway, that his father intercepted him. 'You were satisfied with the meeting, Luis?'

'*Si, Padre.*'

'You are still working on the other matter?' his father asked, resting a big hand with scarred knuckles on his son's shoulder.

'It has my undivided attention.'

'Make sure it has. I will tolerate no excuses, not even from you. You understand?' Iron in every word. The playful slap across the cheek followed. So hard it made Luis's ears ring.

'I understand, Father.' He dutifully kissed the old man and left the house.

21

Winter was bone-weary when he arrived back at Canaveral late on Thursday afternoon. In the gathering darkness a cool sea breeze rippled inland from Cape de la Vela, drifting dust down the airstrip.

He was helping Drummer unload the Dodge when Ugly Charlie came out of the shack, a bottle of Red Stripe in his hand. 'Need some help?'

'Sure. How've you been?'

'Fine. Good trip?'

Winter nodded towards the Panamanian. 'Tell you about it later. Drummer mentioned that Werner Stock still hasn't made it out here.'

'This weekend was the latest update I got,' Charlie said, hefting a crate off the tailgate of the Dodge. 'Jesus, Wint, what you got in here? Gold bars?'

'Picked up some supplies in Santa Marta. Foodstuffs generally.' Winter took the last small crate and dropped it alongside the others. 'You could have been right about the gold, though. Drummer was telling me on the drive back that Santa Marta is the oldest surviving colonial town in Colombia and that the Spaniards used it as a base to plunder the gold treasures of the region.' He stopped talking when the Panamanian disappeared into the shack. He steered Charlie over to the B-25, and they sat under the wing and lit cigarettes. He motioned his head at the old bomber. 'How does she look?'

'Found a new set of plugs in the toolkit inside the plane. Got rid of the mag drop on the left engine. Apart from that, I fixed a couple of oil leaks, and rigged up an intercom, pilot to copilot. Navigation systems. One ADF, one VOR. No way of doing a systems check here, so no guarantees. Likewise the standby compass. Probably needs a swing. Without a landing compass to check it against . . . well, you know.'

'Yeah.'

'No luck getting a plane down south, then?'

'Not unless you want to pay ten times the price.'

'Local pilot?'

'Seems those that are on the market are looking to fly for Avianca, SAM or Satena – the commercial carrier of the Colombian Air Force. Thought I might run into one or two expat flyers – things have changed over the past ten years, Charlie.'

'The political correctness of the nineties,' Charlie laughed. 'When all the men turned into fucking women. Welcome to the Planet Lesbos. Women fucking women, and no one remembers who was supposed to be wearing the dress. Shit, man, like my old buddy Hank Ritter used to say out in Nam, keep the bitches barefoot and pregnant and they'll love you for ever.'

'Go down a bundle of laughs at one of those Women's League meetings, wouldn't he?'

'If he'd come back with the rest of us, he'd probably made a career out of it. Anyway, what about the recce flight?'

'Chartered a Cessna 210 with a pilot. Filmed the entire area at first light this morning. Audio portion has a lot of engine noise. Gives basic info, altitude, speed, temperature, headings, plus local landmarks. We'll hook it up to a TV later, pick the bones out of it. Can't help you with the compass on the B-25. But I bought a Garmin GPS from the 210 pilot. Two hundred and fifty user waypoints. Moving map graphics. I got a lat and long from it one mile east of the target.'

'Pilot didn't suspect anything?'

'Didn't speak English. Told him I was a tourist and wanted some film to show my friends when I got back home. He was happy to sell the GPS and make a few bucks profit.'

'Target?'

'Large house in the mountains – the Cordillera Occidental – one hundred kilometres west of the airport. White. Red roof. Single bush road access. On a westerly heading there's a valley one kilometre to the north. Runs through to the Pacific coast according to the Cessna pilot.'

'Height of the mountains?'

'According to the pilot's map, three thousand metres. Higher stuff south and north, around five thousand metres, but we should be well clear of that.'

'Radar?'

'Airport has primary and secondary. Shift change for controllers oh six hundred hours, might be a good time to go in . . . when confusion is at its peak.'

Charlie stubbed his cigarette out on the sole of his

sneaker. Absently field-stripped the butt, scattering the remnants in the dirt. 'Next move?'

'Get the stores into the shack before they get stolen. Try and locate Werner Stock tomorrow. Flight planning to the strip in Los Llanos.'

'Is that it?'

'Has Maria left yet?'

'No, why'd you ask?'

'The fewer people here when we depart the better.'

'What about Drummer? What do you plan to tell him?'

'As little as possible. Have you eaten yet?'

'No. Drummer usually fixes a meal about this time.'

It was later that evening. Charlie was playing cards with two other American pilots in the shack. Winter was sitting on the steps enjoying the cool evening breeze, trying to sequence events in his mind.

'You have returned!' It was Maria. She sat down beside him, and he detected her faint musky perfume. 'I hear you have been to Cali.'

'I thought you were leaving tonight.'

She lifted her hands in that Latin way. 'Perhaps tomorrow. So how was Cali? Not as humid as here.'

'You've been there?'

'I was born there.'

'Noisy.'

She laughed. 'Oh yes, it is always noisy. Fifty decibels beyond bearable, we always joked. And the traffic, it was fast enough for you?'

'Like the music, all or nothing. As for the traffic lights, I wonder why they bother – no one seems to pay them any attention.'

'Colombian drivers consider them decorative rather than a form of traffic regulation, Mr Winter. Their colours are the same as everywhere else – it is just that my people decipher their meaning more artistically. And your reason for going to Cali? Business perhaps?'

'Sightseeing. The career tourist. Very different from Odessa.'

'Ah yes, you were born there, that is right?'

'No, I was born in Prague. I grew up in Odessa.'

She stood up and went a few paces. And stopped. And turned back to him, hands thrust into the pockets of her jeans, head on one side, long black hair falling across her face. 'Would you like to walk with me?'

'Where?'

'Just to the end of the airstrip and back. Exercise. I do not like to walk alone after dark, you understand.'

They walked in silence for more than half an hour, their arms touching briefly from time to time in the moonlit darkness. It was as they returned to the shack that Winter said, 'You fly for Johnny Shoosh full-time?'

'No, this is my first trip. Why do you ask?'

'I'm looking for a pilot.'

'Ah! And you would like to hire my services?'

'Perhaps.'

'What sort of flying?'

'It depends.'

'On what?'

'Trust. Anyone I hire has to be completely honest with me.'

'What about pay?'

'Five hundred dollars per diem, all expenses, plus

a ten-thousand-dollar bonus and an airline ticket to your home base at the end of the contract.'

'And the length of the contract?'

'Guaranteed thirty days . . . could run to three months. Depends.'

She was silent a long time. Eventually she said, 'Perhaps I am interested. I have a question, though.'

'I'm listening.'

'You said that anyone you hire has to be completely honest with you, that is correct?'

'Yes.'

'And you with them?'

'Naturally.'

'You told me you were returning to flying to make money. If this was true how do you now offer me a job?'

'I didn't know anything about you then. It seemed easier to say that.'

'And you know enough about me now?'

'Not much . . . enough.'

'So, perhaps I should tell you. I was born in Cali, Colombia. Where were you born?'

'I already told you. Prague.'

She stopped at the foot of the steps and turned towards him. The hard, challenging look he had seen before flashed in her eyes. 'Goodnight, Mr Winter.'

'Where are you going?'

'Away from you. Away from your lies and deceit.'

22

On the sloop *Belinda Jane* eighty nautical miles west-nor'west of the Cayman Islands, the Caribbean Sea was calm. The light wind was enough for Williams to lower the main and start the twenty-seven-horsepower diesel. They were running on autopilot now. Edeyrn Owens busy at the three-burner stove in the tiny galley. 'Coffee, boyo,' he called up to the cockpit.

Williams came below and sat on the lower step. 'It's getting a little slick out there.'

'Cast upon a wine-dark sea,' Owens smiled. 'Lucky we have an engine.'

Williams sipped at the coffee. 'The glass is falling slowly. I think we'll get a fair blow in the early hours.'

'Rough?'

'Does that worry you?'

'Quite the contrary – never enjoyed anything so much in my life.'

'Good, we'll make a bluewater sailor out of you yet.'

'Did I hear you on the radio just now?'

'Winter's back at Canaveral. He's bought a large quantity of food supplies and is trying to purchase an airplane from a local drug dealer.'

'Could be planning to move south and go into hiding.'

'My thoughts. Might still have contacts in Bolivia.'

'Any chance we'll miss him?'

'No. I've arranged for the drug dealer to be kept on hold until Monday. He's been told there's another customer coming to town. One who might pay more.'

23

'What is it?' Luis asked Mauricio Becerra, his accountant and financial right-hand man.

'Señorita Rubiano to see you, Señor.'

Luis Figueras looked at his watch. It was nearly nine o'clock. 'Please show her in, Mauricio, then you had better go home to that wife of yours, or she will be accusing me of working you too hard.'

Mauricio, always careful to tread lightly when it came to dealing with members of the Figueras family, wrung his hands and looked distraught. 'Accuse *you*, Señor? No, no, no, she would never do that. She prays for you every day.'

Luis patted him on the shoulder and smiled. 'I am not my father, Mauricio. A joke, I assure you.'

The forty-year-old accountant failed to see the joke. He bowed stiffly and went to let the young lady in.

Ana Lucia Rubiano was still wearing her office clothes. Black skirt and high-necked white blouse. She had been working late at the bank when she made the discovery that nearly made her heart stop. She cleared her desk and ran out into the Plaza Caycedo and took the first taxi to the north side of the river. All the time thinking that she had very nearly lost Luis. Thinking that she would stay poor for ever. Now this. This would change everything.

'Ana, I was meaning to telephone you, but I have been so busy,' Luis said, removing his glasses and kissing her briefly on the cheek. 'You would like a drink?'

'No thank you, Luis. I have something—'

'Before you say anything more, Ana, I must formally apologise. You must forgive my inadequate use of words the other evening. I was never very good at speaking to women . . . the courtroom is different, that I can manage, perhaps because I have an audience and I am indirectly involved in the proceedings . . . With you . . . with you . . . I love you, and I do not know how to say it.'

She smiled. 'You said it very beautifully, Luis. You speak words better than Gabo writes them.'

Gabo – Gabriel Garcia Marquez – the principal figure of Colombian literature. Luis basked in the compliment. He took her in his arms and kissed her gently on the lips. 'You will stay with me tonight?'

'If you want me to.'

'I want you to.'

'Then I will stay.'

'You are sure you would not like a drink? Some wine perhaps?'

'No, really.'

'Coffee?'

'No.'

'Anything?'

White Lie

She bit his earlobe gently, and whispered, 'Just you, Luis.'

He slowly undressed her, gently kissing each part of flesh that he bared. Than he picked her up and carried her to the darkness of the bedroom. They made love half of the night, by which time exhaustion overtook them both.

The piece of paper she had brought from the bank, and which had seemed so important, lay forgotten in her handbag.

24

It was extrasensory. Winter could anticipate a wind change with his ear. Wind increases, creating pressure differences that he could sense, like a driver at Indy seeing a nut on a turn at 220 m.p.h. Something not taught in the classroom. Seat-of-the-pants stuff. Intuition. Like a blind man knowing the difference between five-, ten- and twenty-dollar bills. He felt it now, as he had throughout that Saturday morning.

The young boys who normally helped Drummer had gone. And Drummer had been missing from the previous evening. Perhaps he had gone to collect Werner Stock as he had been promising! Perhaps he should have slipped the Panamanian a grand to keep him happy! But it wasn't that, he knew. You survived in these places by acting mean; macho poker played with hard eyes and clenched fists and guns you weren't afraid to use. One slip, one solitary relapse into something resembling a human being, and your throat was cut from ear to ear; the watch on your wrist would be worth that much – or even the boots on your feet.

White Lie

It was noon when he went to the kitchen-diner. Ugly Charlie was there talking quietly to Maria. There were the two others who had been around all week. Americans. Both suntanned. One young, mid-twenties, thin faced with a ponytail; the other closer to sixty, grossly overweight, thick white hair and horn-rimmed glasses. Both had revolvers pushed into their waistbands. There was a lull in the conversation as Winter helped himself to a bowl of *Cazuela de mariscos* from the pot on the stove. He picked up a chunk of bread and a spoon from the table and took his food outside. He sat on the step and brooded, becoming an entity of his own. Something was wrong. He knew it. Felt it. The airstrip was completely deserted. The sun beating down on an expectant silence. The old bomber the only giveaway that this was an airstrip; the other aircraft still hidden beneath their olive drab netting.

Ugly Charlie, dressed in sweat-stained khaki slacks and shirt, appeared and sat down alongside. He took off his baseball cap and fanned cooling air at his face. 'Anything on the Stock guy?'

Winter shook his head. His mouth was full with the coarse-grained bread. He ate a little of the fish stew and swallowed. 'How long to get that portable building off the airstrip?'

Charlie scratched the tuft of hair on the right side of his head, before replacing his baseball cap. 'On wheels or jacks?'

'Don't know. Think you could get the others to help you . . . tell them you need to do taxi checks on the B-25.'

The old scarred face came close to Winter. 'We got problems?'

Winter nodded his head – his eyes were screwed tight as if he resisted a pain. 'Could be.'

'Like what?'

'Not important. You'd better help me load the B-25 first. Then move the building.'

'Got it,' Charlie said quietly. He knew the voice. Knew when to respond to orders.

It was nearly an hour later, when they had all gone, that Winter went back to their room to check nothing had been left behind. 'Nothing' meaning that even a last scrap of paper was shredded and scattered on the wind. He lit a Particulares and stood at the open window for a moment, watching the distant gathering at the shack on the airstrip. Someone had backed up a truck to it. They all seemed to be inspecting a corner of the building. He couldn't make out what the problem was. He finished his cigarette, tossed the butt out of the window and made his way down the corridor.

He had taken less than five paces from the building when he noticed the dust rising down the dirt road and saw what appeared to be an army truck with men standing in the back. What was more, they were armed. The muzzle flashes came next, a high cacophony of AK bullets overhead . . . flash booms of B-40 rockets, large grenades causing a rash of second booms . . . a .50-calibre machine gun tearing ragged holes in slow, heavy bursts through the hot afternoon . . . a building close to the far end of the strip now in flames . . .

For Winter it was like a charred old memory coming to life. He stood for a moment. Disbelieving. Then

started running towards the plane. Charlie was already
there. The crack-crack-crack of automatic weapons
fire growing closer. 'You get the building moved?' he
yelled.

Charlie made no reply but hauled himself up through
the belly hatch into the bomber. Winter followed,
closing the hatch behind him. By the time he got
to the cockpit Charlie had the battery switch on and,
without checking to see if he had enough voltage,
was pressing the energise switch for the right engine.
Gradually a faint whine started in the Wright Cyclone
as the flywheel built up energy. When the whine had
reached a steady note he flicked the switch across
to mesh. Winter watched as the blade tips slashed
by. Charlie's lips moving as he counted them. One
of those little things on radial engines, necessary to
remove collected oil from the lower cylinders. Pre-
vention against hydraulicking, which can blow a cylinder off.

Ignition ON. Charlie stabbed the prime button . . .
the engine coughed, blade tips chopping through
clouds of blue-grey smoke . . . hand darting to adjust
the throttle . . . then back to the primer switch to
keep everything turning . . . head back from window
to pressure gauges . . . and back to smoky window,
checking for signs of external fuel fire. The engine
settled at a throaty, window-trembling rumble at 800
r.p.m. . . . oil pressure eighty p.s.i. . . . fuel pressure
twenty-one p.s.i. . . . right engine hydraulics hovering
around 1,000 pounds.

Charlie caught Winter's eye as he repeated the procedure on the left engine, all the time looking back
over his shoulder. 'Where the fuck did they come

from?' he screamed as he gunned the engines and the plane rolled slowly forward.

The raw percussion of engines masked the firing now. All that the two men saw was silent explosions growing nearer. What appeared to be the fuel dump had gone up, black smoke towering skyward. Another two camouflaged buildings had been destroyed, as had one of the three American aeroplanes. Winter saw the two Americans who had been in the kitchen earlier crouched behind a stack of crates, returning fire at the truck. They didn't last long. Charlie was turning onto the dirt runway when he saw them cut down in a hail of bullets.

Now the plane had picked up some speed and he was moving away towards the far end of the airstrip. Backtracking to ensure they had enough runway to get off. That was when Winter looked down and back towards the right wingtip. At first he thought it was a soldier and he pulled his gun from his waistband, the other hand yanking the side window open. But it wasn't a soldier. It was Maria. Her eyes wide. Her lips mouthing silent words. He pointed quickly, indicating that she should get alongside the fuselage by the trailing edge of the right wing. He turned and snatched Charlie's hands from the throttles and pulled them back. 'We've got a passenger.'

Charlie swore and hit the brakes. It took less than thirty seconds and she was on board, Winter tugging the hatch closed. Charlie was already moving again, swinging the plane around using differential power. No time for power checks. Maria was strapping herself into the seat next to him, sweat pouring from her face. Charlie said nothing but heaved the throttles forward through forty inches of boost and pointed the plane down the runway. The cockpit side windows were still open, filling the air with a dry clatter that seemed to herald self-destruction.

There was something wrong. The flying controls were not responding. Charlie's eyes did a quick sweep around the cluttered cockpit: supercharger to low gear, booster pumps to emergency, mixtures rich . . . engine temperatures coming up quickly — maybe too quickly. He yanked the wheel again — it was still limp and loose, the rudder pedals flopping meaninglessly. He advanced the throttles to the stops, not even bothering to check the manifold pressures to see if he was overboosting the engines.

Still no fucking control . . . but the plane was swinging left . . . dab of right brake . . . speed through fifty . . . controls . . . feel . . . now they were coming in. Speed eighty-five . . . Charlie squinted ahead in the bright sunlight at the portable building he and the other pilots had only moved as far the edge of the runway. He hoped to God they had enough wingtip clearance. He'd stopped thinking about the truck now. Even so, he continued to hear the dry pecks of gunfire as they found the airframe. He eased the ship as far left as he could . . . the portable building came and went in a blur . . . no collision . . . the end of the runway looming rapidly . . . graded dirt turning to scrub. Without checking the airspeed he pulled back on the controls, and suddenly she was flying. Thirty-four hundred horses breaking free. The scrubland flicked beneath, a few shacks, a dirt road. Charlie let out a frightened breath.

Chest pain. Shit! Too close.

He levelled off at two hundred feet, letting the airspeed build to 140 m.p.h. before reducing power and r.p.m. on the props. Then, checking the compass, he eased the ship onto a northerly course, heading for the Caribbean. He slid his window shut, shutting out some of the noise; smelling, as if for the first time, the stench of his own body sweat.

He turned his head. Winter was by his shoulder hanging onto the pilot's and co-pilot's seats. He looked grim. 'I would have rotated a bit earlier,' he shouted.

'Fuck you,' Charlie shouted back.

'Wings clean?'

Charlie banked the aircraft first left, then right, checking for the telltale vapour of venting fuel from holed tanks. He resumed the northerly heading. 'Checked . . . clean.'

'Give it to Miss Espinosa . . . let's get back and check for battle damage.'

Charlie waved the controls to Maria.

She moved across to the left seat. 'What is our heading to be?'

Charlie looked at Winter for confirmation. 'North. Keep it low for the time being.'

Charlie paused for a moment, using the time to check that the r.p.m., oil pressures and temperatures were normal and laid a hand on the engine control pedestal and felt the slight trembling pulse beneath his fingers; the expected palsies of old age, nothing more. He turned and followed the hunched figure of Winter back into the fuselage, grabbing for handholds as the aircraft bucked its way through the low-level turbulence. The noise was deafening. The heat stifling. Once back in the fuselage he checked the internal fuel tank carefully to ensure that no stray bullets had punctured it, his nose sniffing for fumes. Miraculously, other than a number of holes in the skin, everything seemed intact.

Charlie flopped down in one of the utility seats. He was breathing hard. Light-headed. His hands shaking. His heart thumping painfully against his chest.

Winter sat next to him. Wiped the dripping sweat from his forehead with the back of his hand. 'You okay?'

'I'll be all right in a minute . . . too much exertion.'

Winter put a hand on his shoulder. 'You stay here and rest, I'll go and fly it for a while.'

'So what the hell happened back there?'

'Just another day on the Gaza Strip,' Winter remarked with something that passed as a hint of a smile.

'Army?'

'Looked that way.'

'I thought they never set foot in the peninsula!'

'That's what Drummer told me.'

'But you didn't believe him.'

'You know how it is, Charlie.'

He knew. When in doubt trust to your gut. 'Then again, there's Maria.'

'Maria!'

'Possibly known by the Feds as a drug runner. Now we've taken her on board with us.'

'You're forgetting "grand theft". We just stole an airplane.'

'Perhaps the army will claim they knocked out everything rather than admit they let an unarmed plane get away.'

'Been known.'

'What we going to do with her?' Charlie asked nervously, taking a cigarette from a crushed packet and lighting it, oblivious to the fact that he was sitting next to a massive internal fuel tank.

Winter was quiet for a long moment. Setting himself loose from the world. It was one of those things he did. Almost magical. Creating a void around himself. Concentration. Finally he said, 'We could always take her on as crew. Pay her to come with us.'

'To Los Llanos?'

'Sure.'

Charlie choked on his cigarette. 'And let her in on the entire operation, you mean?'

'Why not? We need a pilot.'

Charlie looked at the Englishman in disbelief. 'You're crazy.'

'What's the alternative? Land somewhere down below and kick her out? Her Aero Commander was destroyed back there, so I don't imagine your friend Johnny Shoosh will welcome her back with open arms. Or will he?'

'I guess not. The "cargo" had been paid for in advance.'

'How do you know that?'

'She told me, when she found out that Johnny and I flew in Nam together. Said that Johnny don't trust his pilots with the folding green stuff; that he wire-transfers it couple of days before the collection is due. So he – or whoever bankrolls him – could be in the hole for a cool million . . . maybe more.' He dropped his cigarette on the bare metal floor and ground it out with the sole of his shoe. 'Anyway, I'll leave it to you, Wint. I'm too tired to care one way or the other . . . Oh, and as you're passing the galley tell the stew I'll have the steak. Medium rare.'

'You want me to check what the movie is at the same time?'

Charlie laughed and pulled his baseball cap down over his closed eyes. And saw a large flock of flamingos on approach for landing in the salt ponds, and pockets of deep blue cut through the shallow flats like lifelines on a weathered hand, and a line of palms reaching out from a strip of white sand. Not such a bad place. When he got back, perhaps he'd buy that boat. Take Nancy on the grand tour.

It was when Winter had dropped into the right seat that Maria leaned towards him. He caught the faintest hint of the familiar musky perfume mingled with the smells of machinery. Looked into her eyes, noticed for the first time the tiny flecks of green against the hazel, sensed in that passing moment he might find something there. He held her gaze a moment longer, then the softness dissolved into nothing more than a stranger's uninterested glance.

'What happened back there at Canaveral?' she shouted.

'Put on your headset.' He found the intercom switch and flicked it to on and pulled on his own headset, grateful for the reduction in noise. 'How'd you read?'

'Fives . . . how me?'

'Fives.'

'So what happened back there?'

'Looked like Colombian Army.'

'You are sure?'

'I didn't ask them, if that's what you mean . . . Hell, I don't know.'

She glanced back down the fuselage. Charlie's direction. 'He is all right? He looked ill.'

'Exhausted. I told him to get some rest.'

'Where are we going? You never said.'

'North for twenty miles.'

'Then what?'

Winter removed the handheld GPS from the nav-bag he had stowed earlier by the seat, connected the aerial lead, wet the aerial suction pad with his tongue and positioned it high on the windscreen in front of him. He switched it on and watched the small screen as numbers and acronyms scrolled across. They needed to pick up a minimum of three satellites – which usually took a few minutes – before it could give them their lat and long position. Once he had that he could plan any course he liked, via any waypoints, to Los Llanos. 'Then we'll probably run west for a while. I'll let you know.'

'How about fuel?'

'We've got two thousand gallons on board.'

'That much!'

'Ferry tank back in the fuselage.'

She looked around the maze of instruments and sweat-corroded switches, most of which carried no labels. 'And no way of knowing how to transfer it. We should climb.'

'Later. Just keep it down here for now.'

She made no reply, her eyes focused on the blue waters of the Caribbean two hundred feet below them, keeping the nose tucked a few inches under the natural horizon, her right hand making small imperceptible movements on the elevator trim wheel.

He watched her for a moment. A hard woman. But there was something about her. Something more than a good pair of hands and a professional flight-deck presence. 'England,' he said, over the intercom.

A brief, sharp glance. 'England what?'

'I was born in England.'

'Why are you telling me that?'

'The trust we talked about.'

'And for that you think I should now fly for you. Is that correct? Because you saved my life back there, perhaps!'

'No, I would have done it for anybody. Besides, what else are you doing?'

'What sort of job?' she asked.

'Military-type operation.'

'What?' That was an attention-getter. She looked at him for a full five seconds.

'Did you ever fly in the military?'

'No.'

'Fly jets?'

'Yes.'

'It could be very dangerous.'

'And the pay?'

'The same deal as I outlined before. A daily rate plus all expenses. The same deal I'm giving to Charlie.'

'And a bonus of ten thousand at the end of the contract.'

'Yes. Plus airline ticket to your home base.'

'Coach or first-class?'

Winter thought he detected a mocking tone in the voice. 'Why not your own private jet!'

She did not rise to the bait. 'And the contract might last three months?'

'Possibly. We won't know until we get to our destination and carry out evaluations.'

'Do clothes come under expenses?' She indicated the jeans and white T-shirt she was wearing. 'Everything I had is back there.'

'We'll sort something out.'

'And the destination?'

'An airstrip in Los Llanos.'

'Es el colmo.' Her hands tightened on the control wheel. The knuckles showed white. 'Los Llanos! That is the country of the guerrilla, Mr Winter. Very dangerous.'

'I know.'

Maria was silent. Her eyes focused on the horizon, darting back to check instrument readings, scanning across the sweat-corroded switches and levers, the gaping holes in the instrument panel where vital information would have once displayed itself to the operating crew; the mildewed and rotting seat harnesses, the smell of decay.

'This military operation. What would it be exactly?'

He outlined the target and the planned mission, keeping everything very brief and very simple.

'Emilio Figueras, the head of the Cartel de Cali! It is suicide. Has anyone told you you are mad?'

'Only Charlie, but then he's been saying that for years.'

'You work for the Federales, Mr Winter? The CIA perhaps?'

'No.'

'So what is your reason? You grow tired of living perhaps!'

White Lie

'The reason is not an issue, Miss Espinosa.'

'Are you a religious man?'

'No. Why do you ask?'

'Your faith is blinding, that is all.'

'Does that mean you'll take the job?'

'*Qué carajo.*' She struck her forehead with the heel of her hand. 'Yes, but subject to an assessment of the equipment we have at the Los Llanos strip. Also there is Charlie – he is wearing khaki. He should change before we land. Jeans and a coloured sweatshirt would be better.'

'Why?'

'He looks like a soldier or a guerrilla, Mr Winter – shooting is the only form of communication between the two.'

'Anything else?'

'Perhaps I should say a prayer for you – for all of us.'

Winter laid his head back and closed his eyes. 'As long as you do it quietly.'

25

A legal mind is a careful mind. None more so than that of Luis Figueras, who on the one hand fought for the rights of the poor in the barrios, and on the other was an unknown legal manipulator, hidden by anonymity, doing the work of headlining criminals. The news he received at his Cali penthouse apartment that Saturday afternoon might have panicked a lesser man. But not Luis. He calmly took notes in a precise hand from the voice on the other end of the telephone a thousand kilometres away, accepting the failure to take out the man Winter with equanimity. He had long reasoned that as a thinker, a strategist, he could accept the principle of violence. As an activist, however, he could not accept participation. Until the advent of his brother's death. A cold wind blowing at the consciousness of being thought so harmless.

He went to his window seat and looked out over the city and reviewed the facts in his mind.

Winter had been in Cali for two days.

Had stayed at the Hotel Royal Plaza on the corner of Plaza Caycedo.

Had gone into Ana's bank, a short walk from the hotel, on the Thursday and changed five thousand US dollars into pesos. Ana had discovered, quite by accident, the foreign currency slip that evening while she was checking balances on the foreign till. That she had failed to tell him that evening when she came to his apartment was not important – the following morning was soon enough.

A phone call confirmed that Winter had checked out of the hotel on the Thursday lunchtime.

Further checking had discovered the Avianca flight to Medellin with a connection to Santa Marta.

At Santa Marta a gringo with yellow hair had been witnessed travelling to the peninsula – Canaveral – where arriving and departing flights were reported by local gamins. The gringo had been travelling with a mulatto – a black man.

Lastly, the mock army raid on Canaveral had failed in its objective, but he had already dismissed that from his mind. The responsibility for that would fall on the real army. A story they would naturally deny. But who would believe them?

The questions came next.

Why was he here?

What did he do in Cali for two days?

More importantly, why would a man change five thousand dollars into Colombian pesos on the day he was leaving the city? The US dollar was an accepted form of currency, especially in the cities. Unless you were a careful man and knew that pesos could be stretched a little further. But for that you would be

planning to stay in the country for weeks, maybe
months – *living off the local economy*!

Even so, the matter would have to wait until Monday. There were more important issues to be dealt
with. The first of which was a telephone call to his
lawyer friend in Washington, DC.

Luis, like his father, was a man seeking the pulse of
the future.

PART FOUR
Eerie 1

26

*Realismo magico . . . verano . . . paquete chileno
. . . doce cuentos peregrinos . . . carajo*! Snatches of
Castellano echoing the uncertain three-dimensional
frames of ribboned gallery forest, thinning rivers,
islands of woodland; flickering in and out of the
blowing dust with the same frequency as the B-25's
shadow.

They were lost. Had been conducting a square search
pattern for an hour now. Seeking a place that had been
designed with a particular bias: *invisibility*.

Winter felt the cold unwanted knot of anxiety in the
pit of his stomach. The sun was low in the afternoon
sky, as if signalling their luck was running out. Luck,
as in: Charlie's take-off at Canaveral, coupled to a
soldier's instinct – living to fight another day. As
in: the two Wright Cyclone engines streaming black
oil down the cowlings at an alarming rate, but still
somehow not missing a beat since start-up. As in:
Charlie who was now dead to the world. An empty
vodka bottle lying on the floor at his feet. Something

that drunks did. Stowed bottles in the bottom of their bags. Emergency rations. Even so, Winter had concluded, with *his* eyesight, he was probably best left to sleep it off.

'Ninety minutes to sunset,' Maria offered, eyes intent on the savannah a thousand feet below. 'I think we should be looking at a place to land.'

'Down there?'

'Unless you feel like taking a stolen airplane into Bogotá and explaining to the police.'

He ignored the hint of sarcasm. 'How soft . . . the surface?'

'What you see down there, Mr Winter, is the accumulation of sand, clay and mud deposited by rivers over millions of years. What grass there is should not be too tall and if the rainy season finished early it should be solid enough.'

Winter looked down and checked the cloud shadows for a moment. 'Wind looks easterly.'

'I had noticed.' She banked the plane around towards the east and went through the prelanding requirements. Props 2100 r.p.m. Manifold pressure twenty-four inches. Mixture – full rich. Gear down . . . three greens confirmed. Flaps – ten degrees. The speed bled back and stabilised at 130 m.p.h. 'We'll do a low pass first and check for obstacles. Okay?'

Winter nodded and watched as she lined the aircraft up on the billiard-table flatness below. As a reference point for what might be an improvised runway she was using a longitudinal fix on the largest ribbon of gallery forest in the immediate area. The one that had been near their initial start point. It was about ten kilometres away. The aircraft sank steadily. Sun aft. Visibility good. Wind easing. Less lifting dust. At about twenty feet she eased the control column back and held the aircraft level, punching the stop watch on the yoke at the same time. Lateral fix.

Winter watched carefully for anything that could prove disastrous to an unscheduled landing. Rocks. Ditches. Debris of any kind.

Patchy grass . . . baked earth . . . flashing by. Distinct possibility.

At sixty seconds she increased the manifold pressure to thirty inches and gently hauled the nose up, easing the aircraft into a rate one climbing turn to the left. 'Next time we will bounce the wheels off the ground . . . see how firm.'

If Winter considered bouncing more than four tons of machinery at a forward speed of a hundred miles an hour off uncertain and possibly dangerous terrain foolhardy, he didn't show it. His eyes were focused on the distant gallery forest sliding through their two o'clock position. His peripheral vision had picked up something. Then he saw it again. Once . . . twice . . . 'Stop the turn, come back onto east. Hard.'

Maria reversed the turn rapidly, commencing a roll out on ninety degrees.

'Ten degrees more. Stop your climb at one thousand feet.'

'What is it?'

'Sunlight caught something in the trees. I saw a flash. Metal or glass maybe.'

'We searched that area before, there was nothing . . .'

'Hold that heading. There it is again . . . see it?' He pointed. 'Right of the nose five degrees. Top of the trees.'

'I have it.' Her right hand reached out unconsciously to select gear up and stopped. Old aeroplanes with a doubtful maintenance history deserved respect. Cycle essential systems as few times as possible. Failure a very real option.

It was on the edge of the ribbon. Camouflaged by trees. What appeared to be a hangar that merged with the colours of the woodland. Except for the glass skylight that reflected the afternoon sun.

The runway was harder to locate, being covered by dirt and debris — twigs and small branches from the nearby forest. Fortunately the dry-season winds had cleared channels at irregular intervals. Waving lines of white concrete. Impossible to detect unless you knew what you were looking for.

A few low inspection passes and they lined up for the landing. Cowl flaps open . . . power back to twenty-one inches . . . check gear still down and locked . . . flaps twenty degrees . . . speed decaying to 115 m.p.h. . . . full flaps . . . threshold 105 . . . flare . . . hold off . . . hold off . . . ninety m.p.h. . . . and touchdown. Irregular dried mud banks perhaps six inches high snatched at the aircraft as the main wheels ploughed through them. Brakes . . . little . . . by little . . . by little.

Both wingtips brushed the branches as they taxied up the sloping access track into a large, partially tree-canopied ramp area fronting a hangar that looked as though it could hold a few decent-sized airliners.

Final instrument check, dead-cut on the magnetos, mixtures to idle cutoff. The props clattered, kicked once on the compression cycle, sighed, and stopped. Batteries off.

And silence.

So absolute after three hours of bracketed mechanical onslaught that the imagination ran riot. Heartbeat wired for sound . . . blood waterfalling through veins . . . dust particles rattling aluminium like too-close machine-gun fire . . . the string-section high-C of spinning gyros.

'Welcome to Los Llanos, Mr Winter. Or at least one little corner of it.'

Winter surveyed the modern-style hangar. 'Looks like somebody spent a lot of money on this place.' He slid his side window open in search of cooling air. Instead the oven blast of a forty-degree-Celsius afternoon hit him.

'Not so much to the people who built it.'

'So what happened?'

'The drug wars of the eighties. The police moved in and confiscated drugs and weapons and airplanes. The cartel bosses disappeared from public life and went to Panama.'

'But not this place?'

'Perhaps they never found it. The plains of Los Llanos cover more than a quarter of a million square kilometres. A very big place . . . Then again, that hangar could be empty.'

'My source said otherwise,' Winter replied, rivulets of sweat streaming down his face, his neck, his chest. He reached for a handhold to ease himself out of the seat. And that was when he saw them. Three men. Standing at the corner of the hangar. One cradling an M-16 automatic rifle in his arms.

He reached across and touched Maria's arm. 'We've got company.'

She looked up. Face impassive. Strands of hair clinging damply to her forehead. '*Llaneros* maybe – local people. Perhaps they are paid to guard this place.'

'The empty hangar you mentioned!'

'They might be using a part of it as their home. In my country the poor . . . *los desechables*, would kill for such a luxury. You have heard of them?'

'"The Disposables" yes, and the death squads who carry out the social cleansing. Funny thing is, when Hitler tried it the world reacted. Colombia does it nearly sixty years later and the world turns a blind eye. Progress, Miss Espinosa, like you said earlier when we couldn't find this place – *paquete chileno* . . . a plan which looks great but turns out very badly.'

'I think that is not the context . . .'

'Artistic licence . . . You want me to go down?'

'You have a gun?'

'Yes.'

'And money?'

'Pesos and dollars.' Winter opened the nav-bag at the side of his seat and took out the Makarov 9mm, checked the safety was off, pushed it into his belt. 'How much?'

In reply she reached into the bag and took a bundle of 500-peso notes, flipped through them, and split the pile into two. She tugged her T-shirt out of her waistband and tucked one half in the front of her jeans, next to her glistening skin, lowering the shirt over it. The other half she handed to Winter. 'About one hundred thousand pesos – a thousand dollars. I'll try them with five hundred first. You hand over the other if and when I tell you. Let me do the talking.'

Winter moved quickly aft to wake Charlie.

He was yawning and rubbing his face. Baseball cap perched on the back of his head. 'This it?'

'This is it. Stay on board, we've got to go and talk to some people. You might want to take your H & K up front and cover us from the cockpit window.'

'Trouble?'

'Three of them. One M-16, could be more.'

'Shit! Army, guerrillas, what?'

'Guerrillas more than likely, but we do have an advantage.'

'We do?'

'Local guerrillas are hotshots when it comes to shooting their mouths off. They've never faced real soldiers, haven't a clue about how they should act if they did.'

'They can pull triggers. What else do they need to know?'

Winter ignored the remark. 'Also they don't know the strength of the opposition. How many on board or what armament we have.'

'Is that it?'

'No – I'm going to offer them a job. Cash in advance.'

Charlie watched from the open pilot's window. Winter's left hand lying casually on Maria's shoulder, the automatic in the other hand at his side. There was much waving and gesticulating and raised voices, especially by the swarthy local with the M-16 – the leader. Then he was smiling, prodding Maria in the stomach with the gun barrel. She stood her ground.

Winter pulled her closer, pushing the automatic into his belt at the same time. He said something to the man in charge, lifted the front of Maria's T-shirt and made a great show of sliding his hand down the front of her jeans. The three men roared with laughter. Then Winter offered the leader what looked like a handful of money. The man took it, held it to his nose for a long moment, grinned, and shook Winter by the hand. 'I'm impressed,' Charlie said, putting his shoulder to one of the six massive steel doors. 'What did you say?'

'Usual macho things that these guys like to hear. The leader, Ramon, thought he'd like to try her out. I said she was my wife – he said that was a shame but as it appeared she was built for speed and not comfort, perhaps it was better he should stick with the woman he had. It got a little coarse when he saw the place I kept my bankroll, but at least he and his friends were amused.'

'Not so Maria, huh? She looked major pissed off with you . . . Where'd she go?'

'Ramon's showing her our quarters.'

'Is that safe?'

'She's a big girl, Charlie. She can look after herself. Besides if he lays a hand on her I'll break his arms.'

'So who are they?'

'They used to work here years ago. When everybody cleared out, they stayed. No money, no prospects. Free home. They grow a few crops, live off the land.'

'Electricity?'

'Diesel generators. They quit operating some time

ago apparently; no one knows how to fix them. Plenty of water in the storage tanks, though.'

'And who are we supposed to be?'

'Guerrillas. I told him the army was looking for us, and how we'd just managed to get out of Canaveral. He'd already seen the bullet holes in the fuselage. I added that we are regrouping, need to work on the plane, and that the rest of our team will be here in a few days . . . strength in numbers, or the promise of.'

The hangar door ground noisily on the runners as both men pushed. Slowly opening onto a vast silent tomb. Smells of metals and oils and jet fuel flowing over them.

It was not that, however, which stopped them in their tracks, but the sight of four silver swept-wing fighters thick with dust. One of the aircraft was nothing more than a skeletal shell, a pile of parts lying by the side of it. Ventral fuel tanks in cradles. Tool shadow-boards. Jacks. Hydraulic mules. Tug with tow-arm attached. Hundreds of feet of cables and hose snaking across the hangar floor. Thin high-pressure main-wheel tyres in tall stacks. But more importantly, along one wall, as many as thirty 500-pound Mk 82 bombs anchored to steel pallets.

Charlie was the first to speak. 'Jesus, Wint . . . Lightnings. Where the hell did they come from?'

Winter said nothing but walked slowly into the hangar. Seeing but not believing. If anything he had been expecting vintage American hardware. But British!

'Not England, that's for sure,' he called back. 'And the only export order of any size went to the Saudi Air Force back in the sixties.'

Charlie walked over to one of them, reaching up, running a hand along the leading edge of the sixty-degree swept-back wing. 'And when the Saudis finished with them, some Arab Mr Fixit sold these off to an invisible shell company in Lechtenstein or Luxembourg or the British Virgin Islands, who then shuffled them sideways to another untraceable company, and another, and another, until the paper trail became so convoluted that nobody could make any sense of it even if they wanted to. In the meantime the hardware was spirited away to Colombia as "Agricultural Machinery".'

'Same sort of game we've played in the past.'

'Except we always played with subsonic equipment. These bitches exceed Mach two, and from what I remember hearing were severely HFD.'

'We don't have to fly them supersonic, Charlie.'

'We don't have to fly them, period,' Charlie answered. 'Highly Fucking Dangerous means exactly that. I flew F4s once upon a time. I was young and hot, but at least it was an airplane. This is a seat strapped to the top of a pair of fucking rockets – just to get around the pattern and back on the ground in one piece needs an inordinate amount of skill. And if that doesn't convince you, what about range? They've probably got an endurance of around sixty minutes in dry power. If you plan to work low level you can probably halve that.'

'Enough time to get to the target.'

Charlie took off his baseball cap and fanned his face. 'And then what? Eject? Those Martin-Baker bang-seats haven't been serviced in God knows how many years, and you're talking step outside. To where? To

what? And even if they work I've got enough problems without worrying about spinal compression. But
just let's back up a minute and figure I was still a
twenty-something-year-old kid with enough empty
space between my ears to figure it feasible to fly the
mission and come out at the other end unscathed.
What about those engines? When do you think they
were last turned. Somebody needed to inhibit those
engines if they planned to use them again. Without
that we need to pull them down and rebuild them.
Parts-wise, career-wise, and otherwise, we're a little
light in all areas.'

'Is that it?'

'No. I could probably keep you entertained with
horror stories all night. One more of which is starting these motherfuckers up. You know how that is
achieved? Sure you do – old-generation jets – but
let me remind you. You press the start button, which
is shortly followed by an unsettling explosion somewhere behind you. That explosion occurs because you
have just ignited an amount of isopropyl nitrate –
known by you Brits as Avpin – inside its chamber,
which in turn hopefully winds up and lights off the
number-one Avon engine. Bear in mind we have two
engines, so we need to repeat the process. Problems?
Isopropyl nitrate is a monocombustible fuel, which
means it can burn without oxygen. Which means it is
severely, and I mean severely, flammable. Controlled
explosions are one thing. As I said before, these ships
have been sitting a long time – too long. Second Law of
Thermodynamics, Wint, relates to a physical quantity
called entropy, which measures the degree of disorder
in a system. Put simply, it states that disorder will

tend to increase if things are left to themselves. The safety margins the manufacturers intended simply do not exist any more.'

'What about the B-25? Could we load it up with a few of those five-hundred-pounders over there?'

'Needs a double engine change before I'd risk going much further with it. The compression checks I ran back at Canaveral were very low – as in imminent failure. That we got here without having to shut one down was nothing more than luck.'

Winter smiled bleakly, turned, and started walking towards the hangar door. 'So what you're saying,' he called back, 'is that we have a no-go situation. That right?'

'Ninety per cent.'

'Only ninety? We'll have a drink on it later.'

'*Woesheil.*'

Winter laughed. '*Drincheil.*'

Ugly Charlie tugged the peak of his baseball cap low over his eyes and watched the Englishman walk out of the hangar into the gathering dusk. He hesitated, then turned back to the nearest Lightning. Another pause, and he climbed the red steps attached to the fuselage, blowing the dust carefully from the glass – you never rub dry dirt and dust: leaves scratches, tiny marks that in combat could appear to be an enemy aircraft closing on you – peering into the hard, merciless environment of a fighter cockpit. Everything was there, as it had been in past years. Different but the same. Flight instruments topped in this case by a linear readout of airspeed, radar, circuit-breaker panel, armament panel, throttles, pins in the ejection seat. And if he could power the canopy open, that smell peculiar to military airplanes the world over.

Hook you for ever, that smell.

He was in there now, drawing a start circle in the air with an index finger to the ground crewman below, hearing the *wheeee-whoosh* of the Avpin starter, watching for overtemping on the jet-pipe temperature gauge . . . ditto on number two . . . taxiing out, running cockpit checks . . . entering the runway, controls full and free, warning lights out, pins stowed – seat confirmed 'live', canopy down and locked. Now a localised thunderstorm at the end of the runway as both engines run up against the brakes . . . now release, and full dry power. Acceleration . . . JPTs . . . airspeed . . . and at 150 knots plus . . . airborne . . . gear up . . . airspeed building and building . . . and building . . . and . . . gone! Thin trails of smoke or wingtip vortices ribboning the place a fast jet had been . . . now twisting and dissipating in the wind.

He remained on the steps peering into the past until the daylight had gone, then reluctantly made his way from the hangar, which echoed his parting words:

'Welcome to Eerie One, Major Riker!'

27

They came through the Bocachica Strait between the two sunset-pink Spanish forts – San Jose and San Fernando – and on into the Bahia de Cartagena. The same route that the tourist boats took out to the archipelago of small coral islands thirty-five kilometres southwest of Cartagena – known as Islas del Rosario – except they would be back now, their passengers returned to their air-conditioned hotel rooms in Bocagrande, showering and changing in preparation for a night of dancing at La Escollera.

Snatches of music drifted over the water, along with a cooling breeze, as Williams, dressed in pale-blue cotton slacks and a short-sleeved white golf shirt, furled the headsail and dropped the main. The Fort of San Jose de Manzanillo slid by on the starboard side, as he finally padded aft to the cockpit to relieve Owens on the tiller.

'Spanish made this place pretty impregnable, didn't they?' he said casually.

Owens smiled. 'Funny, I was thinking more or less

the same thing. It was after our very own Francis
Drake sacked the port in the late fifteen hundreds
that the Spaniards decided to fortify the place. Did
a pretty good job of military engineering by the looks
of things.'

'You looking forward to a night's sleep in clean
sheets on a bed that doesn't move?'

Owens brushed at the caked salt on his white shorts
and sports shirt. 'And a long clean shower – very long.
Nice trip, though, boyo. I can see how it can become
so addictive.'

'What I used to feel as a young kid.'

'But not any more?'

'Once in a while it's nice to be out there and remember. My wife was glad when I left the navy. Reckoned
we were all a bunch of college kids. Said I grew up
when I got a desk to sail.'

'And you?'

'We all have to face up to responsibilities sooner
or later, Edeyrn.' An observation. A regret. The voice
gave little away.

He cut the engine and steered the sloop expertly
alongside the customs jetty on Manga Island and tied
her up. The only sound in that passing moment, water
slapping tiredly on the hull, echoing under the jetty.
He had stowed the spinnaker, removed the battens,
and was covering the main, when a sullen-faced soldier in a scruffy uniform one or two sizes too large,
an ancient rifle slung across his shoulder, appeared
and told them they would need to report to the Port
Captain's office and Customs.

It was fully dark before they had completed the
formalities. They returned to the boat, collected their

bags, and made their way along the lit jetty. The sound
of water being replaced by music and car horns on the
night air.

He was waiting in the shadows by the side of the four-
wheel-drive Grand Cherokee Limited Edition. Overall
white. Plain. He moved back and opened the tailgate,
and the two men threw their bags in. No words were
exchanged until they were driving slowly across the
causeway from Manga Island. Williams half turned in
the passenger seat. 'This is Drummer, Edeyrn. DEA.'
Turning to the man at the wheel, he said, 'Friend of
mine, Edeyrn Owens. Welshman to an Englishman,
Brit to we poor colonials.'

The two men laughed and exchanged greetings.

'Bad news,' Drummer said, his normal Spanish
accent replaced by one that was distinctly lower east-
side New York. 'The strip got shot up this morning.'

Williams froze. Winter was the linchpin that held
his plans together. And the last he had heard he was
back at Canaveral. 'Jesus! Who did it?'

'Army.'

'You're sure?'

'Sure as I can be. I was in Santa Marta overnight
with the German guy Werner Stock, persuading him
to hold off on the plane sale until a new buyer I had
arrived in town. He got the word at dawn to keep clear
of Canaveral. That's when I radioed you on the boat to
check your ETA, and made tracks down here.'

'And Stock said it was the army?'

'Some people read palms, some people read the
bumps on your head; I read eyes. Information carries
a good price in this place, Mr Williams. No point

throwing money at the wall when you can get it for nothing.'

'Any reason the army would hit that place?'

'Hard to say, but I'm in contact with one of my suppliers here in Cartagena. He may come up with something.'

'Any update from Stock since?'

'I phoned him a couple hours back, when I arrived. Only news he had for certain was that the strip was demolished and all aircraft and vehicles there. Except it seems for his airplane. That got away with some of the druggies on board. Two Americans, male, didn't make it.'

'How many were at the strip?'

'Five. Winter and Riker and the woman who brought them in, Espinosa. First time in for her – working for Johnny Shoosh out of the Everglades. The two other druggies were Americans, names of Bell and Daniels. They've been around for years.'

'Any positive ID on the bodies?'

'No. They've been removed by the police to Santa Marta.'

'So it could have been Winter who got out with the airplane?'

'Possible. And his buddy. And the woman.'

'To where? Any ideas?'

Drummer shrugged his shoulders. 'Who knows? As I told you over the radio. When Winter got back from Cali, he picked up about half a ton of provisions in Santa Marta. Food mainly. I got the idea he was going to ground down south.'

'What type of airplane was it?'

'B-25. World War Two bomber. Been rigged with

an internal fuel system. I put two thousand gallons on board, hand-pumped every damned gallon. Figure that would give it some range.'

Williams turned back to Owens. 'Any ideas, Edeyrn?'

'Only that he's a past master at throwing people off his trail. Logically it may appear he's going into hiding but for one thing: why did he go to Cali? Why go all that way down south and back, when he had everything he needed locally?'

'Perhaps the Cali trip was thrown in for that very reason. To muddy the waters.'

'And then again there's Major Riker. What would he want with his old First Lieutenant? An aviation and weapons expert. Better yet, why would Riker, who was living a quiet law-abiding life in Key West, suddenly team up with a man on the run? Something doesn't quite make sense.'

'Might be nothing,' Drummer remarked, 'but when Winter was away, Charlie Riker and I had a few drinks together. We were talking about arthritis – seems he suffers from it like me. I told him the best advice I'd got was from a nurse in Miami, who told me to take one aspirin a day – helps reduce inflammation in the joints. Either that or move to a tent in the middle of the Sahara. He got pretty drunk, asked me if I'd ever been to Los Llanos. I told him you'd have to be out of your mind to go to that place. Guerrilla country. He just laughed, said he'd doubtless seen worse. Asked if it was a desert. I told him only in the dry season.'

'What else did he say?'

'Talked about Nam mainly, the planes he'd flown – how the entire war had been a crock of shit, usual vet gripes.'

'Anything else?'

'Said the B-25 was an accident waiting to happen.'

'Anything specific?'

'Both engines severely fucked, as he put it.'

'What about Los Llanos? What's out there?' Williams asked.

'The strongest guerrilla groups. The FARC and the ELN teamed up in recent years with a dissident faction of the EPL. Formed a guerrilla coalition known as the Coordinadora Guerrillera Simon Bolivar. The government continued to negotiate with the Coordinadora Guerrillera in the aftermath of the Constitutional Assembly, but didn't reach agreement. Negotiations suspended indefinitely. The main change seems to be that the guerrillas have now lost most of their popular support, as well as international support from Moscow and Havana. They now rely on extortion and robbery to finance their struggle. They're also more involved with the cartels and the drug business.'

Williams took the gold Dunhill cigarette lighter from his pocket, flicked up the top with his thumb and lit it. He watched the flame for a moment then snapped the top down. 'So the army raid could have been nothing more sinister than relatives of the government ministers' families killed recently, deciding retribution was long overdue.'

Drummer said, 'Or someone trying to rekindle the drug wars with the government. Up until now we've had an uneasy truce between the Colombian government and the drug traffickers; that truce has hinged on a government pledge not to order the army into the guerrillas' territories. Now that the army has apparently broken that pledge it could give the cartels a reason to try and overthrow the government. Beautiful stuff to the guerrillas, but then they've already been there.'

Williams thought about that for a moment, then said, 'Where we going?'

'I booked you both at the Hotel Caribe in Bocagrande – what they call luxurious neo-colonial. Thought after a few days at sea you guys would both appreciate some serious comfort for a night. The Cherokee's yours while you're in-country. When you've finished with it, just drop it off in the parking lot on Manga Island. Lock it and keep the keys. We have spare sets. One of our guys will collect it.'

'What about you?'

'I'm staying at a little place called the Hostal Baluarte.' He pointed up a dimly lit narrow street with old colonial, balconied houses. 'This is the edge of the Old Town. I'm just up there, at the end of Calle de la Media Luna. I'll call you later when I've met up with my guy. Anything important, we'll arrange a meet. You can decide then what you want to do. Other than that I'll check in with you in the morning. Final item. There's an extensive first-aid kit in the back. Check list here.' He reached up and touched the stowed sun visor. 'Antimalarial tablets, and chlorine tablets for suspect water. Something new that seems to be taking a hold in the poorer areas is bad meat not properly cooked. Causes a killer disease. Goes by the name of neurosysterosis or something like that. Seems the larva in the food migrates into the bloodstream and then travels and lodges in the brain. The tapeworms eat the brain. Symptoms: headaches and numbness and paralysis on the right side. Not trying to put a damper on your vacation, but you might want to be careful.'

'Any meats in particular?' Williams asked.

'No. But they figure pork has the highest risk.'

'Good enough reason for going vegetarian, I guess.'

Drummer grinned, showing very white teeth. 'Or Moslem.'

He braked to a stop in the shadows of the Old Town wall. A few metres away to the left, lights twinkled on the waters of the Muelle de los Pegasos. 'All yours,' he said patting the steering wheel. 'Continue down here, make a left at the next rotary and keep driving. You'll be on the Avenida San Martin. When you get to the end, make a right. The Hotel Caribe is about fifty metres on the left. Can't miss it. Reception's holding two rooms in your name.' With that he opened the door and disappeared into the night.

It was three hours later. Owens was sitting opposite Williams, in his room at the Hotel Caribe. The room was elegantly furnished in blues and pale greys, gilt-framed paintings of the majestic galleons of the Spanish Silver Fleet of 1622 adorning the walls. The only light came from an ivory-coloured silk-shaded lamp on the low coffee table. They had just returned from dinner.

'Feeling the effects of the sea, Edeyrn? It can be very wearing in a small boat, even for those who do it for a living.'

Owens smiled. 'No problems with sleeping tonight, that's for sure. So, what's the plan of action for tomorrow?'

'Depends on what Drummer comes up with. If Winter was one of those taken out at the strip, then it's back to square one.'

'And if not?'

Williams got out of his chair and went over to the window, pulling the curtain back slightly, peering out into the night. In the distance, he could see pinpricks of white lights. Shrimp boats perhaps. He wondered what it would be like to be a fisherman. Not the captain of a trawler but one of the hands. No checking account, no credit cards, no mortgage, no car instalments, just a cash payment at the end of each trip and a series of bars and women and fun. That had been the problem with his life: he had always been an overachiever. He had been conditioned from an early age as a player in the great American game. Everyone was proud of him of course, his mother and his father especially. But his brothers and sisters had become distant, not intentionally: it was one of those big dark voids people sometimes build into their lives. And when they had built them it was too late to add the bridge. The gap was too wide. He turned back to the Welshman. 'I think he could be a hard man to find.'

Owens waved languidly at the nearest wall-hung painting. 'The Spaniards built some good vessels, didn't they? That one for instance was a five-hundred-ton guard galleon. It was a hundred and ten feet in overall length, thirty-three feet wide, and drew fourteen feet of water. It carried square sails on the fore and mainmasts, a lateen mizzen, and set a spritsail on the big seventy-five-foot bowsprit. Other than that it had the ultimate weapons system of the day: twenty-four bronze cannons, most of them sited on the gun deck, which was one level down from the weather deck. That ship was one of four, built for King Philip IV by Alonso Ferrera in his Havana shipyard. Four new ships. Two of which, the *Santa Ana* and the *Nuestra Señora de Atocha* laden with silver and gold, foundered in these waters over three hundred years ago, 1622 to be exact.'

'I take it there's a point to this lesson in medieval Spanish?'

'Always that, boyo. You see, the aircraft which Winter and Riker in all probability escaped in was a B-25. World War Two twin-engined bomber. Unique, wouldn't you say? I mean, how many of those aircraft are flying today?'

'The world's a big place.'

'Not for hiding a vintage aeroplane like that.'

'Assuming they haven't already dumped it.'

'True. And if they don't they'll doubtless need spares to keep it flying. Where would you get those?'

'Stateside. Probably a few hundred different maintenance shops. Too many to monitor.'

Owens looked at his watch. 'I'll sleep on it, Tanner. I always find problems tend to resolve themselves after a good night's rest. What time for breakfast?'

'Seven thirty.'

Owens went to the door, opened it, and paused. 'One might consider a man who leaves a trail of mistakes an amateur, Tanner. What would you call a professional who did that?'

'You still think of him as a master tactician?'

'I think he might be a frightening chess player.'

Williams brought the Grand Cherokee up Calle de la

Media Luna, looking for the San Roque church and Drummer's Ram Charger. The call had come fifteen minutes earlier at 1 a.m., just when he was thinking of turning in. Drummer had simply stated time and place and signal. 'Immediate – Iglesia de San Roque, opposite the Hostal Baluarte, the place I'm staying. The street I pointed out on the drive from Manga Island, Calle de la Media Luna. Park behind the blue and white Dodge Ram Charger. Flash your headlights twice.'

He saw the taillights of the Ram Charger first. There was somebody at the wheel. His eyes shifted slightly right and made out the dark outline of the church. In the daylight he would have noticed that the bell tower of the sixteenth-century building was distinctly crooked, something that had found its way into local legend, telling how the devil had knocked the tower from true. Local colour. Tourist stuff.

He switched off his lights and pulled over to the side of the road. Stopped twenty metres behind the Ram Charger. Flashed his headlights twice. And waited. After thirty seconds he flashed again. All the time watching the street, checking his rear-view mirror. The street was a mixture of activity and none, and his eyes swept around nervously. It was a habit he had allowed himself to forget. Focusing on people whose inactivity seemed to display a purpose. What purpose? But that was an exercise that took time. Something he didn't have. You do not sit alone in a stationary vehicle on the poor side of a city. Especially a Colombian city. In these places they killed strangers who wandered into their ghettos as a security measure, just in case they had some connection with police or army; or hacked off your arm for financial gain – an elegant wristwatch; or ripped off your face for the sport – and those were just the nice things.

He made up his mind in that moment. Took a deep breath and quickly left his vehicle and strode purposefully along the littered sidewalk to the Ram Charger. Drummer was sitting at the wheel. He pulled the passenger door open and slid into the seat, pulling the door closed quickly to cancel the interior light. 'Didn't you see the headlights, I've been—' He stopped as he saw the dark-stained shirt in the light of the dash. The slashed-open throat. The unmistakable sickly sweet stench of blood. 'Oh shit!' One of those chiastic moments. Uncertainty. A feeling he should run back to his vehicle and get out of this fucking place.

That was when training took over. A running figure is more quickly observed in someone's peripheral vision than one moving normally. He slowly checked shirt and trouser pockets. Nothing. Not even a wallet. Seats and floor the same. The glove compartment was empty. He touched the door handle and stopped. And reached up to the driver's sun visor. Instinct, nothing more. A folded envelope fell out. He checked the contents. One sheet of paper, a letter written in a scrawled Spanish hand. He returned the paper to the envelope, folded it in two, and slipped it into his shirt pocket. Headlights swept into the street and a car sped by. Two men had walked out of the Hostal Baluarte opposite and were talking in the lit doorway. Salsa music pulsed from an open bedroom window nearby. The men opposite were joined by a woman, thin, long dark hair, dressed in a skimpy dress. They were looking his way now. A prostitute with her pimp perhaps. On the lookout for trade. Something more?

When in doubt!

He left the Dodge, and with hands thrust into his trouser pockets, and head down, walked very slowly back up the street. Away from the body of Drummer. And the church with the leaning bell tower.

28

Maria Espinosa awoke sometime during the night, tangled in damp sheets, soaked in sweat from the oppressive heat that filled the small room. Her eyes sought out the moonlit single window, panes dirty and cracked, the angled shadows falling across the dusty concrete floor. Winter was sitting in those shadows. She could make out the shape of the soft-backed chair, the profile of his face, his long outstretched legs. The gun in his hand resting on his thigh. She watched him through the patched-up mosquito net for a moment, sensing he too was awake.

Not so Charlie: he would be sleeping like a baby after drinking himself into oblivion. He had been talking to her during the meal they had shared with the local men and their women that night. His words slurred and mostly incoherent – she knew he had been drinking from the moment they arrived, had seen him when he came from the hangar after dark, hands and voice shaking, searching frantically through the boxes in his room, muttering to himself, wandering

off into the trees with a bottle of vodka, coming back
empty-handed – she had only been half listening to
him, picking at her food as her eyes swept the littered
area of the barbed-wire compound on the east side of
the hangar. The tin-roofed buildings which were the
houses of the locals. What had been offices on the side
of the hangar, now converted to makeshift bedrooms
for the new arrivals. Rusted iron bedsteads. Lumpy
sweat-stained mattresses. No pillows. Clean sheets –
a small concession. The squeaking of bats in the top
of a blossoming red flame tree near the smoky camp
fire. The chattering of emaciated, frightened monkeys,
thirsting for water, imprisoned in crudely made small
wooden cages which hung from the lower limbs of the
flame tree.

Charlie's voice had droned on: 'At least they cook
the fucking monkeys here. In Nam I've seen locals
saw off the top of the skull and eat the brains of
the poor little bastards while they were still alive
. . . Something else they went for in a big way was
goats' penises. Said it was an aphrodisiac . . . Know
what they used to say about the Vietnamese? Used
to say, along with the Russians, they were the dogs
of the human race – never liked the little bastards
. . .' Her eyes had moved on. The pockmarked face
and glassy-eyed stare of Ramon, who had had some
of Charlie's vodka, openly fondling the breasts of the
overweight Indian woman who was apparently his
partner. The others eating in silence.

And sitting slightly back, some distance away, on
the edge of the campfire's light, Winter. Very, very
still. She had noticed that before. The way he had of
not moving. Not blinking an eye. And when he did

move, how he appeared to do so without a sound. As though he had lived in the shadows for so long that he had found a way to emulate them. A man who was a mixture of the gentle and the rough. The outward toughness at odds with his incongruous good manners. She wondered how dangerous it was to know such a man.

Charlie had leaned close, his voice no more than a whisper. 'Know what he said about you . . . Wint? When you went off with Ramon . . . asked him if you'd be safe . . . know what he said?' She looked at him and shook her head. 'Said . . . said, "If he lays a hand on her I'll break his arms." Exact words . . . Guess he likes you, huh!'

'You think so?'

Charlie hiccupped. 'Sure.'

There might never be a better time, she had told herself. 'Why is he doing this, Charlie?'

'Doing what?'

'You know what I mean. Why? What is the reason?'

There was a hunted look in his eyes. Drunk, but not that drunk. 'Hell . . . I don't know . . . it's what he does.' He held up the near-empty vodka bottle. 'Want some of this?'

She shook her head. 'You know, but are afraid to tell me. Is that not so?'

Charlie pulled the peak of his baseball cap low over his eyes, as if afraid to meet her gaze. 'He likes you — why not leave it at that.'

And she had. For the time being.

Her eyes watched him now in the darkness. The man

who liked her. Or was that Charlie's imagination?
Drink distorting reality.

Reality:

She knew about drink and drinkers. Her father had
been one. Had walked out on them. Didn't even pack
a bag – went out of the door one evening and never
came back. Left her invalid mother and six children
without a penny, and a pile of bills. As she was the
eldest it became her job to support them. Her father! A
flyer back from Viet Nam. Had come home a different
man. Hardly ever spoke. Drank a lot. Sat in dark rooms
reliving past battles. Dragged his family down for ten
years before he left.

She worked two jobs, and by her early twenties
had enough put by to take her private pilot's ticket.
She wanted to go to the airlines. Always had, ever
since she had been a small girl, when the pictures of
planes had somehow filled the house. She struggled
on and managed to log a few hundred hours' flight
time. After that she got her commercial ticket. And
thought that she may find a flying job. Flying jets. But
no one was interested in a low-time pilot. Especially
a woman. Especially one of South American descent
with a Spanish accent.

Of course there had been promises. Lots of promises.
She had dated a lot of them before she realised that
she was being used like a whore. The last time that
had happened had been with a smooth-talking New
Yorker who had promised her a free check ride in a
Boeing 707, and when that was done, how she could
accompany him to Brazil to fix up and ferry a number
of the old freighters back to Miami. Once they were
there they would be put into service hauling cargo

between the US and West Africa. She would have a permanent job. Flying jets. She had gone to his bed when asked. Accepting it as part of the contract. The next morning as he was packing his suitcase, he told her it was off. That perhaps she wasn't ready to step up to big airplanes, just yet. He would contact her again when he got back into town. She went into the bathroom and wrote a letter on the hotel letter-headed paper, and when he wasn't looking slipped it into his suitcase.

She smiled at the memory. She would have given anything to have been at that remote Brazilian airstrip when he had found the letter. The brief note that had ended, 'It is a shame there is no doctor at the jungle airstrip you told me about. You are going to need one. I'm a whore . . . remember? Pleasant dreams, you bastard.' There would have been fear in his eyes then. It would have been weeks before he discovered he really had nothing to worry about.

It was months later that she met up with Johnny Shoosh in the Everglades. He had flown with her father in Nam, and like her father had been unable to find a decent flying job when he got home. So he had turned to the clandestine operations he had been trained to carry out by the military. He had given her a job. Even so she had never really trusted him. He, like her father, was a drinker.

And another reality:

Ramon's lecherous eyes moving over her body, tongue moving suggestively across his thick lips, raking the end of the rifle barrel violently across her breasts and down her body, stabbing it at her belly, suggesting to Winter that he should at least be offered the opportunity to share in such a pretty woman. Winter's hand moving down to her waist, a gentle reassuring squeeze, then pulling her tightly to him, and hearing him say, 'Maria is my wife, Ramon. You understand?' The voice cold. Unmistakably threatening. And Ramon smiling, and apologising for his mistake.

The last reality:

Marriage had meant protection. Not sharing her bed. Forcing himself upon her as others had done in the past. She had thought to argue the point when they had returned to the room, to tell him she needed no man to watch over her, that she was more than able to take care of herself, but by that time she was too tired to care. He had turned his back as she undressed in silence and slipped, naked, between the clean white sheets, then he had sat in the chair, facing the window.

In the same way he was now.

He was, she decided, the most lonely man she had ever known.

PART FIVE
Contrails

29

Ugly Charlie sat on the edge of his bed, pulling on his trousers. Too much fucking drink last night, he told himself. Gotta watch out for yourself, Charlie boy. Better not touch the holy water today. You can do it. Sure you can. Hell, if you wanted, you could go on the wagon for ever. He tried to stand up but couldn't. His hands were shaking. Jesus, his whole body was shaking. He belched and tasted the sour bile that erupted into his throat. Shit! He didn't like the way he felt this morning. It scared him. Reaching down to put on his sneakers caused more problems, like his head feeling it was expanding, like a balloon being blown up, like any second it would explode. He swore and persevered.

Finally he sat upright for a few minutes. Letting the aches and pains subside to somewhere near bearable. Pulled a shirt over his horrifically scarred upper torso. Slipped on his baseball cap. And tried again. And succeeded. A little unsteady, but he was upright. He made his way to the door in search of water and a few

Advil. Anything to take away the throbbing headache. To wash away the rancorous taste in his mouth.

A dawn breeze was whipping at the dust, lifting it, turning the morning sulphur-yellow. Charlie choked as it found its way into his nostrils, his throat. And the heat as always in these places. Wet heat. Dry heat. It didn't matter which one. It was always there. He looked around the barbed-wire compound, careful not to move his head too quickly. Deserted. The grey ashes of last night's camp fire corrugating in the breeze. Beyond that, through a gap in the trees, the flat savannah blanketed by the all-pervading dust. As Wint had told him. An eerie place. Spooky.

There was a sudden movement in the shadows of the flame tree. He turned and saw Winter opening the wooden cages. Gently lifting out the wild monkeys as though they were children. Giving them fruit. Patting them on the head. Then they were off, scampering away into the trees.

'Didn't anybody tell you it's dangerous to handle wild animals? Those little bastards can give you a nasty bite.'

Winter smiled and took a pack of Particulares from his pocket and lit one. 'Morning, Charlie. How'd you sleep?'

'Fine. Where is everybody? Thought there might be some coffee bubbling in the pot by this time. Doughnuts I figured a long shot, but at least coffee.'

'Gone.'

'Gone? Gone where?'

Winter walked over towards him. His face becoming serious. 'Did a moonlight on us. Packed their kit and headed out just before dawn, about an hour ago. Took more than half our supplies with them.'

Charlie's mouth dropped open. 'How? I mean how could they carry all that?'

'I found some tyre tracks about four hundred yards along the edge of the forest. Seems they had a truck stashed away all the time.'

'You heard them go?'

'Yes. Too late though. By the time I got up there all I saw was a pair of taillights disappearing in the distance.'

'Bastards.'

'Scared, Charlie. You can't blame them. We arrive out of nowhere, telling them others are coming. What would you do if an armed occupying force was moving in?'

'What about our supplies and the money you paid them?'

'They probably thought it was a fair exchange. Their home in trade for a few months' meals. Probably come back when we leave. It's not that that's the problem, though. Once they arrive at their next camp or village the word will doubtless spread that there are guerrillas here. Which means we can expect a visit from the army or a real guerrilla faction. A few coffee-coloured faces we don't really need at this moment in time.' Winter dropped his half-smoked cigarette in the dirt and ground it out with the toe of his boot. 'On the subject of coffee, I found a portable gas cooker in one of the workshops. Couple of bottles of gas as well. I've moved what cargo is left in there.'

'Bottled water?'

'Plenty of that.'

'Advil or Tylenol?'

'In the first-aid kit on the plane. Check behind the pilot's seat. Bit of a hangover, eh?'

'I'm not drinking today, Wint, promise. If you see me with a bottle, take it from me, okay?'

'I'll do that. By the way, there's a block house back there in the trees. Three diesel generators. A few barrels of unopened diesel oil. I've got a feeling Ramon and his boys were not technically adept enough to get them going.'

'Maybe. I'll need to pull them down, though. Pretty gummed up by now. I'll drain some gas from the plane to wash everything off. Need a battery to start it.'

'How about the B-25's batteries?'

'Twenty-four volt. You need a twelve-volt battery to start them, like on a car. Still, I could bypass half the cells and reduce it to twelve. Good job my second profession in life was shade-tree mechanic, huh!'

'Go and bring the first aid kit down to the workshop. I'll get the coffee started.'

'Not going to be as easy with those heavier-than-air machines in the hangar, you know.'

'With your engineering skills, piece of cake,' Winter reassured him.

'Know something that I don't, huh?'

'I'll show you when you get back to the workshop.'

30

Blue signs bearing the name Barranquilla pointed left and straight on. Williams swung the Grand Cherokee left at the last moment. The coast road. He had checked road maps on a sleepless night, not least the notes on the front page: 'The Colombian Caribbean coast extends over 1,600 kilometres from the dense jungles of the Darien in the west, on the Panamanian border, to the desert of La Guajira in the east, near Venezuela. El Caribe, or La Costa, as the Caribbean region is locally known, stretches to the south up to the foot of the Andes. Administratively, the area falls into seven departments . . .'

The sharp left turn awoke Owens, who had been dozing for the past half-hour or so, since leaving Cartagena. 'Everything okay?'

'Sorry, Edeyrn. Last-minute change of mind. Decided the coast road would be quieter.'

'Want me to drive for a while?'

'No, I'm fine now the sun's up. Maybe we'll stop in Barranquilla and get breakfast. Pot of coffee at least.

225

Would have let you sleep longer back at the hotel but under the circumstances . . .'

'Should have woken me earlier.'

'No point. I had to phone some of our guys in Bogotá, let them know about Drummer. They're in contact with DEA people on the coast. They'll pick up the body, sort out matters with the police.'

'You're still convinced it wasn't just a robbery. Bad part of town after all.'

'Thieves don't usually leave cars. Or if they do, they rip out radios and CD players. No, I think it was meant to *look* like a robbery, nothing more.'

'He didn't tell you who he had seen last night, did he?' Owens asked.

'No.'

'Funny thing, that letter, wasn't it? What was it again? "Talk to Werner Stock in Santa Marta about Klaus Barbie and Emilio Figueras. Ask him why the army would commit an act of war against one of the cartels? Especially as the government had given the assurance that the army would stay clear of the peninsula. If the gringo Winter is still in the country Stock will know where he is – Winter, after all, owes him money for his airplane. His price for information is high." Last two points seem logical enough, but Barbie! He was extradited to France years ago.'

'Involved with the drug business in Bolivia, though.'

'I'm trying to put a time-frame to all this. What do we know about this Werner Stock?'

'Very little, other than he's German. And a dealer.'

'Old sparring partner of Klaus Barbie perhaps?'

'A lot of Germans came to South America after the

war with aspirations of rebuilding the Fatherland. Likely Werner was one of them, especially as it seems he had dealings with Barbie.'

Owens said, 'Something I was meaning to ask. How did Drummer get his name? I assume it wasn't his real name.'

'Demosthenes Bolivar. Panamanian by birth. Naturalised US citizen. Used to play drums with jazz bands in his youth. Not *any* jazz bands though, he played with some of the best: Brubeck, Gerry Mulligan, even did session work with Louis Armstrong so I was told. Then he got into drugs. Bad enough to finish his career before it really started.'

'So how did he get mixed up in this business?'

'After the music career took a nosedive, he started dealing the stuff, trying to maintain the lifestyle to which he had become accustomed. Anyway, the DEA picked him up and came to a little arrangement with him. So he became an informer. At some point in time they took him on the strength full-time. Some guys never get the breaks, do they?'

'Never would have made field marshal under Napoleon, would he? *He* always asked the question, "Is he lucky?" before he promoted a general. I suppose our masters consider the adjective "expendable" better suited when faced with such choices.'

They drove on in silence for a while, the sun shimmering on the blue ocean to the left, the green trees silvered with dust, to the right. A brightly painted chiva bus, full to capacity, horn blasting, passed them going the opposite way at speed. Dust settling. The road empty once more. The promise of a carnival atmosphere and rum-based cocktails and tropical music around the next bend. Except a carnival atmosphere was the last thing Williams needed. A good night's sleep was more to the point. A clear head with which to think. The flowers he'd forgotten to send to Sophie; where the hell did that thought come from? Perhaps she wouldn't be there when he got back. Gone to stay with her mother in San Diego. And if she hadn't? Then the sparks would fly. Or the words. Or the crockery. Or the—

He banged the steering wheel with the flat of his hand. 'Shit!'

'What is it?'

'Drummer wasn't killed inside his truck. What happens if you slash open someone's carotid artery and jugular? Blood flies everywhere, right? How much blood in the male body? Five to seven litres? Enough to paint a medium-size apartment! The only blood on Drummer was on his neck and arms and clothing. The inside of the vehicle was clean. Spotlessly clean. Somebody killed him and then put him in the vehicle.'

'You're sure about the blood? It was dark after all.'

'I sat in the passenger seat. I would have had blood on my clothes. I'm sure. The parking lights were on. The instrument lights. How the hell did I miss such a basic thing as that?'

'Exhaustion for one. Long hard working days on a boat with little sleep. Shock. Easy enough to overlook the obvious under those circumstances . . . Even so, why would someone kill him and then put him in the truck?'

'If they were just planning on robbing him they wouldn't. Leave the body wherever and run.'

'Cover blown?'

'More than likely. Probably got to him as he was crossing the street to his vehicle. Killed him in the street. Then put him in the truck.'

'And switched on the sidelights to make it look more natural. Somebody waiting for somebody.'

'Yes.'

'And the letter under the sun visor?'

'What do you think?'

'Dead-letter box!'

'Exactly. Drummer was going to pick it up following a phone call from his contact.'

'But phoned you first and asked you to meet him. Why not after he had checked the contents? Could have waited until the morning, couldn't it? Nothing in that letter was going to hurt for a few more hours – unless something tipped his hand. Panicked him.'

'Something we may never know. Tell you one thing, Edeyrn, I wouldn't be an undercover DEA agent even if they paid serious money, which they don't. Working over the other side. No backup.'

'Unarguable truth,' Owens offered. Remembering the small mining town in South Wales from which he had escaped a millennium ago. A scholarship boy. Jesus College, Oxford. First in Greats. And his father, the miner, who had worked all his life over the other side. No backup. Killed in a pit explosion. There had been no serious money there, either.

The Grand Cherokee flew on down the coast road. Weaving from time to time to avoid potholes. Trailing dust through the hot morning.

31

All things considered, the skies over CALIMA's empire were looking very bright. At least in Luis Figueras's eyes. The United States government had once more come under fire for allowing the CIA to exceed its authority in giving aid and support to what the press (with the help of leaked documents) had deemed reactionary foreign regimes planning to overthrow the government. Bowing to international pressure, Congress had cut off support and passed an Amendment banning covert CIA action in Colombia

Not an unnatural scenario, as Colombia's Gross National Product figures had plummeted in recent years as successive governments had been kept busy resolving emergencies rather than constitutional issues. Fighting to curb drug trafficking in an attempt to pacify the US and other Western Aid agencies. Except they had failed. The nightmare continued. Now, more than ever, politicians had been bought off. Refusal was not an option. Unless you wished to sign your family's death warrant. Drugs and money laundering were on the increase. Something that might have have helped the country in its current financial dilemma, except that black money did not generally find its way into the economy. It was moved offshore to peekaboo financial centres.

One of which now figured in Luis Figueras's plans, where as much as two billion dollars – his father's share – of the cartel's wealth would be laundered into legitimate foreign businesses in a number of tranches.

Difficult if you worked alone. Simpler if you had the ears of governments. And he had.

One of the easier transactions he was working on that Sunday was a ten-million-dollar donation from CALIMA to the Colombian government. The army needed paying. With less money they would become disgruntled. They would slack off. The people would once again become restless – which was something he could not afford to happen. Of course the donation had conditions. Like the government 'selling' to a Panamanian company with a post office box address in Nassau, Bahamas (wholly owned by nominees who shielded the beneficial owner – Luis Figueras), 500,000 acres of land at five dollars an acre; the funds for this transaction being placed in a thirty-day escrow account at a nominated Cali bank. The Panamanian company would then, through its Luxembourg parent company (once again fronted by stooges), make some industrial rezoning amendments to the paperwork, and sell it off to CALIMA at 500 dollars an acre.

And 250 million US dollars would be transferred to a Polish Bank in the centre of Luxembourg. This quarter-of-a-billion-dollar tranche would come from the legitimate trading accounts of CALIMA, with a certificate of origin issued by the Banco Industrial Colombiano, thus reassuring the Federal Reserve who policed the movements of large amounts of money as to its authenticity. The task of repaying the loan from the offshore peekaboo financial institutions in Panama back to the BIC in Cali was not so difficult. Especially with 'paid' assistance from within the banking organisations. Further creative accounting would remove any signs of the large transactions, at least in the CALIMA books, thus negating any questions which might arise from a sudden internal audit. As for the withdrawal from the Panamanian account, which held only a percentage of the cartel's black money, this would be topped up by similar funds from sister companies. This method of 'kiting' money around in circles – robbing Peter to pay Paul – would show up as intercompany loans. On paper at least. By the time somebody checked the paperwork, it would be too late.

As for the 'worthless' land, that would be returned to the government along with the escrowed two and a half million dollars, plus a further seven and a half million, making up the promised donation of ten million.

The clock was now running. He needed to implement phase two of the operation as quickly as possible, before he turned the cartel over to the government in exchange for an amnesty. The quarter-of-a-billion-dollar transaction (with a ten-million-dollar kickback) had been the carrot. He had offered it. It had been taken. The window of opportunity was open wide.

Two hours later, satisfied with his morning's work, he showered and changed. Black lightweight alpaca suit. White shirt. Pale-blue silk tie. Italian leather shoes. Lastly, he gathered up his mother's rosary from the dressing table.

He was going to the Iglesia de la Ermita, where he would light a candle to the memory of his mother and offer his humble prayers to God.

32

The appointment had been made for noon. J.J. Eberhart was ten minutes early. It was his way, even though he had had to slip out of Sunday Mass without taking confession. Now he was browsing amid Oscar Porteous's fine collection of antiques, tilting his head from time to time as he viewed a particular piece. He stopped eventually and considered a titillating painting of a semi-draped young girl.

'Now that brings back memories of my youth. Who's the artist?'

Porteous started at the voice. A distinctive rasping sound, a muffled sandpaper shout which never varied in pitch. The result, so the story went, of severe damage to his larynx in a bar-room brawl in Shanghai forty years earlier. He averted his eyes. The voice had that effect on most people. Taking them off guard. Causing embarrassment.

'Greuze,' Porteous replied. 'Jean Baptiste Greuze. Eighteenth-century French painter. He made his name in the Salon of 1755 with *A Grandfather reading the Bible to his Family,* a piece of Dutch-inspired narrative genre painting, extolling the simple virtues of the poor.'

'Another of those guys who died penniless in some cheap rooming house, huh!'

Porteous coughed into his handkerchief, and managed a painful smile. 'More or less. They say he died in the Louvre looking at one of his works, reliving his past greatness. He was a man of excessive vanity, even when he didn't have bread to eat.'

'Investment potential?'

'His paintings hang in most French provincial museums, as well as galleries in Baltimore, Berlin, Berne, Paris and London. There are also many of his drawings in Russia. He was very popular there.'

'Investment potential?' Eberhart repeated.

'Vincent van Gogh sold only one painting in his lifetime. You can never really tell in this business.'

Eberhart admired the young girl a little while longer and then made his way to one of the conversation chairs by the limestone fireplace. He sat, and Porteous joined him.

'You're quite the authority on antiques, I guess,' Eberhart remarked, hitching his pants off the knee to prevent misshaping in the cut of the cloth.

'I like to think so. I've long been an admirer of European elegance.'

Eberhart placed the folder he was carrying across his knees. The left side of his mouth hooked up in a smile and he grunted. 'Yeah, possibly, European elegance. Never figured it that way. I kind of thought of it as a good investment. More than can be said for the present-day garbage they turn out, wouldn't you say?'

Porteous merely nodded, unwilling to be drawn into small talk. Especially with this man. J.J. Eberhart. Newly appointed Director of the CIA. A man in a dark-grey suit with white button-down shirt and a loud red-and-yellow-striped tie. A flashy gold Rolex, with diamonds set at the cardinal points on the face, prominent on his wrist. A white-haired sixty-six-year-old, who bubbled with a can-do streetwise energy. Nothing, they said, had come easy to the Brooklyn-born businessman, but he had made hundreds of millions of dollars by outworking others, and had, with the tenuous connection of working for Army Intelligence during the Korean War, bought himself the office of Director of the Central Intelligence Agency by heavily supporting the new President's campaign.

Eberhart waved the folder. 'Down to business, then. We're both busy men so I don't intend keeping you long. Simply, Oscar, we have a problem.'

'Problem!'

'The Colombian business — White Knight. Following Congress's Amendment banning covert action in Colombia, I just wanted to check how close we were to getting information on their new export methods.'

Porteous took a Rolaid tablet from his pocket and put it on the end of his tongue. His stomach was causing more pain. 'Indigestion,' he said quickly, noticing the Director's enquiring look. 'Could be very close. Days even.'

'You're pretty confident on that?'

'I was. If we're pulled out we relinquish all initiative.'

'Just as well we have you, then, Oscar. I need you to unofficially stay on the pulse. Keep me advised of any new developments, you know the sort of thing. As that well-screwed phrase goes: a week is a long time in politics. We'll be in a totally different ball game by then, and I do not intend to find myself wanting when the big stick comes back out.'

'I appreciate that.'

'I looked back over the files, you know. Less than twenty years ago we were funding and leading military coups and getting to the point of winning the drug war. Now we've opened the door to the putschists again. Invited them to re-form their paramilitary forces. All that goddamned work and money down the tubes, Oscar. If we allow things to slide much further we'll be in a worse state than we were back in the late seventies.'

Thoughts ran through Porteous's mind: Bleeding-heart liberals, Director, what do you expect? Denouncing prayers in school as unlawful assembly, turning a blind eye to gays in the military. I am glad I'm old. I fear for the future. Silent thoughts. Expressed opinions were noted. Filed away. Used against you at a later date.

Eberhart rambled on. His distinctive, unsettling voice filling the room. 'You know, Oscar, the first few meetings I attended in this new job were full of questions like: Is the CIA going through an identity crisis, wrestling with its role in the world? Were its people dirty tricksters, or were they intellectual high-camp analysts, doing brilliant papers that dazzled the guys who had the security clearances to read them? And you know what? I sat and listened to all this crap going round the table and finally figured everything I heard was a contradiction. The answers seemed to change day by day. I intend to alter all that. I appreciate all the hard work you've put in on this matter, that's why I want you to stay with it. Just keep me informed. Day or night.'

'Consider it done, Director.'

'I also think we need to be very cautious. This isn't something we need going public. Perhaps . . . perhaps you should quietly generate a cover story that I have ordered a stop on all Colombian activities . . . for our own protection, of course.'

'Of course.'

'Now about that painting. Who was the artist guy?'

'Jean Baptiste Greuze.'

'You figure I'd be making a good investment?'

Porteous turned in his chair and peered across at the gilt-framed painting. It was one of those produced in the late 1770s and 1780s to offset dwindling popularity, adversely affected by neoclassicism, the beginning of the end for Greuze. Porteous considered it grossly deficient in drawing and of mawkish sentimentality. That Greuze had died unnoticed, having outlived his time and reputation, elicited no sympathy from Porteous.

'Most certainly,' he confirmed. 'A very fine investment.'

33

It was the blockhouse and the dry clatter of the diesel generator that did it. Recharged old memories of rinky-dink airports in the Far East that had all the hopelessness of a Bob and Bing *Road to Nowhere* movie.

Enough for Ugly Charlie to want a drink.

At noon he could stand it no longer. He went to check they had power at the hangar. They did, and the three of them sat under neon strip lights with a couple of large electric fans stirring the oppressive air, toasting the event with warm Cokes. Then Charlie made his excuses and went back to the blockhouse to work on one of the other generators – they needed a backup in this heat, he assured Winter – but not before he had sneaked a bottle of vodka from his kit.

He found a dark corner, where bricks were removed and a light wind ventured through. And licked his dry lips. And looked at the bottle – couple of mouthfuls wouldn't hurt; shit, didn't he deserve it? – and broke the seal. After two long pulls he was feeling slightly better. He drank some more and felt the aches and pains in his body begin to melt away. The breeze caress his face. The thunder of the generator fill his ears. Like it had been on the flight in: the slipstream through the empty worn canvas gun-sleeves of the B-25, the constant roar of the Wright Cyclones.

Sometime later the half-empty bottle slipped from his fingers and the welcome numbness suffused his body. He closed his eyes and drifted towards sleep, smiling to himself. Not a civilian thing this. Military. You learned to sleep in any environment. Noise was not a factor. But the sleep he was looking for did not come.

Instead he found himself back in *Blue Satin*. The ancient C-47 resurrected for one last war. Turning in the night sky over a place his navigator assured him was Loc Ninh. He studied the ill-defined strip, marked with a handful of gooseneck flares . . . and the tiny flashes of light winking from the jungle boundary. Small-arms fire. Viet Cong. The landing went off without a hitch. Then the waiting while the injured Special Forces guys were loaded up . . . Special Forces guys as in 'Operation Phoenix', a little-known programme run, some said, by the CIA and aimed at eliminating VC cadres by assassination, capture or defection . . . waiting as the bullets found the airframe time after time after time . . . dull little clicks. Sweating it out, waiting for the one that would find him. But it didn't. There was no chance to check for battle damage – you didn't carry a flashlight around looking for holes while you were under fire. You simply checked engines and flying controls responded . . . you simply turned through a hundred and eighty degrees and hauled ass the opposite way . . . praying the blacked-out ghostlike plane was invisible to the enemy . . . praying the trees at the end of the narrow strip were not as high as you believed them to be.

The fire had come sometime later – a delayed reaction to the unchecked battle damage, maybe – on the right engine. They feathered and fired the bottle, but it didn't go out. He had gone cold. On a stifling tropical night he was stone-cold. Dry-mouthed. So much so that he couldn't swallow. How many minutes left? How many minutes before the tanks blew . . . or the wing folded! There was only one way. Down. Down where? The jungle. He lit a cigarette. His last. He knew that with more certainty than he had ever known anything in his life. He briefed the crew and reduced power to the good engine.

Back in some beer-swilling officers' club, full of voices and laughter and cigarette smoke, they said you trimmed for the glide and when you figured you were five hundred feet off the deck you switched on your landing lights. If you didn't like what you saw ahead of you, you switched them off. The thought flashed through his mind, nothing more. Those words belonged to people who had never been here. Here was death. Here was where your sweat-faced copilot was transmitting a Mayday to your base at Bien Hoa. There was even a code for that at the O Club: 'It is better to die in silence than to display the bad form of alerting the world to your predicament'. Macho over a few beers. Here it was different . . . the call going out over and over and over . . . 'MAYDAY, MAYDAY, MAYDAY . . . PARIS CONTROL THIS IS BLUE SATIN . . . GOIN' IN . . . POSITION . . .'

Here was serious concentration . . . no time for slick words . . . no time for regrets . . . no time for prayers . . . no time for picture-book days kaleidoscoping past your eyes . . . no time for anything but total, unblinking, seconds-before-you-died concentration!

Crash checks running . . . landing lights on . . . and . . . a clearing . . . maybe a quarter-mile long . . . longer . . . piece of cake . . . thank the Man . . . he felt his body relax . . . like he was on Valium . . . smooth . . . floating . . . and he was laughing . . . home free . . . shit! How lucky can you get? Shutdown checks on the number-two engine now . . . heightened perception of being in the unknown, in the only glider Mr Douglas ever built . . . only sound airflow shushing over airframe . . . pick your spot . . . pick your spot . . . hold off . . . hold off . . . a second which lasts a minute . . . two . . . three . . . four . . . fi— CONTACT . . . too hard . . . staggering back into the clammy tropical air . . . get down bitch . . . AND AGAIN . . . from a remote somewhere a tearing of metal . . . bracing harder on the controls . . . toes pressing the brake pedals . . . *automaticunfuckingthinkingreaction* . . . no wheels dummy we just did a wheels-up landing . . . hanging on . . . working the rudder . . . keep it straight . . . keep it straight . . . willing the machinery to stop.

Then, the last death-rattle shudder. And silence . . . more than he imagined possible. He sat for a moment asking himself what were the odds of finding this particular clearing on a moonless night? What were the odds of the compass heading being perfectly aligned with the centre line of that clearing from the moment he had initiated descent? What were the fucking odds?

Then he was unbuckling his harness and following
his copilot down the fuselage ... forcing the main
door open ... turning to the crew in the darkness
and shouting orders to evacuate the wounded ... he
shouted again ... and a voice shouted back ... and
again ... and again ... and again ...

And didn't stop.

It caused him a moment's anxiety as he struggled
against the engine sound. Until he realised he was in
the blockhouse. Not an airplane. The voice again. He
looked up and saw Maria, waiflike, dressed in some
of Winter's overlarge clothes, legs of jeans rolled up,
shirtsleeves likewise. 'Winter needs help to get the
tug started,' she shouted, and turned on her heel and
hurried away.

Lighting a cigarette, Charlie stumbled off through
the trees. Taking a mental inventory in his mind.
The equipment Winter had located and had shown
him that morning. The flight-safety equipment room;
spare parachutes, aircrew helmets – bone-domes, lightweight flight suits, gloves, rubber-soled flight boots.
The underground jet fuel tanks on the concrete ramp –
contamination/degradation as yet unknown; certainly
there would be fungus at the surface where oxidisation
had been at work; how deep it had spread was anybody's guess – even so as the fuel was pumped from
the bottom of the fifty-thousand-gallon tanks there was
a good chance it was okay; four fifty-gallon barrels of
Avpin (isopropyl nitrate) in the corner of the hangar;
an indigo-blue Chevy V-6 flatbed truck in surprisingly
good shape except for two flat tyres, pulled into one
of the engine shops at the back of the hangar amid
ground power units for the Lightnings, and racks of

spares, including zero-timed Avon engines in cans; tools; technical library with overhaul manuals on the aircraft. One thing was for sure, these people had been serious. Even so, to carry out engine changes was not an easy matter. The two engines situated in the fuselage of the slab-sided Lightning were placed one on top of the other, leaving little room for fuel and hydraulic pipes, with the result that all these pipes were wrapped around possibly hazardous regions on the engines' outer casings, where temperatures rose to extreme levels in flight. Naturally, both engines had fire-detection and extinguishing systems fitted which could be fired into the affected area; except, as Charlie had tried to explain, the fire bottles were long past their sell-by date. One of many emergency systems made redundant merely by time. Cycles, flight hours and calender date being the maintenance criteria by which aircraft were kept serviceable.

Then again there was the small mountain of weathered equipment at the west side of the hangar – the LOX plant. Never built. Meaning there was no liquid oxygen. And as the Lightning was equipped with a LOX breathing system! Which meant that even though the cockpits were normally pressurised, high flight would be a no-go status, given pressurisation failure at altitude without standby oxygen, resulting in a matter of seconds before blackout and death. Flight would be restricted to about eighteen thousand feet, a place you could still breathe, even though continued exposure to the thin air at that altitude would result in a quite severe oxygen-starvation headache. A lower flight profile causing endurance and range to be seriously compromised. On the plus side it was

quite likely these aircraft had been reassembled and
never yet flown. The chance of a higher degree of
serviceability. The hydraulics systems could be the
worst nightmare, as they were in part responsible for
the power-assisted flying controls. Any failure in that
department left only one course of action open to the
operating pilot. Eject.

Fixing a diesel generator was one thing, playing with
those adrenaline machines something else. Winter, as
always, had thought differently, and had gone back to
the job he had been doing earlier. Playing with wiring
and pressure switches, fuses, and detonators. Five-
hundred-pound bombs didn't go off by themselves.
  More adrenaline.

34

There are such places in every city. In Santa Marta, Colombia's third-largest seaport and oldest surviving colonial town, it was the Hotel Miramar. Apart from being the archetypal gringo hotel and the cheapest accommodation in town, it was the definitive source of information on the city and the region.

It was to this hotel that Williams and Owens had arrived during the mid-afternoon following their drive from Cartagena. After a shower and a change of clothes Williams set out alone to meet with Werner Stock, leaving Owens to an afternoon siesta.

The skies had darkened by that time and a thunderstorm lay over the city. Sheet lightning flickered with the frequency of fireflies in the nimbus clouds. The rain when it started was tropical, a wall of water bouncing a clear foot off the ground. Rivers of garbage flowing along street gutters. Visibility reduced to practically zero.

But by that time Williams was sitting in Werner Stock's study, drinking freshly ground coffee. A dusty,

austere room furnished with a minimum of dark-
wood furniture. A threadbare faded Persian carpet,
predominantly blue, centred on the parquet floor.
A large refectory table which served as a working surface, cluttered with charts and maps. A tall,
glass-doored bookcase, most of the titles in German.
And the majority of one wall hung with framed
sepia photographs of what might have been family
members. Circa thirties and forties, unmistakably
Germany.

Stock himself was a relatively young man, slimly
built, not too tall. Late forties. Straight grey-blond hair,
combed neatly back. Cool grey eyes that matched the
afternoon sky. Classic Aryan features. Flawless pale
skin. His English was particularly good. Too good for
an Englishman. Too textbook. He was dressed neatly
in grey trousers and a grey open-necked short-sleeved
shirt, and black leather slippers with gold eagle heads
embossed upon them. He smoked a navigator's pipe,
its long curved stem designed to keep it out of the way
of the charts while one was working on them.

Stock was filling his pipe with careful precision,
picking up the odd strand of tobacco that had fallen
into his lap and returning it the leather pouch. A thrifty
man, Williams observed, as if he had been raised on
rations of black bread where each and every crumb
had to be accounted for; or a rich man who knew that
waste was a poor man's downfall. 'I am sorry for your
unnecessary journey, naturally, but the aeroplane has
been stolen.'

'Yes, Drummer told me.'

'Ah. You have spoken with him.'

'In Cartagena, yes.'

'He came back with you?'

'No. Said he had business down there.' A small lie perhaps. One of many. One that might bring out other untruths. And if not, nothing wasted.

'But if you knew the aeroplane was stolen, why bother to travel all this way?'

'The guy Winter. The guy who made enquiries about its purchase and who might have taken it during the army raid on Canaveral, I need to find him.'

'What else did Drummer tell you?'

'Nothing. Except he didn't have confirmation it was Winter who got away. He said that two Americans had been killed in the raid.'

Stock went to the refectory table and sorted through the maps and papers. He returned to his chair, handing two photographs to Williams. 'Winter is one of these men?' Voice precise, expressionless.

Williams looked carefully at the black-and-white photographs. One an overweight male with thick white hair. The other, a scrawny kid, hair tied back in a ponytale. Eyes closed. Both bodies riddled with bullet holes. He shook his head. 'No.'

'Police photographs. They are both at the mortuary, here in Santa Marta. And your reason for looking for Mr Winter?'

'As I mentioned, I'm in the antiques business. Mr Winter came to me some months ago with a proposition concerning antique airplanes, warbirds as they're known in America. He convinced me that there was a high profit margin in such dealings. I agreed that should he find an airplane that could be bought at the right price that I'd bankroll the deal.'

'And he told you about my aeroplane?'

'More than that. He faxed me a detailed specification sheet, and a history of the B-25 bomber, along with information on recent transactions in the US on similar. The projected profit margin looked very good. The fax came directly from Drummer – Winter said he was the agent working the deal.'

'May I ask how much he was asking for my aeroplane?'

'One hundred thousand dollars.'

'And the selling price in America?'

'Half a million, according to Winter.'

Stock pursed his lips. 'Wishful thinking, perhaps. And you of course gave him the money to purchase the aeroplane?'

'Yes. Not my normal way of doing business, but it seemed a great deal. He even had a buyer set up in Chino, California. A warbird collector.'

Stock let out a shout of laughter. Slapped his hand against his thigh. 'Forgive my apparent humour, Mr Williams. It is perhaps relief that I am not the only one to be singled out in this – what shall we call it? – con game.'

Williams managed a bland smile. 'There was something else I came across. After I had wired Winter the money, he made no further attempt to contact me. Of course I became very concerned and hired a private investigator to run background checks on him.' Williams paused as if uncertain how to frame what he was about to say.

Stock leaned forward in his chair. 'And?'

'It appears that Winter recently killed a man in America. A Colombian. Someone involved in drugs, according to police sources.'

'And you have the name of the man?'

'Figueras. Francisco Figueras.'

There was a protracted silence. Williams could hear Stock breathing heavily as he fiddled with his pipe. Eventually he asked, 'You know who Francisco Figueras was?'

'My investigator said he was the son of a powerful Colombian family.'

Stock took a few moments to light his pipe. The pipe tobacco had a sweet aromatic smell. 'Perhaps the most powerful Colombian family, Mr Williams. His father is Emilio Figueras, head of the Cartel de Cali. You have heard of them?'

'The report mentioned it, yes.'

'They are dangerous people to be involved with.'

'I don't wish to be involved. I just want to find Winter and get my money back.'

'I think you need to be very careful, Mr Williams. One matter might be inexorably linked to the other. Emilio Figueras would have put a contract out on his own mother, were she still alive, and if he had had the slightest suspicion she was involved in anything underhand. There is no honour there, believe me.'

'You have dealt with him, Emilio Figueras?'

'No. But I knew his partner, who he stole everything from and then turned him over to the authorities.'

The letter in Drummer's truck perhaps. *Talk to Werner Stock in Santa Marta about . . .* He looked directly into Werner Stock's eyes. 'Klaus Barbie?'

A brief look of surprise. Gone in a second. 'I think your investigations have been very thorough. That is good. Perhaps you are more careful than I anticipated.'

'Not so Klaus Barbie, I guess he took too much at face value, huh?'

'Trust, Mr Williams. Klaus Barbie did a lot to help Emilio Figueras. They were like brothers for many years. Quite simply, you do not expect your brother to turn Judas.'

'No disrespect to the German race, Mr Stock, but I hardly think Barbie was whiter than white – his war record for one thing. Seems he crossed the line a number of times himself.'

Stock jabbed his pipe at the air. 'Did you ever serve in the military, Mr Williams?'

'Once. Viet Nam.'

'And you obeyed orders. Yes?'

'Yes.'

'And if you had not? If you had told your officers that you refused to go into the jungle and shoot the Viet Cong, what then? A firing squad?'

'I get the point. What I was trying to say was that perhaps Klaus Barbie should have been hardened to the fortunes of war – any war.'

Stock said, 'But *that* is my point. He was not hardened. He was a soldier who carried out his orders for the Wehrmacht and the Gestapo. If he was a war criminal, Mr Williams, then every soldier is guilty of the same crime. Every civilian in Vichy France perhaps more guilty, yet we did not see what you would have called the traitors of France afforded the same punishment. When he became a civilian after the war, and worked as you may be aware for the American government for many years in their fight against communism, he was what he had always been. A simple man carrying out orders. A trusting man. He trusted

Emilio Figueras. If he had been the arch-criminal the
West made him out to be, do you think he would have
let a Colombian peasant drug dealer finish his life?'

'Perhaps not, although I seem to recollect that quite
a few Frenchmen, the Vichy French crowd you mentioned, were shot at the end of the war.'

'A token gesture to pacify the ignorant masses, Mr
Williams, nothing more, I do assure you.'

Williams finished his coffee and admired the elegant
cup for a moment before putting it back in the saucer.
He didn't need to check for the hallmark of two
blue crossed swords. He had visited the factory near
Dresden in recent years, as part of Oscar's ongoing
training programme. A valuable piece. Not something
one would use on a daily basis. If at all. *Stock checking
his credentials!* 'Meissen?'

Stock nodded. 'Indeed, the very best. A family heir-
loom. One of the few things that survived and were
brought here by my family after the war.'

'Very beautiful,' Williams acknowledged. 'Going
back to Winter. Do you know where I can find him?'

'I was a meteorologist for many years for the
Colombian government. The charts you see on the
table are synoptic charts. Now it is something of
a hobby with me. Albeit an expensive one. I have
instruments in my garden: I take wet and dry bulb
temperature readings, humidity readings, anemometer
readings. I also receive, via e-mail and fax, station
reports from other places around the Caribbean. This
way I can plot weather patterns. Conversely, I could
switch on the television and be told the same information in a matter of seconds; but then I would not
get any pleasure from it.'

More than a few crumbs of black bread perhaps.
'How much?' Williams asked.

'The price of my aeroplane? Let us say one hundred thousand dollars.' No preamble. A meteorologist turned businessman.

'How soon?'

'Before I locate Mr Winter? Difficult to say. One day, one week. One month. Like meteorology being an inexact science, where stated laws of physics applied to an unstable environment are only accurate at the moment of application – anything thereafter being educated guesswork – the weather men still do a reasonable job of forecasting a few days ahead. You can be assured, Mr Williams, that I will find and benefit from those same few days.'

'And will I also get a bill of sale for the airplane?'

'Naturally. I am a man of honour. And even though I would not normally fault a man who killed one of Figueras's family, I do not expect people to steal from me. Like you, I think, principle is sometimes more than money. Even then I think you may have problems retrieving the aeroplane from Winter.'

'I can only try.'

Williams was leaving. Both men were standing at the heavy teak front door of the Spanish colonial-style house. The rain in the courtyard was light now. A cooling breeze rustled through the brightly coloured flower beds as the tail end of the storm drifted inland. The sound mix of car horns and music lifting over the high walls.

Williams said, 'Any reason why the army would hit the place called Canaveral? Drummer told me they never went into the peninsula.'

'That is easy, Mr Williams. Drummer is quite correct: the army never normally go into Alta Guajira. It is a desert land known for its lawlessness. No roads, just a maze of sandy jeep trails. Very difficult to access.'

'Except this time they did. Why would they do that?'

'A good question, I think.' Stock sucked on his pipe thoughtfully. 'The newspapers have been reporting it as government reprisals. The families of two government ministers were murdered by rebels some months ago, here in the north. The army are denying they had anything to do with the raid.'

'Curious.'

'Unless you now consider the man Winter was at Canaveral. An enemy of the Figueras family.'

'You think that had something to do with it?'

'There is a rumour going around that it was the Cali Cartel who mounted the attack on Canaveral, using stolen army equipment. Naturally I pay little attention to such talk, but bearing in mind what you've told me, Winter killing one of the Figueras family, I think Emilio Figueras will leave no stone unturned in seeking the man.'

Williams fingered the Dunhill lighter in his trouser pocket. The feel of smooth heavy gold oddly comforting. His brow was knitted in concern, as he turned towards Stock. 'Let's hope we find him first.'

'That's all we can do.' Stock looked up at the clearing skies. 'And what will you do while you wait? Take a tourist trip to Tayrona National Park, perhaps? The beaches are excellent and some of the bays are bordered by coral reefs. Good for snorkelling.'

'No, I have one of my business partners with me.

We thought we would see what we can find out about pre-Colombian art. Pottery mainly. Funeral jars, ritual dishes and vases. Might ease our losses if we can make a few purchases.'

'You have heard of the Muiscas?'

'Religious jar with a slim neck?'

'Quite right. There are some good examples in the museum on Calle 12 and Carrera 2 – although I doubt the director will sell them to you.'

'I thought most things were available in Colombia, for a price!'

A wry smile. 'You are learning quickly, Mr Williams.'

Williams drove fast along Calle 17. Pluming spray. Window wide open. Breathing what felt like pure oxygen. Light-headed through lack of sleep.

Trying to reconcile himself to the fact that Winter and the Cartel might be playing war games with each other.

Something more than a rumour perhaps!

PART SIX
Squawk Lists

35

'Truth and consequences!'

The only words Ugly Charlie uttered as the hangar doors were rolled open on the pale platinum light which leaked over the eastern horizon.

Friday, the sixth day at 'Eerie One' – so christened by the American who had made up two-foot-high stencils and spray-painted the legend on the hangar doors. A light cooling breeze coursed through the treetops. Optimum time for a test flight. The Lightning that was being towed out, and had undergone a double engine change and essential systems checks, was the T.5 two-seat version.

Winter started a slow walk round, check list in hand. Eyes taking in the things that aviators never really forgot. All engine blanks and ground locks removed. Pitot and standby pitot checked for blockage. Five accumulator gauges, rear right fuselage, readings within limits. Jet pipes checked for signs of molten metal deposits – sign of impending engine failure. Stowed brake parachute, cable of which wrapped around the jet pipes in a figure of eight and secured with clips, and a bolt at the top of the upper loop – degradation of cable usually caused when afterburners in use, result being failure of the chute on landing, the time you needed it. On the left side of rear fuselage, indicators showing fire bottle contents had not been discharged; a moot point as the bottles had not been serviced in years – an engine fire in flight might therefore result in egressing the aeroplane by means of Martin-Baker ejector seats, which had also not been serviced in years. Just two of many technically unserviceable items on a fire-breathing monster capable of sustained flight well in excess of two thousand feet per second. The minutiae of checking continued. All panels secure. No hydraulic or fuel leaks, except for those from designated drain tubes. Tyre condition: check for signs of wear. A very real problem on an aeroplane which according to the book was a handful in crosswind landing conditions, one of which could flat-spot a tyre beyond acceptable limits. With touchdown speeds in the area of 170 knots or close to 200 m.p.h., tyre condition was high priority.

Winter pulled on his bone-dome, thinking about the old prop-driven Skyraiders he had flown and how he had been taught to carry out pre-flights on those – 'you just walk towards it and start counting, one prop four blades; two wings; three wheels – right, you've got yourself a complete aeroplane. Let's fly.' Things had been simpler then. Sure, they would still kill you, but at a respectable speed. What he was looking at landed faster than a Skyraider cruised, near enough. Even the F-86 Sabres had been sedate jets compared with this. And even though he was aware of the problems, it wasn't going to help. The fact was that the optimum speed the human brain was capable of thinking at was around 105 m.p.h., which meant that pilots had to think ahead of their aircraft; the faster the machine the quicker you had to juggle the mental processes to remain ahead. And that applied to young, physically fit pilots. After years away from a cockpit your head would still be at the hangar as you were climbing through ten thousand feet. In fact a vertical burner climb in something like this would get you through ten grand as fast as you could count off incremental altitudes – close to one thousand feet per second.

He climbed the steps to the ten-foot-high cockpit. A pause at the top. Final check over the upper wing surface for fuel venting. Clear.

Charlie was already in the right seat, the instructor's seat, going through the ritual of fastening his harness and leg-restraining straps. Winter lowered himself into the left seat and strapped in likewise, and ran his fingers over the controls, as he had during all the spare moments he had had through the past few days. Touch-drills were a part of staying alive in any aircraft. Reaction time. Mental agility. Emergencies always came when you least expected them. Start-up – not normally a heart-stopping event. Starting a vintage jet that had sat for a number of years by an explosion might well be. Forget the last three starts on the previous day to carry out engine runs and calibration checks. The rules had changed. Where a fast jet pilot was said to be only as good as his last flight, this now applied to the machinery. Every start-up was a journey into the unknown.

Maria climbed the access steps and removed the top

ejector-seat safety pin. Winter reached down between his legs and removed the lower seat pin and handed it to her. She held them both up for him to see and then stowed them, in the same way she had done with the pins on the right seat. Both ejector seats were now live. She removed the access steps and positioned herself by the wheeled fire extinguisher in front of the aircraft.

All main instruments off, Winter selected battery to ON and raised and lowered his seat to check its charge. System – OK. He looked out and raised his left hand, finger and thumb forming a circle, and moved his first finger of his right hand into the circle. Male into female. Connect ground power. Lights flickered on in the cockpit. Throttles full and free movement. Right hand raised, one finger extended, denoting number-one engine, followed by a circulating motion of the finger. Start signal. The wind-up sign came back. Number-one engine throttle forward to open the HP (high-pressure) cock and pull up the rapid-start gang bar. Fuel pumps on line – checked. He looked across at Charlie. 'Ready for this?'

Charlie hooked up his oxygen mask with a shaking hand, disconnected at the business end, but essential because it carried the voice mike. 'I just figured this place out. One square mile bordered by reality.'

'Very esoteric. So what do you think's waiting at the far end of the runway?'

'As Dorothy might have said, the Tin Man looking to pick up a few spare parts, or Kansas City! What d'you think's waiting? Hit the button.'

Winter depressed the number-one start button.

Instantly, the loud hissing noise followed by the explosion as the isopropyl nitrate was ignited. The acrid fumes drifted forward in the light wind, burning Winter's eyes and throat. The explosion ricocheted through the woods. The thunder of the Avon engine following closely behind. He monitored the Jet Pipe Temperature for overtemping. Watched as the r.p.m. increased and the fire lights went out. Oil, hydraulics and accumulators rising. Throttle set to 34 per cent. Gauges checked. Two fingers raised, and start circle for number-two engine.

Systems checked, Winter signalled ground power and chocks removed. Canopy down, warning light out, confirmed locked. Brake pressure checked. Thumb up to Maria. Park brake released. The aircraft leapt forward. Squeeze on the brake lever on the stick, nod of the nose showing both brakes working.

Charlie ran the check list as Winter nosed the aircraft down the sloping taxiway beneath the green canopy of trees.

'Check list complete,' Charlie said over the intercom. 'Make sure you've got that nosewheel straight when you're lining up. According to the book of words it's not self-centring on the ground.'

'You've told me twice already, Charlie.'

'Why I'm still around . . . I worry.'

'You want to do the briefing?'

'Roger that. Dry power take-off. Hundred and three per cent on the r.p.m. JPT 795 degrees. I'll call the speeds. V1 say a hundred twenty knots. Vr – a hundred thirty-five knots. Nosewheel off at a hundred thirty-five and check. One hundred fifty-five knots second rotation – mains off. Confirm positive rate of climb, and call gear up – I'll select and monitor the indicator lights, and confirm up. Careful not to overrotate – we could hit the tail on the runway. Straight ahead climb to ten thousand feet. I'll reduce power to keep you off the Mach. Left turn to south, continue climb one eight thousand and level. Emergency scenario – any warning lights or visual fires before V1, I'll call "Abort, abort, abort". Close throttles, stream the brake chute and hit the brakes. After V1, continue take-off and climb runway heading; if things look real bad I'll call "Eject, eject, eject". If you haven't gone by the time I give the third call you'll be logging solo time. Lastly, as we haven't got g-suits, keep an eye on the g-meter, no future in us both blacking out. Got it?'

Winter read back the speeds and the emergency drills. 'You think the runway's clear enough?'

'Taxi checks I did yesterday blew off most of the crap. Shouldn't be any problem.'

Winter held the brakes on and advanced both throttles to 92 per cent. Turned to Charlie and nodded. Brakes off and throttles forward. And he hadn't been wrong. Kidney-punching acceleration. Feet temporarily snatched from pedals. Drowning in the roar of thundering surf. In fact he was still checking JPT limiting, when Charlie called 130-plus knots and first rotation. Before that was achieved they had passed 155. The wheels came off at 190, by which time they were running out of runway.

'Gear up, my throttles,' Charlie called, easing the power back. 'Approaching ten grand . . . commence climbing left turn one hundred and eighty.'

By now the aircraft had outrun its own thunder. The

storm replaced by a hollow hiss. As though they had blown into soundless space. Ethereal. Winter looked down, a fleeting glimpse of the runway shrinking at a heart-stopping rate.

And moments later. 'Approaching one eight thousand . . . level.'

Winter managed to arrest the climb rate by 19,000. Began easing it back down to 18,000. Trying to come to terms with flying an aircraft after years away from it. It was a strange feeling; control input and response, something he had known intimately, now it felt remote. Alien even. A few brain cells picking at the bones of memory. Flying purely on experience, except the brain was a split second too late in getting the message to the hands. The result: a rough, unpolished, and dangerous performance.

Charlie said, 'Squirts right along like a greased pig, don't she? Okay, we got three hundred fifty knots indicated — fast enough to scare us both. Probably used most of the ventral tank fuel in that little exercise, which leaves us with wing and flap fuel. Try a few steep turns for ten minutes then we'll head back, run an approach with a go-around, followed by normal one-thousand-foot pattern to land.'

Winter looked out for a moment over the vast savannah land more than three miles below. The sun was up now, heliographing its way over the horizon. Warm on his face. The dome of sky cloudless. Perfect. Pale washed-blue in the east. Indigo in the west. He gingerly hauled the Lightning round on its wingtip. First left, then right. Then left again. Pity there were no towering cumulonimbus clouds to climb. To roll and scissor through narrow eye-aching white valleys, wingtips knifing the fluffy edges. Like a kid taking a ride in a magic kingdom. Footprints in the silent wilderness lasting only for the moment of passage, before the traces were smoothed by the mercurial air. Virgin once more. Unsullied. Unspoilt. Something he'd loved with a passion, cloud chasing. Only done solo. You never shared those moments with other humans in the cockpit. You never even spoke of them to other humans. Some things in life were intensely personal.

And at the end of ten minutes he tried a barrel roll just for the hell of it. Somewhere in the inverted position he accidentally unloaded g. Colombian dirt from the cockpit floor drifted down to the canopy roof. Then the g was back as he started to pull through.

'Straight and level,' Charlie snapped.

'Thought you'd like to see the earth the other way.'

'I might. She might not. You simply don't fuck old ladies – not polite, they may write you out of their will.'

Winter got the message. Old aeroplanes were temperamental. The airframe could have been stressed beyond limits on any number of occasions, given its history. The fact that individual excursions of around ten g or so would have produced little or no damage meant nothing. But after a while such excursions began to add up. Aluminium has a memory, and repeated cycles above a certain value take their toll. That toll is a point at which a single excursion will produce a catastrophic failure. The fatigue of a major component could therefore be as little as one or two g-pulling manoeuvres away. The first few flights, then, were shakedown trips. Looking for squawks. Time

and rectification giving them the hoped-for reliability.
'Back to the work element, eh?'

'That's what we're here for.'

'What about bringing the number-one engine back
to idle after take-off? How much increase in range?'
Winter asked.

'I'll check the books when we get back. That's
probably going to be the only way in to the target and
out – bearing in mind you'll have to crossfeed fuel.'
Charlie checked the portable GPS strapped to his left
thigh. 'Time we were going home. Heading . . . zero
four zero. Range . . . seventy-five. Only problem we
might have is with the tail chute on landing. Planned
touchdown speed a hundred sixty knots, a hundred
seventy acceptable, as close to the beginning of the
runway as possible. Wheels on, deploy the chute. If it
fails to stream, get on the brakes – and hope available
runway length is adequate.'

Winter reduced power and initiated descent. The
gallery forest was less than twenty miles now, coming
up fast. Pulling back on the power, the speed came
back through 250 knots. Gear down, three greens
confirmed, fuel state checked sufficient for go-round,
flaps down. Over the west end of the runway. One
thousand feet. Downwind right hand. Over the trees.
A brightly coloured bird visual for a fleeting second,
then flashing by in the overhead.

'Harness – check,' Winter called.

'Checked. Passing abeam runway threshold now . . .
commence right turn base leg. Speed reducing through
two hundred knots . . . good . . . keep it coming all the
way to heading two hundred seventy . . . looking for
one seventy-five on the speed.'

Winter pulled it into a sixty-degree bank, feeding in rudder, feeling prestall buffet through the controls, rolling out rapidly . . . overshooting runway heading by ten degrees . . . nudging it back left. Visual with the runway now. Speed 185 . . . Jinking the throttles back 170 . . . and up . . . 180 . . .

'Looking good . . . airbrakes out . . . and throttle up to maintain speed.'

'Selected . . . and throttles.'

'Fence speed a hundred sixty-five . . . touchdown one sixty on the numbers . . . no trade-off power for height . . . keep it coming . . . back on the throttles a touch . . . okay, airbrakes in, my throttles and go-round time . . . we'll leave everything hanging, make life a bit easier . . . try a left-hand pattern this time.'

Winter rolled in sixty degrees of bank, positioning downwind. Things were happening very fast now. Too fast. Two hundred knots near enough. Visual with the runway. Passing abeam the touchdown point. Rolling back in. Quick check on fuel state and park brake set to off and turning in towards finals at two miles, or forty seconds, to touchdown.

'Three greens confirmed,' Charlie said. 'Air brakes out, my throttles . . . just fly the airplane . . . plant it on the end.'

Winter trimmed back as the speed decayed, holding the reference point on the end of the runway in the same position in the frame of windshield . . . feeling the light buffet through the controls . . . near to stalling speed. Concentration high. Heart rate, higher!

'Speed good, one hundred sixty-five . . . chute handle as soon as we have the wheels on . . . keep it coming . . . down . . . down . . . down . . .' And as the main wheels hit, streaming blue smoke, and the nose wheel followed: 'CHUTE.'

Winter pulled the chute handle as Charlie brought both throttles back to idle. The tug of the chute was positive and, as it deployed, the nose lifted slightly. Winter squeezed the brake handle and the nosewheel dropped back on. And in the same instant the clanging of the audio attention-getters, with associated flashing lights.

Rapid adrenaline surge. Shit!

A moment's panic, then Charlie reached forward and cancelled the audio. 'Air turbine generator dropped off line when I closed the throttles . . . forgot that . . . more brake . . . looking good . . . looking good . . . looking good.' An audible sigh over the intercom, as the Lightning rolled to a near stop. 'Okay, let's turn round and head up the runway. Jettison the chute after the turn. We'll come back in the truck and pick it up. So, what'd you think?'

'I'll tell you when I catch up with it . . . You did a good job on the maintenance, Charlie.'

'Correction. We did a good job. No apparent squawks . . . seems we struck lucky. What's next?'

Winter checked his watch. 'Refuel, refit the brake chute, take Maria for a famil flight before the day gets any hotter – see how well she does. If we stay serviceable we'll try another two slots tomorrow morning.'

'What about the single-seaters?'

'I'll check the logs, see which one we might want to start in on.'

'You know how long it's going to take me to get you marginally operational?'

'You tell me?'

'Minimum fifteen hours. Thirty half-hour slots. We're going to be asking a lot on the serviceability side of things.'

'You take care of the training, Charlie. I'll get up to speed on the engineering side.'

'You were a little hot on take-off by the way. Like thirty-plus knots.'

'I noticed. We'll get it right next time.'

'Plus or minus five knots . . . how much you bet?'

'A dollar.'

'That much, huh! You're on. By the way, all patterns flown will now be south of the runway, away from the trees. We nearly picked up a bird-strike on the first downwind.'

'Never saw a thing.'

'Don't think the bird did either,' Charlie remarked. 'You know, there was a time when I figured I'd never get to fly fast jets again. Makes you feel young, don't it?'

'A young man's occupation, as they say.'

'Or woman's.'

'How do you think she'll do?'

'Maria? Not a chance. A few hours in a Citation is one thing — here we're talking weapons platforms. As I told you a thousand times in the past, a bomb hits the target first in the imagination of the man behind the stick, and only then because he is able to transmit the image through several miles of wires and hydraulic lines that link them to the airplane. Fire-breathing country.'

'But you'll try.'

'It's your money.' Charlie picked up the check list

and started reciting the after-landing checks. Consummate professionals did that. Even alcoholic consummate professionals. Thirty years of mostly single-seat fighter cockpits moulded the man, programmed his every action; three decades of tiny cramped offices scattered across the world. Where wars and rumours of wars always needed craftsmen. A trade, nothing more. From Henry Plantagenet's boisterous storms of war, whose soldiers had exchanged their stallions for aeroplanes, swords for cannons and rockets and bombs. Still killing men, women and children. Sometimes in their hundreds. Never seeing their faces. Or the tears and misery left behind. Consummate professionals did all those things, and more. And never forgot their training. Carried it with them every day of their life.

Sweat stains were spreading from the armpits of Charlie's khaki flight suit as they taxied in to the ramp area by the hangar. His mouth was parched. He needed a drink. Needed the 'buzz'. Thought that if he didn't get a drink he was going to start crying and might not stop. Realised he would have to settle for coffee and a cigarette. And pray he could control the shakes long enough for another launch.

Then again he could always sweeten his coffee. No one would ever know. One shot. Couldn't hurt.

36

Most people had heroes. Even Luis Figueras. Not that he considered Simon Bolivar in the idolised El Libertador light that the common people of northwest South America did. More the complexities of Bolivar's character, the idealist with a poetic mind and visionary ideas; the inspired amateur without any formal training in the strategy of war who had won battles in a manner that still confounded military experts today. The glory and charisma faded after Bolivar's long-awaited dream materialised: the formation of the unified state of Gran Colombia, the joining together of Venezuela, Colombia and Ecuador. The problem that followed was the question of the political organisation of Gran Colombia. Bolivar, then the president, favoured a strong central rule, but the central regime was increasingly incapable of governing such an immense country with its great racial and regional divisions and differences. No amount of impassioned and vehement speeches would save it from its ultimate fate. Where peace was feared more than war. Gran Colombia began to collapse from the moment of its birth.

Figueras therefore knew that *his* manner of winning a financial battle that would confound the experts was the beginning and the end. After it was over there would be no going back. Gone would be legal affairs. Corporate boardrooms. The people he knew. The places he had lived. Even his family name. But then with a wealth of two billion dollars he would need none of them. Few people ever got the chance to cancel out the first half of their lives and start all over again from the beginning.

Now, in the study of his penthouse apartment in Cali, he sifted through papers he needed to carry to Europe – those of a sensitive nature carefully sanitised in the unlikely event of a customs search. The final complex plan which would legitimately transfer – over a period of years – one and three-quarter billion dollars into a Liechtenstein *anstalt*. The end of a paper trail which would begin with the Colombian government and a joint venture with Exxon, developing the Casanare oil fields in northern Los Llanos. A secret deal brought about by his promise of surrendering the entire Cartel de Cali in exchange for an amnesty (the same information he had leaked to the Americans). He being nothing more than a highly respected attorney appointed to broker the deal; one who would transfer one and three-quarter billion dollars (his father's share) of the Cartel's wealth into government coffers, the money being directly available to expand the Casanare oil field development.

His reward: royalties from the Casanare oil fields

over a period of 120 months from the time of the first
of the new wells coming in – of which seismic and
geological data accorded with earlier surveys carried
out on the successful Arauca fields. The amount of
royalties equivalent to the loan he had made to the
government.

Naturally, Luis Figueras knew that there was no
gilt-edged guarantee that the royalties would flow as
unimpeded as the oil. Governments came and went.
Policies changed. It was a risk, however, he was
prepared to take. Especially as the first two hundred
and fifty million dollars of his father's wealth was now
winging its way to a secret account in Luxembourg.

As for the Colombian administration. Kudos. They
would receive all the credit in what the West would
see as a dramatic coup. A positive step forward to
favoured-nation status.

The man Winter was something else. No amount of
investigations by Luis's staff had turned up anything
as to the reason why Winter had been in Cali the
previous week.

They had been slightly luckier in Santa Marta.
They had followed the black Panamanian, who had
been seen a few days earlier with the gringo, to
Cartagena. Monitoring his meeting with two men who
had arrived by yacht from Key West, Florida. Passport
details had been passed. Names and nationality a
matter of record now. Disposing of the Panamanian
– when they confirmed by a telephone tap that he was
a DEA agent – was standard operating procedure. As
for the two new arrivals, possibly DEA, the passports
carried by both of them probably false, they had been
followed to Santa Marta where the black American

had had a meeting with Werner Stock, known for his
involvement with one of the smaller cartels on the
coast. Five days had passed since that meeting and
no one had moved. Which meant they were waiting for
something. Or someone. Winter perhaps? Whatever it
was, they would find out soon enough.

He checked his watch, and called through to Ana
in the bedroom. It was time to leave. He wondered if
he was doing the right thing in taking her with him
to Europe, but it was too late now: she had taken a
few days' holiday from the bank. More simple than
that, she had brought pleasure to a life that had had
little meaning since the death of his mother. Even the
prospect of sleeping alone had become anathema.

He went across the study, simply finished with
cream-coloured carpets, black leather sofas and chairs,
and recessed lighting, through to the bedroom, calling
her name again. She was standing in front of the
full-length wardrobe mirror buttoning her white silk
blouse. 'We are late, Ana.'

She looked at him in the mirror and gave him
a mischievous smile. 'And I was early nearly an
hour ago, Luis, until you decided to take me back
to your bed.'

He laughed and moved behind her, wrapping his
arms around her waist. 'You should not look so
desirable so early in the morning.'

She watched as his fingers undid the buttons, felt
the silk slip from her arms. Watched as her white
lace bra followed the blouse to the floor, his hands
gently cupping her breasts. Felt her nipples harden
to his touch. He turned her towards him and kissed
her temple, her cheek, finally her mouth. His tongue

forcing her lips apart, moving inside her mouth. His body pressing urgently to hers. His mouth moved from hers, tracing a path down her neck, finding her breasts.

'We are late, Luis,' she gasped.

'We own the airline,' he said, lifting her skirt. He turned her back towards the mirror. His knees forcing her legs apart. Bending her over.

Two and a half hours later they were boarding the Gulfstream G-IV at Cali airport. Ana, who had never even seen inside an executive jet before, marvelled at the luxurious interior. The wide, soft, leather seats, burled walnut woodwork, the soft, pastel, coordinated colours. The gold fittings. 'It's beautiful, Luis. I have never been on such a beautiful airplane.'

'Television also.' Luis pointed. 'Plenty of films for you to watch. CD system, telephone, fax. At the back there is a shower cubicle and dressing room. You might want to change into warmer clothes before we land; Milan is very cold at this time of year. You can sit here.' He guided her into a leather seat, explaining the controls that would electrically recline it and extend the footrest. 'The stewardess will serve you breakfast after take-off.'

'Milan, Luis? You said we were going to Zürich.'

'Two days in Milan. We fly to Zürich Monday morning. Is that all right?'

Ana laughed. 'Of course, Luis.'

Luis patted the Compaq laptop computer he was carrying. 'I will be at the back. I have work to do.'

'Why not sit opposite me?'

'And how much work do you think I would manage?
You distract me too much.'

'What about your breakfast?'

'You sound like my mother.'

'You need someone to take care of you. It is not
good for a man to be always working, ignoring his
diet. The body cannot go on indefinitely, Luis.'

'I will come and join you for coffee.'

'And food.'

'I work better on an empty stomach.'

'You are impossible.'

He reached down and placed a hand behind her
neck and kissed her lightly on the cheek, before
making his way to the seat and fold-down table,
inset with a world map elegantly created in gold
leaf, at the rear of the cabin.

They were taxiing out when Luis happened to
look up from the screen of the laptop. He stared
blankly out of the window for a moment, trying
mentally to pick holes in the complex Casanare oil
field project. Complex, because of the risk element
in being paid his commissions. Something his Swiss
advisers would be paid handsomely to handle. Something like a prime European bank underwriting the
Colombian government note. Guaranteeing that the
funds were discreetly transferred to the newly formed
Liechtenstein *anstalt* (an anonymous company with a
single secret shareholder).

His eyes were drawn to a small red-and-white
aircraft that was being refuelled. He stared a moment
longer, unsure why. He had the strangest feeling
he had seen that little airplane somewhere before.
Which of course was ridiculous. He rarely came to

the airport. The last time being to collect his father on his return from Panama some weeks earlier.

He removed his glasses and rubbed his eyes, thinking for a few seconds, then shrugged, and went back to work.

37

In Santa Marta, Williams and Owens had returned moments earlier from La Casa Vieja, a small restaurant on Calle 12, two blocks from their hotel, and a lunch of pan-fried strawberry grouper seasoned with lime and pepper, on a bed of rice and peas. The coco frie, chilled green coconut with the top sliced off, sipped through a straw, had been refreshing.

The windows of the poorly furnished second-floor hotel bedroom were open, the heat of midday beating through; direct competition to the squeaking ceiling fan, aching street-side throb of salsa and vallenato music, muffler-damaged tank-engine blast of cars, artistic interpretation of horns.

'Part of Colombia's charm,' Owens remarked, producing a bottle of duty-free Martell cognac from his suitcase at the foot of the narrow single bed.

Williams was pulling up the two hard-backed chairs to the night stand, which served as a coffee table. 'What?'

'Bloody noise.' He poured two small measures in

toothbrush glasses rescued from the bathroom on the day of their arrival, and used daily – initially at sunset, an hour earlier each day since. A vain attempt to anaesthetise the primary senses.

'What time do we leave to go to the airport?' Owens asked.

'Flight gets in at three thirty. Three o'clock should be okay.'

'You still think our friend Werner is on the level?'

'Paying him a hundred grand for information on Winter's whereabouts, you mean?'

'Easy payday.'

'We'll see.'

'You really think Winter's decided that the Figueras family is going to pay for his wife's murder?'

'If the rumours Werner Stock heard about the attack on Canaveral being the work of the Cali Cartel are true, it makes some kind of sense. A good enough reason for him being here.'

'Granted.'

Williams sipped his cognac. 'You're still worried about handing over all that money?' Williams asked.

'A phone call from Stock yesterday confirming he has the information on Winter, and when he passes it to you no way to verify it, until you actually locate Winter! Still, easy money for him. Compensation for his lost aeroplane. Assuming it was his in the first place.'

'I'm sure he's got title paperwork to prove it, forged or otherwise. A careful man. Like most Germans. Makes you wonder how they lost the war.'

Owens smiled. 'Too careful, Tanner, that's why. Unable to improvise – no, perhaps I'm wrong. Led by a young Alexander they would have doubtless ruled the world.'

'Next time perhaps, is that what you're saying?'

'The professional German soldier was without equal, Tanner. Even our own historians concede that point. With the right leaders, who knows? Even so, handing over a hundred thousand dollars to one of them you've met once and spoken to on the phone a couple of times might be considered at the very least risky.'

'Oscar approved it, Edeyrn. Got in touch with our people in Bogotá. Besides, it's confiscated drug money we're giving to Stock – we take it from them with one hand, and return it with the other.'

'You met your man coming in from Bogotá before?'

'No, he's new. Frank Murchek. Born: Paris, Arkansas. Football scholarship at Oklahoma State. Degree in sociology. Ex-Marine, Quantico-trained. Good all-rounder, I'm told. Should be able to take care of himself.'

Owens looked out of the open window. The clouds were building. The purple bruising, ominous. 'Looks like we could be in for one of those evening thunderstorms we had on the day we arrived.'

Williams dabbed his forehead with a handkerchief. 'Could do with it. Cool the place down at least. Power failure would be nice as well – give the music a night off. You know, after a week down here I'm getting homesick for the snow back in DC.' He finished his cognac. Felt the numbness spreading in his lips. Wished it was his hearing.

They left a few minutes before three, taking the city coast road – Avenida Rodrigo de Bastidas – south to Calle 22. From there fifteen kilometres on the Barranquilla road.

'How old did you reckon Werner Stock was?' Owens asked.

'Late forties. Why?'

'I was thinking about Klaus Barbie and Emilio Figueras. From what he said to you he seemed to know them well, but they were a different generation. Besides which, if he was working as a meteorologist . . .'

'Barbie was extradited from Bolivia in the early eighties – '81 or '82.'

'Possibly one of those expat society things, then, like the Fiancés of Death, whose leader paraded around in an SS uniform. Or perhaps his father was a close friend.'

'Probably right first time. The majority of Germans who came to South America after the war were the high-profile guys escaping a firing squad or a hangman's noose. Although to listen to Werner Stock you'd think that Barbie was a simple soldier who ended up the victim of a witch hunt.'

'For the German kids in South America after the war, Tanner, there never was a thing called the final solution. No Jews went in their thousands to the gas chambers. That was what they were taught. Pretty difficult to accept the Allies' propaganda years later, when they had grown up.'

'Except we have the proof.'

'That's like saying when it comes to homicide the legal system in the United States is fair and just, when we know it is down to money buying the best defence counsel. The best actor. The best orator.'

'That's not the point.'

'What if Werner gave you proof that Klaus Barbie was innocent of all charges, what would you do?'

'It wouldn't happen.'

'But just for a moment, suppose it did. And suppose you also found that we had fabricated the evidence against the Germans.'

'Impossible . . . it couldn't happen.'

Owens smiled. 'And there you have Werner's argument. The mirror image at least. We believe what we are conditioned to believe. Life's a funny old thing, Tanner. You know one of the best jokes I heard in the Far East? Nearly four thousand American POWs never being repatriated after the Korean War.'

Williams frowned. 'You believe that?'

'Not what I believe, boyo. US Army Intelligence reported it. Cold, hard facts. It seems that the Chinese handed over two batches of prisoners numbering nearly four thousand in the truce brokered by Eisenhower in '53; Operation Little Switch and Operation Big Switch to be precise. Your intelligence people stated that was only fifty per cent of the prisoners held. American Chiefs of Staff ordered that *no* POW figures be released to newspaper correspondents in the field. Gagged but not blindfolded. The press boys knew something was not right. Of course their newspapers back home picked up on it, tried to bring the Eisenhower government to book. But like all newspaper stories it eventually lost steam, and the fuss died down. And the missing? Seems quite possible that the Chinese sent them to work camps, Chinese as well as Russian. Extracting biographies along the way for use by the KGB for their own agents. I've seen old black-and-white photographs of a trainload of American GIs being shipped out to Manchuria. Spoke to one of your people about it once, a few years ago. Know what he said? "One man being killed by a passing car outside the White House is a tragedy; the loss of a few thousand soldiers, a statistic – besides it was for the greater good, wasn't it? We won the war against communism".'

'Army intelligence figures have been known to be wrong. Same thing happened in Nam.'

'Not on such a large scale.'

'Perhaps not.'

'But you agree that there could be some truth in the argument?'

'Not without positive proof.'

'In every major library across America, Tanner. All the proof you need.'

'So why hasn't some enterprising Pulitzer-prize-hungry journalist written about it? Exposed the Eisenhower administration as riddled with Marxist or Maoist sympathisers? The enemy within?'

'No one to listen. Korea is the forgotten war. In fact Truman considered it a police action, not even significant enough to be called a war. Quite simply, no one really cares, or those who did are by now dead and buried.'

'And where does Winter figure in this imprimatur on revisionist history?'

'We believe what we are conditioned to believe. Think about that.'

'Monolithic man. You rate him too highly.'

'Do you remember what I said to you when we first spoke about him. You in Washington, me in Florida.

I said one thing that concerns me is that he only operates in Third World environments.'

'Capablanca was considered the invincible chess machine. In a period of ten or more years he lost only one game. Then he stunned the chess world by losing to Alekhine in 1927. Past his prime, Edeyrn. Beaten by age and laziness, and the ascent of a new kind of player. I grant you Winter might have been good in his day, but we all fall by the wayside sooner or later.'

They arrived at the airport a little after three thirty, being held up by traffic over the last two kilometres. Williams eased the Grand Cherokee into a parking space by the kerbside, directly opposite the main terminal. The milling crowds opposite offered little chance of getting into the terminal. Men, women, children, police, soldiers. Voices like their music, full volume or nothing. All vying with each other for space on the sidewalk.

Murchek appeared ten minutes later, lightweight grey suit, white shirt, dark tie, elbowing his way through the crowd. Eyes doing a quick sweep, as though he was reconnoitring a hot LZ that a helo had just deposited him in. Late thirties. Little above medium height. Broad shouldered. Lean, fit. Light-coloured crew-cut hair. Protruding ears. Unsmiling thin lips and dark eyes. Recon Marine. Every inch of him exuding Olympic-class fitness. His eyes fastened on the white Grand Cherokee. He strode across the road. Williams was standing by the rear passenger door.

'How's the weather?'

'A storm is being plotted, the old legends of heathen

mythology,' Williams replied, completing the code sequence. 'Good flight?'

'Known better.'

'You have the package?'

'Affirmative.'

'When you planning to go back to Bogotá?'

'Your discretion. Bill Rice sends his regards and said I was to ask if the ex-Navy ladies need professional field support?'

Williams chuckled and opened the passenger door. 'Sounds like Billy. Hop in, Frank. First beer's on you.'

38

Ugly Charlie had towed the B-25 inside the hangar. He had left one of the hangar doors partially open, along with workshop doors at the opposite end of the hangar. Old aviator's trick. Adapting Bernoulli's theorem, which described lift on an airfoil section. The light evening breeze increasing in speed as it flowed through the venturi tube of hangar. Increase in speed, drop in pressure. Drop in pressure, drop in temperature. Nature's air-conditioning system. Not that the decrease in temperature was much. Unbearable became bearable.

Charlie, satisfied with his application of basic physics to the environment, was now cocooned in the belly of the aircraft taking a quick drink to steady his hands before going back to work on the T.5, which had developed a hydraulic leak after his flight with Maria that morning.

Winter, reasoning there would be no flying the following day, had departed an hour before sunset. Supplies were needed. He had packed a few essentials in the Chevy truck, along with spare cans of gas from the B-25, and water for the radiator. A standby aircraft compass from the spares rack in the hangar, jury-rigged from the rear-view mirror, and the GPS to navigate across the savannah to the nearest road over a hundred kilometres away. His destination: Villavicencio.

Charlie took another pull on the bottle, reasoning with himself that the situation was already becoming impossible. Two flights and grounded. Two forty-minute sorties, and things were falling apart. Of course he had known it all along. A lifetime spent with airplanes teaches you more than the rudimentary principles of flight; teaches you that airplanes were living entities, body and soul, the whole nine yards. And you can't expect airplanes that have been sitting for years to suddenly and quite magically shake off their ills and become healthy. They were no different from people. They needed love and affection. Caring. Which left? Shit, he didn't know. Once maybe. Not any more.

The voice calling his name echoed in the hangar. He ignored it. It continued. He shook his head in dismay. No fucking peace for the wicked, Charlie boy, he muttered to himself. And crawled out through the belly hatch. Sweat dripping from his forehead.

Maria looked at the bottle in his hand and her eyes hardened. 'I thought you were fixing the airplane?'

'Am . . . just taking a break.'

Something of the old mistrust had returned. He could see it in her eyes. 'Getting drunk again, you mean. Letting Winter down – all of us down.'

White Lie

'Dutch courage,' Charlie mumbled, and shuffled away to a work bench littered with tools.

She followed him. 'You think it is wise to be working on an airplane in your condition?'

Charlie picked up a wrench and looked at it. Glassy-eyed. There was a little speech he had stored somewhere in his memory for times like this. 'My condition,' he would say quietly. 'My condition, lady, let me tell you about my condition. I was in Viet Nam before people in the Land of Sam even knew that Viet Nam was on the planet. I was flying night rescue missions in an unarmed beat-up old C-47 before you were even a twinkle in your pappy's eye. I was drinking my breakfast, lunch and dinner because I didn't have anything to make me invisible, and I sure as hell didn't want to feel the bullets tearing me apart. Wise? What's wise? Some old shits in the Pentagon sending Special Forces guys into no-go areas without proper knowledge or training and expecting guys like me to go in night after night to clean up their mess. Sure, why not? Sam gives you a medal and you take another drink and another run at the sky, all the time wondering if this is the night! Everybody had a night, except they didn't know it. On my night I got burned. Sam shipped me home and put me in a hospital for a year and gave me another medal — *and said goodbye*. Sam had no place for cripples. The drink? The drink lessens the pain, that's all. As for Wint, don't worry, I've never let him down yet.' But he didn't say it. What was the point? No one would understand. He threw the wrench down among the other tools and made his way to one of the workshop doors.

Maria watched him go, then turned to the maintenance manual. Mentally running through the work she had helped Charlie with most of the afternoon. The flaps had failed to retract after landing. The ensuing hydraulic leak being traced to a faulty nonreturn valve. They had scoured the spare-parts shelves, but without luck. Which left the dismantled single-seater. She wrote the part number on the back of her hand and went across the hangar. Hopefully, there would be one of the valves amid the unbuilt airplane. Not new. But hopefully serviceable.

One and a half hours later the part was fitted to the T.5. All that remained was to bleed the hydraulic system, replenish, hook up the mule for a function test — and pray it was cured.

She went to find Charlie. Tell him that the work was done.

He was sprawled in a chair fast asleep. Spittle running from the corner of his half-opened mouth. She shook him and he opened his right eye. The left eyelid fluttered with a nervous tic. 'What . . . what is it . . . ?' The nervousness in his voice subsided when he saw her.

'I found a nonreturn valve and fitted it. We can bleed the system and run checks in the morning.'

'Sure it was the right part number?'

'Of course. Did you change the barrel of diesel oil for the generator? It was low when I checked it this afternoon.'

'Morning. I'll do it in the morning.' His fingers plucked at the bottle by his side. He lifted it. Empty. He dropped it on the floor by the side of his chair. Looked up at her again. 'Still mad with Wint, huh?'

'Why do you say that?'

'Because he wouldn't take you with him.'

'I was angry because it is very dangerous. Especially at night. He's got a hundred kilometres before he even reaches anything that passes for a road, near Puerto Lopez, then about another eighty to Villavo. If the Rio Meta has not dried up sufficiently he could get into trouble before he gets anywhere near Puerto Lopez. That first hundred kilometres could take him three hours or more. He will need to drive slowly checking for obstacles. Hidden rocks in the grass. Soft spots. And if he hits anything at speed and wrecks the truck, what then?'

'You told him that?'

'I told him he was crazy, that there were guerrillas in the area. I said it would be safer if I went with him in the daylight.'

'And what did he say?'

'Thank you for your concern, Miss Espinosa. Don't forget to feed Charlie. I told him I was not hired as a cook . . .'

'That it?'

She pushed a strand of damp hair from her glistening forehead. 'He said something like, he was sorry for taking advantage of my sensitive highly strung nature.'

'Sounds like Wint,' Charlie mumbled.

'Then I slapped him.'

Charlie blinked. 'You did what?'

'I do not like condescending men, I slapped him – across the face.'

Charlie closed his eyes and pulled his aching body a few inches higher in the chair. He didn't need any more bad news. He'd had enough for one day. He needed sleep.

'You think I should not have done it?'

'He's having a hard time just now . . . that's all.'

'What does that mean?'

'I need to sleep . . .'

'Not until you have told me.'

What did people want from him? Why didn't they listen? He was old and tired. He'd had enough. 'Go away,' he pleaded. 'Just leave me alone.'

'You are an unwell man, Charlie. A dysfunctional alcoholic. Alcoholics hide bottles, put them in places they think their friends or family would not think of looking. Except I have watched you. I know where every bottle is – every last bottle. What would you say if I smashed them all? What would you say if there was no more vodka. Cold turkey! You know what that means, Charlie Riker. Stomach cramps, knifing pain, somebody kicking your guts out.'

Charlie was gripping the arm rests of the chair, looking sick. 'Please . . . I need it . . .'

'Tell me about Winter.'

Charlie looked around. Darting glances. A way out. Finally gave up on the idea and pulled his knees up into his stomach. The aviator of hours earlier dissolved into a shrunken old man. Eyes downcast. 'He lost his wife. He's taking it hard. Now you know.'

'Lost?'

'Died.'

'How?'

'She was killed some months back – murdered by a street gang . . . druggies . . . in Oklahoma City.'

'Then what?'

'He killed those responsible.'

No surprise. 'He told me he had come back to flying to make money. What did he do before?'

'Teacher. He taught history.'

'High school?'

'University – in Oklahoma.'

'And the Cali Cartel! What have they got to do with all of this?'

'Ask him. You got a problem with this, talk to him.'

A palpable silence. He expected more questions. But when he looked up she had gone.

39

The two local farmers were watching over their herd of cattle five kilometres east of Puerto Lopez. It was the time of year. The dry season. The brief period of activity and prosperity when stock could be transported out to the markets of the highlands. The rest of the year brought hard times for the inhabitants, with storms and floods and impassable roads. Links to the outer world cut off.

The farmers turned their attention to the lone figure in the starlight. He had appeared from the direction of Puerto Lopez, walking east along the unpaved bush road. The next town in that direction was Puerto Gaitan, more than a hundred kilometres' distance.

One of the farmers said, '*Pastuso!*'

The other laughed. Stupid indeed. No one walked out here alone at night. He was about to make a comment to his partner when the lone figure did the strangest thing. He left the road and headed off across the savannah. Moving southeast. And that way there was nothing until you reached Brazil.

White Lie

He was practically out of sight when the next curious thing happened. Lights appeared on the horizon. The faint sound of a racing engine. They watched in disbelief as the lights grew closer, converging on the lone figure. Watched as the vehicle slowed and stopped. The sound of a slamming door reached them as the vehicle accelerated away. Once on the bush road the flatbed truck swung left and passed them, heading back towards Puerto Lopez.

The second farmer said, 'Narcoguerrillas.'

His friend nodded.

Both men, who had had notions of a strange story to tell their family and friends the following morning, decided they had seen nothing.

40

More than two thousand miles away at the White House, and following the standard security check, the Director of the CIA, J.J. Eberhart, was ushered into the Roosevelt Room in the west wing, a place usually set aside for morning staff meetings. Its former name, the Fish Room, came about during Franklin Delano Roosevelt's administration when it had contained an aquarium and mementoes of the President's fishing expeditions. FDR's staff, however, had nicknamed it 'the Morgue' because so many callers sat cooling off in it. John F. Kennedy had continued the tradition of the Fish Room by having a sailfish mounted on one of the walls. It was, however, President Nixon – a firm believer in Theodore Roosevelt's foreign-policy axiom of 'speak softly and carry a big stick, you will go far' – who renamed it the Roosevelt Room to honour the twenty-sixth president, who had made the west wing of the White House a reality in 1902.

Eberhart did not give a damn about history but liked

to know the cost of things. Had been doing some checking. The original west wing had cost $65,196. He'd smiled at that. Wouldn't pay the damned architects' fees today.

The room, furnished in Queen Anne and Chippendale styles, was warmed by a blazing log fire, alongside which stood Jack Downs, Chief of Staff. A tall man with the air of a distracted savant. The charcoal-grey suit, white shirt and black tie giving him the appearance of a funeral home director. In fact he was a retired four-star admiral. A systems analyst. Navy thinker. Former Rhodes scholar. Worse, to Eberhart's way of thinking, a born-again Christian. The CIA Director did not rate him. Too slow. A government servant for too many years. Not seeing the big picture any more. Too full of crap.

'Nice to see you, J.J. The President sends his apologies but he's still tied up with the Chinese delegation. Doesn't look like he'll be through until twenty-one hundred hours. He asked me to brief you.'

Eberhart laid his briefcase on the conference table and selected a chair at the mid-point. He unbuttoned his pale-grey pinstriped suit jacket and sat, careful to ease the trousers up at the knee. Wool stretched. Trousers became misshapen. Eberhart was conscious that presentation was important in business. Private sector or government. A smart man is a confident man. Confidence is exuded in an aura that is picked up by others. Smart people generally succeeded. He was living proof.

Downs sat opposite. 'Concerning White Knight,' he started. 'We need your people out.'

Eberhart was surprised. He hadn't been expecting

this. They were there for his protection. 'All our people are out.'

Downs had anticipated the shouted whisper. The sandpaper monotone rasp. Even so, his eyes involuntarily screwed up. 'We're not talking about the commercial attaché in Bogotá. We're talking about Oscar's people. No one's fault, J.J., I just happen to know they borrowed a yacht from Ike Benson in Key West. He's an old navy buddy of mine. Seems they might have gone on a junket to Cartagena.'

Eberhart flushed, partly in anger, more so because of his own ineptness in having too much confidence in Oscar Porteous. 'Cartagena? You're sure?'

'DEA had some trouble down there. One of their agents was taken out. Seems he'd just met up with two of your people. They moved on to Santa Marta. Bill Rice in Bogotá sent one of his people in to meet with them today. No contact since.' Downs reached up and tugged at his left earlobe. Then rubbed his chin. The hand finally gave up fidgeting and joined the other one on the table. Clasped in prayer-like posture. 'We have a situation developing, J.J. A high-powered Colombian attorney is trying to broker a deal with his government and the White House, the result of which could lead to the extradition of a number of high-powered drug lords to the US for trial. We can't afford the situation to be compromised.'

He slid a document across the table. Eberhart picked it up. It was a sensitive top-secret report from the President's Foreign Intelligence Advisory Board. The six-page report charged that the CIA had been seriously lacking in its intelligence gathering in Colombia and suggested that the diplomatic middle road should be taken. Among those behind the report was the Chairman of the PFIAB. A man whom Eberhart disliked. The feeling, it seemed, was mutual.

Eberhart pushed the document back to Downs, and leaned back in his chair. His eyes angry. 'We're in the process, have been for the past few weeks, of wrapping up the White Knight operation. I'm led to believe that we may be only one or two days away from obtaining the Cali Cartel's new export arrangements. This isn't bullshit, Jack. This is for real. We're about to hand you chapter and verse on how those bastards are shipping thousands of kilos of drugs into this country every week. And now you're telling me some fucking ambulance chaser is *trying* to broker a deal . . . Trying shouldn't cut it, Jack. The figures . . . you want the per-annum export figures? The ones we know at least. Cocaine – five billion. Heroin – two billion and climbing, because they're taking advantage of the transport networks established for the cocaine trade. Then again Colombia is the world's third leading producer of marijuana. The DEA, through the taxpayers' pocket, aerial-sprayed most of the marijuana crop with herbicides back in the eighties. Just about wiped it out. Then we back off, and everything is the way it was. What else do you need, Jack, what other illegal exports? Emeralds! What about animals and birds? Know what a macaw brings in this country and Europe, Jack? Up to ten grand. What about money? You want to know what else is undermining the American economy? Colombia is one of the leading producers of counterfeit notes in the world. About a quarter of all the fake US dollar bills circulating in the world are printed in Cali. And you're telling me that some shyster lawyer is *trying* to broker a deal.'

The Chief of Staff looked away from Eberhart. Nervous. Thoughtful. That morning, as every morning, he had sat down to breakfast and spent a few minutes reading from the Christian Science lesson. The lesson for that day had been: 'Vehemently tell your patient that he must awake. Turn his gaze from the false evidence of the senses . . . look inward.' He had underlined the words, 'Trials are proof of God's care'. And here was a man before him whom he sensed to be one of those trials. Known for his defiant, buccaneering air. Known for saying and doing anything to win a point. 'I appreciate what you're saying, J.J., but we must try and control the situation in a less inflammatory manner. The President made it very clear to me that nothing must stand in the way of this new and very possible initiative.'

Eberhart's fingers tapped a slow rhythm on the table. 'President's making a big mistake, Jack.'

'His judgement is not without reason.'

'Root out the corrupters and the corruption will follow, you mean?'

'Political fidelity to the people.'

'First month of his first term, and he's already laying the foundation for the second, huh?'

'I'm sure he hasn't given that a thought.'

'And if you were not such a gentleman, you'd call that remark asinine. Right?'

'I'm not being kind, or solicitous. I'm merely relaying an executive decision – there can be no compromise. The word is, abort.'

Eberhart stood up, gathered his briefcase and began

to walk towards the door. 'Still reading the *Christian Science Monitor*, Jack?'

Downs managed a tight-lipped smile. 'Yes.'

'Next time Jesus and Moses drop in for a chat, ask them which hooker they'd rather spend the night with. One from their home town, or one from the enemy's. Bottom line, Jack: know who's fucking who.'

Back in his house in Georgetown less than an hour later, Eberhart placed a call to Oscar Porteous. The conversation was brief. *Abort the mission*. He had long ago learned to roll with the punches.

41

Villavicencio.

Red Stevens was waiting at the bar in the Hotel del Llano, when Winter arrived. Two bottles of Cerveza Aguila in front of him. Piped music and conversation filtering through the cigarette smoke, which hung heavy in the air.

'Took your bloody time,' Stevens said, in a deep Aussie drawl. 'I've been drinking for both of us for the past hour.' He slid one of the beers towards the Englishman.

Winter, his blue aircrew shirt and dark trousers covered in a fine layer of dust, pulled out a stool and sat down. Felt the air conditioning chilling the sweat on his body. 'Thought I did pretty well, under four hours.'

Stevens laughed. The same old contagious laugh that Winter remembered. 'I was referring to the Christmas cards over the last twelve or thirteen years. "Have to get together in the New Year for a beer" – that's what you put in all of them. I was beginning to think we'd both be dead and buried before you got round to it. So how's it going?'

'Can't complain. You?'

'Ah, you know, making a buck or two selling aeroplanes, nothing to set the world alight.'

'Wasn't sure you'd be here until I picked up Ramon back down by Puerto Lopez. Said you flew in this afternoon.'

'He's with you?'

'Unloading some gear off the truck. I invited him in for a beer, but he wants to get back to his wife. Said he'd join us for breakfast in the morning. What about the things I asked for?'

The Australian ran his hand across his balding head. 'No problems. Ramon phoned me last week with your message, then faxed me the shopping list from the hotel here. The women's clothes threw me — no way was I going round the stores in Caracas buying knickers and dresses . . .'

'You didn't get them?'

'Yeah, sent my wife out. Silly bitch now thinks I've got a *niña* on the side.' Stevens picked up his beer. 'Anyway, this is long overdue . . . here's to the reunion.' They drank.

Winter took a pack of Particulares from his shirt pocket. The last pack from the carton he'd picked up in Miami what seemed like a lifetime ago. When it was finished he'd quit. The anger had eased slightly. He could manage without. 'Want one?'

'Quit. Five years now. Can't you tell?' He patted his beer gut. 'Put on a couple of stones.'

'No, hadn't really noticed,' Winter remarked. But he had. The layers of fat, behind the slackened muscle of middle age, had removed all traces of the once gangling suntanned younger man. The crop of red hair gone now. What little hair that was left was grey and brittle. The liver spots on the backs of the hands. The sunken, almost lifeless eyes. The dozen years had made more difference than he thought possible. One day, it seemed, you were still hanging on to the last vestiges of youth, the next you had crossed a line you'd suspected was there but had never seen. The truth was he wouldn't have recognised Red Stevens if he hadn't been the only gringo sitting at the bar. Even the canary-yellow shirt and the bright-green trousers wouldn't have convinced him, even though Red had always been one for dressing brightly when out for a night on the town. Perhaps the laugh, if he'd heard it.

Stevens said, 'Remember the last time we had a beer?'

'Caravelle Hotel, Ho Chi Minh City.'

'Yeah, the Caravelle. And that woman who ran the bookshop in Dong Khoi street; you know, the one with the great figure – had the hots for you.'

'I took her out to dinner a couple of times, that's all.'

'Anything to get a discount on all those books you used to buy . . . Yeah, great times. Had some knockout parties at the Caravelle, didn't we?'

'We did that. Owned by one of the generals, wasn't it?'

'Everything was owned by the generals, probably still is. Kick-back for a job well done. Russian advisers in every bloody shadow, hiding around every corner. Always said they deserved each other, the Vietnamese and the Soviets. Rough lot.'

'Paid well enough, though.'

'We could have done better, Wint. How much you think they made on all that ex-US surplus gear we hauled to Iran? Always thought we should have hijacked a couple of those C-130s, full of spares, and flown them to somewhere like Libya; would have got a good price out of Gaddafi.'

'And a bullet in the back.'

'Shit, we still got those waiting. Why d'you think I live under a false name in bloody Caracas? Far rather be Jack-the-Lad back in Melbourne. My kids still stay in touch though, through a series of post office box numbers. Grown up now, of course. One of the clever sods made me a grandfather couple of years back. Now that *does* take the wind out of your sails.'

Winter smiled. 'What else do you do, apart from the aeroplane business?'

'Not a lot. When I quit the merc business, I came back here and tried my hand at the emeralds – a place called Muzo, some way north of here.'

'Any luck?'

'A bad back after two years in a two-kilometre-long gorge digging out a river bed with a bunch of *guaqueros*. Got a few beauts, sort of insurance for old age. Decided in the end that I wasn't cut out to be a labourer, so I headed over to Caracas, found myself a good woman – she's a dentist, got her own practice now – and set up an aviation sales company. Advertised a lot in *Trade-a-Plane* in the States, picked up a few good regular clients over the years. Done a few deals with Ron Connell. You remember him. Kiwi. He's in the aeroplane sales business these days, based out of Corpus Christi. Up-and-down business of course, but it evens out and I get to spend time with the wife. Civilised, after all the tricks we used to get up to.'

Winter watched the barman for a moment, busy making up what looked like a frozen Margarita. Julia's favourite cocktail on a warm Friday evening, when they would meet at a bar in Oklahoma City's Brick Town. And have a few drinks. A meal. And talk about the weekend ahead. Civilised. It had been for a moment.

Stevens continued, 'Anyway, Ramon told me you were holed up at an old guerrilla outpost in the middle of nowhere. Back out of retirement, then, are you?'

'Temporarily.'

'Thought you'd had enough of aeroplanes and airports and foreign lands.'

'Like those tropical islands they use in the rum adverts, you mean? Great to wake up to those bleached white beaches, and greener-than-green palms and aquamarine seas, for a week or two, but after that paradise begins to wear thin. You're craving for the city backstreets and the drizzle and the pollution of a million car exhausts.'

'We were always craving the nine-to-five job at the bank, weren't we? And the two point something kids, and the little woman that was always there? So what happened to the teaching job back in the States?'

A question he didn't want to answer. He compromised. 'Still there. Just let's say that this is my vacation. My few weeks back on the tropical island.'

'Need any assistance?'

'You offering?'

'Depends on how dangerous the tropical island is.

My lady wife'd get real upset if I went off and got myself killed, or something silly like that.'

'Surveillance easy enough?'

'That what the VHF hand-held radios are for?'

'How many did you bring?'

'The four you asked for. Icom IC-A2s.'

The hotel resident band, back from their break, suddenly burst forth into a new set. Local joropo music. Loud enough for the stacked pyramid of glasses behind the bar to rattle dangerously. As of one mind, the two men finished their drinks and moved out of the bar.

'Restaurant'll be quieter,' Stevens shouted, as they went out of the door.

And it was. And nearly empty now. The diners having migrated to the noisier part of the hotel to join in the festivities. A pretty female waitress came and laid out the silverware. They ordered steaks and beer.

'Ramon said he put markers down for you to get out of the savannah. Neat trick, but you want to make sure you pull them up when you go back; you know what these nosy buggers are like.'

'Planned to do that on the return, Red, but thanks for reminding me. What sort of plane did you bring in?'

'King Air B-200.'

'Good range?'

'Couple of thousand miles.'

'Can you afford to be away from your business for about ten days?'

'Not a problem. Just need to phone my sales kiddy and the wife. Let them know I'm doing a demo to a prospective customer over this way – we are talking over this way, aren't we?'

'Cali.'

Stevens pulled a face. 'Shitty place. Could probably do with one or two lads to come in with me – moral support. You know what it's like for us gringos.'

'I'd already decided on that. Need at least three of you to maintain a round-the-clock surveillance. Ramon's got a couple of strong-arm boys, they can go with you. They've fought with various guerrilla factions at one time or another, so they can take orders.'

'Weapons?'

'None needed. Passive surveillance. I've got a couple of books in my kit on wildlife. Covers more than five hundred bird species recorded in Colombia. You're out with a couple of local guides, bird watching.'

'Going back to Ramon, how trustworthy is he?'

'You've been to the tower, heard the babel. You tell me.'

Stevens shrugged. 'Highest bidder!'

'More than likely any bidder. Everybody in this country is on the take, after all. No different from what we had in the Middle East, Africa, South East Asia.'

'His two boys the same, then?'

'Yes.'

'How'd you meet up with them?'

Winter outlined their arrival at Eerie One. How he had found out on the first evening that Ramon had a truck hidden away in the trees. How he'd paid Ramon to take his people out before dawn and lay down a track across the savannah. And how he'd prearranged to meet up with him the following Friday evening a mile south of the road that ran into Puerto Lopez.

'How secure are you out in the bush?'

'I'm hoping a couple of months. Unless Ramon finds someone willing to pay for what he knows.'

'And there was me believing soldiering was still an honourable profession.'

'Not any more, Red. It's changed. I think hookers have more honour – at least you get what you pay for.'

The Australian laughed. 'And sometimes something you didn't . . . So what happens down in Cali?'

'Okay, here's the situation. I need you to position down there as soon as possible. Ten-day surveillance in the bush. You brought the binoculars?'

'Yeah. Seven by fifty. Two pairs.'

'Nothing gets written down, except your bird-watching notes. No taped messages. All observations, timings, changes of personnel under surveillance memorised. Relayed to me one week from today. I'll give you locations and relay details in my room after dinner. I'm quite certain that the group of waiters standing over by the door are just waiters, but I'd hate one to be a lip reader who happens to work for somebody else.'

The waitress returned and served the steaks and salads and beer. Stevens whistled softly as she walked away. 'Nice body. What we used to call a file-under-carnal-knowledge female.'

'We did, and you did.'

They both laughed.

'You mentioned two jocks. Anyone I know?'

'Charlie Riker.'

'Jeez, is he still around? How's he doing?'

'Not too good healthwise, but he's still the best flyer and fixer I know.'

'And the other?'

'A lady driver we collected on the way.'

'Ah, the clothes. Explains it. Pretty?'

'Good hands.'

Stevens cut into his steak and chuckled. 'Now I know you're growing old. Tits and legs suddenly became hands.'

'Tits and legs don't fly aeroplanes, Red.'

They ate in silence for a while. The restaurant empty now. Most of the waiters gone. The girl that had served them standing with another waiter, a young man; both shuffling their feet, glancing at their watches. Waiting to close the restaurant and go to whatever party awaited them. Winter noticed. Briefly envied their youth. Or was it their happiness?

Stevens finished his meal and wiped his mouth with his napkin. 'Best steak I've had in a while. Good as anything you'll get in Caracas. Says something for a place like this. Not so the coffee, though. Had some earlier. Pig's piss. Bloody amazing as Colombian coffee is supposed to be the best in the world.'

'Probably the water. Treated with chemical purifiers.'

'More than not. Anyway, two questions for you.'

'I'm listening.'

'Do I get to know the bottom line on what the surveillance is all about?'

'Might not be wise.'

'I'm thinking of keeping Ramon's two guys in the dark. I can only do that if I know exactly what's going on.'

'And I'm thinking of your safety.'

'Christ, man . . . forget that. Womb and tomb are safe, the rest's a bloody lottery.'

'Your wife . . .'

'Pulling your leg.'

Winter put his fingers to his lips. The waitress returned with the bill.

It was as they were leaving the restaurant that Winter said, 'What was the second question? You did say there were two.'

'Oh, nothing important. Just how much am I going to earn for my ten days on the tropical island?'

'Enough. You can pick up a bit more if you're interested.'

'Go on.'

'Two things, the first of which is: I need details of scheduled cargo flights out of Central America or Mexico into the US. Only slow movers though — piston engined equipment.'

'Time-frame?'

'Say, over the next ten weeks.'

'And number two?'

'Something more than passive surveillance. Still interested?'

'Good money?'

'Phenomenal — plus you get the chance to become a hero.'

Stevens laughed his contagious laugh. 'Ahh! You got me now. Always wanted to be one of those.'

42

It was nine o'clock the following evening when Luis Figueras received the phone call at his luxurious penthouse suite at the Palace Hotel in Milan. The call was from his right-hand man in Cali, Mauricio. Up to that moment, Luis had been enjoying the day: his surprise shopping expedition for Ana, the early dinner served in their suite, the private fashion show which was now in progress, Ana having gone to the bedroom to try on another new dress, followed hopefully by the exotic lingerie he had chosen for her. Even the paperwork before him was a joy. Now the phone call from Cali. It had to be of an urgent nature. Something to bring him back to earth.

He was sitting at the long dining table. Silver candelabra, legal papers in neat individual piles, and a cold half-drunk cup of coffee at his elbow. He removed his glasses. 'Yes, Mauricio, what is it? Problems?' He closed his eyes and squeezed the bridge of his nose between thumb and forefinger. Concentrating.

It was a bad line. Satellite echo making fluent speech difficult.

'My apologies for disturbing you, Señor Figueras, but I thought you would want to know.' A pause.

'Know what?' His words echoed back a millisecond later. As though he was having a conversation with himself.

'A pilot at the airport. He told me that the man you were looking for – Winter – rented his plane for two hours. He told the pilot he was a tourist. He was taking video film of the area west of the airport . . . Señor, you are still there?'

Something clicked in the attorney's mind. 'What day was this, Mauricio?'

'Thursday of last week, nine days ago. Early in the morning. Between seven and eight o'clock.'

'What kind of airplane was it?'

'Pardon, Señor, I do not understand.'

'What kind of airplane? How many engines?'

'I am not sure – you wish me to find out?'

'Immediately, Mauricio, and phone me back. And one other thing, Mauricio, find out what colour the airplane is.'

'Colour?'

'Colour.'

Twenty minutes later the phone rang again. Luis answered it and made a brief note on the bottom of an envelope.

He put the phone down and looked at what he had written. Trying to make sense of it.

Cessna 210. Single engine. Red and white.

The same aircraft that had flown near the house in

the mountains on the morning he and his father had had the meeting with the American, Mr Walker? It had to be.

Taking video film. Why would he do that?

43

Winter struggled through the blinding dust storm. Driving at a walking pace across the savannah, as he had for most of the day. He hadn't found any of Ramon's markers so was navigating on the latitude and longitude of Eerie One programmed into the GPS from the time of their arrival in the B-25. A magnetic heading and range in nautical miles. The elapsed-time information was worthless, as he had to stop every kilometre or less, and get out of the truck and check the surface ahead. Once he went so far ahead, he couldn't find the Chevy for twenty minutes. After that he took the GPS – programmed with the truck's position – with him.

The ground-powder dust seeped through air vents and door frames into the truck's cab. Winter could smell it. Taste it. Hear it – a bombardment of horizontally driven fine dirt particles, not unlike hail, except that the temperature would need to have been seventy degrees lower. Or perhaps the sound was nearer to that of flight through light persistent rain, the rising and falling hiss on the airframe. The opaque windows, dirty cloud. The rocking from time to time, the bumpiness of such a flight. The sweaty-faced reflection in the rear-view mirror a solo aviator looking for a break in the weather. The reassuring glimpse of cross-runways through a hole in the saffron clouds.

Except instead of runways he saw Julia's face. The night she had asked him about his day. And he had told her about one of his students who had stopped at a petrol station the previous evening after class. It was as he was opening the door to get back into the car that the gang of three kids, two boys and a girl – all high on cocaine – had attacked him. The eldest boy had beaten him about the head with an iron bar. Smashing most of the bones in his face. Leaving him lying on the ground, one eye hanging out. Just a story. A sad story. Everyday American life. He wished it had been the cross-runways.

He reached for the water bottle. The distilled tastelessness, clean but foreign, as alien as the unseen plains before him. There had been better days, but he tried not to think about them. Just concentrated on the task in hand. The falling fuel gauge, with the last of the fuel. The rising water temperature gauge. What looked like a slow puncture on one of the rear tyres he and Charlie had repaired. Willing everything to stay together long enough.

In the end, counting down the last twenty kilometres, one by one, by one. Ten hours to travel ninety-nine kilometres. The jaundiced dust was deepening in colour by the time he reached Eerie One. Nearing sunset. He checked the GPS and pulled the truck into the trees one kilometre from the hangar and switched off the engine and sat for a moment. Window open. Listening.

Hooking the sheathed Malayan parang onto his belt, he left the truck and moved off into the trees. No sound. He tried again to pick out the distinctive thumping echo of the diesel generator in the blockhouse. Nothing but the wind moving through the trees. The blockhouse itself was empty. The two generators that Charlie had fixed, cold. Had not been running for a long time. He checked the diesel supply drum. Empty. He went outside and checked the other barrels. Four of the ten were full. Now he knew his instincts had been right.

Charlie leaving messages.

He circled west through the trees towards the opposite side of the hangar, entering it from an unlocked workshop door on the west side. Pulled it closed behind him. Moved silently through to the hangar. Saw the aluminium finish of the fighters caught in the yellow rays from the roof skylights, looking like brass rubbings on a derelict factory floor.

He stood like that for more than a minute. Completely still. Letting his eyes grow accustomed to the fading light, picking out likely obstacles on the hangar floor, then made his way to the far side of the hangar, where the racks of five-hundred-pound bombs were lined up with neat precision. The two nickel-cadmium aircraft batteries, wired in parallel, were exactly as he had left them. He worked quickly and efficiently for close to forty-five seconds, then sat down on the hangar floor, his back resting against one of the bombs.

It was the last cigarette of the last pack. He lit it and waited. Listened to the wind as it whined through a door being opened. Faded as it was closed. Then the light but unmistakable footsteps. Two different treads. Moving apart. Made out the first shape in his two o'clock position ducking silently under the wing of one of the Lightnings

He looked down at the cigarette in his hand. Put it to his mouth. A last red glow in the gathering darkness before he stubbed it out on the hangar floor. Then turned his head in the direction of the first figure and called out, 'Welcome to Los Llanos, I've been expecting you.'

A nervy silence. 'Are you Winter?' American accent.

'Depends.'

'On what?'

'You giving me the right answers.'

'I hardly think you're in a position to be asking questions.'

Winter said, 'And why do you say that? You think two-to-one odds are good enough?'

A pause. 'We have Riker and the woman.'

'Means nothing to me. So who are you? Same guys that were watching me and Charlie in Key West?'

Silence again. Speaking volumes. 'Who said we were in Key West.'

'Old guy in a black Lincoln Town Car monitored a phone call that Charlie Riker made to Johnny Shoosh in the Everglades. Convinced the motel manager he was FBI. First mistake, the manager was an ex-con, doesn't like Feds – just money. I therefore reasoned that if you had been FBI you would have picked me up there and then. DEA, unlikely, as they are inclined to get overexcited, shoot first, ask questions later, besides which a telephone call to a reputed drug dealer in the Everglades would hardly warrant a bust. Which leaves the CIA. The international superbowl players. Do you have a name?'

'Williams.'

'So, Mr Williams, what is it I can do for you?'

'One of the world's most wanted terrorists. Why should we want you to do anything?'

'Terrorist? Soldier, you mean.'

'Is that what you call yourself?'

'No different from you, Mr Williams. We both kill for money.'

'Not my interpretation.'

'Double agents working against *and* for the old Soviet regime. Selling out their country's secrets and personnel behind a cloak of respectability and loyalty to the American flag. Conducting private little wars to enable the dictatorship of a Third World country to be transferred to a White House-favoured front runner – and denying any responsibility for the dead and dying! At least *we* remain loyal to the causes we fight for. So what is it you want? Or perhaps you're here to kill me. Perform the last rites.'

'Might be doing the world a favour,' Williams said.

'Married, are you, Mr Williams?'

'I don't see that has anything to do with it.'

'It might when you go home in a body bag. Still, I'm sure you've left your affairs in order. She'll be well taken care of. Young enough to find another husband, perhaps.'

Williams stared at the shape in the shadows. In a recess of his mind, something stirred. 'You're bluffing.'

'In the same way the gun you are holding in your hand is not loaded, you mean. No, I never bluff. What's the point? Somebody might call you. Quite simply, in my left hand I am holding a pressure switch. That pressure switch is connected to a battery power source on one side, and to a detonator on the other. The detonator is hooked up to the five-hundred-pound bomb I'm sitting next to. Better yet, there are a total of thirty-one bombs lined up against this wall. One second after you squeeze the trigger, Mr Williams, I will release the switch . . .' The words faded.

Williams waited for more. But there was no more. Just silence. Allowing his imagination to go to work. The one-hundred-thousand-dollar information from Werner Stock the previous afternoon, no idea of his source, that was not for sale; but 'guaranteed information' as he had put it. The early-evening flight to Bogotá with Murchek and Owens. Being collected by two local employees at Bogotá airport in two Toyota Landcruisers. Stopping at a hotel for a meal. Then a long overnight drive out of the mountains. Rock falls. Badly potholed roads. Lunatics in buses nearly wiping them out on three occasions. The early-morning drive across flat savannah as the wind began to whip up the dust. Making the old paramilitary base moments before the visibility dropped to zero. Finding Riker and the woman. And a hangar without electrical power. A moment's panic, until Riker had been given a drink, and told them Winter would be back by early afternoon. That he had gone to find spare parts for the diesel generator the previous night. Then the waiting. And the uncertainty as daylight began to fade.

Finally, he was there.

Jesus, they hadn't even seen or heard the guy arrive. One minute they had a lookout staked. The next Frank Murchek had decided to take a walk beyond the perimeter for a piss. And had found a truck half hidden in the trees. Engine still hot. Williams looked anxiously through the darkness towards Murchek now. Couldn't make him out. Then back to Winter. And in his mind Edeyrn Owens's voice chiding him. *Something that concerns me, however, he only operates in Third World environments . . . if you're looking for him he's probably already got you in his sights . . .* 'We'd like to talk to you,' Williams said, finally.

'You've been doing that.'

'We have a proposition.'

'My hand is growing tired, Mr Williams, so let me give you mine. You and your boy both walk over here and lay your guns on the floor. You then go and bring Charlie Riker to me.'

Owens was talking to him again: *. . . so the wise man confounds you by making you believe the opposite . . . I think he might be a frightening chess player.* For Williams it was a moment of tachypsychia — the release of adrenaline causing the body speed to increase and real time to apparently slow down. He witnessed a procession of framed pictures. The tree-shaded street in San Diego where his parents lived. The pretty girl next door he had married, her face, her breasts, her laughter. The faces of brother officers in the wardroom of the USS *Forrestal*. His children playing on a swing. The house in Jackson Place and Oscar Porteous. The stern-faced Alice with the grey cropped hair, who brought him his coffee, and never spoke more than two words. The smiling Edeyrn Owens.

I think he might be a frightening chess player . . .
Bluff.

He needed an additional safety factor. You didn't hand over your weapons to a man like this.

Or did you?

Twenty minutes had elapsed, in which time Charlie had restored power to the hangar complex. Now Winter and Williams were alone in the hangar, sitting in the pilot and copilot seats of the B-25.

Williams had observed the man. A statue's impassivity. An almost terrifying serenity. Owens might have been right: one sensed something here, danger most of all. Not that he would ever admit it. Instead he would overcome it. 'We have a proposition,' he said, his fingers playing with the gold Dunhill cigarette lighter.

'So you mentioned earlier. I'm listening.'

Williams's eyes cast quickly out of the starboard window, taking in the military hardware. From this height not unlike the cramped below-deck hangar space on aircraft carriers he had served on. Even the smells of machinery were familiar. 'We are trying to obtain certain information on the Cali Cartel. We think you may be able to help us.'

'What information, exactly?'

'Francisco Figueras. One of the druggies you killed in Oklahoma City. He was the youngest son of the head of the Cali Cartel, as you may be aware. Whereas we appreciate what you did was of great service to the

322

American people, other government agencies hold different views. Putting that aside for a moment, though, the Cali Cartel, the main player in this country's drug-export drive, has recently changed its export routes. We are attempting to find out what these routes are.'

'Francisco Figueras? What if I said I had never even met the man, let alone killed him?'

'Police work,' Williams replied quickly. 'I'm just telling you what I know.'

'As for the Cali Cartel, what makes you think I would know anything about their business — their export routes?'

'We don't, but as we seem to have a common enemy, we think you may be able to find out.'

'Joint-forces exercise, you mean?'

'Something like that. Perhaps we would try to get you an amnesty. Wipe the slate clean.'

Winter smiled bleakly. 'What if I said your people have a reputation for interpreting democracy's moral and political values with the finesse of Attila the Hun? Not my words, but those of an ex-FBI agent I met a few years ago in Oklahoma City. He was working towards his master's at my university. He also said that most FBI guys he'd known were scared shitless of CIA spooks, reckoned you used people in the field and when their usefulness ran out they were paid off with a bullet in the head. Any truth in those rumours, Mr Williams?'

'We conduct our activities and ourselves according to the highest standards of integrity, morality and honour and according to the spirit and letter of our law and Constitution — you have my word.'

Was that an answer?

'What else?'

'This airplane. We purchased it from Werner Stock in Santa Marta, bill of sale signed by the seller. The purchaser's details are blank, fill in what you like. If that's not enough, we'll turn a blind eye to whatever you have in mind for the collective hardware out there.'

'And if I tell you I'm not interested you'll tip off the cartel boys on my location!'

'No need to do that, the word's already out – how we found you.'

'Expected.'

'Puts you in harm's way.'

'I'm aware of that.'

'We can help.'

'So you said.'

'Is that a yes?'

'An observation. I'm afraid I can't help you.'

'What about your wife, Julia? Don't you think you owe her something? I'm not talking about punitive action against a few people in the Cali Cartel, or a few druggies on the streets of Oklahoma City. I'm talking about a major blow to the drug industry, closing down their shipment lines into the US. Your wife was making a positive contribution to that programme by educating parents as to the problems our children are facing, how schools nationwide have become the target of drug pushers who work on the maxim: start them young and you've got them for ever. Our only hope is to eradicate the source.'

Winter offered no reply, allowing the American to brood on the silence, at the same time staring out through the windscreen, at the way the hangar neon lights accentuated the crazing of the Plexiglas, a thousand tiny veins spreading like crab-grass, growing a little more with every day. Old age, fatigue, it didn't matter which way you viewed it, the aeroplane was a totally unairworthy piece of junk. He wondered how long it would be before the glass gave out altogether. Hoped it would last long enough for what he had planned.

Williams said, 'Only one source maybe, but the biggest. Eighty per cent of the world's cocaine is shipped out of Colombia, most of it by the Cali Cartel.'

'You're wasting your time, Mr Williams. There are only two ways of dealing with the drug problem. One, execute all those involved. No trials or smart lawyers, just a few cents for the price of a bullet. Two, legalise the stuff – the same way you did with alcohol when Prohibition was repealed.'

'Too many government officials are getting rich leaving things just the way they are. Only way I can fight back is by trying to stem the flow. A finger in the dyke today just might result in some honest politicians tomorrow, who will finally do something that is in the interest of the people.'

'Until then it's capricious winds and uncaring Providence, you mean?'

'When has it been any different?'

'And you think a new dawn of politics and truth is just around the corner?'

Williams smiled. 'If I didn't believe that I wouldn't be here now. If you didn't believe that, you wouldn't have wasted six years of your life in the teaching profession.'

Winter was silent a long time.

Long enough for Williams to understand. Something Owens had once told him: love letters carried close to the heart sometimes wore other perfumes. 'An amnesty would give you a new start – legal this time.'

'Guarantees?' Winter asked.

'You have my word – written confirmation if you wish.'

'How long to get the written confirmation?'

Williams rubbed his chin. 'Next weekend.'

'An exchange then. Your amnesty document for information on the Cali Cartel's export operation.'

'When?'

'One week.'

'You'll have it by then?' A hint of surprise in Williams's voice.

'Yes.'

'How can we be certain the information is valid?'

'The source might convince you.'

'And how would you deliver it?'

'A messenger will drop it off to whatever address you say. In exchange the messenger will collect a signed hard-copy CIA document outlining amnesty arrangements for myself. It will also exonerate Charles Riker and Maria Espinosa from any crimes, real or imagined.'

'Agreed,' Williams said. 'What about local support – with the war games you're planning?'

'Who said I was planning war games?'

'These old fighter aircraft and the bombs!'

'Those planes haven't flown in years – need to be

stripped down and rebuilt. No, we're just patching up the B-25. Got a few bullet holes at Canaveral.'

'They say you were in the British SAS, that right?'

'Wrong man, I'm afraid.'

'Kind of you-have-to-play-dirty-to-win outfit.'

'If you need something for your field report, Mr Williams, why not try: aeroplane dealer and his two A & P mechanics restoring classic warbirds.'

Williams slipped the Dunhill into his shirt pocket and struggled from the cramped copilot station. 'Perhaps.' He moved a few feet aft and paused. 'You taught history, is that right?'

'Why'd you ask?'

'I thought your technical background would have led you down one of the science tracks. History is such a dead, dry subject.'

A flicker of a smile on the serious face. 'On the contrary, it's the best-kept secret in the world. All the answers are there.'

44

'Not from the shallow gene pool you imagined, is he?' Owens remarked.

They were driving across the savannah, following Murchek and his team away from Eerie One, routing a different way out of the Meta Department of Los Llanos for security reasons. It was a little after nine p.m. No moon. Snatches of accordion music and static hiss drifting from the radio speakers.

Williams said, 'Anyone can pull a stunt like that. Anyway, I never said he was an idiot.'

'You implied.'

'Perhaps.'

'So what did you find out?'

'Looks like he's planning an airstrike against the cartel.'

'Is he now? He told you that?'

'Not in so many words.'

'You're sure that's not another of his games?'

'An actor, not a reactor, you mean.'

'Some people never reach cognitive maturity, Tanner. I'm inclined to believe, however, that Winter was born with it.'

Williams held his left arm outside the window, enjoying the cooling breeze on his skin. 'There's nothing abstract in revenge. Think about it, Edeyrn. You've been in the mercenary business most of your life, made a lot of money. You see an opportunity to get out before old age catches up with you. What would you do? Retire to a little ranch in South America, find a wife, raise a few kids, and live a long and stress-free life? Or would you go into teaching? Teaching's a vocation, right? A highly stressful vocation. You need a passion to get into that business – it certainly isn't about money. But that's what Winter does. Fulfills a lifelong ambition to teach. And being something of the scholar when it comes to history, he does a pretty good job of it. Then, somebody comes along and takes the six years' hard work away from him, puts him back on the street. On the run. So now what has he got? Other than being raised from the dead and put back into circulation . . . back on all the old hit lists? Enough to spoil anyone's day. So now as an afterthought, he turns to the only other thing he knows how to do. Killing people. And why would you stop at knocking off a few worthless druggies when you have a chance to take out the first team?'

Owens yawned and stretched. 'How about: he could have remained in his teaching job if he hadn't decided to go after the gang members who killed his wife?'

'No, he was worried. Justifiably so. He would have known that as the husband he'd have been a suspect. That the police would have been running their background checks. Trying to pick holes in his alibis. Inadvertently finding out that he wasn't the mild-mannered teacher he professed to be! Maybe if he'd sat quietly he would have got away with it – but that wasn't a risk he was prepared to take.'

'So, what else did he say?'

'I gave him the B-25 and the promise of an amnesty in exchange for information on the cartel's new shipping arangements.'

'And he accepted?'

'Yes. Completion next weekend.'

'You believe him?'

'Why not?'

'What about the amnesty you offered?'

'Official, under certain circumstances.'

'Like living long enough to enjoy the spoils of victory, you mean? You have something in mind?'

'Under consideration. I thought you might have an idea.'

Owens was quiet for a while, eyes drawn to the headlight-lit savannah undulating before them like a gentle ocean swell. The red taillights some way ahead, sending meaningless morse through the clouds of drifting dust. 'Where's Murchek taking us?'

'A little detour to the west, to a track that leads north to the Bogotá road.'

'Sounds like a long night,' Owens murmured drowsily.

Williams tapped his fingers on the steering wheel in time to the faint accordion music, going over the conversation he'd had with Winter again and again. Looking for something he had missed. 'Did you find anything out from Riker and the woman?'

'Might have got something out of Riker, but not

with that young lady at his side. She made it known in no uncertain terms that we were p.n.g. Murchek's gung-ho attitude didn't help either – the Marines don't have a people-skills programme, do they? I offered to make the coffee in an attempt to bring her round, but it seems she has a passionate hatred of all things federal.'

'You think she and Winter . . .'

'Why not? Rough trade, as we used to say in the East, but then any port in a storm. She's probably superseded Riker as first lieutenant – chlamydia and all.'

'Chlamydia?'

'Nice word for VD.'

'Ah.'

'You don't mind if I have a nap for a minute or two? It's been a long day or two – not as young as I used to be.'

'Go ahead.'

'Wake me when you get tired. I'll take over.'

Williams said, 'One last thing. You remember telling me Winter was arrested in Northern Ireland and transported back to England for trial. Do you know how he escaped?'

'Didn't I give you that information when you phoned me in Miami?'

'Not that I recall.'

'Something to do with a light plane,' Owens said, sleepily.

'Accomplices?'

'I imagine so. Why do you ask?'

Williams, concentrating on keeping station with the other Landcruiser some one hundred metres ahead,

said, 'Something he mentioned during our little talk
– perhaps nothing.'

They arrived in the capital before dawn, entering the
centro – the downtown area – along Carrera 7. Bogotá,
a city of spontaneous architecture, where shabby
shacks vyed with modern tower blocks, defying all
rational rules of urban planning. The only consolation
being that the streets, which were a battlefield of
lethal iron during the daylight and evening hours,
were peacefully quiet. Owens, who had not woken
up once during the journey, did so now only because
Williams shook him.

'We're here, Edeyrn.'

Owens rubbed his eyes and blinked at the bright
lights along Calle 19. 'Bogotá? Already?'

'Two thousand six hundred metres closer to the
sun.'

'What time is it?'

'Four o'clock.'

'Four! Why didn't you wake me earlier?'

'Not a problem. Besides I like night driving.'

'Ungodly hour all the same. Is this the hotel?'

'The Bacata. Frank recommended it. Comfort, cuisine,
proximity to the embassy, in his words.'

'Any chance we may get an early breakfast?'

'Doubtful, but we can try.'

'You know, the best breakfast I ever had was at the
Royal SAS Hotel in Copenhagen with an old German
friend of mine, Albrecht Loeffler. You remember him?'
Williams shook his head. 'No, before your time perhaps. Anyway, he was taking an early-morning train
back to Germany. We had an hour or more to kill so

we went across the street to the hotel. Scrambled eggs so fresh they literally melted in your mouth.'

'Sorry to disappoint you, Edeyrn, but we're a long way from Denmark.'

'More's the pity. Europe's nicest people.'

'Especially the women,' Williams added.

'Did I ever tell you my wife was half Danish, on her mother's side?'

'No.'

'No . . .' A brief pause. Recollection. All the harder to bear at four in the morning. 'Anyway, where did Murchek go?'

'He's meeting with Bill Rice at seven. Debriefing him. He'll come by and see us later. One of his guys is waiting in the hotel to take the car keys from us. Seems they have a tight budget when it comes to vehicles. Three written off in accidents in the last two months. These two Toyotas are more or less the entire car pool at present. Having to cover a lot of requirements.'

'The way they drive I'm amazed they have any vehicles at all.'

45

Light flickered thinly along the eastern horizon. In other times artillery flares marking the position of a distant battle. Now, nothing more entertaining than a thirty-minute countdown to sunrise.

Winter had completed the runway inspection in the Chevy truck and laid out the buckets of Avpin-soaked sand at equal intervals. The radio call on his hand-held VHF transceiver was next. Then, holding a flaming torch from the open door of the truck, he sped down the runway, lighting each bucket in turn.

The faint turboprop whistle approached from the east almost immediately. No navigation or landing lights. Nothing to advertise its presence. Then, the double squeal of tyres as the main wheels hit the runway. And suddenly, out of nowhere, the T-tailed shape of a King Air B-200 barrelling out of the flare-lit darkness towards him.

No reverse on the four-bladed propellers – quiet ops. Brake discs glowing red-hot as five tons of machinery slowed, and stopped. Both engines dying in unison. Fading whines. The dry shush-shush-shush of feathered prop blades paddling to a standstill in the cool morning air. The tinkling sounds of hot metal contracting.

The scent of jet fuel.

Winter had the rear airstair door opened in seconds. He made his way forward to the instrument-lit flight deck. 'Good flight?' he called out.

The heavy Australian accent boomed back. 'Getting up at two thirty in the morning? You've got to be bloody joking. The guys in flight clearance had never seen me about so early – asked if the wife had finally kicked me out. Funny buggers.' Stevens laughed at the thought and waved to the copilot's seat.

Winter climbed over the centre pedestal, lit up with orange LED readouts of Omega and autopilot systems, and slid into the right seat. The Australian half filled two plastic cups with steaming coffee from a battered thermos and handed one to Winter. Old aviator thing. You never fill cups to the brim in flight just in case you run into unexpected turbulence. One of those habits that eventually become check-listed parts of everyday life, ground or air. Much like the outdoors man who strikes the match to light his cigarette always using cupped hands. The habit remains even when he is indoors, out of the wind.

Clues to existence.

'Nice runway,' Stevens remarked. 'Concrete?'

'Yes.'

'How long?'

'About seven thousand feet.'

'Jeez. They spent some money, then.'

'You should see the hangar.'

'Next time. You can give me the fifty-cent tour.'

'On your way to Cali?'

'Right. As we discussed up at Villavo. On a direct from Caracas. I flight-planned thirty minutes longer than normal. Hopefully no one will miss me, and if they do I'll get real irate and tell them to check their equipment as I've been calling them till I'm blue in the face.'

'What about transponder squawks?'

'Get real, mate, this place still runs on bloody steam. Like most of Africa. They'll probably give me a code once I get close to the Cali terminal area, then complain they're not picking it up.'

'Nothing changes, eh? Is that why you're wearing the white aircrew shirt with the gold bars? Nobody questions a uniform?'

'Right. Same old head-up-the-arse mentality. Used to like the story you told about Jesus Christ and his mates being the sons of visiting astronauts. Explains why after two thousand years the First World and the Third World are still the same number of light years apart. Two different marks of the human race, never destined to meet, right?'

'Party stories, Red. Something to keep the troops amused on long nights in the bush.'

'Ah, shit! And here was me believing that I was the offspring of some really intelligent people.' Stevens pulled a face. Mock disappointment. Followed by contagious laughter.

'Anything on the cargo flights?'

'You were lucky there. Up until last night not a thing – even the poor boys are operating jets these days. Then I got a fax from an old mate in Merida. You know it?'

'Mexico.'

'Yeah. On the Yucatan peninsula. There's a DC-6 that runs in and out of there every Sunday. Comes in from Gulfport, Mississippi, with bolts of cloth. Leaves a few hours later with made-up men's suits from the previous week's shipment – back to Gulfport.'

'What time?'

Stevens pulled a bulky envelope from a pocket by the side of his seat. 'All the details, plus Jepp charts covering the route. As for the other information on alternative airstrips – only place I came up with is southwest of here. The area is a national park called the Serrania de la Macarena. There's a flat-topped mountain, about a thousand metres above sea level. They reckon the interior is largely unexplored, except the former Medina Cartel put an airstrip in there. Been deserted for years now.'

'Fuel?'

'No. Runway and hangar, nothing else. I'd suggest you hop over there this morning in that old bomber of yours and give it the once over. You might have to airlift fuel in if you plan to use it.'

'Take too many flights. We don't have the time or the manpower. Besides, we need electrical power. We'd have to move half this place there to achieve that. Too difficult.'

'Jeez, when wasn't it? Aviation! Next time I'll come back as a banker or a bloody lawyer. Legalised thievery, and you get to wear a suit and tie, and work regular hours ... I've put the lat and long of the strip on a piece of paper by the way. In the envelope.'

'How did you get it?'

'Greased a few palms. Don't worry – I'll send you the bill.'

'Good intel?'

'If you mean do I trust them, the answer is no. But they know if they lie to me and I find out, I'll kick their bloody heads in. Yeah, good intel.'

'Anything else?'

Stevens scratched the back of his head with both hands. Then yawned. 'Oh yeah. Got rid of your guys, Ramon and Co. Didn't much like the shifty-eyed buggers. Got three of my lads heading over to Cali this morning on a scheduled flight. They're all briefed on the surveillance operation. Should be able to let you have a situation report on Saturday morning. You want me to come here?'

Winter finished his coffee and put the empty cup in the cup-holder at the bottom of the copilot's instrument panel. 'Affirmative. Call up on the same discreet frequency we used this morning. Oh nine hundred hours. If negative reply, return to Cali and haul your guys out p.d.q.; I'll make contact on your Caracas number.'

Stevens looked at the Englishman for a moment, transcribing the last sentence in his mind. 'Things hotting up, then?'

'Not that I'm aware of – contingency measures.'

'Take care of yourself.'

'And you.'

Five minutes later, Winter was standing alone on

the deserted airstrip, listening to the King Air climbing away to the southwest. Still no lights. He'd wait until he was back at his flight-planned cruising level before he put them on.

Careful man, Red Stevens.

46

Rain was pounding the mountain-rimmed city. Unusual, as the rainy season was officially over. The weather men were blaming the higher-than-normal precipitation figures on El Niño: a warm Pacific current of variable intensity that develops after late December along the coast of Ecuador and Peru, sometimes causing – as it was this year – catastrophic weather conditions.

It was not the rain beating on the window that awoke Tanner Williams, however, but the telephone. Murchek. He was on his way over. Nothing more. Except perhaps the note of urgency in his voice.

Williams swung his bare legs out of the warm bed and sat for a moment, head in hands, trying to shake the light-headed feeling and stomach pain that were symptomatic, in the recent years at least, of too little sleep. When he knew it wasn't going to get any better he padded through to the bathroom, pulling on a green silk dressing gown as he went. He turned on the tap and splashed icy water on his face, the cold stinging sensation bringing him quickly back to life. He glanced at the red-eyed, unshaven reflection in the mirror. It reminded him of his father. Old. Worn out.

He took a towel from the heated towel rail and returned to the bedroom, checking his watch on the bedside table: three minutes past eight. Less than four hours' sleep. Perhaps his wife was right. An early retirement. A guarantee of a decent night's sleep.

He went over to the fourth-storey window and looked out on the dismal morning, watching the plumes of rain drifting across the city. Like smoke. The lack of traffic caused him a moment's concern, until he remembered it was Sunday . . . Funny how days ran namelessly into one another in foreign lands.

Murchek arrived twenty minutes later. Dark raincoat and crew-cut hair dripping water. White face with the raw look of cold mornings. He came through the door without a word and went straight to the television, turning it on, selecting an early-morning news programme. Pushing up the volume to what Williams considered salsa levels.

Williams moved over to him. 'Didn't see you arrive.' Virtually mouth to ear.

'No, I came the back way, didn't want to use the lobby. Met with Rice an hour ago. Seems there's been a slew of operational messages going up and down the pike. Bottom line being *what the fuck* is going on?' except Murchek said *wtf* – Marine jargon. 'The word is abort. They want you out – yesterday.'

'Any reasons given?'

A slight hesitation. 'No.'

'Oh come on . . .'

Murchek said, 'We've got a problem here . . . Tanner, this is off the record, understand?' He was talking so quietly that Williams had to strain to hear him above the bleating television. 'It seems there's a deal going down with the Colombians. They're in the process of, or getting close to, extraditing a number of cartel bosses to the US. Sensitive enough, until your name came up as being in-country – right on the heels of Congress pulling the plug on this place. Now everyone's panicking and looking for ways to cover their asses.'

The newsreader had turned his attention to the weather. The tightly wound isobar spring of an intense low-pressure system off the Pacific coast, tracking towards the Gulf of Panama, filled the screen. Williams deciphered enough of the machine-gun Spanish to know it was the worst storm for twenty-one years, and what Bogotá and other inland areas were getting was merely the overspill. 'What about Winter? You debriefed Bill Rice on the situation?'

'He's working on a report now. Idea is to leak Winter's location to the Cali Cartel. Let them take care of it.'

Williams was seriously concerned. If he hadn't been fully awake before, he was now. 'For Christ's sake, Frank, this guy is planning an airstrike. We don't know when and we don't know where, but it's going to happen. We were there – we effectively rubber-stamped the operation. What happens if the airstrike goes ahead before the politicians make their play? What happens when it becomes known that we were involved? And it will. These things have a nasty

habit of backfiring . . . There's no time for fine-tuning
report drafts, Frank. In fact I'd go as far as to say there's
no time for reports, period. Just action. Tell Bill we're
in deep kimchee if we don't move on this – not just
me, him as well. He'll understand.'

'Roger that.'

Williams escorted Murchek to the door. *Roger that*!
What he had expected. No such thing as an *ex*-
Marine.

It was after Murchek had left that Williams went
back to the window. Any relief he should have felt
at the prospect of going home tempered by the red
flags moving gradually in to his field of vision. *War-
nings*: *Your whole life is 'off-line' . . . You are the
deniable link.*

He mentally began to prepare his testimony, scaling
it back, moulding the information to fit what was
already known and what could not reasonably be
expected to stay secret.

'You know what I think?' Owens said.

They were in a taxi heading to Bogotá's El Dorado
Airport. It was noon. The monsoon rain continued. The
cab radio blasted salsa music. The windscreen wipers
beating time like a pair of demented metronomes.

'What?' Williams asked.

'I think it isn't anything to do with intelligence
gathering on the cartel's shipping arrangements, or
implicating members of the Constituent Assembly
who have allegedly taken bribes from the cartel's
lawyers. I think this is a clever ploy to invalidate
the extradition deal offered to Washington. Firstly,
ask yourself who pressured the US Congress into

343

passing an amendment banning covert action by CIA elements here in Colombia.'

Williams considered the question. He lit the Dunhill lighter and stared into the blue and yellow flame for a full ten seconds, before snapping the top down and closing his hand over it. The warmth seeped into his fingers. Eventually he said, 'Lobbyists.'

'Indirectly working for?' Owens asked, stressing the syllables of the first word.

'The members of the Colombian Assembly accused of taking the bribes?'

Owens nodded. 'And the reason?'

'CIA involvement with the rebel faction in the recent drug-war bombings – a covert action reported by the popular press as a plot to overthrow the government.'

'Resulting in the Director of the CIA being sacked and the appointment of a new man. This was an encouraging sign to certain politicians here. All they had to do then was advise the cartel to dramatically change their shipping routes, and leak a minimum of what was happening to the DEA and the CIA to ensure that the new Director would be forced to act. Which he did. Pushing the problem into Oscar's lap, who in turn decided to hand it across to his most brilliant operator – you.'

Williams continued the theme. 'And as I am now in-country, working with a known terrorist, this will suborn all that has gone before, thereby invalidating any extradition treaties. Ergo, protecting the members of the Constituent Assembly.'

'Meaning possibly that one of Murchek's locals who accompanied us into Los Llanos would have to be working for those very same government officials, any one of which could have already contacted the US government crying foul. Lovely world, isn't it, Tanner?'

Neither man spoke for a while. The taxi sped along the Autopista El Dorado throwing up a wall of spray. The rain drumming on the roof with the same intensity as the music.

As they neared the airport, Williams said, 'Except no one factored Winter into the equation!'

'Academic now,' Owens replied. 'Your man Rice will tip off the cartel, who will not make the same mistake twice. Which leaves us with a far graver problem, I'm afraid. Far, far graver. Your future.'

'Or lack of,' Williams said reflectively. 'Of course this is all hypothetical. We're assuming the US government is once more going to prove their ineptitude for foreign policy . . . or perhaps this time they'll cover themselves in glory.'

'Much like you might have done. The day is beset with problems, Tanner, my friend.'

Problems visited again that very afternoon. Flights by SAM and Avianca to Santa Marta being cancelled due to weather. Even so they waited three and a half hours in the hope that conditions would improve. They didn't. All that happened was that the terminal became hopelessly overcrowded with irate passengers.

At four o'clock they found a taxi and returned to the city and the Bocata Hotel. The taxi driver had conveniently forgotten to switch on his meter, and charged them twenty dollars American. Three times the fare they had paid a more honest driver some hours earlier.

Both men, deciding it was likely to remain that sort of day, went to the bar. And remained there all evening.

PART SEVEN
Work-Up

47

Monday. Dawn.

The high overcast was beginning to break up and ahead and to the north there were patches of blue sky. The problem was the undercast. Still solid. Negative ground contact. No sound except for the steady breathing over the ICS.

'Not looking so good,' Charlie said into his oxygen mask.

Winter checked his instruments: 320 knots indicated, altitude 20,000 feet, outside air temperature minus five degrees Celsius. Numbers that when aligned on a pilot's 'whizz-wheel' gave a true airspeed of a little more than 400 knots or 520 m.p.h. The GPS showed a range to the target of seventy nautical miles. Ten and a half minutes. 'Same as yesterday afternoon then.'

'Except that was a dry run.' Concern perhaps for the four 500-pound olive drab bombs under the wings. Safety pins removed. Armed.

'Starting on down.' Winter rolled to the inverted,

easing the stick back. Nose dropping below the horizon.

Both men scanned the area below. Old training. Not immediately looking for 57mm or 87mm anti-aircraft fire, but SAMs – surface-to-air missiles. Initially seen as something in motion out of the corner of your eye coming out of the cloud deck. Relaxing your pull a little, easing the nose up to keep the SAM visual. Working the angle-off. Watching the closure rate. Now the nose far below the horizon . . . aiming to make the missile overshoot. Rolling partially, pulling harder into the buffet with the SAM growing larger above . . . moving aft . . . airspeed nearing 500 knots . . . buffeting through a six-g turn . . . missile closing at a heart-stopping rate . . . pulling . . . pulling . . . *come on you mother* . . . pulling . . . and sliding past the wingtip . . . then it was gone, leaving a multicoloured smoke ring pierced by a corkscrewing white streak . . . the debris passing rapidly from sight astern.

Fighter pilot's lingua franca – *a Zantac moment*!

They were now through 10,000 feet, still inverted. Glimpses of wet forest green, ragged cloud along the hills. Then the narrow valley they had pinpointed the previous day twisting its way to the southwest.

GPS range to target – twenty-five nauticals.

Winter rolled level, dropping down to 500 feet a.g.l. (above ground level), the hills disappearing into the cloud on either side. The 500 feet a visual assessment. There was no radar altimeter, and the basic altimeter suffered compressibility error resulting in a nonlinear overread with increasing speed – for 500 feet at 400 knots the altimeter should read 100 feet, for 500 feet at 500 knots the altimeter should read *minus* 200 feet! Not impossible, except the valley floor was not level. It was rising to a 5,000-foot plateau. Rising and twisting. Only way, visual assessment. Eyeballing it. At something like two football field lengths a second, concentration high. Adrenaline higher.

'Two minutes to target,' Charlie prompted.

'Roger.'

'You're going to have to release horizontally.'

'Roj.' Winter understood. Cloud base too low. A matter of 'winging-it'.

Except it wasn't . . . suddenly they hit a clear patch where the visibility magically increased . . . the cloud base lifted . . . at three miles he could see the target . . . he pulled up and rolled inverted . . . the belly of the aircraft surfing the cloud . . . 3,500 feet a.g.l. . . . target reaching the canopy frame above his head . . . pulling the nose down until the target was in the centre of the windshield . . . stopping the nose now with forward stick and rolling the aircraft back to the upright position using crossed controls (left rudder and right stick to roll the aircraft around the sight axis rather than around its own longitudinal axis) . . . master armament switch on checked . . . holding the pipper on line with the target . . . half a second of track time . . . release point . . . 2,200 feet a.g.l. . . . 450 knots . . . dive angle thirty degrees . . . depress bomb pickle on the stick . . . *one thousand one* (1.2 second count) . . . long enough for the bombs to clear the racks . . . fin-retarded low drag bombs . . . the tail-arming wire being withdrawn upon release from the rack . . . fins popping open like a parachute . . . retarding the bombs . . . giving the aircraft separation from the blast . . . and PULL-UP . . . five g . . . back into the

cloud . . . afterburners kicking in . . . rolling into a
seventy-five-degree left bank onto the escape heading
of northeast . . . quick instrument cross-check . . .
pulling the throttles out of burner, the effect of which
was to throw both men forward in their harnesses
(prior to start-up you pulled every strap until it bit
into your flesh, and still it was never tight enough) . . .
two-minute silence . . . respite from cardiac anomaly
. . . beaded water droplets shivering down the side of
the canopy as they slipped through a band of strata
cumulus . . . silver streamers of supersaturated air
trailing from the wingtips . . . the seconds ticking
by . . . cocooned silence broken only by the ragged
breathing over the ICS.

Returning slowly to normal.

'You want to go back and do a BDA?' Winter
asked.

Ugly Charlie, grey-faced and sweating, snapped
back, 'No fucking point. You were too high . . . planted
them about two hundred metres beyond the target.'

'You sure?'

'Height of the plateau five thousand feet. You needed
to release at seven thousand two hundred, which
would have showed as around six thousand six hundred on the altimeter.'

'What did I have?'

'Seventy two hundred – you forgot the correction.'

'Why didn't you say something?'

'As I'm not going to be there on the big day prompting
from the sidelines, no point. Your decision is the only
one. Just a matter of practice.'

'Pigeons for Eerie?'

'Zero five zero for one two zero miles . . . climb to

two zero thousand . . . when level reduce power to idle on number-one engine.' A brief pause to confirm the follow-up action in the emergency check list. *All fuel – transfer to number-one engine . . . power restore to number-one engine . . . number-two engine shut down* . . . 'This is a fucking nightmare!'

'What?'

'Landing after every sortie with enough fuel in the tanks to fill your Zippo – and besides I'm too old to go scud running in the mountains. Why couldn't we have waited for the cloud to lift, or burn off?'

'All-weather operation, Charlie, you should know that.'

Charlie snorted and peered out at the cerebral grey sky. He needed a drink. They'd been in the tops of the trees on that pull-up. He hadn't noticed that the previous day, how the ground rose sharply at the back – the west side – of the target. He'd almost shit himself. Irony was, if Wint had got the numbers right and hit the correct release height, they would have now been compressed hamburger meat on a Colombian hillside. 'Anyway, how did you find out about that airstrip up there?'

'I told you yesterday, Red Stevens mentioned it. When I ran into him up at Villavo and he helped me out with the supplies. He's coming in this Saturday with intel on the actual target, so you can buy him a beer and talk about the old days.'

Charlie looked vague. He didn't remember the conversation. Hangovers had that effect. 'Good diversion field anyway,' he said. Followed by, 'Fuel transfer complete. Let's bring number-one engine up and secure number two.'

Winter complied. Monitoring instrument readouts before shutting down number two. When that was done he said, 'Red had the same idea for a diversion field. Only problem, no fuel and no power. Probably no water, either.'

'That why we're bombing the crap out of the hangar at the Hill Station back there?'

'You saw the video of the Cali target yesterday morning. Remarkably similar to the place we just visited: your Hill Station – good name. Mountains. Valleys. Only way in low-level.'

'Maybe. Still think that strip would be useful.'

'Logistics, Charlie. It would take us a week to airlift all the equipment we need from Eerie One. Besides, how would we carry sufficient jet fuel up there to be able to continue with the work-up programme? Then again—'

Ugly Charlie interrupted. 'Don't you think that if those CIA spooks found us, the cartel's paramilitary hotshots won't?'

Winter did an instrument cross-check and worried a little over the fuel burn. Anything to take Charlie's mind off a problem that didn't exist. The way he had paid Ramon to quietly leave the base with his people the night they had arrived in the B-25, and contact Red Stevens to set up a meeting; and pass a message to Werner Stock in Santa Marta. The way he had gathered sufficient intelligence to know that Stock belonged to the North Coast Cartel and would therefore have no allegiance to the Cali boys. He, Stock, might, however, pass on the information to an interested third party (at a price) – someone like Drummer. The black Panamanian, who he had

overheard very early one morning on the radio. The
Spanish accent absent. Pure American. New York at a
guess. DEA possibly! The way Williams and his team
had found Eerie One. Half expected.

Trap. Set and sprung.

Need-to-know information. Like Red dropping in
the previous day before dawn. No one else even
aware. Autonomous leadership. The only way under
the prevailing conditions.

'Well?' Charlie persisted.

'If you can come up with a way to move fuel to the
top of that mountain, I'll go along with it. The same
way we're using these hand-held transceivers now
and keeping in radio contact with base. You insisted,
I complied.'

'Common sense,' Charlie muttered to himself. And
tried to reposition his right thigh, which was suffering
from pins and needles, except it was more painful, a
trapped nerve perhaps. The problem with the Martin-
Baker ejection seat. No such thing as a comfortable
position. A rock-hard life raft and emergency equipment formed the cushion in the seat pan, and the way
the seat was configured it practically forced you to fall
forward in your straps. He gave up. He'd walk it off
after they landed. 'You want me to get to work on the
single-seater when we get back?'

'Refuel and rearm first. We'll discuss it over breakfast.'

'What about Maria? You want me to fly her again?'

'Thought you said she wasn't going to hack it.'

'Not in the time-frame we plan to be here.'

'So how long do you need with her? Three months?'

'She's got a few hours in a Slotation for chrissakes!

355

Three months! To get her to do what you just did, six months' seriously intensive training, and even then I wouldn't give her very good odds in the weather conditions we had today.'

'I disagree. I think she'll surprise you. She's got a good pair of hands.'

Charlie raised an eyebrow. 'Even conceding that point, where do you want me to start? Formation flying, aerobatics, air gunnery, dog fighting? How about an abbreviated course on five-hundred-pound bombs, triple ejector racks, daisy cutters, bombsight settings, delivery mode, aircraft dive angle, release height, windage . . . I mean how many civil pilots know that a "mil" is an angular measurement amounting to one sixty-four hundredth of a circumference, or nearly one-eighteenth of a degree? Not many, as civil airplanes are not fitted with gunsights whose settings are in mils. Staying with civilian pilots, we speak a different language. Easy example: say "Break" to a civil pilot and they'll relate it to r/t procedure, a controller indicating he's ending his transmission to you and is going to speak to another aircraft he is concurrently working. Say "Break" to a military pilot and he'll immediately start pumping adrenaline as he hauls his aircraft into a nosedown, hard as hell, last-ditch emergency turn to evade imminent danger.'

'You're looking for problems, Charlie . . .'

'Course I'm looking for fucking problems. You know what they say about the Mongolian ghost trap? By the time the downed pilot has got it erected he's died of exposure. You put her in one of these airplanes solo on a formation bomb run she'll die of inexperience. Probably take you with her.'

'You can teach her a lot in ten to twelve weeks.'

'Not enough to keep her alive.'

Winter took the hand-held VHF transceiver from Charlie, checked the LED readout was still selected to base frequency – 123.45 MHz. 'Eerie Approach, Sibelius, two zero thousand.'

'Sibelius, Eerie Approach, say position.' Maria's voice. Terse. Positioned in the truck by the runway. Checking the runway was clear, no wild animals or flocks of birds to affect a landing aircraft.

'Roger, Sibelius on the two three zero for fifty-one, minimum fuel.'

'Copied, Sibelius, descend at pilot's discretion . . . landing zero niner. Eerie weather is CAVU, surface wind easterly five to ten knots, altimeter setting two niner eight two.'

'Zero nine, twenty nine eight two for the altimeter, Sibelius.'

'Getting to sound like the real thing. Professional,' Charlie said. 'Except you forgot to include aircraft type.'

'We've only got one.'

'Not the point. Start leaving items off the check list today, and you'll leave 'em off tomorrow – when they matter.'

Winter signalled they were going down. Then eased the throttle back on the number-one engine and popped the dive brakes. The Lightning plummeted towards the earth below.

The refuelling and rearming was complete. Ugly Charlie had gone to make breakfast and Winter was towing one of the single-seat Lightnings from the hangar. He backed it up towards the corner of the ramp and cut the tug engine. The silence closed back in, broken only by intermittent bird song and the faint rustling of the leaves in the tops of the trees.

He was sliding a chock behind the left main wheel when he heard the shout echoing from the hangar. He turned and saw Maria coming across the ramp towards him carrying a bundle of white cloth. She looked and sounded angry. As she did most of the time. He went back to the job in hand.

Then she was by the wing leading edge. Hands on hips. Feet apart. Not unlike a drill sergeant welcoming raw recruits to an early-morning session of PT. 'Did you hear me?' The voice was certainly loud enough. 'I quit.'

He finished securing the chock, moved out from under the wing and stood up. She hadn't said anything before when Charlie had been around. Wanted to catch him alone perhaps! 'I was planning to have breakfast. Can I get you something before you leave?'

Hair fell across her face. She brushed it away impatiently. The dark eyes flashed. Her breasts strained against the thin material of the grubby white sweatshirt. Nipples hard. Prominent. 'Perhaps you will tell me how? The next Greyhound bus perhaps!'

He waved a hand towards the B-25. 'All yours. Plenty of fuel, enough to get you Stateside at least. Perhaps you could leave it with Johnny Shoosh in the Everglades. Tell him Charlie will pick it up when he gets back.'

The dark eyes watched him. Full of uncertainty. She didn't speak.

'What's the problem? Charlie?'

White Lie

'You!' she replied, snatching up the bundle of white cloth she had placed on the tug. She threw it at him. 'You think it is funny?'

He caught it. Opened it out. A dress. A skimpy dress come to that. Red Stevens's wife buying clothes for a woman! What else would she buy? Something he had overlooked. Sizes had been easy enough: she was very close to what Julia had been in height and build. Except he hadn't specified what was needed, other than half a dozen complete changes of clothing. 'There are no jeans, sweatshirts?'

She sneered. 'You know very well there are not. I opened the suitcase this morning when I needed clean things. And what do I find? Dresses, skirts, silk blouses, black lacy underwear, nylon stockings . . . high-heeled shoes! What would I need with high-heeled shoes in a place like this? Or perhaps being cook and cleaner is not enough – you want me to dress up for you as well. Something more in the evening – you want to fuck me, is that it?'

'I can explain . . .' Winter started.

'And what lies would you use this time, Mr Winter? Something like the lies you used yesterday about the *federales* – what was it? They were here for information. They needed your help.'

'You don't believe me?'

'Why should I?'

She had had a hard life, he could see that. Every move was defensive. Never letting her guard slip for a moment. 'Yes, perhaps you're right,' he said quietly. 'Something you could do before you leave, however. Fly with Charlie over to Hill Station, the other airstrip – he needs to do a bomb damage assessment.'

'And why should I do *you* any favours?'

'Not me. Charlie. I've got to start work on the single-seater. If you don't go he'll take it solo. And with his eyesight he'll probably kill himself.'

'He is a grown man, old enough to make those sort of decisions for himself.'

And awkward enough, thought Winter. 'A question for you. Ever hear of something called a Mongolian ghost trap?'

'A radar corner reflector – part of survival equipment for pilots.'

'Not civil, though.'

'No, military.'

'How did you know that?'

'My father flew F4s in Viet Nam. I used to read his course notes – other girls played with dolls or experimented with their mother's make-up when their mothers were not watching, I read course notes on air warfare, check lists of modern fighters. Sometimes he would talk to me about flying operations, but not very often.'

'So you'll fly with Charlie.'

She looked up at the T.5. Eyes softening. The covetous look of a pilot wanting fast jet time. 'Perhaps . . . when?'

Winter moved off towards the hangar. 'After breakfast.'

'I'm still leaving,' she called after him.

'I'm not stopping you.'

When he reached the hangar he stopped and looked back. She had climbed the steps and was looking into the T.5's cockpit. She may not be a fighter pilot yet, but she had at least the obsession with flight that was essential. An obsession that in anyone else might be considered a serious symptom of some deeper disorder. That 'anyone else' might be advised to take time off, in the hope of gaining perspective. A fighter pilot has no perspective – a territorial thing perhaps. Obsession with flight total. Lose it and you're on the way to the grave.

He turned and followed the smell of freshly ground coffee. And permitted himself a small smile. Black lacy underwear and high-heeled shoes. He'd forgotten about such things.

Ugly Charlie finished his cigarette and shredded the butt. He was unhappy. They had finished breakfast and were out on the ramp looking at the single-seat Lightning, an F.3, that had – according to the log books – been returned to the British Aircraft Corporation at Warton, England, years earlier and converted to an F.6. Two significant differences being a larger ventral fuel tank than the T.5, therefore increased endurance, and two electrically fired and controlled 30mm Aden guns housed in a gun pack at the front of the ventral tank.

'You're crazy,' he snapped.

Winter patted the radome. Started walking down the left side of the nose, inspecting the rivet lines set in the polished aluminium. 'According to the logs these aircraft came out of Kuwait, from the Kuwait Air Force, with a good few tons of spares. I happen to think the people here did engine changes and never got to fly them, and when they knew they were pulling out, some conscientious A & P mechanic decided he'd inhibit them.'

'And you think draining some avgas from the B-25 and running it through the engines here is going to do the trick, that we can just fire her up?'

'What else is there?'

Charlie threw his hands up in exasperation. I'll do what I can, then I'll tow it to the far end of the runway. You do the engine run by yourself. I'll come and pick up the pieces after the explosion and subsequent fire. Thoughts. Not worth mentioning. Nobody ever listened.

'Oh, and I told Maria you'd be flying with her after breakfast. Thought you might want to take her over to Hill Station and check the bomb damage . . . I'll make a start on this. Tell me what I need to do.'

'Drain twenty-five . . . no, make it fifty gallons of avgas from the B-25. We'll blow that through when I get back. You might start pulling as many inspection panels as you can – I cap-checked a new set of batteries in the workshop, marked "S", you can fit them if you like. We also need to drop the gun pack and check the status.'

'You want it loaded for the test flight?'

'You'll be flying it, you tell me. Need to check weights and c-of-g envelope. Could be critical. Everything else on this bitch seems to be. Staying with the female persuasion, what do you want me to do with Maria – general handling?'

'Whatever you feel like. You're the instructor.'

Fifteen minutes later the T.5 departed. Winter, acting as controller, watched from the truck at the side of the runway. Got the 'Operations Normal' call from somewhere in the climb. Charlie's callsign from their operational days together – *Capone*. What else!

Listened, as the dry thunder gradually diminished. Not quite his classroom. The smell of chalk dust. History books . . . those Cistercian monks again – *Woesheil*.

But a close second.

48

Mauricio Becerra hadn't slept for two nights. Uncertain what to do, he had sought refuge in what was left of the weekend. Especially Sunday. Latin Americans made the most of their Sunday afternoons and evenings. Visiting friends and relatives, taking strolls, sitting in cafés or in the front of their homes. He had worked in his garden putting off what he knew was inevitable.

Reporting to Luis Figueras that his men had failed again.

He had drafted out the telephone conversation a hundred times in his mind. Each time it rang false. Sounding like an apology. An excuse.

'Good morning, Señor, or should I say good afternoon . . . I trust your meetings are going well . . . I have some news . . . your men, led by Rodrigues, who were watching the American and the Englishman in Santa Marta followed them to Bogotá on Friday evening. They were met by two vehicles thought to be from the American Embassy. The vehicles left, heading in the direction of Villavicencio. Rodrigues and

his men followed, certain this might have something
to do with the man Winter . . . unfortunately in the
early hours of Saturday morning Rodrigues collided
. . . crashed . . . with a bus on the mountain road . . .
the bus driver's fault, I assure you, Señor. All five
men in the Mercedes were injured, two seriously.
Regretfully, Señor, I did not find out about this until
late on Saturday night . . . why didn't I call you earlier
than this morning . . . ?'

A question that would be asked. One to which he
had no answer. He was a forty-year-old chartered
accountant with a family, not a gangster. Well, perhaps the small matter of embezzlement when he had
worked for the shipping company in Barranquilla. But
that had been years ago. Many years. And even so
'borrowing' a few pesos was not quite the same as
being involved with a company that operated under
numerous fronts which the street rumour insisted
was to shield the real business of drug running and
protection. Understandably he was afraid. *He* knew
it was not a rumour.

'I . . . I was waiting for Rodrigues to come to the
CALIMA office on Monday morning – this morning
– hoping he had more information! Regretfully this
appears not to be the case . . . the American and his
associate? Disappeared, Señor . . . impossible I know,
but it is true.'

All invalid. All excuses. The Figueras family did not
trade in excuses. One small consolation perhaps was
the fact that he was dealing with Luis Figueras and
not his father. The old man with the big brutal hands
would have acted immediately. Punished those who
had failed him. Those involved in the auto accident

would have been found on the Sunday morning floating face down in the Rio Cali. That was the nice way – two or three bullets in the head. Food for the fish.

Or the brutal alternative.

The Sugar Mill. At the end of a dusty road in the Valle del Cauca. He knew of the accidents to 'workers'. Except he had been in charge of the payroll at the Mill when he had first started work at the CALIMA subsidiary. And during his time no workers were killed; he had still paid the same number of men week after week. So who were the 'accidents'? It did not take him long to realise that they always coincided with the arrival of Emilio Figueras in the grey dawn light. On those days the workers were given an extra break for a cigarette while the boss inspected the machinery. The old man with his entourage of bodyguards would disappear into the plant. The whines and rumbles of electrical motors and roller mills would follow – Mauricio listening from the open window of his tiny office.

He knew all the sounds.

He had made it his job to know how the sugar cane was processed, more from a time-and-motion study to make the factory more efficient, more cost-effective. He did not intend to be a glorified wages clerk for the rest of his life.

Sounds. The raw sugar cane being loaded onto the cane-feeder table, which slowly transported it towards the slashing blades which cut the cane into chips . . . to the cane shredders, hammers which reduced it to a fibrous structure . . . to the pressurised rollers which extracted the juices.

Sounds that might disguise a man's screams as, through taped-open eyes, he watched the rapidly revolving cane knives shred his feet, his ankles, his legs . . .

Mauricio had shuddered at the violent pictures his mind conjured up.

Finally, at nine o'clock that morning, he had placed a call to the private bank in Zürich. A secretary with a hard German accent explained that Señor Figueras was in a meeting. Could she take a message? She could. He left his name and number. And put the phone down with a shaking hand. Relief. Temporary.

He sat at his desk for the next thirty minutes, transfixed with fear. Thinking perhaps he should leave the office and take a short walk. Fresh air to clear his head. Perhaps he could stop at a café and take a double *aguardiente*. Courage. He didn't. He remained, trying to hide inside his own skin. Eyes never leaving the grey telephone on his desk. And when it rang he felt his heart bounce painfully off his chest.

He took a deep breath and picked it up. 'Becerra.'

It was the girl on the switchboard. He knew before she spoke, heard the music in the background. She always played music. 'Someone is trying to reach Señor Figueras. I explained he was not here but they said it was very urgent.'

Mauricio let out a small sigh of relief. 'Thank you, Beatriz, put them through.'

The call was brief, with Mauricio Becerra doing all the listening. His features slowly changing from uncertainty to disbelief to pure unbridled joy.

He looked at the words he had written on his desk pad. Read them twice over. Then picked up the phone and dialled the number for Rodrigues. Rafael Rodrigues, known as Raf, one of CALIMA's behind-the-scenes musclemen. Recruited from the Easy Money School, whose diploma could be awarded in a matter of minutes or as soon as the student could recite the school's first and only lesson: 'The law is the major stumbling block to your happiness. It's a waste of time and energy learning to read and write. You can live a richer more secure life as a criminal than a tax-paying citizen.'

Raf, who had already fouled up on the Canaveral raid, certainly would not want to be found wanting a second time. The car accident had happened certainly but Rodrigues, through his many contacts, and although injured, had perservered. Found the location of the man Winter. An anonymous telephone call could just as easily have been received by Raf, could it not? Therefore why shouldn't Raf receive the praise for his endeavours? And should anything go wrong . . .

One hour later the rambling six-foot-two Raf Rodrigues, with shoulder-length black hair and matching beard, skinned knuckles, and bandaged left arm and sticking plaster above his left eye, had been briefed and had spoken with Luis Figueras in Zürich. Brilliant work. Luis Figueras had been very happy. Ecstatic even. Mauricio Becerra had smiled quietly in the background. He did not seek any reward. He never sought to lead or to be the last. Security lay somewhere in the middle.

White Lie

Rodrigues thanked the accountant warmly as he left his office, assured him he was in his debt. Mauricio likewise assured him it was not necessary.

The accountant tidied his desk and left a few minutes later for an early lunch. Aware of the conversation he had overheard. That the man named Winter, who had killed the youngest son of Emilio Figueras, would by the end of that very day be dead himself. Simple justice.

He pushed it out of his mind and thought of lunch. He was suddenly very hungry. Perhaps he might even take the double *aguardiente* he had considered earlier.

By way of celebration.

49

The Boeing 737–300 was packed to capacity, as was every other flight out of Bogotá, the airlines working to clear the backlog from the previous day when more than forty domestic flights had been cancelled due to adverse weather conditions.

Williams and Owens had managed to get the last two first-class seats on the lunchtime Avianca flight to Santa Marta. Owens said, 'Nice of Frank to call you this morning, wasn't it?'

'Bill Rice directive,' Williams replied. 'Survival instinct is never so strong as when it is your own life on the line, Edeyrn.'

Owens leaned closer. 'When will they have confirmation?'

'They're monitoring the situation. Said they'd keep me updated.'

'What about Stock? What do you intend telling him when we go to collect the car?'

'That we drove out to the base and I had a very amicable discussion with Winter. He explained how he had escaped from Canaveral by the skin of his teeth when the army raided the place. He has since been working to patch up the B-25 which was damaged by gun fire. When that was done he was planning on flying to Santa Marta to pay Werner for the airplane before contacting me and taking the plane on to Chino, California, to sell to his customer. As we of course now have the title paperwork, he has agreed to wire our initial funds back to us as soon as he arrives in the States, followed by the agreed profit from the sale.'

Owens chuckled. 'Williams' Law: "When you subtract infinity from infinity the answer can be anything you want; when you subtract truth from truth, likewise".'

'A smokescreen, nothing more.'

Thermodynamic arrows of time. Pricking the memory. 'It was two planes!' Owens said suddenly.

'What?'

'You remember asking me about Winter's escape the other evening. When he was arrested in Belfast, Northern Ireland, and escorted back to England under armed guard . . . I just remembered. Harry Tait in London used the same word when I called him. Smokescreen. Apparently it was a little trick the SAS boys used to infiltrate enemy territory. They called it "Hearse Cover". Winter modified the concept. Seems he had some loyal friends in the ranks who arranged for a couple of light planes to be made available. Harry didn't give me the exact details of the escape other than the first aircraft, on the pretext of doing a night charter trip from England to Belfast, filed a flight plan and took off. It seems the second plane with Winter on board climbed away from a farmer's strip nearby and formated under the first plane. That way the controllers would only see one legitimate flight moving along the airways on their radar scopes. When it descended into Belfast, the other aircraft broke away at low level and landed in a small field somewhere. Leaving Winter to slip across the border into southern Ireland. Then the two planes returned to England using much the same procedure.'

'How did the authorities find out?'

'Vigilant security man or something, or maybe it was a controller. Thought it was odd that a small charter plane should fly in from England empty, land, and file a flight plan straight back to its point of origin without picking up any passengers. As the word had gone out concerning Winter's escape, Special Branch were put on alert. They questioned the pilot when he returned – apparently he didn't hold up too well to the interrogation.'

The airliner began its descent. Vibrating as it hit a patch of clear air turbulence. Chimes. FASTEN SEAT BELT signs illuminating. Dull little clicks of belt buckles being mated.

'Interesting.'

'Very. But surely you didn't think he was going to use the same plan after he'd carried out his private litle war with you know who.'

'Why not?'

'Returning to the States! Florida?'

'Last place anyone would think of looking for him. Once there he could obtain whatever false papers he needed, adopt a suitable disguise, and leave the country as a legitimate airline passenger to anywhere in the world.'

'Yes . . . perhaps. Didn't Drummer say that the B-25 had a great deal of fuel?'

'He did.'

'So flying back to the States might not present too much of a problem.'

'Probably not.'

'But where would Winter have found his other aircraft? The one to formate with.'

Williams stared at the gold cigarette lighter in his hand. As though it were a crystal ball about to offer up a plethora of secrets. 'The sixty-four-thousand-dollar question . . . a hypothetical one come to that. Something we don't have to worry about any more. Right?'

'Game, set and match – I agree.'

'What made you change your mind on his invulnerability?'

'You, more than anything. When you mentioned he was growing older, prone to error perhaps. Much like the cowboy pictures I used to watch as a boy at the local Hippodrome cinema, always a faster gun around the next corner.'

'I can't imagine you watching western movies.'

Owens visualised a small raggedy-arsed boy playing in the grimy streets of a 1940s Welsh mining town. Happy days. Poor but happy. 'Another lifetime,' he said reflectively. Then, moving quickly on, 'Anyway, Oscar will be pleased that he's survived one more day. Have you spoken with him?'

Encrypted voice circuit to Washington. Bounced off a satellite. The future had crept up on all of them. 'Indirectly. Through Bill Rice. I'll contact him again from Cartagena.'

A pretty young flight attendant walked slowly backwards through the first-class cabin, bestowing smiles and checking seat backs in the upright position and tray tables stowed. Owens glanced out of the window and saw the coastline a few thousand feet below. Blue sea, green trees, red-roofed houses. Picture postcard.

'Are we leaving for Cartagena tonight?'

Williams said, 'If you feel up to another night drive. The sooner we get back on the yacht, the happier I'll feel.'

'Lunch first?' Owens suggested.

'Why not. After we've collected the car from Werner.'

'Just as well he offered to lock it up in his garage while we were away. Can you imagine what we would have found if it had been left in the street by the hotel?'

'An IOU in Spanish painted on the sidewalk?'

They both laughed.

An hour and twenty minutes later they had nothing to laugh about. Werner Stock was not at home. The gates to the courtyard were chained and padlocked.

They redirected the taxi to the low-key Hotel Miramar on Calle 10C. Jairo Portillo, the friendly manager, explaining that there were not so many gringo backpackers that week – except that for gringo he said foreign – as he gave them their old rooms back. Bake-heat afternoon and throbbing streetside salsa and vallenato music included in the daily five dollars American charge.

Owens once again rescued the toothbrush glasses from the bathrooms and opened the bottle of Martell.

50

Luis Figueras's mind was spinning. The result of a fourteen-hour business day. One that he was replaying in his mind even now as he sat at his tiny work station in the rear of the G-IV executive jet which was climbing away from Zürich Airport. Tapping coded information regarding the Casanare oil field project in to his Compaq laptop computer.

Two working days compressed into one. That is all it had taken. Contracts drawn, signed, sealed. He had been more than a little impressed with the Swiss bankers, all the more for the background information he had gleaned over a working lunch. How the bank, along with a group of Swiss arms dealers, had succeeded in the eighties in selling war planes to the Iranians even though Swiss law actually forbade the sales of arms to any country at war or located in a troubled area. The bank had found a way around the problem by claiming that the planes were trainers and therefore not war material. Converting the trainers to war planes requiring detailed reference to a complex conversion manual – which the arms dealers, on advice from the bankers, included in the terms of sale. Luis had laughed at that.

It got better.

The same bank had had a hand in the OPEC embargo against South Africa, when they orchestrated an operation where a Liberian-registered oil tanker picked up a load of oil from Kuwait. Destination – Europe. The ship secretly unloaded the oil in South Africa, before proceeding up the coast where it had an 'accident' and sank. Fortunately the entire crew had time to pack their bags and lower the lifeboats before the distress signal was sent out. More than $40 million received for the oil also disappeared, refined through the Swiss bank. Then of course there was the insurance . . .

And better.

His royalties from the Casanare oil field had been underwritten by a major German bank. Even when he had taken into account clauses on charges, interest-rate increases, rescheduling fees, and terms-of-trade deterioration, it still meant that he was totally safe. Inviolate. Better to pay a major bank a little, his advisers had cautioned, than get caught up in a complex web of phony invoicing which could lead to problems at a later date.

And lastly.

How the following Monday, when he had handed over the final documentation to the Colombian government on the Cartel de Cali, he would fly to Madrid and renounce his Colombian citizenship for that of Spain, whose extradition treaties with Colombia, as that of the US and the majority of other countries around the globe, prohibited the extradition of a Spanish citizen who had committed a crime in another country before becoming Spanish. A technical point, nothing more. As would be the changing of his name.

Which left?

He closed the Casanare file in Microsoft Word, and opened the Lotus Word Pro program (where all his personal files were stored), moving the cursor to: Create a New Document from a Smartmaster. He selected Letter 1. A personal letterhead with his name and address appeared on the screen.

He began writing. A short letter to the president of the University of Southern California, Los Angeles – his alma mater. His last philanthropic gesture in the name of Luis Figueras. A donation of ten million dollars, to be set up as a trust fund to benefit the Law Centre.

They, who had taught him so much, deserved to be rewarded.

It was when he finished the letter that his mind focused on the news he had received earlier that day from his man Rodrigues. Everything was finally coming good. All of his experiences in life had taught him that luck runs in cycles. He was deeply in a good-luck cycle now. Even the Winter situation, where Rodrigues had discovered his whereabouts: hidden away in the wastes of Los Llanos working on military aircraft, trying to make them flyable perhaps; there are many bombs at the base also – perhaps he is planning to start a war; a small joke, Señor. They had both laughed. And when the laughter was over Luis had ordered immediate action. As many men as was needed. No failures this time.

Something that would prove to his father that he

was more of a man than he had been given credit for. That because a man chooses not to marry, wears glasses, and has fine manners, he should not be accused of being a gay boy – worse than a simpering woman – a disgrace to his family name. That lack of physical strength in a son should not be an excuse for physical abuse from a father. Perhaps when the old man was in an American prison he would have time to reflect. To think about such things, to realise how wrong he had been. How he had seriously underestimated one man in particular. Especially the way he had failed to care for his wife in her old age – that most of all. Perhaps a letter from the Holy Father in Rome, excommunicating him. Something that could easily be arranged, with money, and the right sympathetic ear in the Vatican.

The final blow. Cast adrift with the sinners. No landfall.

Ana appeared, carrying two crystal glasses of champagne. The merest hint of expensive perfume reached out to him. He looked up and gave her a tired smile. Heard for what seemed the first time the hiss of slipstream and the aircraft's pressurisation system. Funny how the mind could totally block out background noise. Funnier that now he had focused on the sound he could hear nothing else. 'A celebration?'

'I have decided that fifteen hours of work in one day is too much,' she announced. 'I have made up the couch into our bed. The flight attendant has gone forward to her quarters, and I've given her instructions to wake us with breakfast one hour before we land in Cali.'

White Lie

He logged off the computer. Removed his glasses and rubbed his eyes and stretched and yawned. And accepted the champagne. 'I am most impressed,' he replied, raising his glass.

The glasses clinked.

'I thought you were watching a movie,' he said.

'I changed my mind.' She took his champagne glass and put it on the desk, then, taking his hand, said, 'Now, come with me and I will undress you.'

'How high are we, Luis?'

They were in the narrow fold-down bed. Both naked, except she had kept on her lacy garter belt and black stockings and high-heeled shoes – she knew that excited him. He looked up. Through one of the windows he could see stars. So many that they seemed to fill the night sky. 'Perhaps ten thousand metres . . . twelve, thirteen.'

'How many miles?'

His tired mind struggled to convert kilometres into miles. 'Six . . . seven. Possibly more. Why do you ask?'

She ran her hand down his body, across his stomach. He felt her fingernails. Sharp. Exciting. Tantalising. Then she was holding him. Gently squeezing. Lightly massaging. And as tired as he was he felt his manhood coming alive in her hand. 'That is nice, Luis?'

He grunted in the darkness.

She continued massaging him, feeling the hardness growing in her fingers, faster and faster until she could hear him gasping. Then she took her hand away and went down on him with her mouth. Gently at first, her tongue playing games; gradually more violent, the tongue being replaced by teeth biting into him. Finally, when she thought he could stand it no more, she pulled her mouth away and threw off the blanket and straddled him. Guiding him into her wetness. Slowly riding him. Arching her body back. Sighing with pleasure. Stopping from time to time, to lie on him and smother his face with kisses. Telling him it was too nice and she did not want it to stop. And he, pushing her back up, hands reaching for her breasts, fingertips flickering over the erect nipples, moving down to her slim waist, fingers intertwining with the garter belt for better leverage, lifting and lowering her body in time with his. Until finally it was too much and she flung herself down on him in a series of pounding gyrations, crying out over and over again in the darkness.

They were wrapped in each other's arms. Exhausted. Drifting towards sleep. Across space.

'Why did you ask how many miles?' Luis mumbled.

She stirred and kissed his ear. 'Something I once read. Making love in an airplane, it is called the mile-high club.' She kissed him again. 'Does that now mean we are members?'

He held her close. Skin to skin. Exchanging body heat. 'Perhaps . . . perhaps there is a club for five miles.'

She smiled contentedly and nestled her head into the hollow of his shoulder and let her hand slide down his stomach. Until her fingers lay on his limpness. She stroked the velvety skin for a moment.

Then slept.

51

Ugly Charlie was sitting in the blue Chevy truck watching the T.5 line up on the runway about seventy-five feet from the rubber-scars of previous landings. His earlier flight with Maria had further convinced him that he could never get her up to operational readiness in the time-frame allowed. He had argued the point with Winter again. That he wasn't going to waste any more time. That the airplane was dangerous enough; putting a civilian at the controls – suicide. Winter had smiled in what Charlie referred to as his St Francis of Assisi manner – reserved for children and dumb animals – and suggested he fly with her; if she was as far behind the lift/drag curve as Charlie suggested, they would rethink their strategy.

The T.5's engines rose to a crackling thunder, black smoke trailing from the jet pipes, as the pilot pushed the throttles forward and released the brakes. He felt the sound vibrating against his chest. Blocking out all thought until about half a mile down the runway when the nosewheel came off. Then the mains. Then

a shallow climbing turn to the left. Rolling out on a
southerly heading. Rapidly disappearing beyond a veil
of dust which drifted off the savannah. The light to
variable surface wind picking up slightly, something
he needed to keep an eye on. The last thing they needed
was a dust storm. Wint had made it very clear that
a diversion to Hill Station would lose them a full
day, if not more. Flying fuel and possibly a spare set
of batteries up there in the B-25 to enable a visual
recovery when the weather cleared.

Two minutes later he received the 'Operations Normal' call on his hand-held VHF transceiver. Thirty-
five minutes tops before they returned. Hardly worth
heading back to the hangar to do an engine run on the
F.6. Might as well wait for them to get back – keep
an eye on the weather. He picked up the near-empty
bottle of vodka from under the seat and took a couple
of swigs. Then lit a Marlboro and laid his head back on
the seat.

The imagery was not that far off Da Nang in the
mid-sixties. Perimeter tree line. Sound of jets. Smells
of jet fuel and dust. Heat. All it needed was a village
of SEA (South East Asia) huts and stacks of body bags
baking in the sun.

Like it had been the last time he had seen the place.

On the day he had been taken off operational flying
because he was due to go home in seven days, and the
powers that be had decided that the last seven days of
a pilot's tour were the most dangerous. Which was so
much fucking horseshit. It was *all* most dangerous.

He'd made a phone call to a friend at Bien Hoa.
Colonel Frederick Cagliari was an old and eccentric
Anglophile known as Fast Freddie because he flew one

of the slowest multi-engined airplanes in Viet Nam —
the Gooney Bird, also known as Puff the Magic Dragon,
or less imaginatively by the Douglas planemakers as
the C-47. A near antique airplane which had served
through countless wars during its long history and had
now found a place in South East Asia. A place with an
Air Force operation known as Black Magic. A kind of
exclusive flying club for majors and above. Three matt-
black aircraft. Unarmed. Their role to carry out night
penetrations into the North to pick up Special Forces
teams who had been parachuted in on intel-gathering
missions.

Riker had flown for Fast Freddie before. Had been
checked out on the C-47. A phone call was all it took. If
he could scrounge a ride to Bien Hoa he had a seat that
very night. Another call and Riker, with overnight bag,
was on board a MARLOG flight in a C-117 (Hummer)
with a bunch of hollow-eyed, battle weary, thousand-
yard-stare, Marine grunts, heading south.

Fast Freddie, complete with his trademark white
pith helmet and handlebar moustache, met him on
the ramp at Bien Hoa and briefed him as they strolled
across the crowded tarmac. 'Loc Ninh . . . little place
up north . . . no VC for a hundred clicks . . . piece of
cake, old boy . . . have a drink when you get back . . .
celebrate your return to the real world . . . when is it
you're leaving? . . . weekend! . . . lucky bugger.'

Jesus, he even sounded like an Englishman.

Riker wandered off and found a cup of coffee and
a cigarette. Did a preflight on his aircraft. Sat in the
pilot's seat, elbow out of the open side window. Waiting for his crew to show. And in between airplane
engines running up and down, the Ray Conniff Singers

with a smooth rendition of 'Smoke Gets In Your Eyes' drifted from the speakers in the makeshift hangars. Return to the real world! What the fuck was that? Los Angeles and the Hippie Cult. Being spat on by a bunch of long-haired, flower-haloed weirdos. Adjusting to civilian life. Applying for a job with Pan Am. A few million miles of subsonic straight-and-level until retirement.

And he suddenly realised this was it!

This squalid piece of real estate on the other side of the planet *was* the real world. A Never-Never Land. Complete with miniature yellow-skinned Captain Hooks. Wendys by the hundred in the downtown bars distracting your taste buds from the crap taste of formaldehyde-laced beer. Tinkerbells back home in the Pentagon, magnanimously dispensing fast jets and fuel and bombs like largesse from a gyro-toppled Welfare State. Shit, you could stay young for ever in a place like this.

For ever! A long time in any language.

For ever! A priceless commodity in any currency.

For ever . . . broken by the distinctive *whop-whop-whop* of Huey helos, the flat sound thumping down out of the afternoon sun . . . medevac flights no doubt . . .

He opened his eyes and knew something was very wrong. The Hueys were still there. The two-blade vertical sound moving closer. Except Bien Hoa had been swallowed by space and time. No such thing as a static universe.

Fuck.

He snatched up the hand-held and began transmitting. 'Sibelius, Eerie Approach.'

Silence.

'Sibelius, Eerie . . . how do you read?'

Nothing. Out of range.

Which left making a run for the trees. Hiding out. For what? A bunch of soldiers to hunt him down and pick him off? He'd told Wint it wasn't safe, that they should have moved the operation to Hill Station . . . no use crying about it, Charlie boy, better start doing something . . . A run to the south maybe, over the savannah, away from the base . . . How far would he get over open terrain? Few miles!

He started the truck and slammed his foot down on the accelerator. A wheel-spinning turn back towards the hangar.

Ugly Charlie wiggled his oxygen mask on his sweaty face, said a silent thank-you to whoever was running the Universe today, and reefed the F.6 into a seventy-five-degree bank.

It had taken him five minutes to grab his bone-dome, kick out the chocks from under the Lightning's main wheels, strap in, and do an internal battery start. Amazingly, everything had gone by the book. Even the afterburner take-off (a mandatory check-listed item on the heavier F.6), which had scattered the flight of three Huey helos hovering in the blowing dust at the west end of the runway.

He was at ten thousand feet. Breathing hard. A little shaky. He tried the hand-held again. 'Sibelius, Capone.'

Carrier-wave silence. Followed by the calm voice of Winter. 'Capone, this is Sibelius, go ahead.'

'Roj. We're under attack . . . we got a flight of three Hueys one click west of the base at five hundred feet

. . . look to be firing two-point-seven-five-inch rockets
. . . got some smoke from the hangar, over.'

'You airborne?'

'Affirm.'

'What you flying? B-25?'

'Negative . . . the Six.'

Another silence as that computed. Then: 'Are you
still visual with the helos?'

'Affirm . . . what are your pigeons?'

'On the one six five for fifty – be with you in less than
five minutes.'

'Roger that. Suggest you make a run on due north to
cross west end of the runway – should be able to ripple
all three. I'll keep you updated on change of status.'

'Sibelius copied.'

The silence flooded back. Charlie reduced speed to
conserve fuel and tightened his orbit. He was down
to five thousand feet now and could just about make
out the helos' blades glinting in the afternoon sunlight. The hangar was burning at one end, a pall of
black smoke drifting slowly skyward. Something flickered at the edge of his field of vision. One of the
Hueys was moving up over the gallery forest, closer
to the hangar. Which made him realise it was Amateur
Afternoon on the Los Llanos Gunnery Range. Shit, if
you couldn't hit a stationary target from five hundred
metres perhaps you should be looking for another line
of work.

And speaking of easy targets. He was carrying 240
rounds of 30mm HE (high explosive) cannon shells.

They used to say in Viet Nam a pilot's most dangerous time was his first and last week on ops. And as
Charlie Riker looked down, burning the battle scene

into his imagination, he was cast back across the time-lines of war. And once again and quite inexplicably, his fear disappeared. His hands steadied. He even imagined his eyesight had miraculously reacquired 20/20 capability. And he was back in his F.4 Phantom making a run at the guns at the mouth of the Mu Gia Pass. Unconsciously separating himself from his own gravity, a kind of Chandrasekhar limit for airmen, where death ceased to be the enemy, merely another participant in a game he did not want to end. If he had thought about it a little more he might have concluded that his psychological buttons had been pushed and he was once more Pavlov's dog – a recipient of military programming so thorough that he was more given to dying for his country than going home to it. But he didn't. Major Charles Riker was back where he belonged. An ageing fighter pilot who had been readmitted to Never-Never Land. A last chance to arrest the inevitable advance of his own tomorrows.

He selected 'Guns', and rapped the stick against his right knee to break into a roll . . . holding the inverted . . . lowering the nose fractionally below the horizon . . . lining up on the single Huey which was manoeuvring to fire another salvo of rockets at the hangar.

'*Playboy in hot.*' A mouthed transmission as he rolled level. His old callsign. He was young again. Strong. Pain-free. The days he had known how to laugh.

The Huey filled his sights . . . no need for lead . . . the target was stationary . . . he recited the catechism in his mind . . . one more of those pithy jingles for ever branded into his memory cells – *same . . . half*

. . . *pause* . . . *shoot*. Something you did when radar ranging was not an option and you needed to eyeball it. At around a thousand yards the small circle in the centre of the gunsight should be the *same* width as the target, an indication to start tracking it. At five hundred yards – *half*-width – you eased the pipper up to the target (the front if it was moving, the centre if it was stationary) – *pause* – until range passed through four hundred yards. Then *shoot*.

At 350 yards and 350 knots he thumbed the gun button . . . two streams of bullets converging on the helo which for a moment appeared immune to high explosive . . . a hologram through which cannon shells passed harmlessly . . . then a bright orange fireball . . . a silent explosion . . . gone . . . blood and bone and flesh and metal and plastic vapourising in an instant . . . MAGIC . . . no kill like a 'guns kill' . . . he pulled hard into a five-g break . . . momentary grey-out as the blood supply to his brain shut off . . . then rolled and dropped back down towards the airstrip . . . one down, two to – Something was wrong . . . something . . . no audio attention getters with associated flashing lights, but the controls were stiffening . . . quick check of the instruments . . . normal . . . all normal . . . *Bad Day at Black Rock, shit*!

'Sibelius, Capone.'

Momentary pause.

'Go ahead.'

'Roj, got some problems here . . . controls stiffening up . . . no cockpit indications of anything significant . . . heading two seventy . . . about five miles west of Eerie . . . angels seven.'

'Stand by . . . stand by . . .' A matter of seconds

flashed by. 'Okay, you're tally . . .' More seconds. 'Coming up on your left side . . . you've got a rear-end fire, Charlie . . . number-two engine . . . suggest you eject while you still have control . . . we'll come back and pick you up when we've dealt with the three helos.'

'Two . . . I splashed one . . . problem with the ejection . . . never got around to pulling the pins.'

An *Oh Shit silence* this time. Upper case.

'Can you reach back over your head and get the top pin?'

Once maybe. The scar tissue on my body, webbed beneath the armpits. I can only lift my arms to shoulder level. 'Negative . . . I've tried.' Charlie looked out of the cockpit and saw Wint's Lightning off his left wing. He raised a gloved hand in salute. 'I'll try for a landing below. Slowing up to two fifty now . . . check my gear.'

The T.5 slipped lower and aft. Winter's voice: 'Negative on the gear.'

'Wheels up then.'

They both knew that was a bad idea. Belly landings were a thing of the past. Primary reason being the engine location on most military jets. Behind the pilot. And whereas the strongest and heaviest elements in the aircraft were the engines and their attach points, the cockpit area was the lightest and weakest. In an impact the cockpit section decelerates and crumples while the engines with their greater momentum tend to rip away from their mounts and continue forward through the cockpit. Reducing the pilot to hamburger patties in the process.

Charlie was descending through three thousand feet now. Flying straight ahead. No r.p.m. indication on the number-two engine. Speed 230 knots. Focusing on a touchdown point in his twelve o'clock. Hoping that the same charmed life which had worked for him before would do so again. The wind had eased, that was something. No lifted dust. Good omen. No time for recriminations about flying totally unserviceable airplanes which had had no maintenance checks, that would come later.

Outside glance at the endless dome of blue sky. Pretty day. Mares' tails of clean white cirrus etched high above the western horizon. For all the world like a squadron of sailing ships lined up for the start of an ocean race across the heavens.

Inside glance at the flight instruments, catching the ghostly reflection of his bone-dome and oxygen mask in the glass of the artificial horizon. In a place like this he carried no deformities. In a place like this he was the young steely-eyed ace he had often dreamed about in his dusty rooms in Key West. The lost boy he had shed vodka tears for.

He had both hands on the stick, fighting to keep the stricken aircraft honest when the fire, which was now consuming most of the rear fuselage, finally burned through the control rods.

The Lightning hesitated, shuddered slightly, then rolled gently over. Departing controlled flight.

Spiralling towards the earth below.

Charlie was amazed at how beautifully blue the sky suddenly appeared as the aircraft rotated from sun to shadow and back to sun. Like flax fields he had once seen in Europe in his youth. An Air Force detachment to Germany. And a long-legged Austrian girl with waist-length blonde hair who had offered him . . .

52

No thanks, no tears, no prisoners.

There were better codes to live by, but not here. The life of a fighter pilot is transitory at best. It is also the wildest adrenaline-pumping game so far invented. A grand addiction. The protagonist always looking for that one 'big' mission beyond the next line of clouds. Talk to him about going home to find a respectable job, and a wife, and to raise one point seven rug-rats and you will sense his ambivalence. It's not that he doesn't want to go back to the real world, more that he's taken that one fatal step over the edge. He belongs more to Never-Never Land than any of Barrie's fictional characters ever did. Peter Pan *is* a fighter pilot. Afraid of growing up. Afraid of growing old.

In some cobwebby recess of his mind, Winter would later find comfort in those thoughts. How, indirectly, he had been Charlie's salvation, sparing him the final years of loneliness trapped on the ground. A gift of wings. A Viking funeral.

But that would take time. Now, grim-faced, he carried out a low pass over the wreckage which burned on the windswept Colombian plain. A dip of the wing. An airman's valediction. The best — *all* — he could offer. Then he pulled up, climbing on course for Eerie One.

And the enemy.

53

'Leticia? A small town on the Amazon River, at the southeasternmost tip of Colombia, on the tripartite border with Brazil and Peru. Something of a tourist attraction these days. People come to see the local Indians and buy their handicrafts. Years ago the rulers of Empires sent their undesirables to such places; now tourists! Next I think, a jungle Disneyworld.'

Tanner Williams was drinking coffee in Werner Stock's study and getting a short dissertation on Colombia Amazonia from the German who had arrived back in Santa Marta late that Tuesday morning, following an extended weekend trip to visit his sick mother. Williams, who had been telephoning Stock's house at hourly intervals, had finally contacted him at eleven o'clock, one hour earlier. He had left Edeyrn Owens at the hotel to pack for their journey to Cartagena. *Tripartite border*. Very exact, very German. 'You said your mother had been ill. Nothing too serious, I hope.'

Stock finished his coffee and began filling the bowl of his navigator's pipe, pausing to pick up a few strands of loose tobacco that fell into his lap, returning them carefully to the worn leather pouch. Almost a re-enactment of his last visit – even the light covering of dust on the furniture seemed unchanged, as did the piles of yellowing synoptic charts and papers piled on the long refectory table. 'She is eighty years of age, Mr Williams. The slightest ache or pain gives her concern for her life. Of course I fly there and expect the worst every time, and every time she is in better health than me. Of course I have asked her to come here to live, but she is more accustomed to the heat and humidity of the jungle.'

'But you prefer the coast and the sea?'

'I find it cleaner, fresher. Don't you agree?'

Had he mentioned the yacht the last time he was here? And if not, Drummer might have done so. 'Certainly. A sailing boat on the ocean is one of the few pleasures I get out of life, blows away the cobwebs of being confined to an office cataloguing antiques.'

'But still it is a good business I think.'

'Antiques? Yes, reasonably profitable. Except when you slip up and do a bad deal. Then it becomes expensive.'

'Like the aeroplane.'

Williams laughed. 'Oh, I've made worse mistakes than that Mr Stock, and in areas I'm considered expert in.'

'But you met with your Mr Winter and got your money back!'

'We made an arrangement, yes. He's working to make the airplane serviceable and then plans to fly it to California, to the customer he has. Once there I will get paid.'

'You are sure?'

A small shrug to emphasise his concern. 'Not altogether, but I had little choice in the matter, and as I'm not a pilot.'

Stock shook his head thoughtfully, and took a book of matches from his trouser pocket, lit one and worked at lighting the long curved-stem pipe. Satisfied all was well, he puffed contentedly for a few moments before putting the matches on the coffee table, alongside the leather tobacco pouch. 'More coffee?' he asked, getting out of his chair. 'I will make a fresh pot.'

Williams, initially eager to collect the Grand Cherokee and be on his way to Cartagena, accepted. He had sensed it the last time he had been here. This time, more so. The fact that something was not quite right. Not what it seemed to be. As for Frank Murchek's warning: *The word is abort. They want you out . . . yesterday.* All in good time.

Satisfied Stock was in the kitchen at the other end of the house, he went over to the refectory table and leafed through a few synoptic charts on the top of an untidy pile. The other papers turned out to be old letters written in German. He ran a finger along the edge of the table, through the dust, before moving over to the only window in the room. He prised the slats of the Venetian blind wider. A small garden at the rear of the property, flower beds laid out in neat precision, a number of trees partially obstructing the sunlight. He eased the slat back, brushed the dust from his fingers, and went to the wall covered with framed photographs. Groups and portraits, thirties-style civilian clothes, uniforms of the Third Reich. A young blond-haired officer standing in the conning tower of his U-boat – Stock's father perhaps! A group of laughing young airmen, an Alsatian lying at their feet, next to a line of World War Two fighter aircraft. What might have been a nightclub setting with a beautiful blonde woman in a low-cut evening gown raising a glass of champagne to the camera – in the background, slightly out of focus, a stage and a white grand piano. It was signed in the lower right-hand corner, the faded ink difficult to decipher, the first line: *Ich bin Feuer und* – the next line unintelligible, the name beneath, Madelaine. He lifted the picture from the wall and turned it over. Removed the back carefully. Checked the photograph, before slipping it back in the frame. Finally he returned to his chair, picking up the book of matches from the coffee table as he sat. Glossy green with gold lettering. A hotel in Leticia – the Parador Ticuna. Tel: 27241.

It was half an hour later. He was backing the Grand Cherokee from the garage. 'Something I forgot to mention to you earlier,' Stock said to him through the open driver's window. 'Another rumour, but an interesting one. Emilio Figueras is offering five million dollars reward for information leading to the whereabouts of Mr Winter. I think perhaps information means his head.'

'A lot of money.'

'If it is true, but even then such a man would never pay. A safe journey, Mr Williams.' Stock held out his hand.

'No honour, you mean?'

'Precisely that.'

'When did you hear about it?'

White Lie

Stock knocked out his pipe on the palm of his hand, and scattered the ashes on the flower bed. 'This morning,' he said, sucking at the empty pipe to check for blockages. 'As I was changing planes in Bogotá. All the airport workers were talking about it. More money than they have ever dreamed of.'

Williams watched him in his rear-view mirror as he drove away. A man dressed in pale grey, to match his hair and eyes. The dust in his house. Almost invisible.

Back at the hotel Owens watched Williams hook up the hotel phone to his laptop computer. The never-ending pulse of music seemed fainter today. More distant. 'What are you doing?'

'Sending an e-mail message to Frank in Bogotá.'

'You think he may have more information on Winter?'

'I don't know. I just have a feeling there's something wrong. Why would Emilio Figueras offer a five-million-dollar reward, when Frank has already tipped off the cartel on Winter's location?'

'You did say it was a rumour.'

'Call it a gut feeling.'

'You sound like a policeman.'

'I feel like a policeman.'

'And our old friend Werner? You think a layer of dust in his house portends graver things?'

'The synoptic charts were more than three years old. I checked the dates. They were all in sequence.'

'And the letters were the same vintage, so you said. Why not an old bachelor who never gets around to unpacking, to filing paperwork, to doing housework?'

'You don't *do* housework here, Edeyrn. You hire

help. A few dollars a week, no more. Every household has its servants.'

'But not Werner?'

An observation. So normal as to be overlooked. 'He has a gardener. The gardens are immaculate.'

'Perhaps that's where he spends all his time, working with the soil.'

'His fingernails are manicured. His hands are very soft. A meteorologist turned businessman, maybe. A gardener? I don't think so.'

Owens, affecting a very passable Californian accent, said, 'And we are investigating Werner *because . . .*'

Williams smiled and shook his head. 'There was a framed photograph of a beautiful-looking woman, taken back in the early forties. I commented on it as I was leaving. Asked if it was his mother, who now lives in Leticia. He said it was. The point is he was lying. Earlier I'd noticed the photo had a wrinkled appearance. I took it out of the frame when he went to make a pot of coffee. It was a cutting from a German magazine. The page had been carefully folded and pressed into the frame. Apparently she was a famous nightclub singer in the thirties and early forties – killed in a night air raid on Hamburg in 1942. The piece was her obituary.'

'So Werner recruits a few more socially acceptable or attractive people to hang in his family tree, as opposed to *from* it. Nothing new in that.'

Williams said, 'I didn't say there was. I just want to know what he's hiding.'

A car stopped on the street below their open window. The radio so loud the floor seemed to shake. Owens reached for the Martell.

54

Emilio Figueras was looking out of the window, surveying the old city centre across the river, as Luis entered the boardroom on the top floor of the CALIMA building. Dark wood panelling. Period lighting. Gilt-framed oil on canvas, a job lot picked up from a New York art dealer. An imported Adams fireplace with an elegant silk screen – purchased from a Sotheby's auction in London years earlier. Bookcases of legal and corporate volumes – unread; an interior designer's attempt at European elegance. The long mahogany table which could seat thirty-six people, twinkling in the sunlight which slanted through the Venetian blinds. The smell of beeswax.

'Ah!' The old man spun round. 'The great general has returned.'

Luis immediately sensed the danger. His father, the enraged bull. Neck straining at his collar. Huge red hands hanging at his side, clenching and unclenching. Violence crackling around him like a summer storm.

Luis said, 'A pleasant surprise to see you, Patron. I was planning on calling at the house this evening.'

'To report your failure, no doubt.'

Failure? Winter! Los Llanos! What else? Now Luis
had a frame of reference for this unexpected visit from
his father, he quickly collected his thoughts, assemb-
ling them with legal precision. How he had diverted
the company jet on the previous evening to Bogotá,
where he had learned the mission to kill Winter might
have failed. This had taken time and although his crew
had been willing to fly him to Cali, he had insisted
that they get a good night's sleep. They had left Bogotá
only a few hours earlier. Less precise thoughts – how
he had dropped Ana off at his apartment, where she
had spurned his playful advances as she unpacked in
the bedroom, promising to cook him dinner, to get his
strength up for the long night, sending him off to the
office in a shower of kisses before she weakened. 'I was
told that one jet crashed. Was shot down. It is possible
that Winter was flying that plane.'

'And we lost two helicopters and ten men. Not good
odds, would you say? The problem with anonymous
information. What was it your accountant Becerra told
me? Winter and his men were working on a number of
broken airplanes, trying to make them flyable – there
was no threat. So you decide they were sitting ducks.
You did not consider to confirm the information first?'

'I was aware of the great urgency, Patron.'

The old man snorted. 'I have sent my men to scour
the wreckage. For your sake I hope that the body,
if there is a body, is that of the murderer of your
brother.'

Luis removed his glasses and rubbed his eyes, before
taking a handkerchief from his pocket and absently
polishing the lenses. 'I . . . I heard in Bogotá that you

have put out a five-million-dollar reward for the man Winter.'

'Something I would have expected you to do. Too simple, was it, Luis? Too simple for your superior-educated mind to get hold of? All that money I spent on educating you, sending you to fine universities, and the result? You talk law like a textbook, you use big, clever words, you make members of your own family feel like simple country fools. And out of all that, no common sense, not one gramme. Now I, your simple uneducated father, have millions of people looking for the gringo. *Millions*. Dead or alive. And what, you ask, will I do when I am presented with the assassin's body? Will I pay the reward? Of course I will pay the reward . . . with a smile on my face, even. Like my old friend Pablo Escobar I am charitable to the poor. I will publicly hand over the money and my heartfelt gratitude . . . that the poor unfortunate is killed and robbed in the next street will be of great sadness to me as I'm sure it will be to his family and friends.' The old man had been moving towards Luis as he spoke. Now he seized his arm in a fierce grip, and hissed, 'Your brother Francisco would have cleared up this matter long ago.'

Francisco had liked killing people. His father's son. 'I understand, Patron. I will not let you down.'

'But you have.' His face came very close. Close enough for Luis to smell the sour odour of garlic on his hot breath. 'You *have* let me down. This was a simple task. There were only three gringos at the airfield in Los Llanos – three! How can anyone fail to destroy three people? Armed or not.' The huge red hand came up and patted Luis on the cheek. 'How?

Because you were in Europe instead of being here directing the battle plans.'

'I . . . I was . . .'

Another pat. Harder this time. 'And your reason for going to Europe? Surely as the chairman of this vast company I am allowed to know how its money is being spent!'

Luis, who had written down all the possible questions and rehearsed all the possible answers, said, 'I have formulated a new way to *reinvest*' – he never used the word launder, or any other word that might imply black money – 'company funds. Legitimately, through an oil field development with a joint venture partner. The joint venture partner is one of the major international oil companies. The project will run for twenty years and will be underwritten by a German bank. I think you will be pleased when you see the business plan.' All true of course. Except Emilio Figueras would never get to see the plan. By then he and his cronies would be on board a private jet airliner being whisked towards the United States. A lifetime's incarceration. Or what was left of a lifetime.

'Bottom line?'

'Minimum increase on gross profits to the group a quarter of a billion US dollars per annum.'

'And when will I see this business plan?'

'Next Monday, Patron. The documents will be brought to your house – for your approval of course.'

The brutal face came closer, breathing its hot garlic stench. 'Do not make the mistake of thinking that improved financial arrangements will absolve you from this. You failed me over the Winter matter, you understand?' The coarse red hand tapped his cheek. A playful pat. Father to son. And was that a smile on his father's face?

Luis relaxed slightly. 'I understand, Patron.'

'No more chances,' the old man hissed. 'Now I will be watching you even more closely than before.' The huge hand crashed into the side of Luis's face, sending him reeling across the room. 'No more chances,' he repeated to himself as he left the room.

Luis stumbled around for a few moments, looking for his glasses, which had flown off with the force of the blow. He found them on the floor beneath one of the windows. He picked them up and pulled out a chair from the conference table and sat down. His body was shaking. He was afraid, more frightened than he could ever remember, but at least he had survived. He ran his tongue carefully around his mouth, tasting the blood. Thankful that there were no broken teeth. A thread of spit dribbled from the corner of his mouth. He wiped it with the back of his hand. Not much longer, Luis: you can last another five and a half days. One hundred and thirty-two hours, then you will be free of him for ever.

He remained sitting in the chair for a while, until the shaking had stopped, and the headache had become more bearable, then he left the boardroom and took the elevator down to the second floor. There was still work to be done. The CALIMA accounts would be first.

Mauricio Becerra's office was empty. A half-drunk cup of cold coffee on his desk. His computer screen, on screensaver, was blank. Luis went back through the door and down the corridor to the reception area. The girl on the switchboard was sniffling. At first he thought she was suffering from a head cold, then he realised she was crying.

'Beatriz, there is something wrong? You are not well?'

The girl looked up quickly, fighting back the tears. 'I am sorry, Señor Figueras, please forgive me. It is Señor Becerra, I have only just heard.'

A pinpricking sensation of the scalp. 'Heard?'

'He is dead – an accident.'

Luis stared at her, his mouth dropping open. 'Dead! A car accident? What? What happened?'

The girl had taken a handkerchief from her handbag and was dabbing at her eyes. Smudging her mascara in the process. 'At lunchtime, Señor. He was at the sugar mill . . . they said he was talking to the manager about purchasing some new equipment . . . it seems he slipped and fell . . . into . . . into one of the machines . . .'

Luis listened in disbelief. Momentarily closing his eyes, trying to ward off the brutal image of his father.

Like his pet dog (a present from his mother) had been poisoned when he was a boy. No one knew anything about it, except his father, who hated animals. He gloated for days.

Like his mother, who had died for the simple need of a few pills. His father had hated her as well.

Now Mauricio, for no other reason than his son counted him as a friend.

A warning. He was next.

PART EIGHT
Tally-Ho!

55

The airstrip at Hill Station was little more than that, a two-mile concrete gash on the plateau of a table-top mountain. A derelict hangar on the north side of an east–west runway – frameworked angular steel with the majority of the roof cladding rusted through, leaving gaping holes which mirrored the changing sky. The whole was threatened by the deciduous trees and lush vegetation of a subtropical rainforest. Even so it was better than the savannah they had left, where the dust and heat could become so strong it was difficult to breathe.

Better! Winter thought about that as he heated water on the hobo stove he had fashioned from an empty five-gallon drum, and remembered the cold plains winters in Oklahoma: the campus drifted with snow, the vivid colours of buildings and cars and evergreens against the eye-aching white, the stamping feet of students in the corridors, books, chalk dust, a peace that was almost tangible. He missed it, much in the same way on those bitter winter nights he had sometimes missed the heat of these places, the powerful smells of rotting vegetation mixing with those of hot aeroplane engines, fuel, grease; the choreographed flame and thunder and check-listed precision of the military life. Two nostalgias face to face, and it took returning to one of them to make him realise that the past was a lie and that memory runs inexorably forward. No refundable deposits on days. No action replays. Even his life with Julia had in the final analysis been an ephemeral truth.

And if that was true, what of the Midas touch he had once possessed? Gone! How could he have overlooked the very real possibility that Ramon would sell him out at the first opportunity, especially as Red Stevens had replaced the Colombian and his men with his own crew? He should have anticipated. But he hadn't. He had merely considered the monthly bonus payment to Ramon of $1,000 – every month until the operation was complete – to be adequate compensation. Even Charlie, without that knowledge, had sensed the bad karma. Had warned him.

He opened two instant-coffee packets and emptied the contents into the water that was beginning to bubble in the mess tin. The smell seemed to revive him. As it did Maria, who crawled out of her makeshift shelter rubbing her eyes. 'What time is it?'

'Seven.' He poured some of the coffee into another mess tin and handed it to her.

'You like early mornings, don't you?'

'Best part of the day.'

'And all this!' She indicated the two lean-to shelters he had erected in the opening of the hangar, along one wall; the wooden reflector walls he had cut and bound together – the principle being only surfaces facing an outdoor fire are warmed by it and a reflector not only reflects heat but makes smoke go upward; the plastic bags he had tied around the ends of a number of healthy, leafy branches, leaving the trees to draw up moisture from a water table as deep as fifty or more feet; evaporation from the leaves producing a condensation that collected in the bags – a supplemental to their rationed emergency water supply. 'You are very good at surviving in the outdoors.'

The usual contempt in her voice was absent. That worried him. 'Camp craft, something I learned in the army.'

'So, I learn something new about you. And what did you do in the army?'

'Prepared for war.'

'And when there were none, you went away and started your own.'

'Is that what you think?'

She made no reply. For a moment he thought she was about to immerse herself into one of her angry silences. But she was looking up at the overcast sky. Inspecting it. 'What happens now? What if this Red Stevens does not arrive this morning?'

'What makes you think he won't?'

She looked back at the sky. 'The weather. It looks as though it might come down.'

'Not according to the barometer – I checked the altimeter in the B-25. A slight rise from yesterday evening.'

'And the Lightning? Without fuel I think we have a very big problem.'

Winter shook his head. 'That's where Red earns his money.'

'Except you said he was going to the old base.'

'True. We might have to launch in the B-25 and wait in the vicinity of Eerie, in the event that he comes into Los Llanos a different way than I anticipate. Other than that he'll be there.'

'You are certain?'

'Yes.'

'In the same way you were certain we were safe at Eerie One, even though the *federales* had found us?'

So that was it. Back to Charlie's death. Totally unnecessary according to her. Totally unnecessary if he had paid attention to Charlie's warning about moving out. 'My mistake,' he said in a quiet voice. 'The last one, I assure you.'

'And I am supposed to accept that?'

'You can leave with Red this morning. He'll take you over to Venezuela. From there you can get an airline back to the States.'

She sipped at the coffee, and pulled a face at the bitter taste. 'And the alternative? We have hardly any water and the only food is the survival rations from the plane.'

He said, 'You can come back with me tomorrow night to the States.'

Her eyes flew wide. 'Tomorrow! How?'

'I've brought the mission date forward. Tomorrow afternoon in fact. Subject to Red getting sufficient Jet A-1 up here to refuel the Lightning.'

'What about range? You were planning to take the F.6 because of the better endurance.'

Winter looked across the ramp to the T.5. They'd refuelled and rearmed the Lightning after he had scored a lucky hit with one of the four 500-pound bombs he'd rippled over one of the Hueys. The other helo had fled at zero feet in a northerly direction. With precious little fuel they had landed and taxied into the hangar ramp. Forty-five minutes to refuel and load up another four bombs, as the flames inside the hangar spread rapidly. With the hangar doors closed, the pressure build-up was phenomenal. Enough to blow out the two large roof windows and send them whirling skywards. So high they disappeared from view. Then Maria had started the B-25. And he had followed. They were airborne before the racks of Mk 82 bombs in the hangar exploded. Even so he felt the teeth-rattling shock wave as he was passing one thousand feet, turning left for Hill Station. Fear, adrenaline, shakes: it never got any better. 'I checked the map – about three hundred kilometres to the target.'

'And the same back. And then you have the low-level segment to consider. High fuel burn. I think it is not possible . . . unless . . . unless you did not come back here at all.' She looked at him for a moment.

'Go on.'

'You continue west to Buenaventura. Across the bay, about twenty kilometres further west there is a place called Pianguita beach. Very long. Very flat. I could position there in the B-25, wait for you to come overhead and eject. Then I could land and pick you up.'

Suicide. What were the chances that the ejector seat would work after . . . how many years since it had been removed and serviced? But what was the alternative? 'You've been there? This beach.'

'My grandparents used to live in a village nearby, La Bocana.'

'What about tidal levels? We'd need to check on that. Also, how soft the surface is.'

411

'Your friend Red Stevens could do that. Where are we going in the States?'

'Initially to Merida, Mexico.'

'Then Buenaventura would be perfect. We could fly up the Pacific coast towards Panama and cross over to the Caribbean. Daylight or dark?'

'Late afternoon, dusk at the beach you mentioned. Dark by the time we're on our way up the coast. What about Panamanian radar?'

'They have primary and secondary, but I think they will not pay much attention to an unidentified paint, especially on a Sunday evening. They will either be just coming on shift after a day with their family, or going off duty and looking forward to a Sunday dinner. It is a good day for us. You could overthrow the government on a Sunday and no one would pay the slightest attention.'

'It's still risky. You understand?'

'Yes.'

'If we're caught on that beach . . . it's a death warrant.'

She pursed her lips. Then looked at her hands. Back and front. Then curled the fingers over and inspected her nails. They were full of dirt. 'Have we any spare water?'

'Water! For what?'

'To wash. We have a visitor coming. Perhaps you also have a clean sweatshirt I can use.' Her eyes were suddenly bright. The last few days of boredom consigned to a deferred defects list at the back of an imaginary tech log. The prospect of flying again. Of action. The tip of the arrow.

* * *

Red Stevens arrived in the overhead thirty-three minutes later. Unannounced. Winter was out at the B-25
doing a walk-round inspection, considering the fact
that they were going to have to get airborne and position
over to Eerie to stand any chance of making radio
contact with him, when the T-tailed King Air appeared
out of the grey sky and sailed over the airstrip at no more
than a thousand feet. Winter ran back to the hangar and
grabbed his hand-held transceiver. 'Tyler, Sibelius.'

Nanosecond delay. 'G'day, Sibelius. Had a feeling I'd
find you here. Which runway you using?'

Winter checked the smoke from the camp fire. 'Two
seven. Wind out of the southwest, about ten knots. You
want the altimeter setting?'

'If it's handy?'

'Need to get it from the B-25. Give me a minute.'

'Naah, that's okay. Tyler's finals now. All green.'

Winter marshalled the King Air alongside the B-25,
then went back and opened the rear airstair door.
Stevens had completed the shutdown checks and was
there before the props had stopped turning. 'Shit!
Had me worried,' he said, coming down the steps.
'You okay?'

'Fine. What did you hear?'

'Got into town last night. Preparation for the planned
launch this morning, as we'd discussed. Went over to
the airport weather office to make sure it was going
to be clear and overheard there'd been a small shooting war out this way. Planes and helos shot down.
Jesus, to listen to those guys you'd think you'd just
stumbled on the opening salvoes of World War Three
. . . Anyway I figured it was you, and that if you'd

survived you'd have made a bolt for this place. Good guess, eh?'

Winter led him over to the hangar area and the camp-fire. Maria, face and hands scrubbed clean, was making coffee on the stove. 'Red, Maria . . . Maria, Red.'

The Australian grinned and shook her hand, then looked through the open hangar doorway. 'Charlie about?'

No easy way. 'He was shot down, Red. Killed. Caught a missile . . . lucky shot I'd guess.' A distortion of the truth, maybe, but getting dinged in combat was eminently better than forgetting to pull your seat pins – you could do that on peacetime ops. And that is what would be remembered. Not that he got airborne in a totally unserviceable aeroplane and splashed one of the enemy. And gave his partner a chance of survival. Just that he had made a fundamental error and paid the ultimate price. Something they called 'pilot error'. Charlie deserved better.

A catch in the throat. 'Ah, Jeez, real sorry to hear that. I was looking forward to splitting a beer with the old bugger.' He took a corona cigar from his shirt pocket, bit off the end and spat it out, and crouched down to light it from the fire. His free hand going to his eyes – brushing away hot ash, or smoke . . . or a tear!

When he stood up he caught the questioning look from Winter. 'I know, I've stopped smoking. Call this a temporary mental aberration. Something to calm me down . . . So when are you planning on getting out of here?'

'Tomorrow. Need a few supplies.'

'No problem. Give me the list and it'll be done.'

'What about getting jet fuel up here?'

'How much?'

'Enough to refuel the Lightning.'

'Mate of mine's got a Caribou, based at Caracas. I'll get onto him, probably have it here first light tomorrow morning. Cost you a bit extra, though.'

'No problem with that. What's the status at the Cali end?'

'Okay. Basically, you've got eight fairly well-concealed guard towers around the perimeter at approximately three-hundred-metre intervals. They form a part of the surrounding wall. From what I can tell they've got Zip-u's in each tower . . . fourteen-point-five-millimetre, belt-fed, very lethal to low-flying aircraft. Nothing heavier observed, but I wouldn't discount some type of hand-launched missiles – knowing these guys, if they have them they'll be the best money can buy. Laser-guided stuff. About a hundred troops on the ground, dispersed around the compound.' He drank some of his coffee. 'Yesterday afternoon just before I left, a convoy of trucks arrived. They weren't unloaded so at this point in time we don't know what they are carrying. Other than that, the big chief, Emilio Figueras, rarely leaves the house, and if he does he's always back well before nightfall. He's got a son, apparently, a lawyer, works in the city. Haven't seen him out there at all. That's about it. Oh, there's a tall radio mast at the back, the west, of the property, about three hundred feet a.g.l. No other obstructions – except of course the mountains.'

'Not much room for manoeuvring, then?'

'I'd say a one-shot deal. If you have to make a go-round and line up for a second run, they'll be waiting for you.'

Winter handed the Australian an envelope. 'Before we discuss the contents of the envelope, here's what I need doing by fourteen hundred hours tomorrow . . .'

Twenty minutes later, Red Stevens took a last puff on his cigar and threw it into the embers of the campfire. 'Don't get shot down or anything bloody silly before you pay me, will you?' The contagious laughter was noticeably subdued. The news of Charlie.

'I'll try not to.'

'I only mention that because those guys in the weather office at Cali also mentioned something about a reward. I didn't catch much of that part of the conversation and being a gringo I wanted to blend into the background best I could. But at a guess I'd say you and Maria here could be up on a local wanted poster. Not good news if you have to use your chute and land among a bunch of locals.'

'I'll try and keep it simple.'

'Sure.' He turned to Maria and added, 'Nice meeting you, Maria, safe trip tomorrow – oh, and I hope the clothes my wife picked out for you were okay.'

Momentary uncertainty flickered in the dark eyes. 'Clothes? Oh, yes, they were fine . . . perhaps you will thank her for me.'

'Sure I will.'

A hand on Winter's shoulder. 'Sorry again about Charlie . . . one of the best.'

A ghost of a smile. He'd have liked that. 'Thanks.'

Stevens said, 'We'll be doing the DJ thing tomorrow then. Don't get brave up there – just get on and off the target in a hurry.'

*   *   *

Minutes later the King Air was gone. The faint whisper of the Pratt & Whitney Dash 42 engines lingering for a second or two in the clouds, then nothing. Aviation people. Fast movers.

Maria was looking at him with some of the old anger burning in her eyes. 'The clothes! I am expected to apologise to you?'

Winter was busying himself extinguishing the morning campfire, slightly later than usual. Red's visit. An excuse. Not good enough. He was beginning to see his own mistakes shining through everything else. What else had he missed? What else was he going to overlook between now and the mission launch?

'Well?'

He hadn't heard. Hadn't been listening. 'I'm sorry, what did you say?'

She pushed past him, striding across the ramp area to the B-25. The Spanish might have translated to, 'Screw you, Winter, screw you!', but he couldn't be sure.

Certain the fire was completely extinguished, he began the long walk down the runway, to the job he had been working on over the past few days. A large granite boulder, halfway down the strip, a few yards off the left side of the runway, partially hidden in the tall grass. One that he had decided would be Charlie's memorial stone. Close enough to his final landfall. When complete the simple inscription would read:

RIKER
Woesheil

A familiar scenario. Leaving friends at the end of the world. Only problem was there weren't many left.

56

At Manga Island Williams and Owens were preparing for sea. Checking the yacht's engine, electrical supply, navigation and radio systems, and stocking with provisions. Water slapped tiredly against the hull. Faint salsa music pulsed on the morning breeze, distant enough to be bearable – as was the low-eighties heat.

'You still think we should stay the extra night?' Williams said, dropping down into the galley.

Owens had poured out two plastic cups of fresh orange juice. 'You asked my advice, I gave it.' He passed one of the cups to Williams. 'Ever spend any time in the Arctic?'

'No.'

'The Inuit used to use huskies to pull their sleds. Then the snowmobile was invented and they transferred their allegiance to the internal-combustion engine. Problem was they inherited an unforeseen problem. More fatal accidents. Falling into deep unseen fissures that had opened up on the snow fields. You see, the husky, like all wild animals, possesses a sixth sense, an ability to smell danger and therefore avoid it. The dogs would simply stop running when they approached a hazard. The snowmobile has no such powers.'

'And you think Winter will still produce the information he promised me on the Cali Cartel.'

'He's not going to stop running. Besides, what hazards has he encountered?'

'The raid at Los Llanos!'

'Which according to Frank's e-mail to you was something of a débâcle. Something that would only strengthen Winter's resolve and, it seems, the cartel's. Why else the five-million-dollar reward? And if you're worried the Los Llanos raid might be attributable to you, don't be. Didn't you tell Winter that the word was out, that's how we'd located him?'

Williams took the gold Dunhill lighter from the pocket of his sports shirt and turned it over in his fingers. 'You're missing the point, Edeyrn. I don't need to be here. Frank's e-mail meant nothing. No cover memo. He's acting as the whipping boy for Bill Rice. He was as good as telling me, "Of all the people in the world who might have to take a fall, you have been voted the most qualified in history".'

'Moral dilemmas, is it, boyo? You've broken the rules, probably the law. And the blood on your hands will raise the investigative questions about the White House, the CIA, Congress, the political temptation of covert action, the fakery of plausible deniability. Except you're assuming the worst.'

'You said it yourself, Winter's still running.'

'Unseen fissures.'

'Like what?'

'We wait another day for the information. Give him the seven days you promised.'

'You think he'll trade without the amnesty paperwork?'

'*He* might not, but I doubt *he's* going to be the messenger boy. Even so, if he delivers, I think your concerns might lie in a different direction.'

'Like what?'

Owens sipped at his orange juice. 'Think about it. What other reason, apart from an amnesty document, might he have had for doing a deal with you? Buying some kind of protection from the CIA perhaps, enough time to complete his little war with the cartel.'

Williams became very still. 'And when the information is delivered he has no more need for such protection – meaning whatever he had planned has been executed.'

'One more day,' Owens said.

'Perhaps I should contact Bill Rice.'

'What can he do?'

'Same as me. Have a sleepless night.'

57

It was a breath of much-needed fresh air for Oscar
Porteous. He put the phone down and went over to
the window. Watching the snowflakes swirling against
the glass. A DO officer instinctively savoured a moment
like this; praise from the top, even if it was from a man
like Eberhart. In such obedience there was a comforting,
almost exhilarating, recognition of being a part. He had
put himself out on a limb many times in his career. This
had been the farthest he had been. Some might have
said too far.

He took his handkerchief – tucked into his jacket
sleeve – and held it to his mouth, failing to suppress
the coughing fit that came upon him. Blood speckled
in the greyish-yellow phlegm. What was it the doctor
had called it? Coffee-ground emesis? Whatever it was it
was getting worse. As was the stomach pain. Bleeding
ulcers, he was sure. Perhaps when this was over he
would take some leave, check into a private clinic for
the EGD that had been recommended. Why ever not? A
few weeks recuperating and he would be a new man.

He walked slowly back to the *caquetoire* he had turned to face the limestone fireplace, and sat and watched the flames from the log fire dancing up the chimney. Twisting the edge of the handkerchief between his fingers. Going over the STU conversation in his mind. Right down to Eberhart's obscene whisper.

'Congratulations.'

'What for?' he had asked suspiciously.

'That memo on handling the news media over the White Knight business – dumb bastards have been so busy trying to nail us to the fucking cross that they missed the White House coup. President's very pleased, Oscar.'

'Glad to have been of service, Director. Everything went according to plan then?'

'Off the record, Monday is D-day. A few i's to be dotted, a few t's to be crossed – extradition will take place Monday night. There'll be a private gathering at the White House later in the week. Drinks. Pats on the back.'

Drinks. Pats on the back.

Porteous closed his eyes, feeling the soothing warmth of the fire on his face. Lately he had been trying to last until midday before he had his first cigarette. Today he felt he might make it.

58

Night skies.

If you needed perspective for the *so-called* enormity of what you were about to do, this was always a good place – staring out across the vast tracks of empty space where galaxies piled upon galaxies, where time was measured in Euclidean space curves, where black holes lay in wait like hunters' traps, and gamma ray quanta replaced primitive voice communications between pilot and ground controller.

Winter walked across the starlit ramp and climbed the steps to the Lightning's cockpit, lowering himself into the left seat, trying to lose himself amid the smells of sweat, mildew, hydraulic fluid, burnt wiring, jet fuel. Running through tomorrow's mission sequence in his mind. Looking for the kinesthesia he felt in flight. He'd been able to do that once. Sit in an aeroplane and close his eyes and imagine every detail of past missions, and superimpose them onto the imaginary one. The one that had yet to happen. But not any more. Whatever magic he had once possessed had gone. And from out of the darkness, mixed with night sounds, Charlie's voice came to haunt him:

'*It's a young man's game . . . me fly an airplane? Shit, we'd both end up in a fireball at the end of the first runway I tried to negotiate . . . what about those Martin-Baker ejection seats, when were they last overhauled? . . . did anyone ever tell you you're fucking crazy? . . . it's your deal if you want to go home on your shield . . .*'

And he realised that in the last seven years he had paid his final dues to life, including growing old. And if that's not war, he thought, it can only be death. It was a supposition so convincing that he identified it as a premonition. That was when his hands began to shake. His legs. His entire body. Adrenaline rush. It would go soon.

But it didn't.

It was nearly an hour later when he left the aircraft and made his way to the hangar. To Maria's shelter.

'Wint?' Alarm in her voice.

'Yes . . . who else?'

'There is something wrong?'

'Can I lie with you?'

The alarm, the concern, evaporated in an instant. Replaced by the familiar bitterness. 'You want to fuck me, is that what you are asking? What soldiers always do before the battle.'

'No – just lie by you.'

She threw back the solitary blanket and made room for him on the narrow wood-framed cot he had built on the evening of their arrival, and he lay with his back to her, his head sharing the bundle of clothes she had rolled into a pillow, feeling her body heat through his shirt.

'You are shivering, you are unwell?'

'No, I'm fine. Just cold. I'll be okay in a minute.'

She put her arm across him and pulled herself closer. 'You have had malaria?'

'It's not that.'

'What then?'

'Mortality.'

'I do not understand.'

He almost laughed. He didn't think he did. 'I never called you Maria, did I? Always Miss Espinosa.'

Her voice lightened. 'Very proper. Very English.'

'Yes, I suppose . . .'

'Tell me something.'

'If I can.'

'Your callsign, Sibelius. Where did that come from?'

His mind clicked at the combination of memory. Athens? Jeddah? Sharjah? Any one of them, or a dozen more. He couldn't be certain. 'Old flier I once knew, Jack Crane. He was a lover of classical music. He introduced me to Sibelius's works . . . said that as a person I was like the composer . . . more complex than was generally supposed . . . someone sensitive to criticism and yet his own worst critic.'

'And so he gave you the name.'

'So he gave me the name.' He didn't add: a seemingly infinite capacity for evolving new material from simple germinal ideas. That had been a long time ago. A different man perhaps.

She kept talking to him, softly. Asking him questions. Until tiredness took over and he found himself slipping towards sleep. The shaking stopped. The warmth of her body comforting him. A half-recognised familiarity.

He awoke briefly in the night, uncertain of his surroundings, aware only of a dream: driving down a yellow dirt road and finding a black tar pit, the skull of a prehistoric animal preserved in the black liquid watching him. Then a hand was caressing his back, and a voice was making gentle shushing sounds, as a mother to a child.

He slept again. And dreamed of Julia. He was telling her about his student. The one who had been beaten by the druggies. Severe head injuries, brain damage. Such a brilliant scholar. Such a waste.

'The police?' she asked.

'They like chasing people in cars, handing out speeding tickets. No stomach for dealing with real crime.'

'Would you, for ten dollars an hour?'

'Is that all they get paid?'

'A little more perhaps.'

'It's the schools,' he said then. 'The pushers are there every morning – they don't sell at first. They give. Get the kids hooked, until the kids are stealing from their own parents to pay for the next fix.'

And later on another night.

'How is your student? The one who was beaten with the iron bar.'

'I went to the hospital today to see him – his room was empty. The nurse asked if I was family. Historically so, I told her. I don't think she understood – she told me he died in the early hours of this morning.'

'Oh, I'm sorry.'

'Yes, and me. Can you understand what's happening?'

'Perhaps I should talk to my producer, see if I can do

a series on pushers targeting metro area schools. What do you think?'

He was falling asleep. He mumbled, 'The next time it might be Hemingway . . . or Steinbeck.'

'What did you say?' She shook his shoulder.

He repeated it.

'Good angle . . . great angle. Might work.'

The beginning and the end. Lying with her night after night. Caressing her body. Talking to her about the vulnerability of schools. *Preparing her for the executioner.*

59

Luis Figueras was lying awake staring into the darkness, going over the final stages of planning which had consumed three years of his life.

Sunday: Ana departs at 6 a.m. in the new BMW 540 (he had bought it for her two days earlier, a belated Christmas present he had insisted; she had been delighted). In the trunk of the car, four suitcases, two briefcases, and a change of clothing. Destination: Bogotá.

A simple precaution in the event his movements were being monitored and reported to his father.

At noon, leave the apartment and drive to CALIMA building. Tell security guard you are going to your office and are not to be disturbed for any reason. Once in office, close Venetian blinds and switch on desk lamp. Change into street cleaner's blue-denim clothes, including cap (which have been hidden there for the last six months). Wrap own clothes in brown-paper bundle and leave office, locking door. Exit building through rear delivery entrance. Take a sequence of three taxis to airport, essential to check not being followed. At airport go to toilets and change back into casual clothes – dump denim in trash bin. Check in for 2.45 p.m. flight to Bogotá. Ana waiting at Bogotá's El Dorado airport at 3.30 p.m. Drive to Hotel La Bohème – north of the city in the Zona Rosa. Room service – champagne naturally.

Monday: 7 a.m. – Leave for meeting. Instruct Ana to remain in hotel suite until noon, and speak to no one.

7.30 a.m. – Meeting with two senior members Constituent Assembly and Director of Criminal Investigation. Hand over all four suitcases. First suitcase contains hard-copy documents which will incriminate every member of the Cartel de Cali. Other three suitcases packed with American one-hundred-dollar bills – tell them a million or two in each suitcase, you haven't counted. Suggest that the 'black' money can perhaps be used as evidence! They will nod sagely and agree (both sides will know it is vote-buying money, as in an election year when politicians raffle off home appliances in exchange for electoral favours). Coffee and iced water offered. Small talk. Then a government limousine to airport. Charter jet standing by. Destination: Madrid, Spain.

Luis glanced at the bedside clock. The luminous numbers showed 4.10 a.m. He yawned and buried his head in the pillows. Perfect plan. Prelude to a new life. Quite perfect. Every aspect checked and double-checked. Much in the way he had chosen Ana Lucia from a carefully selected short list. And she was enough in love with him and his money to obey without question. That he would never return to the hotel suite in Bogotá meant little to him. Her social status had always precluded her from being anything other than a highly paid whore. Acting like one was quite acceptable, provided you knew when to stop and become a lady.

She did not. Upbringing.

60

'I think you have a problem with the fuel!' Maria said.

Winter looked up from the bowl of water he was shaving in. A bonus to the jet fuel – and two drums of Avgas to top off the B-25 – they had received from the Caribou crew that morning: a fifty-gallon drum of water. Enough to wash out a pair of flight suits, socks, shirts, pants. The washing was hanging on a makeshift line between the B-25's right engine propeller and the nose. They were both sitting under the wing of the B-25 – shade from the noonday sun. 'Like what?'

'You told me this morning that with full fuel you needed a lot of luck to make Pianguita beach. That is so?'

'More or less.'

'What weight are you using for your calculations?'

'Seven pounds per US gallon.'

'Because that is what you were using at Eerie?'

'Yes.'

'Except the fuel at Eerie One was JP-5. Higher flashpoint and therefore a higher weight than, say,

JP-4, or what Red's people brought in this morning, Jet A-1.'

Winter's brain dug up some half-forgotten theory about a jet engine deriving its thrust from the weight of fuel burned, not the volume. Thus one does not refer to range in terms of miles per gallon, but miles per pound. 'And the weight of the Jet A-1?'

'According to Red's people, six point six pounds per gallon.'

'You asked them?'

'Of course.'

Another mistake. Small enough to be overlooked. Small enough to be fatal. 'So working on the total fuel capacity of the T.5, how much range am I losing?'

'Difficult to say as you are planning a hi-lo-hi profile, with the high-level segments on one engine. What level do you fly at on the high-level cruise?'

'Twenty thousand – bit more maybe.'

'Speed?'

'Three sixty knots.'

Maria ran her finger across a graph taken from one of the aircraft's technical manuals and scribbled quick calculations on a piece of paper. 'Allowing three minutes' low-level for the bomb run, plus the climb back to cruising altitude, and assuming the temperature remains at ISA plus fifteen, I think you will flame out four minutes before Pianguita beach . . . twenty-four miles.'

'What if I went up to forty thousand for the high-level cruise?'

'With no standby oxygen! I think it is a dangerous idea.'

'Pressurisation system hasn't failed yet.'

A shake of the head as she returned to her calculations. Hair falling into her eyes. An impatient flick of the hand. 'Two minutes' reserve at Pianguita – not much.'

'Enough.'

She poured half a cup of coffee from one of the thermos flasks she had prepared that morning before the campfire was extinguished. Passed it to him. His hand touched hers. He left it there for for a moment, looked into her eyes. She smiled.

He said, 'You're clear on the plan after Merida?'

'Yes. We formate on the DC-6 and follow him up Amber 770 towards Grand Isle . . .'

'You have the airway charts?'

'Yes.'

'And my ETA at Pianguita beach?'

'Seventeen forty-five alpha.' Military phrasing for local time.

'If I'm not there by seventeen fifty, go on alone. Understand? Could be that I run out of fuel earlier than planned. In that case I'll be ejecting somewhere over the mountains and making my way out on foot.'

He could see that she did not believe him. He hurried on: 'If that happens, you have Red's contact numbers in Caracas. Call him once you're back in the States. He'll know of my whereabouts – I'll be two-way radio with him on the run this afternoon. In fact if I have to eject prematurely he'll probably be the one to pick me up. Also he's been instructed to wire you funds if you call him from back home.'

'You have no intention of coming.'

'I have every intention, but I've lived too long not to have a backup plan . . . Have we covered everything?'

'Fuel, weather, both aircraft preflighted . . . nothing yet on the Pianguita beach state.'

'Don't worry about that, that's the way we operate. If Red had found problems he would have got a message to us. The fact that he hasn't means it's okay to use as a landing strip.'

'How long before take-off?'

He looked at his watch. 'Four and a half hours – I'll be thirty minutes behind you.'

Her eyes were on him. Watching his fingers run back through his blond hair. The startling blueness of his eyes. He had been here with her all this time, and yet it was as though she sometimes saw him from a different angle, as though it were the very first time. It always took her breath away. She said, 'What about the shelters in the hangar? Perhaps we should take them down. What did you call it – leaving no trace?'

He looked up and smiled. Boyish. Something she had not seen before. 'Slash and burn.'

In the same way they had loaded the B-25 with anything from partially filled oil and fuel drums, to spare survival rations. Piling it all in the bomb bay along with the life raft and ELTs (Emergency Locator Transmitters). A simple matter of house cleaning, leaving no trace of their presence in this place.

They walked across the concrete ramp to the open hangar door. Hands brushing hands. The sun beating fiercely down. No wind, but the altitude helped. Made it a dryish heat. Almost pleasant.

She crawled into the darkness of the shelter and sat on the makeshift cot. He joined her. Sitting close so that their bodies were touching. His hand moved automatically to her waist, gently squeezing the flesh beneath the thin cotton T-shirt. An electric silence stretched between them, until neither of them could stand it any longer. Then they flung their arms around each other, lips seeking lips with something close to an act of violence.

They undressed quickly, then she was pulling him on top of her, her legs lifting and wrapping around his waist, guiding him quickly and expertly into her. A small moan. Nothing more. No words passed between them as their bodies moved together with an urgency that surprised them both.

Later they lay side by side, facing each other in the semidarkness, sweat-covered bodies pressed tightly together. He kissed her neck and her shoulders, memorising the faint scent and the silkiness of her skin on his tongue.

And finally slept.

And dreamed he was back at his university. Five thirty on a raw winter's afternoon – already dark – a mist from the river lifting as a jaundiced smoke against the lit windows across the campus lawns, coalescing on the dark boughs of blackthorn trees as glittering necklaces, softening the severe geometry of the concrete pathways; more cleverly time-slipping the place east to the Greenwich meridian where it became a corner of the old country, and all because of the silent collision of temperature and dew-point on a near winter's day. Even so it was not an unpleasant illusion to him as he made his way along the footpath. The country of his youth often beckoned across the years. It was not so much that he missed England, just that he sometimes came face to face with her faded pictures. A nod of recognition, nothing more, and they would go their separate ways.

Except on this day there was more. Charlie Riker calling out of the darkness. Welcoming him. Telling him that his ejector seat pins *had* been removed . . . that the seat had failed . . . that all the ejector seats were inoperative.

'Not on the T.5, though,' Winter said.

'You're not fucking listening again,' Charlie snapped. 'Why do you think you're here?'

'At the university, you mean?'

Charlie laughed. 'University! You gotta be kidding. Y'know what this place is? The DEW Line. Distant Early Waiting. It's all fucked up – like the world you just left. We have to wait for the inspection team to categorise us for onward transportation.'

'Left! You mean I'm dead?'

'The ejection seat . . . I told you about it. Warned you. Great device . . . zero-zero capability . . . hell, you can eject while you're sitting on the chocks . . . providing it's serviceable in the first place. Except it never was, Wint. That's why those planes had never flown. The seats weren't wired up. They were waiting for parts.'

'You're sure?'

'You wanna go back and try again?'

'Can you do that?'

Ugly Charlie's muffled laughter drifted out of the fog. 'Crash and burn? Sure you can.'

He awoke covered in sweat. In the same kind of semidarkness he had just left. Frightening. It was for a moment.

'Wint . . . you are all right?' Maria's voice, a whisper in his ear.

Disturbed by the noise of dead people. How all right is that? 'A dream, I was having a dream.'

She kissed his lips, then ran her mouth slowly down
to the hollow of his shoulder. And after a while was still,
but for the steady rythmic breathing of sleep. He lay in
the hot darkness, checking his watch from time to time.
Counting off the minutes. Concentrating on the task that
lay ahead. Reading off the mental checklist.

Pushing Charlie's warning from his mind.

Above 40,000 feet the sky was a deep indigo blue
offering a glimpse of deep space. A total detachment
from the earth below, a temporary relief from the problems that being on the ground brought. For Winter
especially. Nothing else mattered – at least for these
few moments.

Even his *raison d'être* had been relegated to a far-off
place: the face of the young Francisco Figueras which
he had observed down to the last detail – gone, as was
the Colombian's arrogant voice when he had tried to
buy Winter off, thinking he was nothing more than a
mugger after an easy pay day; how he had offered him
a job working for him, better pay, all the women he
could handle – like the one he had raped and killed
some days earlier, a pretty TV woman with nice tits
he had taken his knife to and who had kneeled naked
before him promising him anything, and how she had
given him the best blow job he'd ever had, and how
he'd fucked her for six straight hours before cutting her,
piece by piece.

Deep space. Being that close was a kind of benediction.
A cleansing of body and mind. Something that existed
only for the passage of flight. Something that reached
out and touched all aviators. Changed them for ever.

Here and now Winter was that changed man. A cool clinical technician going about his job. Unconsciously iconoclastic because of the underlying realisation that complacency was the implacable enemy. He had reprogrammed the GPS and was on a 'direct' to the target, his natural instinct to detour to the north of Cali and drop down into the mountains as a means of radar evasion being overruled by fuel/endurance considerations. The last thing he wanted was to flame out and eject over inhospitable terrain with the prospect of possible injury and having to walk through the mountains for days. Besides, he had reasoned, even if Cali airport primary radar picked him up they would first consider him high-level overflying traffic. And if and when they plotted his descent and made whatever telephone calls were necessary to whatever military bases, he would be off the target and long gone.

He confirmed the frequency on the VHF hand-held – 123.45 – before depressing the transmit button. 'Tyler, this is Sibelius, how do you read?'

Instant response. 'Sibelius, Tyler, fives, go ahead.'

'Sibelius is five zero east of you, heading two six five, angels four zero.'

'You planning a straight in?'

'Affirm.'

Momentary pause from the Australian. *Don't get brave up there.* Untransmitted thought. 'Okay, weather over target good. Scattered cumulus three to four thousand a.g.l. Make your run on a heading of two eight five following the bush road . . . advise one five miles inbound.'

'Roger, call you fifteen miles. Confirm packet delivered to Cartagena.'

'That's affirm. Negative reply though.'

'Expected . . . confirm emergency landing strip operational?'

'That's Charlie.'

'Sibelius commencing descent . . . we'll advise at one five miles.'

'Roger. Matter of interest, just had four vehicles arrive . . . looks like a full house.'

Winter gave a double click on the transmit button, and with both throttles back at idle, selected the airbrakes and lowered the nose. The spine of the Cordillera Central had passed aft. Ahead the Cordillera Occidental and beyond that the blue of the Pacific washed pink by the lowering sun.

Time check: 1725 alpha.

61

The only mistake Luis Figueras had made was being kind to the wrong people. Especially to the likes of Raf Rodrigues. The tall, long-haired minder did not respond to a gentle hand. He had been raised in the Cali slums and beaten every day of his life by a drunken father. Genetics and environment conditioning him to respond to brutality in all its forms.

So it was that when Luis Figueras had taken over the day-to-day running of the CALIMA empire from his father, Rodrigues had been in something of a quandary. The lawyer was softly spoken, gentle as a woman. Some even sniggered that he was a *marica*, an arse bandit. Perhaps. But then the poorly educated Rodrigues was wise enough to know on which side his bread was buttered. If he had to protect and work for a gay boss, so be it. As long as the gay boss never tried anything with him. He hadn't. In fact he sometimes went out with women. Something that had greatly relieved the minder.

Things might have continued in that uncomplicated

vein had he and his men not failed in their latest attempt to capture the gringo Winter at the Los Llanos airstrip. Instead he had returned sheepishly to Cali expecting to find the softly spoken lawyer waiting, ready to accept his excuses in that gentle manner he had. But he wasn't. It was his father, Emilio Figueras, the most feared man in all Colombia, who greeted him. And he had known in that passing moment that his life was over. That he should have died with his men out on the savannah. It was out of a clinging-to-straws kind of desperation that he mentioned the street cleaner's clothes. The ones Emilio's son had sent him out to buy some months earlier. Not new, though. They had to be soiled. Showing signs of wear. The clothing he had found and returned to his boss, who had rolled them into a bundle and placed them in a drawer in his office – under lock and key. Why would anyone do such a thing with dirty old clothes? 'I am not for one moment suggesting anything, Señor,' he had begged. 'Although I am certain that Mauricio knows a great deal more than me . . .'

A lucky guess. Rodrigues knew that the accountant spent a great deal of time at his boss's apartment. It therefore seemed natural to assume Mauricio would know more. And he had, except what he knew had nothing to do with street cleaner's clothes, more about accountancy. How Luis Figueras had constructed a second set of books for the CALIMA empire. Creative accounting, Rodrigues heard someone remark, except to him it seemed a fancy way of saying thieving. Which was more or less Emilio Figueras's spin on the short-lived meeting, as he had pounded his big red-raw hands together in uncontrolled anger.

John Templeton Smith

It was after a white-faced Mauricio had been taken away by a small army of bodyguards, that Rodrigues had his audience with the old man. The order was simple: keep a watchful eye on my son, and report anything unusual.

Which was why that Sunday morning he had been asleep in an old van parked in the underground car park of Luis Figueras's apartment building off the Avenida Sexta. And had been awakened by the sound of voices. Had watched as the lawyer and the beautiful young woman (whom he recognised as Ana Rubiano, an employee at the Banco Industrial Colombiano) humped a number of heavy suitcases over to a new BMW saloon and loaded them into the trunk. A brief kiss on the cheek and the woman had climbed into the car and driven away.

Rodrigues followed. North from the city. A short drive, he had thought. After a hundred kilometres he was worried if he had done the right thing in leaving the lawyer alone. But it was too late now: he was committed to following the woman. To finding out what was in the suitcases. A gas station would be the likely place, he decided. Except when she reached the town of Armenia she kept on driving. Now he had a problem. His fuel gauge was down to a quarter. The next town was Ibague, which he doubted he could make. Which left only one course of action. He overtook her on a dangerous mountain bend, forcing her to stop. Sunday morning was a good time. The mountain road was deserted. He was out of the van in seconds, gun in hand.

Opening the suitcases and finding three of them

stuffed with money was the shocker. To the woman also, it seemed. But he put that down to a bit of play-acting, the kind of thing he would do when he had screwed up. He questioned her, but all she would say was that she was going to Bogotá to meet someone.

Now came the question of what to do with her and the money. He enjoyed a few moments fantasising about white beaches and long-legged girls and a life of pleasure. But he knew what happened to such people.

The Cartel de Cali had long arms.

The phone call had been the right decision. The old man's anger was directed elsewhere, not at him, thank God, especially when he arrived at the mountain fortress and Emilio Figueras opened the suitcase containing the company documents.

The old man had spun around to face Ana, a big calloused hand reaching out to stroke her cheek. 'There are two ways we can handle this,' he said threateningly. 'You can tell me everything you know right now, and walk free. The other way, I leave you to my men to get the answers from you.'

Ana Lucia, arms pinned behind her back by Rodrigues, repeated what she had already said, that she was taking the suitcases to Bogotá for his son, Luis. That he was going to meet her there. Emilio Figueras chose not to believe her and she watched as the big hand slid down inside her blouse, tearing away buttons from the white silk, ripping away the bra strap so violently it cut into her flesh. Then the iron fingers grabbed her right breast in a vicelike grip. She cried out in pain. The grip tightened. She gasped for air. Somewhere amid the pain and confusion she knew that Luis would arrive shortly and explain to his father that it was all a mistake, and everything would be all right, and they would leave together, he patting her hand gently, showering her with loving kisses. *Please God.*

When the old man took the knife from his belt she whimpered and tried to back away. Strong arms prevented it. Her eyes were drawn to the gleaming blade as it gently stroked down her exposed breast, the point flickering over the erect nipple with an almost mesmeric fascination. The second time the pressure increased and she saw the thin trail of bright red erupting from her skin. Then the blade suddenly turned and slashed and she felt the searing white heat of excruciating pain.

That was when Rodrigues let her go and she dropped to her knees before Emilio Figueras. Tears flowing from her eyes. Her mouth completely dry. So dry she couldn't swallow. And the pain. She reached a hand to try to stop it, looking down at the same time at the bloody mess that was her right breast. Her fingers trying to staunch the bleeding. That was when she realised the nipple was gone. That was when she fainted.

When she came to she was sitting in a chair in the same room. Someone was standing over her. Pushing a needle into a vein in her arm. She felt light-headed, sick, but at least the pain was not as bad. The wound she noticed had been covered with a white gauze dressing. Taped neatly to her skin. A few islands of pink spreading as the blood soaked through the bandage. The man who had given her the injection handed her a glass of water, and left the room. She drank it, dropping the empty glass on the carpet. And closed her eyes. And tried to make sense of what was happening. What had Luis done? What was the meaning of the suitcases full of money? What did they want from her? What else could she tell them? How long could she endure all of this?

The answer came a short time later. She opened her eyes to find Emilio Figueras squatting before her. Wild dark eyes locked onto hers. The knife was in his hand. The blade stained brown with her blood. At the edge of her vision the tall bearded Rodrigues hovered.

'Much easier to talk, Ana Lucia. What I have done to you is nothing compared to what this man will do.' He waved the blade towards Rodrigues, who stepped forward and reached down and began to remove her torn and bloodied blouse.

That was when she screamed. And started talking. Saying the same thing that she had said on two previous occasions. Word for word.

And when the words finally ran out in a series of sobs, Emilio Figueras helped her gently to her feet, barking orders at Rodrigues, who ran from the room, then turned back and buttoned her torn blouse, explaining that he had had to be sure she was not lying. Then he escorted her out into the compound, into the warm afternoon. She breathed deeply of the fresh mountain air. Freedom. Thank God. She watched as a number of cars started their engines. Thinking that one of them would be taking her back to the city.

Instead they all left. Rooster tails of dust trailing down the long mountain road.

A uniformed guard came up behind her, grabbing her roughly by the arm and marching her away to the back of the property. It took her less than a minute to realise what was happening, but by then it was too late. Her clothing was torn from her body piece by piece and she was flung to the ground. And the group of men standing over her began unbuckling their belts. It was a few minutes past one o'clock.

By five o'clock Ana Lucia Rubiano had been raped and beaten by no fewer than forty-four of Emilio Figueras's guards. The forty-fifth, angry that she was unconscious, beat her some more, until one of his friends pulled him off, explaining that she was dead.

They took the blood-smeared naked body and threw it in a shallow ditch near the west perimeter. No one even bothered to shovel loose dirt over it, leaving it instead to be picked over by wild animals and birds.

It was exactly 5.25 when the fleet of four Mercedes arrived back at the mountain fortress. With the guards was Luis Figueras, who had been picked up at Bogotá airport, and put on the company jet and returned immediately to Cali. The cars had been waiting on the ramp at Cali International when the jet landed.

Now he was escorted up the stairs to the east balcony, where his father, purple-faced with rage, stood before a table. On the table lay a solitary suitcase. The guards left the two men alone.

Luis stood before the old man and watched as the big hand reached out to slap his face. He lifted an arm to protect himself. A feint. The hand balled into a fist and hit him in the stomach. Hard. He folded. And dropped to his knees, trying desperately to breathe and be sick at the same time.

The old man grabbed him by the hair and pulled him violently to his feet. Luis stood, holding his stomach, as his father threw open the suitcase.

'Money perhaps I could understand,' the old man began in a low voice. 'But to betray your family . . . your friends . . . the memory of your mother . . .'

'Leave my mother out of this,' Luis snapped, his voice raised in uncharacteristic anger.

A small laugh. Full of bitterness. 'Ah, the boy has teeth. A bit late in the day.'

'For you it is,' Luis said.

'What does that mean?' A shout now.

Luis said nothing.

The big hand arced through the air, connecting with the side of Luis's face, sending him sprawling across the verandah. 'You think you can hand over your family to the Nortamerican government, just like that? You think I have not enough men loyal to me who will spend the rest of their lives tracking you down?'

Luis crawled to his feet, wiping blood from his lips. 'It was for my mother,' he whispered, spitting out a broken tooth.

The old man mimicked his son, 'It was for my mother . . . Shit, you are a feeble excuse of a man. How did I ever father such a . . . such a . . . ?'

He was still searching for the word when Luis said calmly, 'Perhaps you didn't.'

The dark eyes blazed savagely. 'What are you saying, you *cabron*.'

'The reason you killed her, perhaps!'

'Killed . . . killed!' The old man lunged forward and

grabbed Luis by the throat. 'With my bare hands will I take the life that I gave you – with my bare hands.'

It would be the only time in his life that Luis Figueras used physical violence. A result of being pushed to his limits. And a little way beyond. Although a hundred pounds lighter than his father, the pent-up frustrations of a lifetime suddenly erupted in a high-pitched scream and with it a physical strength so awesome that he threw the body of his father a clear ten feet through the air. The old man, eyes wide with momentary surprise, roared and leapt to his feet. Head low. Arms outstretched. Luis backed away, pushing his hand in his pocket, looking hopelessly for a weapon. Instead his fingers closed on his mother's rosary. He pulled it from his pocket, slipping the metal cross between his first and second finger, winding the beads around the base of his fingers. Clenching his hand into a fist.

The old man stopped as he saw something in his son's eyes. Something he had never witnessed before in his life. The wild killing rage of a mad man.

Now it was Luis who was advancing on his father.

The sudden shouting from below, followed by the eruption of automatic-weapons fire had no effect on either of them. They were gradually inching closer, each convinced he would kill the other. Each totally blinded by rage.

Had they turned their eyes to the east and followed the line of fire from the guard towers they would have witnessed the chilling sight of a fighter aircraft glinting in the late-afternoon sun, rolling inverted. Diving straight towards them.

62

'Tyler, Sibelius, one five miles, tally-ho the target.'

'Roger, Sibelius, we have you contact. Make your run on two eight zero, left pull-out . . . confirm you're going to ripple the whole load?'

'Negative . . . dropping in pairs.'

'Copied, Sibelius, be advised we observe small-arms fire.'

'Roger that.'

Winter dropped down to zero feet, following the bush road into the target area. At more than seven miles a minute airspeed it was all down to preprogrammed action . . . final checks . . . master arm on . . . gunsight on checked bright; eighty-seven mils . . . quick check of the GPS . . . coming up on two miles . . . NOW . . . nose up forty-five degrees . . . passing two thousand feet . . . roll left 135 degrees pulling the aircraft around on to its back . . . good, looking good . . .

'Sibelius in hot.'

. . . okay apogee of the manouvre now, 3,200 feet inverted check . . . looking down on the target . . .

muzzle flashes in the afternoon shadows . . . figures running for cover . . . two figures on the verandah looking up, gun position? Hard to tell . . . shadows . . . target reaching canopy bow . . . pull nose down until target middle of windscreen . . . got it . . . check the nose with forward stick . . . roll back to the upright position using crossed controls . . . pipper on line with the target . . . steady . . . half a second track time . . . altitude 2,200 feet . . . speed 450 knots . . . dive angle thirty degrees . . . RELEASE . . . 1.2 second pause for bombs to clear the racks . . . five-g left pullout . . .

'Sibelius off.'

Aussie voice up. Jubilant. 'Outstanding! *Outstanding!* Right on the money, Sibelius . . . you gonna play dumpex with remainder?'

'Negative . . . we'll just make sure.' *For you Charlie boy.*

'Copied, put 'em on top of your smoke.'

'Tyler, any ground fire?'

'Negative. Could have some unfriendlies up in the hills though . . . keep an eye open for missiles on your outbound.'

Winter eased the Lightning back down the bush road. The dusk was gathering fast now. The air silky smooth. Above the mountains dissipating puffs of cumulus. He climbed and rolled and commenced the final dive towards the pall of black smoke that drifted skyward. The last two 500-pound Snakeyes bull's-eyed the smoke.

'Sibelius off target at three six, winchester.'

'Roger, Sibelius, cleared feet wet on this frequency. Tyler will overfly in about three hours to check you're clear.'

'Thanks for the assistance, Tyler, next beer's on me.'

'Pick a better bloody place next time, Sibelius.'

'You'd better get out of there.'

'Copied. We are moving. Tyler out.'

At forty thousand feet the indigo blue had deepened. Approaching night. Stretched out below, the Pacific coast. Buenaventura, lights already winking in the gathering darkness.

Winter completed the fuel transfer, and brought the number-one engine up from idle. Monitoring instrument readouts before shutting down the number-two. Time check: 1740 alpha.

He picked up the hand-held. 'Tricky Five-Five, Sibelius.'

Carrier wave for the smallest part of a second. 'Sibelius, Tricky Five-Five, go ahead.' He sensed the relief in her voice. Two-way.

'Descending out of angels four zero, visual with recovery area . . . ETA four four.'

A small laugh in the voice. 'One minute early.'

'Didn't want to keep the lady waiting . . . Have you checked the landing area?'

'Did a fly-by seven minutes ago. Looks okay close to the water line. Earlier smoke indications give a slight westerly wind . . . about five knots. State your intentions.'

'How long's the landing strip?'

'Best area seems to be southeast corner of bay, half a mile at least.'

Winter looked down at his fuel state. Critical. 'Roger, looks like we have negative fuel reserve – will make a direct pass down beach at three thousand feet . . . ejecting on your instruction . . . have you got me visual?'

'Negative.'

'What's your position?'

'Holding one mile south of the southeast point of the bay at three thousand feet.'

'Copied that. I'm showing eight miles to run on the GPS . . . passing angels one zero . . . and we're tally with the corner of the bay.'

'I have you contact . . . continue present heading . . . turn right at start of bay . . . landing area commences from that point.'

'Sibelius copied. Talk to you on the ground.' Winter slipped the transceiver into the leg pocket of his flight suit. Range: four miles . . . speed back to 240 knots . . . out of six thousand feet.

Seconds remaining. Seconds to run through the manual separation (mansep) drill in the event that the seat failed to separate by itself. Best ejection altitude ten thousand feet, the height the barometric device is designed to release the body from the seat and deploy the chute. Should it fail you have a number of seconds to activate the mansep handle to get rid of the seat, before pulling the chute D ring. Ejecting at three thousand feet gives little chance to go to plan B. But then ejecting at a higher altitude might mean drifting out to sea. *Trade-offs.*

Three miles . . . ease a little right . . . try to cut the corner . . . through 4,700 . . . fuel one hundred pounds in the right wing . . . *seconds'* worth of flight remaining.

Winter leaned back against the headrest and lowered

his chin. Spinal posture for the mammoth kick that was about to come.

One mile . . . 3,500 feet . . . fuel zero . . . not good . . . should have left the descent a few seconds longer . . . better go now while we still have control.

He raised the nose and slowed the Lightning to nearly two hundred knots, and grabbed the yellow and black seat pan handle between his thighs with his right hand. Left hand holding his right wrist. A deep breath. Okay, Wint, looks like you're in for a swim. Ejecting. Three . . . two . . . one . . . *Go!*

He heard the dull blast as the canopy went. Then nothing. Adrenaline super-slow-motion clock. There was a moment of something close to anger-annoyance-fear as he realised that he was going to die trapped in this ageing fighter. Just as Charlie had warned. Then nearly one second after the canopy had gone, the seat fired.

The two-hundred-knot slipstream slammed into him. Spinning the seat. He didn't feel the seat separate and was searching for the mansep lever, when the parachute deployed with a hard jerk at his crotch and chest. He let out the breath he'd been holding since he'd activated ejection, and reached up for the parachute risers. Looking up to check the chute was properly deployed. It was. Multishaded white, green and orange. New favourite colours.

Some days it seemed were better than others. As he looked down through the remaining two thousand feet of air, he noticed he was drifting towards the shore. The opposite direction than he had expected from Maria's smoke sighting some time earlier. A localised occurrence at this curved end of the bay perhaps. Lucky. It was at this point that he remembered the aeroplane, and started looking for it. But it had gone. Probably dropped into the sea seconds after he'd ejected. Pity, he'd grown quite attached to it.

Two hundred feet and he was closing on the surf that ran along the beach. He'd almost succeeded when the breaking waves began expanding rapidly. Holding the risers, he twisted his body around so he was facing away from the direction of travel, avoiding the possibility of smashing his face into submerged rocks. Checking down and forward at the same time, gauging impact. Knees, ankles together. Slightly bent. He went in to about twenty feet of water, releasing the parachute fittings as he came up. Striking out for the shore.

It was as he crawled exhausted up the wet sand that the B-25 curved onto a low final approach.

PART NINE
Feet Wet

63

Cartagena de Indias airport is three kilometres north-east of the old city, in El Crespo, and is serviced by Avianca, SAM and Aces. It was the last Avianca arrival of the day that brought a worried Frank Murchek in from Bogotá. The time was 1955 hours local.

He was now sitting with Tanner Williams and Edeyrn Owens in the white Grand Cherokee parked by the front of the terminal building. The partially rolled-down windows catching the whines and thunder of arriving and departing jets. Kerosene-polluted air.

'Funny thing about the Winters of this world,' Owens said, during a lull in the conversation. 'Death beckons them for years, as stridently as a Cicero whore calling to a cash customer, but they somehow keep slipping the noose. Somehow keep coming back, a little frailer in each incarnation, but still as lethal.'

Williams rubbed his face vigorously with both hands. Willing away fatigue. Then turned towards the back seat. To Murchek. 'What else did Billy Rice say?'

'Reckoned Winter or one of his associates tipped off

the local television station on the raid. How else would they have had a helo taking live pictures of the bomb damage by six o'clock, minutes after the event? Other than that he wanted me to confirm the e-mail that you sent at seventeen hundred hours.'

Williams said, 'In the briefcase, next to you. Chapter and verse on the cartel's new export arrangements.'

'No argument. Without the amnesty document you'd promised.'

'The package was delivered by a Venezuelan national. He just handed it over and took off. There's a covering letter in the envelope.'

Murchek opened the briefcase and took out the large manila envelope. He held the covering letter up to the interior light. Reading out loud. '"I had my doubts about the official piece of paper certifying that I am free to walk the streets again, but that's not important. What is, however, is that you act on the information I'm enclosing. A few more fingers in that dyke of yours." What was that about? Fingers in the dyke.'

'Winter has a passionate hatred for the drug pushers of this world. That was how I recruited him. Have you read the PS? Page two.'

Murchek pulled out the second page of airmail-weight paper. '"As you reneged on the amnesty document, I intend to pass all this information to the media. I have enough contacts through my late wife. I will, however, give you fourteen days' grace. Fourteen days to get your clean-up campaign underway. After that you will be made accountable." Shit, what can we do in fourteen days?'

Williams said, 'Look at the info he's given us first.'

Murchek sifted through the handwritten papers.

'Jesus, this looks pretty good. Names. Canadian mining companies. Ships. Department of Transport officials, for God's sake.'

'Enough to pacify the White House when they find out tomorrow's extradition is not going down? That we were involved in a covert action against the Cali cartel?'

'Bill Rice is working on that. Based on information you passed him on that guy Werner Stock in Santa Marta.'

Williams flicked at the wheel of his Dunhill lighter. Sparks showering the darkness. 'What's Werner got to do with it?'

'Last field report you sent in, you mentioned he'd been in Leticia. Gave us the name of a hotel you thought he might have been staying at. The Parador Ticuna. We did a bit of investigating. It seems the hotel operated another place called the Monkey Island Lodge on the Isla de los Micos, as well as its own travel agency. Then we found out that the owner, a US citizen, was recently charged with drug trafficking and ended up in a Miami jail.' Murchek paused. 'Think we could drive to that hotel of yours? I haven't eaten all day, and I've got the feeling this is going to turn into a long night.'

Williams started the Cherokee and slipped it into drive. 'You were saying the owner of the hotel ended up in a Miami jail.'

'Except he wasn't the sole owner – apparently had a sleeping partner . . . Werner Stock.'

'So Werner goes down there from time to time to keep an eye on his investment. What's unusual in that?'

'Your report mentioned him visiting his sick mother. You thought he might be lying. You were right. Records show she's been dead for twenty years.'

Williams, clear of the airport traffic now, accelerated down Avenida Santander. On their right pinpricks of white lights on the water. 'You mean he's still running the operation as a cover for drug trafficking.'

'Him and the North Coast Cartel. Seems they've got a number of clandestine laboratories in the jungle where they refine the cocaine paste, before distributing the pure product Stateside. Looks like another Tranquilandia, the operation the Medellin guys ran in the eighties.'

'Forgive me for being a bit slow tonight, Frank, but I still don't see where all this is leading.'

'Tomorrow's newspapers. *El Espectador*, *El País* and *El Occidente*, to name but a few, *could* all be carrying the raid as their lead story. Responsibility for the raid being claimed by the North Coast Cartel.'

Williams looked back at Murchek in surprise, and almost ran off the road at the bend a hundred metres before the Hotel Bellavista. The only bend on that long stretch of coast road. Owens's hand reached out and eased the wheel anticlockwise. Williams muttered a hurried thanks, and concentrated firmly on the road ahead. He said, 'And they would do that *because*?'

'Bill Rice asked them.'

'Asked who?'

'Werner Stock.'

'What about the rest of the North Coast Cartel?'

'He's taken over as the boss, now that his partner is serving time in Miami.'

'So why would Werner open himself up to God

knows what kind of shit, not only from the other cartels, but the government?' Williams's voice was strained. He'd heard it all before and didn't believe a word of it.

'Three reasons. Number one, he hated Emilio Figueras with a passion, as he did all the Figueras family. Number two, we have agreed to protect him personally from any government interference – to the best of our ability, naturally.'

'And the third?'

'Stock is not his real name. His real name is Werner Barbie – the son of Klaus Barbie.'

No one spoke for quite a while as the enormity of what Murchek had said slowly sank in. Williams continued down the coast road, skirting the old town, heading for the Bocagrande district. Then it was Murchek again. 'Your first field report mentioned that Klaus Barbie had once been a partner of Emilio Figueras, and that Werner Stock had fiercely contested Barbie's apparent guilt of war crimes when the issue was raised. The fact that Figueras turned his father over to the Bolivian authorities, who in turn handed him over to the French, might be enough to sell Werner on the idea. Revenge. Simple. Werner being seen as the new strong man, letting it be known that no one crosses any member of his family and gets away with it, no matter how long it takes.'

'What else?'

'What d'you mean, what else?'

'Oh, come on, you don't really believe Werner's going to put his life on the line for a headline in a newspaper – or protection from us. We're the Great

Satan, for Christ's sake – so how did we establish our bona fides? It's certainly not a shipload of powdered milk, or a lifetime subscription to Medicare for him and his men . . . What are we offering, Frank?'

Murchek said, 'Assistance in building up their infrastructure. Three-year turnkey project. Realpolitik, as Bill put it.'

Williams nodded understanding. Survival was all that mattered. Self-image. Moral credibility. Besides, in their concealed world, the agency never said what it really meant anyway. 'The real world, sure. So how did you find out who Werner really was?'

'By accident. Your last report mentioned his mother. When we checked back we found a cross reference. Stock and Barbie. Stock was his mother's maiden name.'

Owens, who had been quietly listening and taking everything in, said, 'Do you know who was killed in the bombing raid on the Figueras home in the mountains?'

'No. But being a Sunday when all Colombian families gather, I'd guess the entire family.'

'But only the one family. What about the other cartel members? I was just thinking of the likelihood of the extradition going ahead tomorrow.'

Murchek laughed. 'You can kiss that goodbye, Ed. Every last one of those guys was on a jet to Panama the moment the news hit the TV screens.'

Williams slowed as they ran into heavy traffic on Avenida San Martin. He lowered his window. Snatches of car horns and vallenato music on the night air. 'So we could all come out of this smelling of roses, is that what you're saying, Frank?'

'Close. Except now you've got this guy Winter about to go off like a loose cannon, media will have a field day with that sort of information.'

'Not if we stop him.'

'How?'

'A hearse cover manoeuvre he's known to use in escape plans. Tell him, Edeyrn.'

Owens half turned in his seat, and recited the story of Winter's escape from the British Army. And how he had fled back to Northern Ireland.

'So you figure he'll go back to the States.'

'The B-25 he has, which you gentlemen gave him, apparently has internal fuel tanks. No reason to think to the contrary. Besides, where else would he go? A gringo who has just killed one of Colombia's major drug barons – a man who was doubtless revered in many quarters – might find it difficult to find a safe haven in this part of the world, at least in the imminent future.'

'Where in the States exactly?'

'Florida. Point of origin. Could be that he knows that Johnny Shoosh character in the Everglades.'

'Except to do that and avoid radar, he'd need a second legitimate aircraft going the same way to formate with.'

'I didn't say I had all the answers, Frank. Just a few. I suggest you alert Customs aircraft and all radars in that particular area.'

Williams reached the end of Avenida San Martin, and made a right. 'I agree with Edeyrn,' he said. 'Time is now twenty thirteen. What time did the TV guys put that raid at?'

Murchek said, 'Approximately seventeen thirty.'

'Okay, so Winter lands his fighter at some pre-arranged spot and is picked up by the B-25. Speed of that is around two hundred twenty knots. Close to four miles a minute. Which would put him five hundred miles closer to the States as of this very minute.'

'You're sure of the speeds?'

'Surfed the Internet this week – amazing what you can find there, Frank. Yes, I'm sure. In the same way I found out that the range of the Lightning without air-to-air refuelling is pretty short. Something like six hundred fifty nautical miles. What we need to do now is look at a map and plot possible direct routes from the Cali area to Florida.'

'Long shot,' Murchek said, as they stopped outside the front of the Hotel Caribe.

'All we've got. We'll go up to the room and order sandwiches and coffee from room service. Anything to add, Edeyrn?'

'You said that the B-25 had a speed of two hundred and twenty knots. What speed do jet airliners fly at?'

'Figure five hundred knots. Why?'

'Just a thought. Perhaps your customs chaps could run a check with the air-traffic controllers. See what legitimate flights they have coming in from the south – other than jets, that is.'

'A lot of ground to cover in a short time,' Williams remarked.

'Not if you concentrate your effort in the southern Florida area, surely.'

'Worth a try. What do you say, Frank?'

The ex-Marine said, 'Do you mind if I have a steak and fries instead of a sandwich?'

64

One hour earlier, Oscar Porteous had watched the CNN news with horror. Listened as words spilled over images of battlefield scenes . . .

'Narco-terrorism resumed late today in Colombia, when an airstrike by a squadron of jet fighter-bombers totally destroyed the mountain fortress home of the world's most powerful drug czar, Emilio Enrique Figueras.

'Casualty figures have been estimated in excess of one hundred men, women and children. It is believed that Emilio Figueras — head of the notorious Cali Cartel — died in the raid along with other members of his family.

'As yet no one has claimed responsibility for the airstrike, which is being seen as a return to the drug wars of the 1980s when Pablo Escobar led the Medellin Cartel through one of the most bloody eras in Colombian history . . .'

Porteous held out the remote controller and clicked the power button. Instant silence. He momentarily closed his eyes. His complexion was even whiter than usual. He had lost more weight in the preceding days, and now, unable to take any solids without suffering severe pain and vomiting, was reduced to a diet of nonfat milk, water, Zantac and Advil tablets, honey-and-lemon cough syrup, and a varying number of cigarettes. He ignored the increased blood in his stools, as in the phlegm he frequently coughed up – or at least assured himself it was not getting any worse.

One day! Twenty-four hours before the cartel members were due to be extradited. *No one has claimed responsibility*. Chilling words. He looked up from the *caquetoire*, eyes moving slowly along the lines of antiques arranged in careful order. A millimetric precision. The way he had endeavoured to conduct his life. And now? Now he had become the town's leper! The outcast!

He heard his own voice, cracked with pain. 'What have you done to me, Tanner? Why have you destroyed me?'

He gathered up his overcoat and gloves, cast a last covetous glance at the antique-filled room, and went out into the snow.

The drive to his home in Fredericksburg, Virginia, had taken an hour and fifteen minutes. Driven at speed, oblivious to snow and ice, to other road users. His car phone blinked a green eye at him. A message. But he never answered it – he knew it would be the Director, Eberhart, and *he* was the very last man he wanted to talk to.

White Lie

The driveway to the rambling eighteenth-century estate was deep in snow, so he abandoned his Lincoln by the open gates and trudged wearily towards the house. No lights. No one there to welcome him. Not that he minded too much – there had been no one there to welcome him for years.

He paused at the front of the house, peering up at the Doric columns and entablature. His mother's passion – classical architecture. She who had fostered within him a deep appreciation for European elegance. He moved on slowly, eyes taking in things in the stone-coloured moonlight that he fancied he hadn't seen in years. And then he was at the back of the property, looking across the snowy courtyard to the old stables with the Florentine arches.

He removed a glove and pulled a white linen handkerchief from his sleeve as he felt a coughing fit coming on. And when it had passed he lit a cigarette. Eyes still surveying the Florentine arches, remembering when he was a boy and how he had tied ropes to the metal hooks the gardener had driven into the masonry, and made swings between them.

He stubbed out the cigarette on an ice-crusted stack of flower pots, shivered at the east wind which whimpered through the skeletal trees, then moved purposefully towards the stables.

65

They had routed low-level in darkness up the west coast of Colombia, across the Darien Gap, climbing to 12,000 feet over the Caribbean abeam the Archipiélago de las Mulatos, and on through a clear night, briefly overflying the Honduras coastline at Laguna Caratasca. Now, four hours and thirty-seven minutes since taking off from Pianguita beach, they were approaching the Yucatan peninsula.

'You must have loved her very much,' Maria said, after a long silence.

Winter, who was nursing back pain – not from the ejection, but when he had moved aft to change into a dry flight suit after take-off, and had somehow twisted his body and trapped a nerve under his left shoulder blade – moved his lips. As though he was about to answer. But he didn't.

'Charlie told me . . . about your wife, what happened in Oklahoma.'

'I thought he might.'

'I am sorry.'

'No need. It's all over now.'

'I said a prayer for you, when I was positioning to Pianguita this afternoon.'

A small smile of thanks and he closed his eyes. Closed out the world. Confined his thinking to their escape. Looking for the unforeseen.

And a short while later.

'Thunderstorms,' Maria said, indicating distant lightning flashes on the nose.

Winter opened his eyes. Looked out. 'Over Merida?'

'Possibly.' She leaned forward and checked her watch in the red glow of the instrument lights. 'You did say the DC-6 had an ETD of twenty-three thirty?'

'I know, it's going to be close. What's our ETA?'

'Twenty-three nineteen.' She glanced across at him. Concern in her eyes. 'What if they left early?'

'Airliners, Mexicans, Sundays . . . you'd get better odds in Las Vegas. Besides, you said it yourself ten minutes ago when I told you the track we were making good would take us straight through the Estacion Aeronaval danger area – *wars only Monday to Saturday, sunrise to sunset* – so if the navy can't be bothered to defend the country on a Sunday, what chance the airport workers?'

She laughed. And looked beautiful. 'Point taken. You want to change seats now?'

'No, you can stay there. I'll fly it from this side when the time comes.'

'Traffic twelve o'clock high . . . right to left.'

He looked up and watched the white strobes drifting across the heavens. 'What do you think?'

'Probably a four-jet heavy inbound to Guatemala, nothing to do with us – too high.'

Winter peered out of the side window of the cramped cockpit, listening to the dry roar of engines, watching the splatter of white flame from the exhaust stubs. Very much aware that they were entering the most dangerous phase of the operation. Not so much the possibility of being picked up on radar and being intercepted by an Air Force fighter, but more the formation join-up on a dark and stormy night. How long since he had done something like that! How long since he had maintained night formation for more than five hundred nautical miles! More than two hours of intense mental concentration.

He looked down. They were over the peninsula now. Chinks of lights from isolated farms. Beacons of safe places filled with safe people. Different worlds.

'You never told me how you came up with this hearse cover manoeuvre,' Maria said.

'Not me. Something I borrowed from the British Army, and which they pinched from the Navy. It was based on the premise of having to disappear and reappear without being seen. Someone came up with a naval skirmish at the Battle of Jutland when a German vice-admiral by the name of Boedicker laid down a smoke screen and allowed his light cruisers to escape from the British, and modified it to aerial use.'

'But why the name hearse?'

'Aviator's black humour. A coffin is carried inside a hearse, in this case the second aeroplane is as close to inside the first as makes no difference. Any mistakes by the number two, like accidently ramming the leader, means you transfer to the real thing in no time flat.'

*   *   *

White Lie

It was 2322 alpha. They had descended to four thousand feet to avoid the scattered storm clouds. Even so it was a bumpy ride. Squally rain showers mixed with light hail driving against the windscreen. Creaks and groans from the airframe, making the bomber sound like an old sailing ship being pounded by heavy seas.

Maria saw it first though a break in the clouds. The pale twinkling dust of city lights. 'Merida,' she announced. 'One o'clock. What now?'

'Take up a right-hand orbit, as tight and as slow as you can.' He reached forward and switched the radio to Merida Approach frequency. 'You monitor the Tower frequency on your hand-held. According to the paperwork the northbound flight operates under the callsign – Southern 221, possibly 221 Alpha. Usually gets assigned eight thousand feet up to Grand Isle. I'm going to call Approach and tell them we're a Piper Navajo en route Kingston, Jamaica, to Corpus Christi, Texas, that we're at six thousand five hundred feet and requesting any traffic information to the north of them.'

'What about their radar?'

'As far as they're concerned we're fifty miles northeast of them – hopefully on the limits of their primary. Then again, there's a lot of rain clutter in the area.'

'And if they ask you to squawk?'

'Transponder's u/s . . . quit on the way out of Kingston.'

'What about a tail number?'

'What year were you born?'

'Nineteen fifty-nine.'

'November 1959, then.'

'What if they paint our present position?'

'Stay in the heaviest rain showers, in a tight slow orbit. As they're not expecting anything six miles from the field, they might put down an intermittent almost stationary paint as an anomaly.'

'And I suppose you have worked out ETAs all the way to Corpus Christi for this imaginary flight.'

'History of aviation from the time of the Wright brothers if they want it, but this is still Mexico on a Sunday night.'

It was that easy. Keeping the mike away from his mouth gave his transmission a weak, strength-three quality, something you would expect at a range of fifty miles. A surly-voiced Mexican queried their position once, then advised they had a DC-6 departing northbound in perhaps twenty or thirty minutes, that was all.

Winter acknowledged, saying they would be clear to the northwest by then, and thanking the controller for his help. The Mexican didn't even reply.

He turned to Maria. 'You get any of that?'

'Departing in twenty to thirty minutes, yes. Problem is, we could be getting tight on fuel if it is much longer.'

'How tight?'

'Very tight. All the internal fuel has gone. We are now back to wing tanks only.'

Winter removed his headset and unstrapped and climbed out of his seat, grimacing at the back pain.

'Where are you going?' she shouted.

'Backup plans,' he mouthed, and moved aft into the darkness.

66

There were three of them. They had a combined age of 175 years. Old timers from the piston-engined era. Flying cargo in an ancient DC-6A freighter. They had left Gulfport, Mississippi, that morning carrying 22,000 pounds of cloth to Merida, and were returning that night with 7,500 men's suits.

The pilot swung the big Six onto runway 10, while the copilot read back the clearance from Merida Tower. 'Southern 221 is cleared destination – Gulfport – flight planned route . . . climb and maintain eight thousand.'

The pilot pressed down hard on the top of the rudder pedals for maximum braking, then advanced the throttles to thirty inches of manifold pressure on each engine. The engine noise became a steady din and the nose dipped slightly from the pull of the big propellers. The copilot reached overhead to turn on the four ADI (antidetonation system) switches while taking a final look at the engine gauges.

The skipper drawled, 'Max power – wet,' then

released the brakes as the right-seater eased the throttles forward to fifty-nine inches. The noise increased and the freighter accelerated slowly down the dimly lit runway. At eighty knots the copilot called, 'Instrument cross-check.' Followed shortly after by: 'V1 . . . Rotate.'

The big Six lumbered slowly into the stormy Caribbean sky, turning on course for the low-altitude airway, A770, which would take them 493 nautical miles across the Gulf of Mexico to the Grand Island radio beacon, and onward to Gulfport. The pilot completed the after-take-off and climb checks and lit a cigarette.

Twenty minutes later, the big Six levelled off at eight thousand feet. In cloud and driving rain. Imperceptible rumbles of turbulence. The Pratt & Whitney R-2800 engines throttled back to a comfortable snore. The flight engineer poured steaming black coffee from a thermos and handed it round.

'Shitty weather,' the pilot complained. 'No one else dumb enough to be out here at this time of night, flying in this.'

The crew concurred. Unaware of the dark shape that had slipped into position line astern; nose bobbing directly beneath their tail section.

67

The US Customs Service E-2C Hawkeye, callsign Hawk 07, had been on patrol for four hours, tracing the first two legs of a giant triangle in the night sky; the domed radar antenna on top of the aircraft looking down from 17,500 feet over a 200-nautical-mile radius for targets. Not for incoming enemy aircraft or intercontinental ballistic missiles, but for light airplanes laden with illegal drugs trying to creep into the southern states under cover of darkness, and especially on that night one particular aircraft thought to be routing into the southern Florida area from Colombia.

The Hawkeye, an ex-navy machine, was ideally suited for the role, having three primary sensors — radar, Identification Friend or Foe (IFF), and a passive detection system for electronic-warfare support measures — which were integrated with a general-purpose computer to accomplish its missions. The onboard equipment was able to track simultaneously more than 250 targets and control up to thirty interceptors. Apart from that, the plane was old, having been built by the Grumman Aerospace Corporation of Bethpage, New York, in 1964 and delivered to the Naval Air Station Miramar, California, in the same year. Twenty-six years and seventeen thousand flying hours later, she had been handed down to the Customs Service.

Tag Elliot, a recently retired navy CPO, and now a radar operator with the Customs Service, massaged the cramps in his neck, his eyes flickering occasionally to the dim green radarscope, checking for a target. Nothing. That was the way it had been for the past 239 minutes with the exception of a couple of false returns and a low-level target booming along at over six hundred knots; possibly military, but whoever it belonged to no one would ever know. It was off the scope before anyone could make up their mind – he decided it was some young navy hotshot *dragging* the Gulf. He adjusted his noise-attenuating headset in a vain attempt to block out the roar of engines and checked the twenty-four-hour clock under the Radar Video Select panel. One minute and they would be turning northbound. Returning to their base at Pensacola.

He went back to reading his ops manual, very much aware that he was still on probation. Any fuck-ups, they had warned him, and he'd be checking baggage at JFK or LAX. '*The Customs air interdiction operations are coordinated by two C3I (command, control, communications and intelligence) centers. An administrative facility is located in Oklahoma City. The West Coast C3I center is at March Air Force Base, Riverside, California, the East Coast center is located in Miami . . .*'

He felt the aircraft roll into a right-hand turn and glanced across at Johnson, his partner on the next scope. He was asleep. He was about to say something, but thought better of it. The guy had just got married and from the look of the dark circles around his eyes wasn't getting much sleep. The ribald comments from the rest of the crew, not forgetting the guys back at base, would last at least another month, before transferring to some other unfortunate with a situation worth exploiting.

He pushed the manual aside and reached for his coffee. It was cold but he drank it anyway. It was as he was putting the cup back in the holder that he noticed the weak return on the very edge of his radarscope. He quickly scanned the radar set control panel above the scope. His left hand went forward, fingers slowly increasing the LG pulse gain. The target brightened slightly before being absorbed into rain clutter. A minute later it was back. He tracked it carefully for the next five minutes, then adjusted his mike. 'Jonno, check this out, will you?'

Johnson stirred, rubbed his eyes, and looked around. 'We landing?'

'No, still two hours out. Got a slow mover at two hundred miles bearing two seven zero. Paralleling our track.'

Johnson yawned, muttered, 'Shit!' and lazily flicked a few switches. 'Taco Air Force lost again!'

Elliot said nothing. He doubted it was military, Mexican or otherwise, no IFF. And the speed it was moving meant it wasn't a jet.

'Looks as though he's heading up Amber 770.'

'To where?'

'New Orleans maybe.'

'So what do you want to do?' Elliot asked.

Johnson laughed. 'Hey man, you got the job – lighten up. We do nothing – he's still in international airspace.'

'What about the alert status in the Florida area?'

Johnson consulted his watch, which was set to GMT – six hours ahead of Central Standard Time. 'It's zero seven zero eight. That situation was valid to zero seven hundred . . . Whoever they were hoping to catch obviously thought better of it and has left it for another day. Either that or he fooled us all, and is now sitting in a bar in downtown Miami.'

'"Slow mover, possibly in close formation with legitimate airways traffic" . . .,' Elliot recited from the report in front of him.

Johnson looked at him for a moment, sighed, and unfolded an airways chart, poring over it for a minute. 'Okay, monitor his progress. If he maintains present heading he'll cross the FIR boundary at Dolph . . . twenty-eight north, ninety west. That's where you need to set up your intercept.'

'Got it.'

'Tag, me bucko. It pays to lead a quiet life. Creating too much unnecessary paperwork pisses off the boss. He retires this year . . . likes to get away from the office and play golf.' The conciliatory tone did not go unnoticed.

68

'Houston Center, Houston Center, Southern Two Two One, position.'

'Southern Two Two One, this is Houston, go ahead.'

'Roger, Southern Two Two One is Kehli at zero six fife one, level eight zero, Dolph zero seven four niner, Grand Isle next.'

'Southern Two Two One checks, Kehli zero six fife one, level at eight zero, estimating Dolph at zero seven four niner, Grand Isle next, confirm.'

'Two Two One, that's charlie.'

Ritual whispers.

That had been the last position report the B-25 had monitored twenty-five minutes earlier. Winter, whose instrument scan had long since transferred to the white taillight and massive tail empennage of the DC-6, coeval with the staccato thunder of rain and the intermittent bouts of turbulence which pitched and rolled the flight deck, was fighting vertigo, convinced that they and the lead aircraft were slow rolling all the way across the Gulf of Mexico.

Maria's near-continuous patter of position, fuel state, and engine instrument readings helped to keep him from dwelling too long on the problem and possibly trying to correct for a flight condition that didn't exist.

A radio transmission added to the noise of engines and slipstream, faint enough to be partially missed by Winter as he fought to maintain station on the jinking white light.

'Who was that?' he asked.

She glanced at him. Saw the sweat-sheened face in the instrument lights. The intense concentration. The hands feeding in minute control corrections, almost, it seemed, by the second. 'Houston Center . . . told 221 they are not receiving his squawk . . . he is recycling.'

'What frequency are we on?'

'One three two point six five.'

'Position?'

'A hundred and eighteen miles south of the FIR boundary at Dolph . . . about thirty minutes.'

Winter watched as the white taillight suddenly dropped down his windscreen. *Shiiiiiit!* He stabbed the controls forward, lost the light for a second. Eased back up . . . searching . . . waiting for a collision . . . the tiny orb of light flickered through the grey cloud like the limiting mass of a cold star . . . sigh of relief almost painful in its intensity . . . back in the top centre of the windscreen . . . the sensation that he was rolling came back, worse this time . . . hands fighting brain . . .

'Fuel state?'

'Difficult to say . . . According to my calculations perhaps one hour to dry tanks – perhaps as much as ninety minutes.'

'Can we lean off any more?'

'No – the cylinder head gauges are near the red line now, especially the left engine . . . I think we need to run a little richer . . . or open the cowl flaps.'

An argument that had persisted for two hours, when he had realised that the DC-6 was cruising faster than he'd anticipated. Close to two hundred and forty knots. He'd thought the DC-6 crew might reduce to compensate for the weather. Not so. They were pushing on, turbulence or not. And that had meant flying at maximum power in the B-25. The worn-out engines being stressed to their limits, or what had once been their limits. Opening the cowl flaps would reduce their speed by enough that they would fall out of formation – running richer, depleting the fast-dwindling fuel reserves, enough perhaps for both engines to die before they even reached the coast. 'We can't,' he said, as they ran out of the weather into a patch of clear sky.

'We must.'

'A few minutes longer.'

'Then what?' A little of the old anger was back in her voice. 'What happens when one engine seizes up – or both? Besides, you told me that if the *federales* had any idea you were coming back to the States they would be concentrating their search in southern Florida. Is that right?'

'Diversionary tactics.'

'How? You never explained.'

'I left a note for Williams – the CIA guy – telling him I was turning over the story to the US media. As this will implicate the CIA in an apparent covert operation against the drug cartels, they should get understandably concerned.'

'But they could not be sure we were planning the flight tonight.'

'If he researched his subject and read between the lines, I'm sure he does.'

'And you intend giving the story to the media?'

'No.'

'So it was nothing more than a threat. Something to get him to look for you.'

'Yes.'

'In southern Florida.'

'Yes.'

'But he was never going to find you because you came this way. What if you had never told him anything about the media in the first place?'

'Then I wouldn't have known what he was thinking, or possibly doing.'

'So perhaps there are no customs radar planes out here tonight – perhaps they have all been sent to the Florida area.'

What a lovely idea. 'Perhaps. Try and tune in the Grand Isle NDB – in case we lose the GPS and our escort.'

She reached up in the red-lit darkness and fumbled with the coffee-grinder ADF, accidently finding a music station that drifted in and out on waves of static. And a slightly distorted metallic-sounding voice moving through a slow ballad:

A glass house no one else can see
Full of struggling demons and dreams of you

Frequency drift, as the voice changed to the musical cadence of morse – too fast for Winter to pick up.

Shipping perhaps! Who else used the morse code to send messages? What speed was that operator sending at? Twenty w.p.m.! Charlie had been good at that, would have sat in this very seat and read it off word by word. The message, whatever it had been, slipped away into the night, and the haunting voice returned. Weaker this time . . .

> *In the night of the fight where you're fallen*
> *And wounded . . . and bleeding . . . and*
> *Silently screaming . . .*

The voice was lost behind the drumbeat of rain and hail. A lightning flash backlit the stark outline of the DC-6 against silver rods of rain. From a range of thirty feet it filled the sky. A dark rivet-lined hulk. Ominous. Frightening.

The tension was mounting as they approached the reporting point at Dolph.

Winter's voice was strained. 'How're the gauges?'

'Left engine is now at red line. I think we will lose it any minute – an engine fire even.'

'Can you take over?'

'There is more bad weather coming up – I can see the lightning. I don't think I could stay this close in turbulence.'

At least she was honest. 'How far?'

'Hard to tell . . . five miles perhaps.'

'I'll be back by then.'

'Where are you going?'

'Check the life-raft.'

'You think we are going to have to ditch?' More

than concern now. Now it was visions of ditching in a stormy sea. At night. Few aviators got away with that one.

'We'd better get ready. You might want to drop a few feet lower. Keep his taillight as your reference point, though – keep it in the same position in your windscreen at all times.'

She wanted to reach out and touch him, feel his hand on hers, his lips on hers. In case it was the last time.

But he was gone. Back into the darkness.

69

On board the Hawkeye, Houston Center came up on frequency.

Johnson took the message and jotted down the information. He looked across at Elliot. 'False alarm. Seems it's a DC-6 bound for Gulfport. The crew have been having a few radio problems. Old ship probably leaks like a sieve, and with the rain we've been having tonight . . . You still plan to send 02 in?'

Elliot, who was guiding Spookship 02 towards the DC-6, said, 'He's still slow-moving airways traffic.'

Johnson laughed and shook his head from side to side. 'You will go far, Mr Elliot . . . They say Fairbanks can be very nice at this time of year.'

Elliot raised a hand for silence. He was setting up the Citation for a vis-ident. Calculating closing speed.

Stopwatch.

Timing rate of closure over fifteen-second increments. If the Citation closed on the contact by 250 yards in this time it meant the contact was flying thirty knots slower. If 1,000 yards was covered in the same period it meant a closing speed of 120 knots. As a further check at 900 yards, Elliot would attempt to get the Citation flying co-speed with the target in order to reconfirm his calculations. Difficult enough in daylight-clear conditions. On a dark stormy night something entirely different.

Stopwatch.

'Zero Two, this is Hawk Zero Seven, you are now at two thousand yards . . . closing at nine zero knots. State conditions.'

'Er, roger that, Hawk Zero Seven . . . Zero Two is Popeye at this time . . . maintaining heading three fife zero.'

Popeye. On instruments. Elliot was beginning to sweat. The rain clutter in the vicinity of Dolph was excessive. Possible thunderstorm. He lost the target for a few seconds . . . then Zero Two was gone as well. Shit! Time had expanded alarmingly. Seconds becoming minutes. He ran through the intercept procedure again in his mind: Zero Two performs vis-ident, relays aircraft details and possible tail number. This information passed immediately to C3I-Miami to be verified on computerised records. The technicians at Miami then monitor the chase on their radar, if within range. Once suspect aircraft reaches land, the technicians electronically place sectionals, geological charts, or road maps behind the radar screen and use that moving-map type of display to guide chase aircraft to probable landing sites.

Zero Two emerged from the rain clutter. Time up.

Stopwatch.

'Zero Two, you are now one thousand yards, reduce airspeed by nine zero knots, report new airspeed.'

'Roger that, Zero Two, reducing by ninety . . . new airspeed will be two three five true, go ahead.'

'Advise steady.'

More seconds. 'Okay, Zero Seven . . . Zero Two is now steady two three five.'

Both radar paints remained exactly the same distance apart over the next quarter-minute. Elliot needed a cigarette. 'Copied, Zero Two . . . increase your speed to . . .'

The pulsing sweep tone from 1,600 hertz down to 300 hertz that screamed in Elliot's headset nearly ruptured his eardrums. Or so it felt. He wrenched the headset from his ears and shook his head, then gingerly eased one earpiece halfway over his left ear. 'Spookship Zero Two, you still on frequency?'

'Zero Two, affirm. Picking up ELT on Guard.'

Guard the emergency communications channel – 243 MHz on UHF or 121.5 on VHF. And someone's Emergency Locator Transmitter had gone off. Someone had experienced an instant velocity change of at least 3.5 feet per second. *Somebody had crashed.*

'Roger, we have that also, Zero Two – enter right-hand orbit and stand by.'

Elliot turned to Johnson. 'Check with Houston on the status of that DC-6 . . . What's his callsign?'

'Southern 221.'

'Yeah, 221 . . . See if he's got troubles.'

It took two minutes.

Johnson said, 'Two Two One's okay. He's got more radio problems than earlier – didn't hear an ELT go off because he's down to one radio now.'

'It's not the DC-6,' Elliot said excitedly. 'I think it was the traffic we were looking out for earlier . . . Anyway, he's down, two miles north of Dolph.'

'You sure?'

'I only ever had one target painting – the DC-6 – and as he's still there, where did the other one come from? Unless he was flying close formation on the Six.'

'And something went wrong.'

'Big time. Sweep tone indicates he's stationary – as in ditched.'

'What are the crash parameters of those ELTs?'

'Crash worthiness in the region of one hundred g's for twenty-three milliseconds, from six directions.'

'Poor bastard. Rather him than me . . . rough seas. Where's Zero Two?'

'Looking for signs of wreckage.'

'Coast Guard?'

'On their way.'

'We staying?'

'Skipper said he can give us twenty-four minutes maximum. It seems our earlier diversion toward Dolph has screwed up our reserves. They're launching the other Hawk by the way. He should be on freak any minute now.'

That was it. Night's work nearly done. Pissing rain. Level-Five thunderstorms. And somebody taking an unscheduled swim.

They were still holding five minutes later – between reporting points Ivone and Viper – when the Citation, Zero Two, came up on frequency.

Elliot responded. 'Go ahead, Zero Two.'

'Okay . . . Zero Two is at two hundred feet, on the Leeville 169 for fifty miles. We think we identified what could be an inflated life-raft . . . might be over-turned . . . no sign of survivors . . . looks like they got out of the airplane, inflated the raft and activated their standby ELT in the raft survival pack, before being washed overboard . . . real bad sea . . . fifty foot plus swells, over.'

'Copied, Zero Two. Can you continue the search?'

'We're trying, sir. Pretty bumpy down here.'

'We got that. Be advised that Hawk Zero Seven is RTB – Hawk Zero Eight is airborne. We'll hand you over to him shortly.'

'Zero Two standing by.'

Elliot turned to Johnson and shook his head.

'Shitty sorta night to die,' Johnson said, reading his thoughts.

'You gotta believe.'

'What about the DC-6? You think he was in on it?'

'Our guys are waiting for him at Gulfport. They'll soon find out.'

'You still think it was the Colombian traffic?'

'B-25? We'll have to wait for the Coast Guard to pick up some wreckage.'

'Want a bet?'

'What odds you giving me?'

'Three to one.'

'Ten bucks.'

Johnson whistled through his teeth. 'That much, huh!'

The two men, both young, both ex-navy, fast becoming friends, kept up the light-hearted banter all the way back to Pensacola.

70

Tanner Williams got his victory later that morning, at 0800 CST. It came in the form of a coded operational message, via e-mail, from Bill Rice in Bogotá.

williams.t.
fyi-nar
gives me pleasure to confirm your hunch paid off. b-25 carrying winter and his associates crashed in the gulf of mexico, approximately 50 nm south of new orleans, early hours of this morning. us coast guard have located crash site and have salvaged minimal wreckage, including inflated life-raft. no bodies recovered. search continues but all on board presumed dead. message ends.

Williams passed the plain-English version to Owens as they board the yacht *Belinda Jane* at Manga Island. 'Not my hunch, Edeyrn, yours. I'll clear that up when I get back.'

The Welshman smiled. 'You'll do no such thing,

boyo. Praise and honours are wasted on old men –
you use it to get where you want to go.'

'Did Frank leave the newspapers?'

'He did. North Coast Cartel grabbing the headlines
in every one. Seems your Billy Rice is in line for a
promotion as well.'

'Nice morning for an ocean voyage.'

'No pressure this time. Perhaps we could stop at
Grand Cayman?'

'Any reason?'

Owens laughed. 'I've had an offshore account there
for twenty years. Thought I might like to see who's
taking care of my money.'

'I'll make sure you get a consultancy payment for
all of this.'

'Not necessary, Tanner. It's been a holiday. Wouldn't
have missed it for the world.'

'And Winter?'

'What they would have once called a good soldier
gone bad – these days I'm not so sure. Even so, he was
a devious bugger, wasn't he?'

'An ex-sergeant, Edeyrn, always that. As I once
told you, he may have been good dealing with Third
Worlds.'

'But he never really stood a chance, is that what
you're saying?'

Williams took the gold Dunhill lighter from his shirt
pocket and turned it over in his fingers. 'Naval officers,' he said. 'Better equipped because of command
at sea. You have to make instant decisions; you learn
there is no one else out there in a pinch. You learn to
be cool, whether on the bridge of a destroyer or here.
They're the same.'

John Templeton Smith

'So what do you intend to do now? When you get back?'

'Easy. Retire. I'm taking my long-suffering wife on a world cruise.'

The *Belinda Jane* put to sea thirty minutes later, exiling herself from the faint sounds of salsa and vallenato music that carried on the warm morning breeze.

The white sails bright against a green sea.

71

At that same time in Fredericksburg, Virginia, a home-health nurse from a local agency found the driveway to the Porteous mansion blocked by a black Lincoln town car.

Concerned it may have something to do with her patient, she hurried to the house. The bedridden old lady, Ursula Porteous, pushed the oxygen mask from her mouth and in a frail voice suggested that it was perhaps her husband's car, and asked the nurse to check his bedroom at the back of the house.

The high-ceilinged room filled with priceless antiques, much like the rest of the house, was empty. The bed had not been slept in. The nurse, curious to see what lay at the back of the rambling great mansion, tiptoed over to the window and looked out. Black trees pressed on a white landscape of rolling hills. What she would have given for such a view, especially in the spring; she could only imagine how beautiful it would be then. What she would have given for such a house. At nearly sixty years of age, and with an income of twenty-two dollars an hour, an impossible dream.

She was turning to leave as her eyes lowered to the courtyard and the stables. Tiles missing from some of them. No horses. The wind lifted the snow in a thin white mist, drifting it across the courtyard. Something moved. She took her driving glasses from her uniform pocket and looked again. For the smallest part of a second she didn't believe what her eyes were telling her. Then she cried out once, and ran from the room.

The movement continued. A dark shape swaying gently in the wind and snow. A frozen body, hanging by a rope from one of the arches.

Debriefing

The small airport at Stennis was originally built with NASA in mind: to be used as a site to fly Saturn booster engines into. Instead it ended up as a general aviation airfield. Its single north–south runway set in the midst of a buffer zone of southern pines – a 200,000-acre woodland area developed by NASA to protect people on the northern side of the plantation in the event of explosions during testing of their booster rockets.

It was to this general aviation hideaway, in the Magnolia State of Mississippi, later that Monday that a King Air B-200 with a foreign registration – and on a VFR flight plan from Fort Lauderdale, Florida – landed and taxied to the hangar at the north end of the runway.

The cold front had cleared at midday. Now, weak sunlight sparkled from the pools of standing water on the ramp, as the owner of the maintenance facility came out to greet the pilot. They stood by the tail of the aircraft talking for a while, the pilot lighting a cigar. The other man, more elderly, clenching an unlit pipe between his teeth.

It was ten minutes or so later that a maroon Cadillac pulled onto the ramp, and a man and a woman got out. The pilot's passengers it seemed. Both dressed in smart city clothes; the dark-haired woman clinging to

the man's arm, looking up at him from time to time.
A contented smile on her face.

The talk and occasional laughter continued.

Anyone overhearing that conversation might have
concluded they were listening to a group of ex-navy
veterans, especially when the subject matter ran to
submarines, and how wartime submariners had con-
ceived the trick of firing oil and clothing, and anything
else that came to hand, from their torpedo tubes in the
hope of convincing a destroyer patrolling the waters
above that they had sunk.

It was as the sun was sinking over the plantation that
the group split up. The pilot and his two passengers
boarding the King Air. The old man, pipe jutting from
the corner of his mouth, watching as the turboprop
climbed away from the southerly runway, turning
left towards the east, and Florida. And when it had
disappeared from view he went back to his hangar.

It was a vast, untidy emporium littered with airplanes. Mainly warbirds. His speciality. He looked
up at the old B-25 bomber he had just bought, engines
leaking oil, flaps drooping, bomb doors hanging open.
The left propeller feathered: an engine failure minutes
before landing. Fuel tanks so empty he'd been surprised that the one surviving engine had kept turning
long enough for the pilot to clear the runway and taxi
to the hangar.

Other than that he had been made aware of its
dubious background. Had given shelter to its crew.
Had fed them. Loaned them his car to drive in to New
Orleans to buy some clothes. All without ever knowing
their names. Even so, he could be relied upon to keep

his mouth shut. He was known in aviation circles to be that kind of man.

As for the price of the airplane, that had been an unexpected bonus. He thought they were joking right up to the time he was handed the bill of sale.

Hell, you couldn't buy a gallon of gas for one dollar these days!